NOR THE MOON BY NIGHT

ALICE LANG, a young English hospital nurse, flies to South Africa to marry Andrew Miller, the Senior Game-warden of Velaba, a Wild Life Sanctuary in the making which is being opened up by Andrew and his brother Rusty.

Alice has always been strongly drawn by the lure of Africa, but till now she has been tied at home by circumstances beyond her control. The story is concerned with her physical, mental and emotional reactions to the dangerous and unfamiliar setting in which she finds herself. It explores not only the wild bush and forest of Velaba, but the undiscovered territory of a woman's passionate heart inhibited by years of severe self-discipline and now suddenly set free.

The action takes place over the period of Alice's trek across the Sanctuary, which is the scene of sinister violence. She falls under its spell on her first night in camp as she looks across the moon-drenched thorn-veld to the sombre mountain range rising against the luminous sky.

" This is a strange night, she thought, my first in Velaba. *I will lift up mine eyes unto the hills, from whence cometh my help. The sun shall not smite thee by day, nor the moon by night* . . . The sun and the moon of Africa were not like the sun and moon of England. They were potent and dangerous . . . Far away she heard the thunder of the lion's roar . . ."

It is against this primitive background, haunted by crime and witchcraft, that Alice learns to know her own heart and body, her capacity for fear and suffering and for courage with which to face her final ordeal.

NOR THE MOON
BY NIGHT

JOY PACKER

THE BOOK CLUB
121 CHARING CROSS ROAD
LONDON, W.C.2

FOR OUR NAN

*This book is printed in Great Britain
by Wyman & Sons Ltd.,
London, Reading and Fakenham*

Contents

NOR THE MOON BY NIGHT

" I will lift up mine eyes unto the hills, from
whence cometh my help . . . the sun shall not
smite thee by day, nor the moon by night.   The
Lord shall preserve thee from all evil: He shall
preserve thy soul."

Extract from Psalm 121

Author's Note

MANY THOUSANDS of square miles of well-watered bush and grass-lands have been set aside in various parts of Africa for the preservation of wild life. In these sanctuaries it is intended that wild creatures should live in their natural state, secure from the guns and snares of men, with their water and grazing as far as possible assured.

I have spent many happy and fascinating holidays in the famous Game Reserves of Southern Africa, and have enjoyed the hospitality of Game-wardens, Rangers and their wives and families.

Velaba, where Alice Lang learns to know herself and her lover, is no particular Sanctuary. It is a territory in the Union of South Africa which exists only in my imagination. Its Bantu people belong to no specific tribe, and the native words and names they use may come from one dialect or another—or none at all. Their superstitions and temptations, however, are those of every native living in lion and elephant country and surrounded by edible but protected game.

Of all my characters, white, black or animal, only Dumela, the Rogue Elephant, is not fictitious.

JOY PACKER.

Claremont,
  Cape.
1957.

1

First Step

MEG BROEKSMA stood at the barrier at Jan Smuts airport waiting for the London-Johannesburg airliner to land. Her two little boys, aged four and five, danced up and down beside her, the elder keeping up a running commentary on everything he could see with wheels or wings, and the younger echoing his brother and clasping a toy monkey to his breast.

" Look ! " cried Johnny. " There she comes, there, there, zoom-zoom ! "

" Zoom-zoom," came the refrain from Dicky. " Look, Lily, look at the big plane ! "

" It's landing—it's down. They're running the steps to it ! "

" It's down—they're running the steps to it. Look, Lily ! "

The blind glass eyes of Lily, the toy monkey, watched the passengers stream out of the aircraft, among them a thin, dark young woman in a blue linen suit with a tweed coat over her shoulders and an outsize handbag under her arm. She wore no hat and her short hair in the late afternoon light was blue-black and glossy. Small and dark, Andrew Miller had said in that extraordinary telephone conversation when he had asked his sister, Meg, to meet Alice Lang. Twenty-six years old and a hospital nurse, a Londoner.

Who was this Alice Lang ? Meg wondered when and how she had come to know Andrew ? And how, in heaven's name, had that hermit of a man induced her to fly across half the world to visit a place as remote and uncivilized as Velaba ? Meg's mind seethed with questions and forebodings. She noticed that the dark girl walked fast as if she were in a hurry and as if she knew where she was going.

" Which is her, Mommy ? Which is Alice Lang ? I want to show Lily to Alice Lang."

" I think that might be her—the one without a hat, Dicky, the one who walks fast."

" Why ? " Johnny flung his ' why's ' into conversations

haphazard as a rule.   He found that they altered the direction of talk like changing the points on his model railway, sending the engine off on another course for no particular reason.

" Because hospital nurses walk that way."

" Why ? "

" Because they are not allowed to run."

" Why ? "   He knew the third ' why ' would receive no reply, and before his mother could stop him, he darted forward and intercepted the hatless young woman just as she reached the entrance to the Immigration counter.

" Are you Alice Lang ? "

He looked up into a pair of wide-set brown eyes under well-defined brows that lifted at the outer corners.   When she smiled those eyes were like pools with the sun on them, and Johnny smiled too.

" Yes," she said, " and who are you ? "

" I'm Broeksma.   We've come to meet you.   Uncle Andrew told us to."   Johnny had recently begun to attend a real school and the use of his surname without a prefix made him feel old and superior.

Meg and Dicky came up with them.

" Then it *is* you," said Meg.   " We guessed."

" This is Lily."   Dicky held up the monkey for admiration. It was old, threadbare and gruddy, much mauled by love.

" How do you do, Lily."   Alice shook its limp paw, and received from Lily's owner a smile of such sweetness that her heart contracted.   She looked up over the two fair heads of the little boys and said :   " How very kind of you to meet me, Mrs. Broeksma.   Andrew cabled me to expect you."

" My name is Meg," smiled Andrew's sister.   " I'm not as formal as Johnny, who is very surname conscious at present."

She had red-gold hair, amiable blue eyes and a snub nose. Her fair skin was dusted with freckles.   " I'm going to take the boys over to the bookstall while you get through the Customs and Immigration formalities.   Then we'll be on our way and we can talk in comparative peace."

All round her Alice heard Afrikaans spoken.   The officials who examined her passport and yellow fever and vaccination certificates, and who stamped her light, new-looking luggage spoke with an accent strange to her, and she had the feeling that she had arrived in a foreign country rather than a British Dominion. It seemed fantastic to her that only twenty-four hours ago she had been in London. Only yesterday! A black porter took her bags to Meg's car, and within half an hour of landing she was speeding across the highveld towards Pretoria. Meg drove the big American car fast and well, and the two little boys bounced about in the back where Johnny kept up a volley of questions about the aeroplane, and Dicky echoed them from time to time.

" Be quiet, boys," said Meg. " We're talking."

There were a great number of things she wanted to ask Alice Lang, but she hesitated to do so. Her brother's telephone call two days ago had left her bewildered. He had put through a personal call from the Police Post at Poinsettia just outside the northern limit of the great new Wild Life Sanctuary of Velaba. Andrew was the Chief Game-warden of Velaba and it was seldom that Meg heard from him.

" Listen, Meg, I want you to do something for me. Will you meet a girl called Alice Lang at Jan Smuts airport the day after tomorrow—flight one-six-two, Springbok—give her a bed for the night and put her into the Duikers' Drift train at Pretoria."

" Yes, of course. But who is she? What is she to you? "

" She's English—a hospital nurse. Her mother died a few days ago. Alice has been taking care of her for the past four years. Now she's coming to Poinsettia Mission Station."

" A few *days* ago——? "

" Yes."

" Is she a missionary? "

" No. But the Missionary and his wife will put her up."

" Is she . . . a particular friend of yours? "

" Very particular. But that's entirely confidential, Meg. It is possible that, if we like each other, we will get married."

"*If* you like each other! But if she's a particular friend——"

" I know it sounds mad. Ask her about it when you meet her. She'll tell you better than I can over the phone."

Meg was consumed with curiosity, yet this was not the time for confidences. And Alice Lang did not invite questions. There was something separate about her in spite of her friendliness. She was self-contained and exact. Whatever her relationship with Andrew might be, Meg sensed that it had not as yet quickened into life. It was there, but still very much in embryo.

" This marvellous light . . ." said Alice. " The sense of light and distance . . ." She was looking out at the limitless landscape of dry grassland, at the high cloudless sky, and the sun on the sultry horizon—a flat raspberry disc swelling as it sank.

" We need the spring rains. The grass-fires have been bad this year. Do you know South Africa ? "

" No. I've dreamed about it for years—most of my life. I've read about it and thought about it. The idea of Africa has always put a spell on me—bewitched me—and now I'm actually here ! I can't quite believe it."

" I suppose you met my brother when he was at Oxford just before the war. But no, you'd have been too young——"

" I've never met him. Didn't he explain ? "

Meg shook her head. " He said you'd tell me."

" He published an article on Velaba about two years ago. I happened to read it and I wrote and told him how much I had enjoyed it. I wanted to wish him luck in his enterprise. A great tract of land—thousands of square miles set aside for the preservation of wild life—it's such a wonderful ideal."

Meg's face hardened suddenly.

" Ideals are all very well, but putting them into practice . . . Oh, never mind ! Tell me what happened. Andrew answered your letter, I suppose."

" He did indeed—and asked me to write again. We got involved in a correspondence."

" How like Andrew ! He's a born writer, but he won't try to commercialize the gift. He'd much rather write for one sympathetic reader than settle down to a series of popular articles or stories. It's not often he bursts into print."

" He writes wonderful letters. I guess we were both lonely in our different ways, and we found an outlet in writing to each other—discovering and exploring each other's minds, finding how much we had in common. He wanted to know what was going on in London. He calls it the heart of civilization, and I wanted the exact opposite. I dare say it was escapism on my side . . . his letters took me out of a very sad atmosphere into the land I've always longed to see."

It seemed to Meg the dry skeleton of romance. But she said : " So now you felt you must meet each other."

" We have felt that for a long time. We've known each other for two years . . but I wasn't free to come to Andrew sooner. My mother needed me. Fortunately I'd qualified before she was taken ill—incurably ill. As a matter of fact I'd been accepted for a post in the Colonial Nursing Service—a hospital in Swaziland—but naturally I stayed to take care of Mother."

She spoke bluntly and without self-pity, but Meg had a sudden vision of broken dreams and young vigorous years sacrificed to nursing a hopeless case and doing most of the household chores into the bargain. Four years of servitude—a long time by Meg's standards. She stole a glance at her companion, at the clear olive skin moulded close to the fine small bones, the carefully controlled red lips, and eyes that must often have blazed in rebellion, for in Alice Lang Meg sensed a woman hungry for life. She said gently :

" It must be heart-breaking to see someone you love suffer without hope."

" There could be nothing sadder."

From the back of the car came the excitable voice of Johnny. " There's Pretoria. Look, Alice, there's Pretoria ! "

Dicky echoed : " Look, Alice ! look, Lily, there's Pretoria ! "

To Alice, exhausted after her journey, Pretoria's importance as the administrative capital of the Union of South Africa was reduced to a mauve dream. The surrounding amethyst hills and the violet dusk were reflected in avenues of leafless jacarandas laden with mauve blossom ; even the sidewalks were carpeted with the mauve confetti of flower petals. She had glimpses of old colonial houses, of modern blocks of flats, an open, attractive shopping centre, and on the heights above the city stood the magnificent Union Buildings. On every side were gardens ablaze with flowering shrubs.

Meg turned the car into a short drive and ran it into a garage built under a single-storeyed house. She sounded the hooter and a native boy in a neat white uniform came and fetched the suitcase Alice required for the night.

" We'll leave the rest of the stuff in the car," said Meg. " Your train leaves at nine tomorrow morning. Pity you can't stay a few days before you move on."

As they went round to the front of the house a big man with a full, dark beard hurried out to meet them.

" My husband," said Meg. " Danie—this is Alice Lang."

Alice felt her hand lost in the warm grasp of a huge paw.

" Welcome to our country. Did you have a good trip ? "

Danie Broeksma spoke with the same foreign accent she had noticed at the airport and she was reminded that, like many South Africans, his roots were in Holland, not in England.

" Yes, thank you. Very comfortable. It was all rather strange to me. I've never flown before."

He laughed. " That's the least of it. You'll find Velaba very savage, I'm afraid. It's unfortunate that Andrew can't meet you at Duikers' Drift. The Chairman of the Board of Sanctuary Trustees has chosen this moment to visit Camp Three at Poinsettia, and Andrew can't possibly get away. He has arranged for Rusty to take you through the Sanctuary to him."

If Alice's heart sank at his words—if she felt suddenly sick and faint, as if someone had struck her a severe blow—she made no sign. Her lips tightened and her voice was calm as she said :

" That's very disappointing. We've waited a long while for our meeting."

" It's only postponed for a short time," said Meg. " It's about three days' trek from Duikers' Drift in Rusty's station-wagon."

Danie laughed. " If Rusty is giving Miss Lang a lift it'll take just as long as is necessary to complete his surveys and inspections. You know what Rusty is ! "

Meg wrinkled her snub nose at her husband.

" Don't make it worse for Alice, Danie."

She led the way into the house. " Rusty is my younger brother," she said. " Andrew's assistant—but of course you know that—and, like all the men of my family, he puts his horrible animals before everything else. He's in love with the Sanctuary. Now, would you like a drink, or would you prefer to go straight to your room ? A bath and a rest, perhaps ? "

Alice smiled. " A bath and a rest, please."

She wanted to be alone, to pull herself together and recover a little from a disappointment that was not only intense but somehow frightening.

She followed Meg into a light, pretty bedroom leading into the garden. The air was heavy with the scent of stocks.

"You have your own bathroom," said Meg. "We eat at half past seven, but join us earlier for a glass of sherry. No need to change. We are quite informal."

Johnny and Dicky, who were frisking at their mother's heels like puppies, cried out with one voice : "Isn't Alice going to bath us ?"

"Certainly not. She's very tired, and she's going to bath herself. Maybe she'll come and say good night to you." She laughed as she turned to her guest. "Being invited to the bath ceremony is a great compliment. You've made a hit."

The little boys were awake when Alice went to say good night to them. They looked up from their pillows with glowing faces. Their fair heads gleamed in the light that streamed through the open door. Their beds were only covered with a thin blanket each, for the spring night was warm.

Dicky shared his pillow with Lily and a tattered lion. A springbok lamb, made out of real springbok hide, lay on its side at his feet. Johnny occupied his bed alone.

"No cuddly toys for you ?" Alice asked him.

"My things are on this table by me," he said. His 'things' were mechanical—a varied assortment of miniature racing motor-cars, tractors, aeroplanes and speed-boats. Alice glanced at Meg.

"How different they are—your sons."

"Like my brothers. You could hardly find two characters less alike than Andrew and Rusty. Yet their main interest is similar—wild life."

Meg turned to Johnny.

"Have you said your prayers ?"

"We were waiting for you."

"Waiting for you," added Dicky. "We'll say them now."

In a moment they were kneeling by their beds, palms together, lashes flickering over half-closed eyes to observe the effect of their devotions on Alice.

"You have rather a lot of people to pray for," remarked Alice when the final Amens had been said.

" We pray for our animals who have gone to Heaven," said Dicky, unexpectedly taking the initiative. " God takes care of them."

As Alice bent down to kiss the little boys she felt their soft, responsive lips with a maternal thrill she had never before experienced. She let her hand linger on the warm, silky head of the child with his toy friends about him. Andrew must have been like this once—with his animals tucked up beside him in bed. A memory of the children's ward in St. George's touched her—sick children falling asleep clasping grotesque toys like Lily. She had been good with children, able to soothe and comfort them, and then children had gone out of her life with so much else. The starved, sacrificial years of her young womanhood seemed to crowd upon her in this nursery. She had hungered for a man of her own during those years. Out of ink and paper she had created a lover and breathed life into a dream. Soon, soon he would be flesh and blood, bone and sinew, arms to hold her, lips to kiss her and a virile body to take hers and possess it and give her children of her own.

Meg saw her eyes soften and glisten. The child looked up at her with his slow, piercingly sweet smile.

" I will lend you my lion," he said. " He can sleep with you on your pillow. His name is Ratau. He is called after Uncle Rusty."

" That is very handsome of you," smiled Alice, accepting the well-worn lion the child offered her. " But Ratau . . . ? "

Meg laughed. " Ratau means Lion of Lions. It is the name the natives give Rusty. It suggests strength and mastery."

" What do the natives call Andrew ? " Alice asked.

" Inyanga. That means Medicine Man. It implies wisdom and a knowledge of medicinal herbs, even rain-making. Andrew knows a great deal about plants and their curative properties, and of course he dispenses the white man's medicines as well, so they regard him as a healer. And, when he was taken prisoner at Tobruk, he was wounded in the leg. Since then he's had a limp which is more marked before rain. They don't know about things like a touch of arthritis. They find something rather special about a bone that can predict rain. Andrew plays it up. He knows his Bantus inside out."

Meg kissed her sons good night.

"Let's go into the garden for a few minutes," she said to Alice. "There's something I have to say to you because I like you and I saw just now that you love and understand children."

She linked her arm in Alice's as they strolled across the lawn.

"You'll hate me for this," she said. "You'll think I'm trying to queer your pitch—but, Alice, don't marry my brother!"

In the light slanting out from the french windows of the house, Alice saw that Meg's placid features were intense.

"Why do you say that?" she asked. She had withdrawn her arm from her companion's and they stood a little apart staring at each other.

"You don't know Andrew," said Meg fiercely. "What can you possibly know about a man with the wilderness in his blood? I know the men of my family and what they expect of their women! My grandfather was an ivory hunter. Afterwards he became one of the first Rangers in the Kruger National Park. That was long before it was developed into the most famous Wild Life Sanctuary in the world. In those early days my grandmother was often left entirely alone for days on end—even weeks—in lion and elephant country with only a few natives to talk to. When my grandfather was away on one of his patrol trips she had a miscarriage and a fatal haemorrhage. She could have been saved if they had been anywhere near civilization. Instead of that he came back to find her dead with her three-year-old son—my father—crying his heart out and trying to warm her hands while the old house-boy pulled up the floor boards to make a coffin."

Alice felt her fingers tighten on the soft body of Dicky's toy lion. "How dreadful. But things are different now."

"They are in the Kruger Park, but they won't be in the places Andrew will take you to. As soon as there is some sort of a life in Velaba—people, tourists, a bit of company—he'll be off to some new wild territory. I know these men. The wilderness is their love and their wife, and its creatures are their children! I was born in a Ranger's outpost and when I was still a child my mother was bitten by a mamba in our garden. By the time the boys had found Daddy she was dead. A mamba's poison kills in a matter of minutes"

"Perhaps your mother was luckier than mine," said Alice sadly. Meg looked startled.

A shadow fell across the lawn as Danie Broeksma joined them. He put his massive arm about his wife's shoulder.

"What is Meg telling you?" he asked. "She has her angry face—the face we seldom see."

"She's giving me some idea of life in the wild."

"She hates it. She's not like the men of her family. They've been hunters and Rangers for generations."

"They've broken the hearts and the health of their women for generations, too," said Meg fiercely. "I want Alice to know what she's in for if she marries Andrew. You can't educate your children in Velaba. You'll be parted from them at an early age, you'll be left alone, you'll live with fear knocking on your door day and night. You'll learn the meaning of the word loneliness. Rusty's wife couldn't stand it and you won't stand it either——"

"Come now," said Danie gently, "we are not all alike, thank God. Alice is tired and I'm sure she's hungry. Let's go in and have a glass of sherry." He turned to Alice. "My wife works herself up on this subject. She was brought up in the Kruger Sanctuary, and, luckily for me, she hated the life. There were some very dashing Rangers there, but she settled for a humdrum Pretoria lawyer. Not so, Meg?"

"And a normal home-life," she added.

As Meg glanced up at her big, bearded husband, Alice noticed that her smile had the same quality of extreme tenderness that was so striking in her younger son's expression. She thought of the toy animals in the little boy's bed, and with a flash of prescience she knew that yet another generation was destined for wild life and lonely places. But surely, if a woman had love and courage, she would not hesitate to share her man's solitude. What, after all, was loneliness? Alice had known the absolute meaning of that word among London's millions. Loneliness was the need for a lover, for a comrade and mate. With Andrew to love her there would never again be loneliness.

2

Rusty

THE train from Pretoria to Duikers' Drift was in no hurry. It crept peacefully across the vast dry grasslands of the highveld and stopped at every little *dorp* among the windmills and willows.

Alice gazed with delight at clusters of mud huts adorned with strange geometrical designs, and at stately native women carrying burdens on their heads and babies slung on their backs or over one hip. The women wore gaily printed wrap-over skirts and little bodices that were always open so that the baby might be suckled whenever it cried. Their necks, arms and legs were adorned with brass and bead necklaces and bangles, and their frizzy hair was often bleached with cows' urine and plaited with grass, or it was worn high in a sort of busby. The coiffure, whatever it might be, had its special significance and denoted the status of matron or maiden, but to Alice the wearers were just extraordinarily picturesque and dignified. The piccaninnies had a natural gaiety that entranced her. They danced and postured grotesquely for the benefit of the train. They waved little pink-palmed hands and yelled Bantu greetings.

Towards noon the heat increased and the scene changed. A wide river foamed down from the rocky blue mountains between citrus and paw-paw plantations. Orchards of mangoes, bananas, and avocado pears fringed the line and bougainvillaea and poinsettias blazed in the gardens of white bungalows with dazzling tin roofs. But always there was the sense of light and space that had been Alice's first impression of Africa. It was the essence of her new-found freedom. It was infinity.

She ate the sandwiches Meg had given her and bought coca-cola at a wayside station. She was no longer keenly disappointed that Andrew could not meet her at Duikers' Drift. She was content—even glad—to wait. She realized that she was afraid of the moment she had so ardently desired—the first meeting with her stranger lover. That morning, just before her departure, Meg had given her a letter from Andrew. " Lucky

he expressed it," Meg had said, " or it would have missed you."
It was a fat letter, sensible and tactful, yet it had left her with
an odd hollow feeling under her heart. She took it from her
handbag now to re-read it. He had said nothing about not
meeting her. That complication had evidently arisen later.

" I can't believe that you are really on your way to Velaba
at last ! I have arranged for you to go to the Mission Station
at Poinsettia for a few days. Poinsettia is only two miles
from Camp Three, just outside the limits of Velaba, and
Dr. & Mrs. Hurley—the missionary and his wife—are good
people. They are trying to establish a small hospital and to
train a few native orderlies. Ostensibly you are going there
to give them a hand.

" Only Meg and Rusty and Dr. & Mrs. Hurley know the
real purpose of your coming here. No one else. Even from
outposts like this a ' story ' could leak out to so-called civilization. Can you see the headlines ? ' GIRL WEDS PEN-PAL IN
WILDS ', or, quite possible, ' GIRL FLIES TO WED PEN-PAL.
SAYS " NO ! " FLIES HOME.' Maybe you wonder who else
would be interested. There are our farmer neighbours,
policemen and store-keepers, a bunch of scientists working
on nagana in the tsetse fly belt, Rangers and their relatives.
One way and another our love story might spread quite fast.
And if it doesn't end right we'd feel rather stupid.

" Letters, after all, are only a mental approach, and the
world I live in takes little account of the mind. So little
that it sometimes shakes my confidence in this matter of you
and me. In the animal world it is the shape, the smell, and
the right mating-call that matters. So far my mating-call
sounds good to you but when we meet you may change your
mind. I'm not an easily frightened man, Alice, but I think
I'm a little bit frightened of you ! . . ."

Frightened—she thought—that makes two scared people.
Or does it ? No, I refuse absolutely to be scared ! According
to Meg, I'll have plenty of cause for fear without including
Andrew. The shape and the smell . . . well, there's nothing
wrong with my shape, even if it is a bit on the skinny side, and,
as for the smell, I've got that right here ! She drew a little
bottle of perfume from her bag and took out the stopper. It

was a woody scent, light and fresh. Nothing sweet or cloying about it. Would it appeal to him? Or would he prefer the rose and jasmine type of woman? And what about him? She knew that he was lean and rangy with greying hair and a narrow bony Stewart Granger sort of face, but even the most expressive photograph could hardly convey the subtle individual emanation of a human being. Did he smell of tweed and tobacco, leather and horses, or maybe just sweat and toil? Hardly that. She had already learned that sweat and toil in Africa were the prerogatives of the black man.

Alice tried to laugh at her own reflections, but her heart was beating fast and anxiously. What was he really like—the feel of his skin, the touch of his lips, the sound of his voice? All these were as yet unknown to her.

The afternoon was well advanced when the train drew into Duikers' Drift terminus. A few people waited on the platform and a handful of natives wrapped in blankets squatted against the red-brick station wall.

A broad-shouldered man in khaki shorts and a belted bush-jacket with four large pockets, short sleeves and an open neck, came towards her. He swept off his wide-brimmed felt hat, banded with a narrow snake skin, and his crisp, coppery hair was burnished by the sun; his sturdy legs were clad in gaudy stockings of a diamond pattern, and he wore ostrich-skin veld-shoes.

"You are Alice Lang," he said. It was a statement, not a question.

"And you are Rusty. How did you know me?"

He laughed and his blue eyes were lost in a ray of tiny lines. "Look around you."

She saw a brawny woman in a crumpled cotton dress, a tall blonde in slacks, half a dozen men in shorts or khaki slacks, and one or two children.

"Do you want tea?" he asked. "We have a long way to go. Three and a half hours' drive."

She shook her head. "Let's go. I have no baggage in the van. It's all here."

"Only three pieces?"

She smiled. "I didn't bring any ball dresses."

He called over his shoulder to a tall young native. "Nimrod

is my special Game-guard," he said to Alice. " He'll bring your stuff."

Nimrod wore khaki shorts and a bush-jacket with brass buttons and a black lion badge on the left pocket.   Attached to his leather belt was a knife in a sheath fashioned out of the hind-foot of an antelope.   The brim of his hat was turned up on one side, and Alice thought that his ebony-black face was one of the most arrogantly beautiful she had ever seen.

Rusty led her to a station-wagon parked in the dusty area outside the little terminus.   As he opened the door a dog sprang out, whimpering with pleasure.   It was more or less the build of a fox-hound, but taller and heavier, and its smooth snuff-coloured coat was lacerated with old scars.

" This is Smokey," said Rusty, " my best friend.   Wherever I go Smokey and Nimrod go too."

" What breed is Smokey ? " she asked.

He grinned.   He had a blunt, attractive face like his sister's, but it lacked Meg's gentleness.   It was, Alice thought, rather ruthless.

" Just dog," he said.

" And the scars ? "

" Clawed by a lion.   Our dogs don't hunt the fox, they are bred to fight lions."

Nimrod and a porter appeared with Alice's luggage.

" Could you stow it flat ? " she asked Rusty.

" Flat, and right side up," he said.

Ten minutes later the little *dorp* of Duikers' Drift lay behind them and they were heading towards a distant mountain range, flax blue in the pure light.   Alice was beside Rusty in front and Nimrod and Smokey sat behind with the luggage and provisions and the guns.

Rusty drove the powerful car, which he called ' Sweet Sue ', at a steady, fast pace over the corrugated earth road.   Seventy miles an hour.   His hands on the wheel were strong with square, well-kept nails.   His profile had an obstinate, hot-tempered look about it.   The forehead was broad, the chin square and slightly cleft, the space between nose and upper lip short.   His narrow eyes were light clear blue under level brows darker than his hair.   A few freckles dusted his deeply tanned skin.   Ratau, the lion, a tawny man, proud and without fear.

He said : " I'm an outspoken man, Alice Lang, and I want you to know straight away that I think this business—this pen-friend romance—between Andrew and you is crazy. I heartily disapprove of it. To contemplate marriage with a man you have never met—never even seen—is sheer lunacy. And it's madder still to imagine that you could fit into the bushveld life—an English girl, a city girl like you. One has to be born to it."

" Your sister, Meg, was born to it," she said sharply. " That doesn't mean it suits her. The fact that I was born on the outskirts of London doesn't make me a Cockney at heart. One can be born again—born to a new life."

He shot a quick look at her—the firm, clear-cut profile, the glossy blue-black hair waving from a wide brow, the slim, wiry figure in the neat printed cotton dress. Her complexion was a clear, pale olive, smooth and innocent of make-up save for the vivid lipstick that added a touch of defiance and sophistication that he found oddly provoking. She knew what she wanted. She wanted the Africa she had dreamed up and the man who symbolized it. He could imagine her notion of Africa—the noble, savage, exotic scenery, the incongruous comfort of the wilds depicted in *safari* novels about strong white hunters panting over the charms of some modern Eve in a primitive paradise where woman is the rarest animal. Well, in Andrew's absence, Rusty would have to introduce her to reality.

The introduction came sooner and in a cruder form and far more horrifying than he could have guessed. On the road ahead they saw a cloud of dust advancing rapidly towards them. Rusty frowned. He half turned his head and said something to Nimrod in the Bantu language. The boy answered quickly and Alice caught the word ' jeep '.

" It's the jeep," said Rusty. " Nelmapius's jeep. Nelmapius is the Ranger in charge of Camp One. Now what the devil is he doing on this road at this time of evening ? He should be in the Camp to meet us."

As they drew abreast, Rusty put on the brakes and killed the engine. The oncoming jeep pulled in behind him on the same side of the track. A young man sprang out of the driver's seat and hurried towards them. His face, framed in ' Sweet Sue's ' window, was round and red and bearded, not with a strong growth like Danie Broeksma's, but with the soft, yellow fluff of a boy recently come to manhood and anxious to appear more mature.

"This is Jan Nelmapius—Miss Alice Lang," said Rusty.

The young man acknowledged the introduction with perfunctory politeness. Then he said: "You must excuse me if I speak to Rusty in Afrikaans, Miss Lang, but something dreadful has happened. What I have to say is not right for you to hear."

It seemed to her that he spoke the foreign language quickly and with considerable indignation. As Rusty listened she saw the square bony line of his jaw tighten until finally, with an exlamation that sounded like an oath, he jumped out of the station-wagon and went over to the jeep with Nelmapius. Nimrod and the dog followed him.

Alice too got out to stretch her legs. She did not attempt to join the men, but strolled some way down the earth road and back again. They had been driving along the ridge of a high escarpment flanking the bushveld. Below them the bush glowed in a tawny tapestry picked out with the feathery white of the wild-pear, the burning scarlet of an occasional kaffir-boom, the yellow of mimosa and the ethereal mauve of bush-wistaria. Along the banks of a dark jade river the foliage of the trees was emerald green, a lush winding line of verdure in the parched landscape. Here and there she picked out a huddle of mud huts thatched with tamboekie grass or reeds and contained in a hedge of blue-green sesal or prickly-pear. In the clear air she could hear the cries of little naked herd-boys bringing home the humped, long-horned cattle. A phrase from one of Andrew's letters came to her mind.

"A Bantu's prestige is measured by the number of his cattle and of his wives. He loves his cattle as you or I love flowers. He doesn't want to eat them—only to admire them. From his wives he desires daughters—the source of more cattle. The bride-price for a girl is from fifteen to thirty head of cattle depending on her standing and her beauty."

Alice turned as Rusty strode towards her, arms swinging wide. "We have a casualty," he said, "one of our best Game-guards, a boy called Amos. We think he may be dying."

" What happened ? " She walked beside him to the jeep with the scurrying speed of a nurse on duty in an emergency —not quite a run.

" His tongue has been cut out. And he has been blinded." The implication of his words and the grim way in which he spoke them made her shudder.

In the back of the jeep, sitting bolt upright, an impassive elderly native supported on his knees the head of his companion whose recumbent body was covered with blankets. The head lolled sideways on a roughly contrived cushion of torn, blood-stained sheeting, blood oozed from the blue, swollen lips, and the empty, brutally wounded eye-sockets were bandaged.

Alice felt for the ice-cold wrist under the blankets and took the pulse, which was fast and faint. Rusty said :

" Nelmapius was patrolling on horseback in the direction of Camp Two at daybreak this morning when suddenly the dogs went after something in the bush. It turned out to be this poor devil, Amos. He was bleeding terribly from the mouth. Nelmapius and Job here managed to sling him across a pack-donkey and get him to Camp Two, where they picked up the jeep. There's a hospital at Duikers' Drift—but tough as these natives are, I doubt if Amos'll make it alive."

Alice was appalled. Injuries such as these could only have been the deliberate mutilation of one human being by another. But her voice was calm.

" He's in a shocking way. He must have suffered great agony and loss of blood. What time did you say he was found ? " She tried to keep her voice calm.

" About six this morning."

" Nearly twelve hours ago. And it'll be about two hours more before he can reach Duikers' Drift . . ." Alice said. " If we could give him some glucose water—sugar would do."

" That's easy."

Rusty shouted an order to Nimrod, who hurried away to ' Sweet Sue ' and came back with a mug, sugar and a flask of water.

" I was afraid to give him anything to drink," said young Nelmapius, as Alice dissolved sugar in the mug of water. " He was bleeding so badly."

" You were right," she said. " But at this stage he needs

something, poor man. It was lucky he was able to crawl, and that you slung him over the donkey face-down."

She did not lift the bandage from the eyes, but she washed the blood-stained lips and chin gently; then, a very little at a time, she dripped the sugar solution into the cruelly damaged mouth. After a while she gave the mug back to Nimrod and felt the injured man's pulse once more. She released the limp hand and drew the blankets gently over it.

As she straightened her back and turned to the young Ranger, Jan Nelmapius, the golden evening light fell full on her face and shone in her dark eyes grown soft with compassion. She had a look of strength and tenderness that moved Rusty to reluctant liking and respect.

"You couldn't have done more for him," she said. "If he recovers—and I think he will—he will owe his life to you."

Nelmapius flushed with pleasure at her praise. The day had been long and anxious. He was a lad with a keen sense of responsibility to the Bantu Game-guards under his charge, and Amos was one of his best men.

"If he gets well I suppose he'll be dumb for keeps, Miss Lang?"

"Not necessarily. I've nursed amputations of the tongue. You'd be surprised how little seems to be essential."

"It won't be the same. Their language is so full of subtle sounds. Amos here was a grand story-teller."

"No. It won't be the same."

The light, that had spun a web of drifting gold over her black hair, began to fade as the sun slid down behind the hills.

Nelmapius sprang into the jeep with a swift, athletic movement. "I'll see you again at camp," he said. "I should be back around midnight. We'll meet tomorrow morning."

"By the way, Rusty," he added, "I got your brother on the radio-telephone this morning. He knows about this. He'll be calling you at eight tonight as usual. *Tot siens*."

He waved his hand and the jeep moved away in a cloud of dust. The Bantu, Job, sitting with his injured companion's head across his lap, remained immobile as a primitive wooden statue.

Rusty and Alice watched them out of sight.

"Terrible things like that don't happen by accident," she said.

"No, Alice, they don't," he agreed, putting 'Sweet Sue' into gear.

She sat silent while he engaged in a quick conversation with Nimrod. A certain word occurred again and again. Tokoloshe. What, or who, was Tokoloshe?

The great red globe of the sun had vanished and the swift dusk enveloped the scene in veils of dove-grey. Alice put her tweed coat over her shoulders.

"What happened?" she asked.

"It's a curious story and it makes very little sense. But to get truth out of a native is never easy. Either he has something to hide or he tells you what he thinks you want to hear, or he drowns his facts in sorcery and superstition. In this case sorcery has the upper hand."

"Those horrible mutilations were committed by a human being," she said flatly.

"According to Job and Nimrod the Tokoloshe was responsible."

"Tokoloshe?"

"The Tokoloshe is a hairy dwarf who inhabits reedy places near a river or a water course. He is a raper and a killer, more dangerous to women than to men—unless he is actuated by jealousy. The suggestion is that Amos planned to meet a woman near a certain river and was attacked by the Tokoloshe."

"Do Job and Nimrod believe that?"

"I wouldn't be sure of the answer to that. The brain rejects what the instinct accepts. But the point is that I do not believe one word of it."

"What do you think?"

"I think that Amos stumbled on to a poacher's cache of smuggled guns or something of the sort, and someone decided to make an example of him. If he lives he will be a walking warning to every man in the Sanctuary that it's rash to see or talk too much. Better to be blind and dumb. We'll look deeper into this matter tomorrow. Forget it now—if you can!"

They were snaking down the long escarpment into the bush-veld. Fires were springing into life, the signs of human habitation—fires that would burn all night to keep the lion, the leopard and the hyena at bay.

" Down there—all that bushveld world—is Velaba," said Rusty. " We haven't far to go now."

She looked at the mysterious, unknown world gathering darkness about it like a cloak—hiding what primeval violence and tragedy ? Till now she had imagined Velaba as a natural Paradise to be explored and shared with her lover. But now she knew it to be the home of dark, uncomprehended, terrifying forces.

A picture of the cottage on the outskirts of London rose before her eyes, and in spite of all the sad memories it held for her—memories she was determined to exorcize or crush—she saw it once again as she had seen it in her early childhood when the garden wall, overgrown with rambler-roses and honey-suckle, had been the symbol of security. Later, ah, later, it had become a prison wall, but in the age of innocence she had played, safe and happy, in its shadow. There was the little summer-house that had been her special refuge, a place to take her toys and her friends, a place to be cunningly defended from the intrusion of her waspish half-sister, Harriet, a place where only a short while ago, she had read and re-read her precious letters and dreamed of Africa and Andrew.

" I am in love with you, Alice . . ." he had written. " We are not children any more, and the years are slipping away . . . I want you to join me here . . . I fully appreciate your position but something *must* be done to free you . . ."

Something must be done. . . . She had folded the letter with a sharp pang of sorrow and a strange bitter-sweet joy. He wanted her. She had stood in the open doorway of the summer-house knowing herself loved, all her senses heightened and receptive, tasting autumn in the air, inhaling the scent of bonfires and leaf-mould, hearing the lowing of Farmer Bur-ford's cows going home to be milked and the screech of the Colonel's peacocks from his garden across the meadow. Tomorrow it would rain. You could always hear the Colonel's peacocks when the wind was from the west.

How far away the cottage seemed, how safe ! Yet even there, in that quiet little summer-house, she had not really been immune from hate and danger. The rustic walls had not shut out the dreadful sounds of the blitz that had killed her scientist father, nor the shrill, venomous voice of her half-sister. And there, at the last, she had examined the inmost secrets of her own heart and dissected with naked honesty the final scenes of a mounting horror.

She drew her coat more closely about her shoulders. There is no safety anywhere, she thought, neither here nor there. That is life. Danger is the core and the currency of living. I have waited for four years to begin to live. Very well, then. Here is danger, here is life—and I welcome it!

3

Voice of the Lion

THE Camp was entirely surrounded by a high, thick thorn-fence which contained the Ranger's house—a bungalow with a green galvanized-iron roof, and behind it a windmill—a few white, mushroom-shaped thatched *rondavels*, each with a brick fireplace outside it for cooking; and a separate area of native huts for camp servants, the fire-squad, gardeners, lorry drivers, and the few Game-guards who were not out in lonely pickets in the bush. Adjoining this hutment were the stables where the horses and the pack-donkeys spent the night with the dogs and the domestic fowls behind a triple barrier of thick thorn to keep out marauding lions and leopards.

The primitive outdoor sanitation that served the *rondavels* was cunningly concealed at the end of a little track between trees and bushes.

" This is only a beginning," said Rusty. " One day we'll have hot and cold water and electricity like the Kruger Park. And a store and a restaurant and all the trimmings. That's when Andrew will decide to move out. This is your *rondavel*. Mine is the one next to it."

Alice followed him into the round, self-contained bedroom lit by a hurricane-lantern which stood on a wooden shelf under a small mirror. The furniture was simple—an iron bedstead neatly made up with clean sheets and an army blanket, a wash-stand with an enamel ewer and basin, a wicker chair, a small

R—B

table, and a few wall-pegs behind a curtain. The door and windows were screened with fly-proof wire. There was a rush mat beside the bed. The light of the lantern shone up into the shadowy, conical recesses of the thatch and was reflected off the smooth, white walls.

" A boy will bring you hot water," he said. " And I see you need a towel and some soap."

" I have soap in my dressing-case."

He grinned. " Keep it there."

As he spoke a camp-boy in a green cotton tunic and shorts came in with a jug of hot water, a towel and a bar of soap. Alice thanked him and he smiled at her with a flash of white teeth in surprisingly pink gums.

" I'll leave you now," said Rusty. " When you're ready we'll eat outside—chops cooked on a wood fire—what we call a *braaivleis*."

" That'll be lovely."

She stood in the doorway and watched him cross to his own *rondavel*, which was only separated from hers by a short, thatched verandah furnished with a wooden table and two chairs. She could see the camp-boy piling wood in a horseshoe-shaped clearing banked by a dense hedge of flowering cabbage-trees and euphorbia. The dog, Smokey, ran about sniffing and exploring, whippy tail wagging. On the far side of the *rondavels* ' Sweet Sue ' was parked under a spreading ebony tree.

It's beginning, thought Alice, the new life is beginning !

She changed into linen slacks and a plain blue shirt and slipped a woollen cardigan over her shoulders. Her hair sprang up round her head in a halo as she brushed it, for the air was dry and electric. She smoothed it into place with her palms and stared at herself in the mirror. Her eyes were dark and deep in the thin frame of her face. They were a stranger's eyes. Who are you ? she asked them. She had the eerie feeling that she was no longer herself but somebody else— somebody she had yet to discover and learn to know. She went to the east-facing window and looked out at the fire burning against the leafy screen. The wood ash was silvery and glowing sparks drifted up into the night. Behind the horn-shaped hills the moon rose in a red-gold orange, nearly at the full.

It seemed unbelievable that only three days ago nightfall had meant the twinkling lights of houses and the loom of London. In England now this same moon would be shining down upon the pale stubble of the reaped fields and on the autumn blooms in the little garden where so recently she had spent most of her leisure hours working with old Thrift, the one-legged jobbing gardener who was as proud of his peg-leg as he was of his ribbons of World War One. Tomorrow the cottage and its contents would be put up for sale. She supposed she should have waited for that. Who would be the new occupants of the little home so full of sad and disturbing memories for her? Would they keep old Thrift on? She hoped so. He was really only good for light work, of course, but he could make things grow. He talked to his plants and they listened to him. He was the sort of person who could conjure a garden out of the wilderness. So, for that matter, was she. Andrew's bungalow in the thorn-veld would soon be standing in a garden bright with the English cottage flowers she intended to plant. But she would miss old Thrift's warnings and suggestions; and his grumblings, too. He was a great grumbler, like all good gardeners. And how he hated Mrs. Withinshaw!

" That bag o' poison," he'd say of Alice's big, raw-boned daily help. " Dips 'er tongue in the midden, 'er do. Get rid of 'er, Miss Alice ! "

Alice would like to have taken his advice, but it would not have been easy to replace Mrs. Withinshaw. She had needed a capable woman with strong arms to help her with the many needs of the patient who was quite unable to do anything for herself.

Alice smiled as she thought of old Thrift. What would he say if he could see her now? She could imagine his bushy eyebrows climbing his forehead in amazement. " 'Er's out there in Africa with all them savages—black as yer 'at, can't trust 'em an inch ! "

And Mrs. Withinshaw? She shivered. Mrs. Withinshaw would have something to whisper. " She's a deep one, is Miss Alice—seems so quiet, but there's a man at the back of this flying off to Africa in such a hurry. You mark my words ! "

Alice had sometimes suspected that Mrs. Withinshaw read her letters. There was a key to her bureau, but once, when she

had mislaid it, she had found that a hairpin was just as effective.
Perhaps Mrs. Withinshaw had made the same discovery. She
often intercepted the postman and brought Alice's letters to
her. " One of them foreign letters, Miss Alice. These
animal stamps is real uncommon——" And Alice would put
out her hand for the thin air-mail envelope with assumed
indifference, hoarding it unopened to read later in the summer-
house at the bottom of the garden.

What a comfort it had been ! What an escape—this queer,
long-distance friendship blossoming steadily into something
deeper. Each letter had been a little more personal, more
revealing of the writer's inner self. The scope of their common interests had widened ; she had sent Andrew books from
time to time, or reviews of plays she had managed to see. She
had given him indications of the bondage that held her chained.

" I have less and less chance of getting up to town these
days. Mother needs constant attention, though the doctor's
wife, Mrs. Manfield, stands in for me occasionally. (She
was a V.A.D. in the war and is kind and competent.) I love
the theatre—lose myself in the make-believe. When I was
a student-nurse I used to go whenever I could. My friend,
Betty Swanson, and I used to queue for the pit. Ballet too.
Do you like ballet ? How could you though ? In your
sort of life there's no opportunity for cultivating a taste for
ballet ! "

But he had answered with rather a beautiful letter which
showed her the ballet of the breeze in the branches of the
thorn-trees ; the whirling Dervish dances of the ' dust devils ' ;
the rhythm of giraffe cantering through the veld, ' their long
necks swaying like the masts of fishing boats in a swell ' ; and
the soaring Pegasus flight of a herd of leaping impala.
" Nature's own ballet is right here if one has eyes to see it," he
had written. That was when she had first fallen a little in love
with him.

Outside, the boy had placed the table from the stoep close
to the fire and set it for two. Near to it, on a smaller table, he
had put a tray of drinks. She saw Rusty help himself to a
brandy and soda. He was wearing grey flannels and a thin,
white shirt with a gaily coloured cotton bandana round his

neck. A vervet monkey with a little wizened black face was perched on his shoulder, and its tiny black hands went through his thick coppery hair. The boy suspended a wire grill over the fire. On it were chops and potatoes in their jackets, and soon the tempting aroma of roasting meat made Alice realize that she was hungry.

" What shall it be ? " said Rusty as she joined him. " Brandy or gin ? With water or soda ? There's some squash, too, if you prefer it."

" Gin, squash and soda," she said. " Not much gin."

" You must be tired."

" I don't tire easily."

Amusement sparkled wickedly in his eyes. He laughed, and she noticed that his strong, square teeth were set a little crooked in his upper jaw. He handed her the glass which he had just filled. The measure of gin was generous in spite of her protest.

" You wouldn't admit it if you were."

" Hospital nurses are hardy animals."

" They need to be, I suppose. Well, what is the toast to be, Alice Lang ? Good hunting —— ? "

She looked at him steadily. So that was it. So he thought she was pursuing his brother, chasing him to the ends of the earth, hunting down her quarry—her man. Well, maybe she was. But she wouldn't stand for Rusty saying as much. Her head went up, proud and high.

" I'll toast Velaba, where the human hunter—or huntress—has no place." Her red mouth smiled, her eyes challenged the mockery in his.

" As you wish. Shall we say, then . . . to the love affair between Alice Lang and—Velaba ! "

She raised her glass. " I'll drink to that."

The grey monkey had jumped off Rusty's shoulder and was astride the dog, examining his smooth coat for ticks and fleas. Smokey accepted his attentions tolerantly. They were old friends. The air vibrated with the high shrilling of cicadas and the chirping of crickets. Fireflies flitted to and fro among the leaves and glow-worms lit and extinguished their tiny candles now here, now there. Then, somewhere out in the bush a lion roared.

It was a long, resonant, cavernous roar followed by a series

of short coughs.   It sounded infinitely menacing and frighten-
ingly near.   Alice's fingers had folded into her palms and the
nails bit into the flesh as she waited for the mighty voice to
thunder again.   The dog had risen with hackles bristling, and
the monkey had scampered up a tree.   A strange, expectant
silence held the bushveld in its grip, as if all life were suspended.
The King was on the prowl.   Once more the roar shook the
night and died away in deep grunts, and then, suddenly, the
hush that followed was broken by innumerable echoes.
Baboons swore and scolded from their sleeping place, hyenas
uttered their curious *whoosh-whoosh*, the jackals barked *ha-ha*
on a higher note, and down by the stable *scherm* the camp dogs
bayed.   Smokey growled in his throat, but Rusty was
unconcerned.

" That lion is some way off," he said.   " A couple of miles
at least.   His voice carries in the wind.   You needn't be
afraid."

" I'm not," Alice said.

He looked at her and saw that her emotion was not one of
fear but of intense excitement.

" You're a strange girl," he said.

" To me that was the voice of Africa," she answered.   " We
invoked it with that toast of yours."

He laughed.   " There's plenty of lion-magic in Africa.
There's a witch on the borders of the Sanctuary who is famous
for invoking lions."

" What does she do ? "

" She sells them for five pounds apiece.   If I have an enemy
I can go to Ndlovukasi and buy a lion.   It won't be a three-
dimensional lion when she gives it to me.   It will be a piece of
paper with a ferocious picture of a lion on it.   But I can blow
life into it, murmur an incantation and one day it will materialize
and kill my enemy."

" And does it ? "

" Frequently.   You have to remember that all this is lion
country and that Bantu witches are good psychologists.   It is
essential that my enemy should know that I have bought a
supernatural lion in order to destroy him.   This creates great
fear and horror in him, and a sense of Nemesis, and when next
he meets a lion he will act stupidly, stand paralyzed, scream or

run wildly, and the lion will react to his terror and spring on him. Sometimes Ndlovukasi's lions run amok and kill other people as well as the intended victim, and then she charges ten pounds to recall the animal."

" How thrilling to substantiate a paper lion ! "

" Very, very dangerous," he said. " Never try it."

He glanced at his watch.

" We must eat. Andrew will be on the radio-telephone in twenty minutes from now. You'll want to talk to him."

He did not see her face as he stooped over the fire and put two chops and a potato on a plate for her. Bread, already buttered, was on the table.

The faint colour had drained from her cheeks and her hand rushed to her throat in sudden panic.

" The radio-telephone ? " she said faintly.

" It's very unprivate. Have some mustard. Anyone can listen in if they know the Sanctuary wave-length and the hours at which the Camps are in communication. And a lot of people do—farmers, store-keepers, missionaries. They find it rather entertaining to hear us talk our sort of shop. Andrew hasn't told anyone about you and him—except Meg and me and Mrs. Hurley, the Missionary's wife, as you are to stay there—so you'll have to be pretty guarded in what you say."

" I've never used a radio-telephone."

" It's quite easy. I'll show you."

" I'd rather not. Could you say I'm tired—that I've gone to bed . . ."

He put his elbows on the table and leaned forward, chin on hands, to look at her. This time there was genuine apprehension in her expression. The left corner of her lower lip was trembling and she had not touched her meat. His eyes were narrow slits and his smile was a shade contemptuous.

" I told you this thing was madness, Alice."

" What thing ? "

" This setting your heart on a man you don't know. You're trying to substantiate a paper lover, my dear. You've got half-way with your magic. The words are written, the picture is drawn, and now you are afraid to hear the voice. That is the next stage. The voice. The incantation."

He saw her face strengthen as he watched it. It seemed to

him that the bones hardened and pressed against the clear skin in the firelight, the lips came firmly under control, and the fathomless eyes met his challenge squarely. He could see determination take command of her whole being, casting out the moment of doubt and misgiving.

"Of course our voices must meet," she said. "You are perfectly right. That is the next stage. I will talk to Andrew when he calls."

4

Andrew

ANDREW MILLER stood in the doorway of the shack that served him as an office and stared across the untidy garden to his house. Through the moon-bleached leaves of the trees he could see the overhead electric light bulb shining on the stoep of his bungalow. I should get a shade for that, he thought. She won't like that naked light. Still, she's lucky that we make our own electricity. For the last four years he had taken his comfortable, shabby house for granted, he had inhabited it with a deep contentment in his surroundings. Now, during the past week, it had begun to fling its shortcomings in his face. The very walls had cried out "Alice won't like this, she won't like that!" And Maxim? How would she get on with his house-boy, who was a moody, self-opinionated old rascal if ever there was one? But Maxim and his master understood one another's ways. Andrew did not want to lose Maxim.

Andrew Miller was tall and loose-limbed, he walked with a slight limp—the souvenir of the Desert Campaign that for him had ended with three years 'in the bag'. During the time he was a prisoner of war he had made the best of his wretched circumstances by studying Natural Science, Zoology and Bantu customs and languages. Thus, in his own way, he had asserted his faith in the future and his intention of one day making his life among primitive people under primitive conditions.

At thirty-five his dark hair was already lavishly streaked with the same pewter-grey as his humorous, long-sighted eyes. The Bantu people of the district loved and venerated him, for this man knew them as no Native Commissioner or missionary had ever done. He was their friend and ' Wise Father ', and he had their interests at heart. But, of Andrew's many ' children ', some were good and some were bad, and they often gave him more headaches than satisfaction. He studied his black ' family ' unceasingly, and generally with amused or exasperated affection. He was as familiar with the complex ramifications of their inherited litigation as they were themselves ; he neither mocked at their superstitions nor frowned upon their marriage rites, but there were certain ancient survivals among their customs that he could not condone. Terrible survivals. For his ' children ' were old in time but young in civilized humanity.

As he stood staring across the garden, disturbing thoughts milled around in Andrew's brain. Three problems in particular played leapfrog through his mind—the shocking mutilation of Amos, who might indeed be dead by now ; the presence of the girl he loved in Velaba, the young woman whose arrival threatened to disrupt the entire manner of his life ; and the insistence of the Sanctuary Board of Trustees that Velaba should shortly be opened to tourists.

Amos. Had he been deliberately silenced in such a terrible manner because he had stumbled upon some secret of the increasingly active game poachers ? Or was it possible that a certain old Chief, well known in the district, had begun to feel that he was losing his grip ? Amos had been famed as a humourist and story-teller, and vision and eloquence were qualities much esteemed in a Chief. If the Elders of the Tribe, advised by the Witch Doctor, had felt it necessary to ' strengthen ' the Chief, they would have selected just such a victim as Amos, so that powerful ' medicine ' might be made of his sharp eyes and golden tongue.

Alice. Everything being equal, she should be here at Camp Three the evening after tomorrow. All that had been dear but nebulous for many months was about to become substantial. A bundle of letters, an inexpensive studio portrait, and a few snapshots of a slim, dark girl were imminently to be exchanged for a living, breathing woman with a right to make demands

upon him and turn his household upside down. Only yesterday the Chairman of the Sanctuary Board had taken up her
photograph on the desk in his study.

" Interesting face," he had remarked. " Your girl friend ? "
Andrew had hesitated. " Just a friend."

" There's character here," the Chairman had said. " Fine
eyes and good features. Reserved, I should say. Not one of
your chocolate-box beauties." He had turned abruptly and
looked at the younger man over his half-lensed spectacles.
" You need a wife, young fellow. It's a lonely life here in the
back of beyond. Work is a good friend, but a woman is
a better one—if she's the right woman."

" I'm not the marrying sort." As he had said the words he
had wondered with momentary horror if they were not absolutely true. He had lived too long without a woman of his
own. Alice, the far-away girl of the letters, had been the
outlet of his lonely hours. He had visualized her, hoped one
day to show her this primitive paradise that had already captured her imagination. He had desired this unknown woman
with a man's fierce necessity, yet now that she was on her way
to him he was harried by nervous misgivings. In a way he
felt that he had, with half a dozen words, denied her.

" So you're not the marrying sort," the Chairman had repeated slowly. " Perhaps not. Being a prisoner of war, and
then leading the life of a hermit in the wilds don't make for
sociability. And not many women are suited to be the wives of
Game Rangers and Wardens. Though, once the Tourist Camps
are established, it won't be so lonely any more. Not really."

The Chairman had harped continually upon that aspect of
the Sanctuary. Tourism. He had urged Andrew to draw up
plans for the necessary visitors' organization. He must start
on those plans tomorrow. Hateful prospect. But the Board
required his views before their next General Meeting.

Andrew looked at his watch. It was solid and luminous on
the flat, thin part of his wrist above the prominent bone. The
hands showed seven fifty-five. If Alice was indeed with Rusty
at Camp One she would expect to speak to him. What could
he say to her ? There was no privacy on the radio-telephone.
Anybody with an ordinary wireless set could listen in on the
Sanctuary wave-length, and often did. The Police Posts at

Poinsettia and Duikers' Drift always did. The Mission Station certainly would tonight. After all, Alice was going to be the guest of the missionary and his wife. Young Thea would be interested . . .

He switched on the light in the office and went over to his desk. On the table beside it was the radio-telephone set, already tuned in. He had only to turn it on and begin to speak.

He pulled up a chair, turned a small black knob and drew a long breath.

"Q.R.L.3 calling Q.R.L.1—Q.R.L.3 calling Q.R.L.1.—Over to you, over." He switched it to reception.

Through the grille on the wall above his head the loudspeaker answered in Rusty's deep, warm voice.

"Q.R.L.1 to Q.R.L.3. Can hear you loud and clear. Go ahead. Over."

Automatically he switched to transmission. "Is Alice Lang with you? Over."

"Yes. She is here at my side. Will you speak to her now? Over."

"No, later. Have you any news of Amos? Over."

"On our way from Duikers' Drift to Camp One, about six-thirty p.m., we met Nelmapius in the jeep with Amos and Job. Amos was in a bad way. Alice Lang gave him sugar-water, he seemed better. Nelampius hopes to get him to Duikers' Drift hospital safely and will report to the Police Post there. Over."

"Any idea how it happened. Over."

"Nothing new. Job blames the Sweet Spruit Tokoloshe. Over."

Andrew recognized the guardedness in his brother's tone. If the old Chief should happen to be listening in at his kraal the less said the better. He had a battery wireless set which was his most cherished possession. He kept it on most of the time at full strength. The Chief might well be involved in this matter.

"Anything else to report? Over."

"A lion attacked our stables last night. Game-guard Esau had to shoot it. A fine male, lamed by a trap. Esau reports extensive snaring in Wit Vlei area. And Job reports a solitary elephant seen on the lower Fulene. Over."

"What route do you propose to trek tomorrow? Over."

"I shall inspect the Mahogany Grove road construction.

From there I intend to take the long circuit to Camp Two. Over."

"Fine. There's nothing new here. Poinsettia Mission will expect Alice Lang the evening after tomorrow. Over to Alice Lang. Over."

As he turned the knob, nearly three hundred miles away in Camp One, he heard a little gasp and a girl's voice whisper "What do I do?" and Rusty's curt, "Talk! I'll do the switching. Every time you're through just say ' Over '."

Funny, thought Andrew in that brief moment; I've been charged by lion and rhino in my time, I've gone into battle and been taken prisoner, but never before have I felt my bowels turn to water quite like this. She's scared too, poor kid. Does she realize that this is *not* a private line? Rusty will surely have told her. I want to say kind things, welcoming things, even loving things, and all I can do is bark, or the whole world—our wilderness-world—will be on to the situation between Alice Lang and me, tearing at it like a pride of lions on a zebra's carcass . . .

There was an endless pause. And then from the little grille came a voice that was low and clear and very English.

"Alice Lang calling Andrew Miller. I am very glad to be in Velaba. Thank you for arranging to have Meg meet me at Jan Smuts Airport. She sends her love. They are all well. They were very kind to me. Over."

"Sorry I couldn't meet you myself. I hope you didn't find the train journey to Duikers' Drift too hot. Over."

"It was fine, and I thought it all very interesting. Rusty was there to meet me . . ." Her voice faltered and faded.

"Over," put in Rusty.

There was nothing they could say that didn't establish their intimacy for the listener—nothing that wasn't personal, something particular to him or her. Yet Andrew did not want to lose her voice. Even her few trite, conventional words had vibrated with overtones of youth and excitement—and nervousness, great nervousness. Was she afraid of this unfamiliar machine, the radio-telephone? Or was she afraid of him? He wanted to say, "Alice! Let's *really talk* . . ." Instead he said: "Did Meg give you a letter from me? Over."

"Yes. Thank you. Over."

He thought he detected a flatness in her voice. Had that letter struck her as a withdrawal? He had not meant it so. The frustration of this difficult conversation overwhelmed him.

" Listen," he said. " We are waiting to welcome you here. They look forward to seeing you at Poinsettia Mission. Over."

" I look forward to coming. Over to Rusty . . ." Rusty came in quickly : " Anything more? Over."

" Nothing. Call me from Camp Two this time tomorrow night. That's all. Good night."

He turned the knob with finality.

The silence inside the shack was the more complete for the sounds of the night beyond it. Cicadas shrilled on a high, monotonous note and a night-bird called with a curiously animal grunt and was answered from farther down the garden. The motor throbbed as the dynamo generated electricity for the Camp, and up in the boys' quarters Andrew could hear the beat of drums and occasional gusts of uninhibited song or laughter. There was a beer-drink in progress.

Andrew sat with his elbows on the table and his head in his hands; his fingers were doubled into his palms and his knuckles pressed against his closed eyes. Against the dark background, shot with falling patterns, he could see a picture of Alice and Rusty as they might be now—standing by the dead box-like machine in Jan Nelmapius's little office. She would look up at his brother with puzzled, disappointed eyes, wondering no doubt at the bleakness of that short, impersonal conversation. Nothing that he had said had given her the least inkling of his longing for her, of the tumult within him, or even of the awful doubts that arose at times like nausea at the thought of his own inadequacy. What had he to offer this young woman who had journeyed so far to meet him? This unpretentious home in the *bundu* that till recently had served all his small wants so well and that now seemed bare and shabby. Himself. A man already past his first youth whose knowledge of women was as narrow as his understanding of his Bantus was wide. A handful of white acquaintances spaced many miles apart and possibly uncongenial to this London-born, city-bred girl, and a population of black tribesmen whose language and habits would be as incomprehensible to her as those of the ferocious wild beasts who were paramount in the little kingdom of Velaba.

He ought to have learned by Rusty's example. Flora had taught them both that this was no life for a woman of sensibility. Now it was too late. He and Alice were both committed.

Was Rusty being kind to her? Rusty, once so easy-going and cheerful, had changed greatly in the past ten years. He had grown into a hard-bitten young man, a soldier of fortune, good value in men's company, attractive to women and ready to take what fun came his way and forget it. Only with children and sick or wounded animals did the tender streak show in the tough meat. Rusty had disliked the idea of this long-distance love-affair with Alice Lang when Andrew had confided in him.

"It's madness," Rusty had said. "What do you really know about this woman—except that she writes a pleasant letter and is interested in your life out here? You know damn all about her."

"I know her well enough to want to marry her."

"It's lunacy!"

"Why? Our ancestors in this country married women they had never seen—had never even heard of. Boat-loads of brides arrived for settlers, and it was a case of a lucky dip. Marriage is like that. Yours was an unlucky dip——"

"Leave me out of this! Leave Flora out of it!"

How deep that wound had gone, poisoning Rusty's whole outlook, his faith in love and in himself. Andrew had said no more. But the brothers had chanced to be together at Camp Two when he had received the cable telling him that Alice's mother had died—that she was free and ready to join him.

Poinsettia Police Post had broken in on the evening session when Jan Nelmapius had come through from Camp One. Sergeant van Wyk could create greater disturbances on the radio-telephone than anyone living. If he had something to say he made you realize that he was there, trying to get a hearing. Andrew recalled the rumbling Afrikaans voice when Poinsettia had at last come in. "K.X.Z.2 calling Mr. Andrew Miller. Post Office has sent a cable from Alice Lang, London. Post Office wants us to contact Andrew Miller and relay the cable if so desired. Over."

Andrew had said, his heart pounding, "Yes. Read it, please. Over."

The Sergeant had cleared his throat and repeated the simple message. " Do you still want me to come to Velaba ? Love, Alice." There had been a pause. Then the Sergeant had added : " Any answer ? Over."

Andrew had known at once what the message meant. Mrs. Lang was dead and Alice was free to join him. She had promised, " When I am not needed here any more I will let you know without delay."

He had considered quickly, aware of his brother's dismayed, questioning look. He had said into the waiting instrument : " Yes, there is an answer. I would be obliged if you would remit it to the Post Office, Sergeant van Wyk. Stand by." He had given the address and the reply, conscious all the while of Rusty watching him with silent but intense disapproval.

" Arrange fly Johannesburg as soon as possible. Cable arrival date. Leave rest to me. Love, Andrew."

" So she's coming all this way to get her man," Rusty had said bitterly. " She must be a mighty determined woman ! "

Andrew had been furious with his brother—and with himself. For months he had been urging Alice to come to him, yet now that she was able to join him he was seized with sudden panic. What if, after all, they were not suited to one another ? How would they face a trek of three days if in the first few moments they found themselves critical of one another ? *It could happen.* And she could hardly reject him on the station platform. Nor could he return her like goods on approval that failed to come up to standard.

Then fate had intervened. Almost on the eve of his departure for Duikers' Drift there had been a tip-and-run raid by biltong-bandits. These gangsters had driven a Land Rover over the border at night at a particularly lonely spot between Camps Two and Three. They had dazzled a herd of wilde- beeste with their powerful lights, drilled them full of machine- gun bullets, cut up the carcasses, and were back on the Johannesburg road all in the space of a few hours. By the time the native pickets could report the incident, the veld was both dangerous and tragic with shockingly wounded animals that had escaped death but must be tracked and destroyed as soon as possible.

At the same time the Chairman of the Sanctuary Board of

Trustees had wired that he would be passing through Poinsettia by car on his way back to Pretoria from a Rhodesian tour, and that he proposed to spend twenty-four hours at Camp Three to discuss various urgent matters with the Senior Warden.

Andrew had had no choice but to ask Rusty to meet Alice at Duikers' Drift in his place and to bring her through the Sanctuary to Camp Three. Rusty had consented with reluctance. Over the radio-telephone Andrew had heard the antagonism in his brother's tone and ignored it. But it had intensified his own doubts, and with every day that passed these multiplied until they seemed to buzz about his ears like a swarm of bees.

And now Alice was really on her way with Rusty.

He had heard her voice, the low-pitched English voice of a stranger; he had sensed her disappointment in the letter Meg had given her from him—a sensible letter, not a love-letter, one that might perhaps have chilled her. She had no one but him in this savage land, and if he failed her she would be lost indeed. He was determined that he would not fail her.

5

First Night in Velaba

ALICE warmed her hands over the fire. Although the spring night was mild she was deathly cold. Her teeth chattered. Rusty had made an excuse to leave her alone after he had brought her back from Jan Nelmapius's office and she was grateful to him for his tact. Before he had left her he had fetched her tweed coat and put it over her shoulders.

" I won't be long," he had said, " and when I come back we'll have some coffee. I've half an hour's work to do in the office."

When the dog, Smokey, had made as if to follow him he had said " Stay ! " and the animal had remained obediently. The vervet monkey had gone to sleep in the branches of a tree, and in the shadows, a little distance away, she was aware of the camp-boy squatting or getting up from time to time to feed the

fire, moving silently on bare feet. Nimrod had disappeared.
" Nimrod is my brother of the veld," Rusty had said. " He is
no house-boy or camp-boy." My brother of the veld. A
strange term.

So she had spoken to Andrew. So the second stage of
substantiating her ' paper lover ' had begun. She felt exhausted and extraordinarily crushed. Rusty had warned her
that the radio-telephone was not private—" It's worse than a
party-line. Don't imagine that you and Andrew can talk freely.
Don't be disappointed if he sounds aloof. He's a shy man."

Even so, the formality of their conversation had been a
desolate experience. It had affected her more profoundly than
the letter she had received in Pretoria. She had recognized
the sound, good sense of that letter. After all, Andrew and
I are not Romeo and Juliet, she had thought, we are two
perfectly rational adults. We cannot expect to spring into
each other's arms at the first meeting and rush for the nearest
parson crying " Marry us, instantly ! " Our love has been a
plant of slow, wintry growth, we can't expect it to blossom into
a tropical plant overnight. But, underlying the practical
estimates of her brain, her heart said " Does he want me ?
Does he *really* want me ? "

And his voice—the timbre of it—had been lighter than she
had expected. But then it was always impossible to match
a personality to a voice. She had often listened to the seductive
resonance of some radio commentator's voice and endowed him
mentally with the physical glamour of a film star, only to
discover that he was a scrawny little man with a bald head and
spectacles. This evening the opposite had happened. She
had long since set the pictured face and figure of Andrew
Miller to the music of an imagined voice—and then the real
voice had been a tenor instead of a baritone. And, because it
had momentarily surprised her, the whole image of her lover
had gone awry. Perhaps she too had sounded strange to him
—as distant in manner as in space.

How little I know him, she thought, how much we need to
learn about each other ! Everything.

Rusty found her sitting forward in the wicker chair, hands
outspread to the warmth of the fire. The glow had an X-ray
effect and he could almost see the fine bones under the firm

flesh. Her narrow fingers with the square, unpainted nails might have been those of a pianist. The firelight washed the cleanly-carved lines of her face in rosy colour, and her downcast lashes lay thick and silky against her cheeks. She seemed lost in thought.

It occurred to Rusty as he watched her that she was a woman who tackled her problems with her intellect rather than her emotions. He was aware of her strength of purpose, her undeviating intention to marry his brother, and resentment flared up in him.

The iron kettle suspended over the fire was boiling. Rusty put a spoonful of coffee essence into each of the two cups on the table.

" Do you take it black or with milk ? " he asked. " The milk is out of a tin."

" Black," she said, as if he had wakened her from a dream.

The boy brought the heavy kettle and poured water over the coffee essence.

" Sugar ? "

" Please."

As she took the cup from Rusty and stirred the coffee she emerged from her mood of abstraction. Her smile suggested that she had rejoined him after a brief spiritual absence.

" Don't you find it rather an odd situation," he said, " travelling thousands of miles to marry a stranger ? I should say it belonged in the period of captive princesses—of caravans crossing the desert to unite remote African kingdoms through the medium of a man and a girl——"

" Or of Henry the Eighth and the Flemish Mare," she put in with a little grimace that pulled her mouth downwards at the left corner. " Poor Anne of Cleeves didn't quite make the grade, did she ? "

" You risk disillusionment," he agreed with a grin. " But I suppose there's no real reason why a marriage of diplomacy— or suitability—shouldn't work out. Just as marriages for love very often don't."

She wanted to say, " But we *are* in love ! " And then the words died on her lips. Love between men and women was not a matter of letters and photographs alone. No one would know that better than Rusty. Rusty had his feet on the ground. He found her romance with his brother ridiculous and incredible and he had not hesitated to say as much. Suddenly she felt raw and vulnerable, her confidence in the future shaken. She wanted to hurt Rusty.

" Your marriage, presumably, was for love ? "

" Yes. It was for love and it was a failure. The fault was mine."

He rose and took a leopard-skin tobacco pouch from his pocket. He plugged his pipe and lit it.

" Can one assess blame so dogmatically ? " she asked.

" I think so. We were both very young. Flora was Italian. We met in Italy during the Italian campaign. We were married on the shores of Lake Como just after the war. The South Africans were among the Occupying Forces. I was a fool not to realize that this was no life for a highly cultured Florentine girl—but I believed in love."

There was bitterness in his voice and his blunt, attractive face assumed a harsher mould.

" And now you don't believe in love any more ? "

" Of course I do. But I know that it's not all-powerful. Love can't surmount every obstacle.

" There are many sorts of love."

" Yes. And the spiritual brand is the most satisfying to some people. To missionaries, for instance—perhaps to nurses. It was written in your face when you were doing what you could for Amos—the love for humanity, for the sick and suffering."

She shook her head and laughed.

" The love of all mankind . . . That's a nice ideal, but I assure you hospital nurses are just like other women. They're as liable to lose their hearts and their heads as the next girl."

" Did you—before Andrew ? "

" I had my juvenile crushes, but there wasn't much opportunity after I left the hospital and . . . went home. I was only twenty-two then—four years ago—and boys soon lose interest in a girl who is never free to go out with them and who can't entertain them in her own home."

" Men are selfish animals." A picture grew dimly in his mind of her young years of work and sacrifice. " You were caught in a trap," he said.

She looked up quickly.

"That's what Betty used to say—my great friend, Betty Swanson. She was the only person who knew about Andrew. We were trained together. We used to hunt in couples in our student days. She was a wonderful friend to me. She often came to the cottage to help me out. She was there the night my mother died—with me when I found her next morning . . . when I couldn't wake her . . ."

She shrugged her shoulders, shaking off the burden of a sad and haunting memory. He helped her.

"Your friend Betty will miss you."

"Oh, no. Betty is going to be married—as soon as the young house-surgeon she's engaged to can get a few days off for a honeymoon."

She recalled the day—only a few weeks ago—when Betty had told her about Jack. A mean little stab of jealousy had pierced her heart. Now indeed she would lose her friend.

"I'm so happy, darling," Betty had said. "But we are keeping it secret till we can get married."

"It must be a great strain—seeing him every day at the hospital—trying not to show what you feel about each other."

"It is. But it's thrilling too—that secret between us. Of course, we are lovers in the full sense of the word. You understand that, don't you?"

Alice had nodded, with a pang of sharp, feminine envy. Her friend had crossed the Rubicon into the realm of love fulfilled. It could not be otherwise. Betty was the last person to withhold herself from the man she intended to marry. Her morality was in many ways elastic.

"It'll have to be a Registry Office affair for us," Betty had added regretfully. "Jack was married before. He's been divorced. For you it'll be a wedding at the Mission, I suppose. A white crinoline and a tulle veil."

"A plain white dress, and a few synthetic gardenias masquerading as a hat," she had answered. "If it happens at all."

"You must *make* it happen! You're caught in a trap here. Get out before it's too late. While you are still young."

"Betty—please!"

"I'm your friend and I have to say this. You know very well that this illness of your mother's can go on for years and years—till you are withered, dried up and finished! Are you

going to give up your life to this one hopeless case that doesn't
even exercise your skill and experience——"

Alice had flared up. " This one hopeless case is my own
mother ! As to my skill and experience—they are the least
one could have—and you know it."

" I'm sorry," Betty had said. " Forgive me."

But afterwards, when Alice was alone, her whole body had
been torn by terrible dry sobs. It was true. She was in a
trap set by duty and devotion. There was no way out. The
unresigned spirit would continue to fight and struggle, sus-
taining its cruel, secret wounds, accepting its plight without
the Christian resignation that might have made it bearable.

The moon, impaled upon the topmost branch of a thorn-
tree, bathed the bushveld in radiance. The shadows it cast
were long and exotic. The twisted silhouettes of euphorbias
and spiky palms reached out towards the *rondavels* behind
Rusty and Alice. She had travelled a long way physically and
emotionally since death had released the jaws of the trap.

" What did Betty think about your coming here ? What do
your other friends think ? " Rusty drew on his pipe. He
was not looking at her.

She said slowly : " Betty approves of my joining Andrew.
I didn't consult or confide in anybody else. I have no idea
what they think."

" They'll be speculating quite a lot, I dare say. You'll have
them guessing."

" I suppose there'll be talk. I hadn't considered it."

" In the heart of a city or out in the *bundu* there's always one
thing you can count on. There'll be talk. Even if it's only
one old nigger gossiping with another."

" There's the postmistress," said Alice. " For two years
she's been mailing letters and books and magazines to Andrew
for me ; there's the Colonel's schoolboy son who collects
stamps and always waited for my animal stamps from South
Africa ; there's the doctor's wife who teased me about my
mysterious boy-friend out in the blue ; there's Thrift, the old
gardener who used to chat with the postman at the cottage
gate ; and Mrs. Withinshaw, our daily help, who lives for ' a
bit of news ' as she puts it. She's a ferret for scandal. I
believe she read my letters——"

Alice broke off, frowning. There had been one letter in particular that she had missed, a letter she knew by heart that had vanished from her desk. " I am in love with you, Alice ... I want you to join me here. It is terribly important for us to get to know each other as human beings ... I fully appreciate your position but something *must* be done to free you ..." On the strength of that letter she had gone so far as to enquire about air-passages to South Africa.

" You'll need a yellow-fever certificate," the clerk in the travel agency had said, " that is, if you are leaving soon."

" I'm not leaving soon, as far as I know," she had answered.

" Well, remember you'll have to have the injection at least ten days before you leave here or they quarantine you at the other end."

" How long does the immunity last ? "

" Immunity ? Oh, about three years, maybe four."

I want to be ready, she had thought. When the time comes I must be quite ready. She had arranged to have the injection. The needle under the skin, the burning sensation of the serum had given her a curious thrill—like the first touch of a lover's lips.

She heard Rusty say : " You've quite a start there for a bit of gossip. What about relations ? You didn't mention your family."

" I have none. Only my half-sister, Harriet Carver. We don't get on. To be frank, we detest each other."

Alice shivered. The last time she had seen her half-sister, Harriet Carver, had been at her mother's funeral. She could smell again the lingering sickly-sweet scent of the few wreaths and crosses that had covered the coffin before the cremation, and see the rain falling outside the casement window. She could hear the dry voice of the family lawyer reading the short, pathetic will as if it were a brief sermon on the subject of poverty and parsimony.

" ... and to my younger daughter, Alice Mary, in grateful thanks for her constant devotion and professional care, the sum of two thousand pounds over and above her aforementioned share in the estate ..."

That was when Harriet had gasped aloud and her rat-faced husband, Cyril Carver, had leaned forward with his sharp teeth showing. Even their dreary little daughter, Mabel, had realized that something was amiss and dragged at her mother's black skirt. Afterwards they had cornered and attacked her. Here was genuine fuel for Harriet's consuming jealousy of Alice, the child of the man her mother had loved. Harriet had always resented her mother's second husband—the tall, austere scientist who had given his wife love, happiness—and Alice. She had pressed her narrow face into her sister's, her thin lips writhing spitefully.

" I never knew Mother had two thousand pounds tucked away. I suppose *you* knew, Alice ? "

Then Cyril had chimed in, " Of course Alice had endless opportunities of influencing the poor soul when her mind was failing."

" I never saw Mother's will ! " Alice had cried. " I didn't know about that two thousand."

" And what will you do with your . . . *unexpected* windfall ? " The rat-teeth were bared.

" I shall go to Africa."

" Why Africa—of all places ? "

" It's a long way from here ! "

A very long way, thank heaven.

Rusty's deep voice cut across the memories that distressed and disturbed her.

" We must make a fairly early start tomorrow. We'll have breakfast over at Jan Nelmapius's place at seven-thirty."

" Will he be back ? "

" Sure. He'll leave Amos at Duikers' Drift hospital, report to the police there and come straight back. You'll probably hear the jeep about midnight."

" I shall be asleep, I hope. And I doubt if anything will wake me."

He stood up and knocked out his pipe against a tree. The dog woke and watched him.

" A night-cap before you turn in ? "

" No thanks. Good night, Rusty."

" Good night. And sleep well."

Alice undressed by the light of the hurricane-lamp. She pulled on her blue silk pyjamas and a light woollen dressing gown, creamed her face, turned down the lamp and drew aside the curtains of the window. She opened it wide and looked towards the far mountains rising in moon-drenched radiance against a luminous sky.

This is a strange night, she thought, my first in Velaba. *I will lift up mine eyes unto the hills, from whence cometh my help ... The sun shall not smite thee by day, nor the moon by night. ...* The sun and moon of Africa were not like the sun and the moon of England. They were potent and dangerous. It was as well to pray for protection against their power.

How still the night was ! Even the cicadas were silent. How fresh it smelt—of grass and leaves and wood-smoke. She breathed deeply, inhaling the purity of the bushveld air.

Far away she heard the thunder of the lion's roar, followed by the deep, throaty grunts—only one of the many unfamiliar voices of Velaba.

She crept into bed, pulling the sheets up close around her chin. At home, thousands of miles away, the wind might be from the west, carrying the cries of the Colonel's peacocks across the meadows of her childhood. A rain wind probably. Home ? The cottage would never be home again. It belonged to the past. She wanted to put it right away from her with all its accumulated weight of unhappiness, frustration and friction. She felt, with a swelling of the heart, that her spirit had returned to forgotten haunts and love long lost in the mists of time.

6

Drop of Poison

FLURRIES of rain beat against the mullioned windows of the ' Blue Boar ', only a short walk through the red-gold October woods from the cottage Alice Lang had so recently left.

Harriet Carver and her rat-faced husband sat on either side of the big open fireplace adorned with warming-pans, copper kettles, fire-irons and all the other trappings of a low-raftered Tudor kitchen turned ' Visitors' Lounge '. They were glad to have the place to themselves, for the child, Mabel, was asleep in their bedroom upstairs and they could not have talked without waking her. Mabel was a nervous child.

The bar had just closed and the landlord put his round, rubicond face in at the door.

" Have you everything you need, Mrs. Carver ? "

" Yes, thank you, Mr. Jenkins. Especially now that the bar is closed and we have peace and quiet ! What a din people make when they are drinking ! "

Mr. Jenkins came in and warmed his seat at the fire.

" Noise—within reason—is a sign of good cheer." He winked at Cyril Carver. " A silent bar would be a sad place, wouldn't it, sir ? "

" It would indeed. But my wife and I have a good deal to discuss." Carver spoke pointedly.

" Of course," agreed the landlord. " The sale and so on. Let's hope it clears up by tomorrow. Rain puts bidders off. Pity Miss Alice couldn't stay to see who buys the cottage. She'll be in South Africa by now with all those Mau Mau, I suppose."

" She should have arrived in Johannesburg yesterday," said Carver. " And, for your information, Mr. Jenkins, there are no Mau Mau in the Union of South Africa."

" Not as yet. But, from what I've read, South Africa is a dreadful country—all the blacks in concentration camps and the whites armed to the teeth."

" Do you really believe all you read in the sensational press ? " asked Harriet tartly.

The landlord chuckled. " If it's exciting enough. I like a bit of blood and thunder with my breakfast. Adds spice to the eggs and bacon. Give me a really lively morning paper with lots of crime on the front page ! "

" Don't stay up on our account, Mr. Jenkins." Harriet was scandalized, but she suspected that Mr. Jenkins was pulling her leg and resented the idea.

When the landlord had taken the hint and left them she turned to her husband. " Sordid. But that's the way they are. Always sniffing out something evil."

Carver took a cigarette from his case without offering one to his wife. She neither smoked nor drank. He had arrived from London less than half an hour ago—just before closing-time fortunately. He was tired and disgruntled. The business that had kept him late in town had not gone satisfactorily.

" Find everything tin-dish over at the cottage ? " he asked.

" I suppose you might say so. The stuff was all stacked in lots. If you want to buy one thing you have to take several other things you don't want. The furniture won't fetch much. There are a few decent pieces but most of it's junk."

" Pity your dear mother didn't go when second-hand furniture was fetching a fortune. But one can't arrange these matters to suit oneself."

" Can't one ? "

Carver glanced at his wife sharply. Her face had its ' burrowing ' look—the eyes pin-points, the long, thin nose twitching, ready to drill into some dark earth in search of—what ?

" What's on your mind, Harriet ? "

" There's been a lot of talk," she said.

" Talk ? "

" About Alice. Flying off like that before Mother's ashes were cold."

" She gave it a week. Time to get an air passage and a nice advance on that two thousand pound legacy. What was she to wait for ? "

" The sale."

" Why ? She'll get her fifty per cent of that automatically." Harriet's thin mouth pursed. " It was indecent haste."

" What was her hurry—in your opinion ? "

" There's a man in this somewhere."

Cyril Carver's upper lip, decorated by a narrow line of blond bristles, drew back from his teeth. The noise he made was a titter.

" Alice ! Where could she pick up a boy-friend ? Even if she has what it takes in certain ways, the simple factor of opportunity was missing. Your mother was a full-time job, as you well know. And you didn't help, my dear. If you'd taken your share of the rough you'd have picked up your share of the smooth. As it is, that two thousand—clear of death duties—went to ' my younger daughter, Alice Mary, in grateful appreciation of——' "

" Nothing would have made any difference," Harriet chipped in. " Mother always favoured Alice. She loved Alice's father and hated mine. And, anyway, those savings had belonged to Alice's father. We thought Mother had spent them. That's where we were wrong."

" I dare say Alice would just as soon have had the old girl spend them on getting in a paid nurse—two nurses if necessary —leaving her free to follow her own fortunes."

" And when the two thousand was gone, what would we have done ? By then Alice might have been in the heart of Africa—married perhaps."

" Why not ? If *you* could catch a man, *she* might." It amused him to taunt her.

The look she gave him was venomous. It did not disturb him. He was used to it.

" That is exactly what Alice has gone to do," she said deliberately. " She has gone to South Africa to catch her man."

He leaned forward and put another log on the fire. The crackle of the dry wood and the patter of the raindrops on the window-panes were the only sounds in the room.

" Where did you get that theory ? " he said at last.

" When I went to the cottage this afternoon Mrs. Withinshaw was there—checking up on things she wanted to bid for."

" That bag of gossip ! "

" She certainly keeps her eyes and ears open—wide open." Harriet shivered and drew her chair closer to the fire. " She had a few things to tell me."

" Such as ? "

" She declares Alice had . . . a . . . secret life."

She stared into the flames, seeing again the big raw-boned woman standing in the little bedroom that had been the invalid's, hearing the coarse voice, the sinister insinuations.

" Not much worth 'avin' 'ere," Mrs. Withinshaw had said. " Dismal it is with the days drawin' in and winter on the way. I s'pose where Miss Alice is the sun'll be shining."

The woman's tone had irritated Harriet. " Where do you imagine my half-sister is ? "

" I expect Mrs. Dimble at the Post Office could take a guess. There's talk, Mrs. Carver, talk."

" What sort of talk ? "

" Your sister was a deep one, Mrs. Carver. Deep as the sea. She didn't blab 'er affairs around—not by a long chalk !—But rumours get about."

" Rumours ? "

" Miss Alice 'ad 'er *secret life*. For more'n two years Miss
Alice 'as been communicatin' with a gentleman friend in Africa
—letters and books and goodness knows what not all passin'
between 'em regular as clockwork. It's my belief he was urging
'er to go out there to join 'im—to marry 'im——"

" To marry him ! "

" So you didn't know nothin' about it ? I didn't think you
would, Mrs. Carver."

" Did Miss Alice confide in you ? "

" Miss Alice wasn't one for giving 'erself away. But I knew
'er better than most—comin' in daily and 'elping with your
poor Ma. Mind you, when I comes in she usually takes 'er
chance to go shoppin' in the village, rain or shine. Gave 'er
a bit of an airin'. Real outdoor person, she was. That rascally
old peg-leg, Thrift, used to say she had the green fingers.
Mad on 'er patch of garden. Sometimes I used to wonder to
myself if Miss Alice was really cut out to be a nurse. You need
patience nursin' an 'opeless case, day in, day out. She 'ad to
force 'erself to be patient. She *was*, mind you, but it didn't
come easy. I could see that ! She never let 'erself go. Might
'ave been better if she 'ad. But, if you ask me, 'er secret life
kept 'er going."

" Exactly what are you getting at ? "

Harriet had clutched the back of the stiff little armchair by
the bed as she shot the question at Mrs. Withinshaw. The big
woman had remained unperturbed, leaning against the wide
window-sill, facing into the room, her gaunt form silhouetted
against the wet, grey daylight. Harriet could not see Mrs.
Withinshaw's expression, whereas her own was exposed in all
its searching malice, tempered with dislike of discussing family
matters with this woman who was playing her curiosity like a fish.

" This trip to Africa. Let me tell you something. A person
can't just fly off at a moment's notice, Mrs. Carver——"

" My half-sister did—at very short notice, anyway."

" That's just it. My nephew—just come back from 'is
national service with the Mau Mau—he was in to see us a couple
of days ago, and 'e says to me, 'e says, ' Look, Aunt Eliza, if
you want to fly to Africa these days, there's *formalities*. You
gotta 'ave a certificate to say you've been vaccinated and another

to prove you've 'ad the yellow-fever inoculation. And that isn't done in a flash. You gotta 'ave the yellow-fever all of ten days before leaving—or they don't let you in the other end.' Miss Alice *knew* that, Mrs. Carver. Miss Alice *'ad* 'er certificates. *She was ready to take off before ever your poor Ma breathed 'er last.*"

" How can you say that for sure ? "

" I'm thorough when I dusts. When Miss Alice came back from 'er 'oliday in London a fortnight or so before your Ma passed on I was dusting 'er bureau and there I sees a passport and in it a loose slip of paper with ' yellow fever ' printed on it. It's only afterwards the little things add up. Miss Alice was takin' no chances with 'er secret life. She had it all planned, if you ask me."

" You don't like my half-sister, do you, Mrs. Withinshaw ? "

" Miss Alice and me may 'ave 'ad words once or twice, but I suited 'er an' this place suited me. We got along."

" You spied on her."

The silhouette framed by the window had swelled and lengthened as Mrs. Withinshaw drew herself up to her full formidable height.

" I don't like that word, Mrs. Carver. I'll ask you to take it back."

" Very well, then. You used your powers of observation. What else did you notice—besides the passport with the yellow-fever certificate in it ? "

" The morning after your Ma passed on—nobody knows exactly when she went, but it was in 'er sleep that night— something *does* strike me as peculiar. Very peculiar—if you're interested."

" I am extremely interested."

" Well, I was a bit late comin' in that day—all unsuspecting of what I'd find ! My Jackie was in bed with one of 'is sore throats, and I 'ad to go by the school and explain, so it was nearer 'alf-past ten than 'alf-past nine when I comes in. Imagine the shock I gets when I finds your poor Ma 'as gone in the night, and Dr. Barnet—that's the new young one who is taking Dr. Manfield's place while he's on holiday—has been in already an' given the death certificate, while Miss Alice is just finishin' the layin' out with Miss Swanson to 'elp her.

You know Miss Betty Swanson, that young nurse from London, Miss Alice's great friend. Well, I will say they was making a good job of it. I seen plenty laid out by the District Nurse, but never a tidier one or more peaceful lookin' than your Ma. I never seen 'er lookin' so contented in life, poor soul, an' I thinks when I sees her, there's a merciful release ! "

Harriet had nodded. It had indeed been strange and unfamiliar—the expression of rest and calm that had descended like a benediction upon the haunted features.

" Miss Alice meets me, cool as you please, not a tear—just very pale with 'er face thin and hollow. ' Mrs. Withinshaw,' she says, ' I have a great deal to attend to. Please go ahead and clean up as usual.' *As usual !* But then I will say Miss Alice always 'ad 'erself in hand. So she settles 'erself by the telephone an' gets ahold of Mr. Pitt, the undertaker, an' the lawyer, the paper, the florist an' so on. She'd wired you already, I think. And I gets on with the cleaning. Naturally I comes in 'ere to the bedroom first in case people come to visit your Ma. I sweeps an' dusts an' empties the waste-paper basket . . ." Here Mrs. Withinshaw had paused for what seemed to Harriet an interminable time. A pause for effect. Harriet had cut it short with a sharp " So then ? "

Mrs. Withinshaw had continued : " I've 'elped in this house day in, day out for years, Mrs. Carver, before ever your poor Ma was taken ill. I know the 'abits 'ere like the back of me 'and. Every night, regular as clockwork, before Miss Alice turns in she gives your Ma an injection an' throws the empty vial and the cotton-wool swab into the waste-paper basket, under the table. She was never one to leave bits and odds and ends lying in the kidney-dish. Always tidied up those little things. *But on this particular morning what do I find ?* "

A gust of wind shook the long tendrils of the honeysuckle creeper outside the window so that they tapped against the pane like futile fingers knocking for admission.

" What did you find, Mrs. Withinshaw ? "

" I found *two* empty vials and *two* used swabs in the basket. Your Ma had *two* injections the night she died in 'er sleep, Mrs. Carver."

" What about it ? This Dr. Barnet—Dr. Manfield's locum —had probably increased the dose."

The woman had shaken her head. "Oh no, it wasn't as simple as that. Miss Alice 'ad been very upset for quite a time because your poor Ma was gettin' fancies. She was frightened of all of us—except Miss Swanson. I must say Miss Swanson 'as a way with 'er. She could do anything with your Ma, but then she wasn't there so very often. But your Ma had begun to be scared of everybody—even Miss Alice. And only a couple of days before the end I finds Miss Alice with 'er pinched look, and she says to me, ' It's so sad, Mrs. Withinshaw—there's so little we can do for Mother any more. Even the night injection can't be increased. I've asked Dr. Barnet, but he says Mother is getting the maximum dosage.' So you see, Mrs. Carver, the night she passed on your Ma got *double the maximum dosage*."

Cyril Carver saw his wife begin to shiver violently as she sat crouched over the fire in the Visitor's Lounge of the ' Blue Boar '.

"What's up with you ? " he asked. "You might have a fever the way you're shaking."

Her fingers trembled as she opened her handbag. She took out a match-box containing two transparent, empty vials and two cotton-wool swabs that no longer smelt of ether or spirit, and a South African air-letter-card closely written in a neat, slanting hand.

"I exchanged these with Mrs. Withinshaw for the armchair in Mother's bedroom," she said.

Cyril Carver opened the folded air-letter-card and the words that caught his eye made him draw in his breath with a low whistling sound.

"I am in love with you, Alice. We can't go on like this much longer . . . the years are slipping away. . . . I want you to join me here. . . . It is terribly important for us to get to know each other as human beings—not merely on paper. . . . I fully appreciate your position but something *must* be done to free you. . . ."

He began to read the letter slowly and carefully from beginning to end. At last he said : " So this was her secret life— this was her love-life—the written word and no chance of turning it into flesh and blood, a man, marriage and children."

" You sound as if you were sorry for her." She had stopped shivering. She was herself again, spitting the words at him.

" I've never been sorry for anyone in my life," he said. " If I were the pitying kind I'd pity myself. Hadn't you better tell me everything that happened at the cottage this afternoon ? "

When she had done so she said : " You see it all adds up—as Mrs. Withinshaw suggested."

" Adds up to what answer ? "

She did not reply. She sat over the fire with her bony shoulders hunched, her sharp face brooding.

Carver said : " I wonder why Mrs. Withinshaw waited this long to talk to you."

" I asked her that. She said she was waiting to see if Alice was really going to Africa."

" Allowing the motive to establish itself. I see. I'd rather like a talk with Betty Swanson."

" She was married in a Registry Office yesterday. She's gone to Paris on a four-day honeymoon. She rang me up to ask me to bid for the French clock in the dining-room. That was before Mrs. Withinshaw . . ."

" Dropped the poison into your ear. Well then, let's see what Mrs. Withinshaw's conclusions add up to. Let's put the weights in the scales against your step-sister, Alice Lang, the perfect nurse and daughter. What have we ? A legacy of two thousand pounds that would certainly be useful to anybody. A love-letter begging her to abandon her duty and join her lover ; evidence that she was sitting pretty with a yellow-fever certificate before there was any reason to suppose she might make a journey ; further evidence that a lethal injection could have been administered by her hand. All small weights that may not amount to much. But there is one big weight that could fairly be added to that lot—one that might well turn the scales. Can you guess it, my dear ? "

She hesitated, frowning. " Alice has always been crazy to go to Africa. Would that be it ? "

His lip was drawn back from his sharp teeth in the smile that resembled a silent snarl.

" Oh, no, my dear. But then this big weight in the scales would never occur to you. You don't study people as I do. Your imagination moves in the limited grooves of the egoist."

" I know Alice," she snapped. " She had good reason to want her freedom—to take it."

" And to *give* it, perhaps." He spoke slowly and with emphasis. " Have you ever considered the pain of watching another human being suffer—someone you love and cannot help—someone beyond all hope of healing ? "

There was no sound in the room save the rain pattering against the mullioned window. Even the dying fire was silent.

" Think about it ! " he said.

7

Sunrise at Camp One

ALICE woke with the dawn. Through the open window of the *rondavel* she could see the scimitar-shaped screen of bush and trees that only a few hours ago had been illuminated by fire-light and moonshine. She could hear the sleepy twittering of birds.

No, she thought, this can't be true. I'm not really here in Velaba. If I close my eyes and open them again I'll see the beech trees nodding outside my window at the cottage. She tried closing her eyes and fell softly back into a light doze. When she opened them once more the sun was rising in a blaze of ruby red and the camp-boy was humming to himself as he cleared away the table and coffee cups from the space beside the blue-white wood-ash of last night's fire.

She sprang out of bed, throwing back the blanket and sheet to strip it all in one movement. Even here the old habits persisted. She pulled on her dressing-gown and slippers and called to the boy that she would like hot water to wash in.

" Yeez, Nkosikasi," he said, in his rumbling voice, and disappeared to fetch it for her.

She dressed in brown linen shorts and striped shirt, and brushed her hair till it gleamed. The face that looked back at her from the mirror was young and fresh and rested. She hardly knew it. She was not the same person any more. She was no longer a tired, frustrated nurse with the monotonous

R—c

chores of a long day's work before her and a suspicious and unhappy patient to care for and cheer. She was a young woman with a life of her own to lead, and a man of her own waiting for her.

As she went out into the sparkling, sweet-scented morning all her doubts of the night before evaporated. Everything was going to be all right. In the dust round the *rondavel* she saw the spoor of nocturnal visitors—the delicate hoof-prints of buck and a pug-mark she took to be Smokey's. A host of yellow buffalo-weavers, metallic blue-black starlings, and speckled hornbills fluttered and twittered among the branches of a spreading umbrella-thorn covered with fragrant white blossom.

" Good morning. Ready for breakfast ? "

Rusty, in khaki shorts and bush-jacket, looked scrubbed and aggressively healthy. His tanned skin had a glow on it, and his thick, springing hair was burnished where the sun caught it.

" I'm hungry as a wolf," she said.

" Or a hyena," he remarked, with a glance at the dog-like spoor in the dust. " Somebody prowled round here last night to see if we'd left any pickings from our *braaivleis*. Come along then, Alice, Jan Nelmapius is expecting us for breakfast. He arrived shortly before midnight. He left Amos in hospital doing comparatively well, you'll be glad to know."

They strolled over to the Ranger's house. Half a dozen snuff-coloured puppies ran out to greet them. " Smokey's progeny," remarked Rusty. " They are first-class bushveld lion-dogs."

Smokey sniffed at the puppies with paternal patronage and greeted their mother with obvious pleasure.

Young Nelmapius came on to the stoep with the vervet monkey perched on his shoulder.

" Come along in," he invited eagerly, and then apologized for his home. " I'm afraid it's not very civilized. The last Ranger was a family man, and when he left I didn't try to furnish all the rooms. You see, I'm not here very much."

Indeed, the place was scarcely furnished at all. It had a derelict air of neglect, but Alice saw at once that it could have been made not only habitable but attractive. He needs a mother or a sister, poor boy, she thought ; he hasn't a clue.

The living-room, in which they ate an excellent breakfast of eggs and bacon, was dominated by an enormous paraffin refrigerator ; a pile of old magazines was heaped on a couch with a broken spring, and a little battery wireless set stood on an upturned packing case.

As they finished their coffee, Alice heard an extraordinary commotion from the direction of the kitchen—grunts and snorts and a thumping noise as of some considerable weight battering against the door. Rusty's blue eyes had narrowed with laughter and Jan looked disconcerted.

" I told Piccanin to keep him out," he said to Rusty. " I thought William might come as a shock to Miss Lang."

" Shock or not, William wants to come in," said Rusty. " And he is accustomed to getting his own way. Any moment now, Alice, you will see why Jan doesn't over-furnish his house. William is impulsive—some might think him repulsive—and when he's in a hurry he pushes through things, never goes round. In fact, he'll have that door down in a minute if Piccanin doesn't open it."

The half-grown piccanin who had served their breakfast was evidently of the same opinion, for, as Rusty spoke, the door opened and William made his entry. He paused for a moment in astonishment at the sight of strangers, and then trotted rapidly up to Jan Nelmapius, tasselled tail erect. In all her life Alice had never seen any creature so grotesque and engagingly hideous as William the Warthog. His tiny piggy eyes gleamed intelligently from a fantastic grey face loaded with curving tusks. The tufted cheeks were adorned with warty excrescences and the small, stiff ears twitched as did the flat snout which resembled that of a vacuum cleaner. Jan offered William a piece of toast, which he received with enthusiasm, and, as he ate it, the vervet monkey sprang down from his master's shoulder and landed neatly on William's sturdy back.

" Jan's family," said Rusty. " And there's a hornbill, too, but he's probably outside with the fowls, eating their breakfast. I think we should be going over to the office now. We haven't much time to waste."

Alice was helpless with laughter as she went out into the sun with the two men. William, goaded by his improbable jockey, trotted rapidly ahead of them and presently disappeared among the thorn-trees.

Hanging on a line against the thick thorn-fence were strips of meat drying in the sun.

" Lion-meat for the dogs," said Jan. " That lion got into the stables the night before last and one of our Game-guards shot him. He'd been caught in a trap and the poor beast must have gnawed through his own foot to release himself. He was too lame to go after his natural game. He was a beautiful black-maned fellow."

" Do the Bantus eat lion-meat ? " asked Alice.

" Some will, some won't. There are all sorts of contradictory lion superstitions among the natives. Some won't even skin a dead lion. They are afraid that a lion will get them in revenge. Others believe that if they eat lion-meat they will have the strength of the King of Beasts—something of his power."

She turned suddenly to Rusty.

" Have you ever eaten lion-meat ? " She had a fanciful notion that Rusty—Ratau, the Lion of Lions—might not be altogether immune from native superstition.

He laughed. " I sometimes suspect that Nimrod has flavoured my game stew with lion. Nimrod always likes to include me in his magic, with or without my knowledge."

And you are not averse to it, she thought. You are something of a wild man yourself—something of a Pagan.

" Want to come into the office, Miss Lang ? " asked Nelmapius. " We could show you a map of the Sanctuary. It might make your journey more interesting."

" Thanks," she said. " I'd like that."

The Ranger's office was as bare as his home. Only the absolute necessities were in evidence—a desk, two chairs, wall-charts and maps, a corner shelf with a few basic medicines for the use of sick natives, epsom salts, castor-oil, penicillin ointment and a snake-bite outfit. Over a filing-cabinet was a gun-rack holding a ·303 rifle, a heavy ·375 Holland and Holland, and a ·22 for small game.

" The poacher's favourite weapon," remarked Rusty, touching the ·22. " It's light and almost silent—just the thing for buck. I believe that someone is smuggling these guns to the natives on the borders of the Sanctuary."

" Buck biltong fetches a high price on the Rand—in any

town," said Nelmapius, "and our herds along the border are being depleted. Look, Miss Lang, it's a long border to patrol —practically three hundred miles. Unfenced, of course. It would cost too much, and in any case the game must be free to seek their water outside the Sanctuary in time of drought."

He spread a chart on his desk.

"See what a long, narrow strip Velaba is," said Rusty. "Here to the east, we are bounded by the Black Mamba Mountains—our main watershed—and to the west we have the Native Territories and a number of farms who draw their labour from the neighbouring kraals as we do. The farmers sell us all the farm produce we require because it is impossible for us to do any serious cultivation in country given over to wild life. There is a Police Post at Poinsettia in the north and another at Duikers' Drift. So we depend almost entirely on our own Game-guards and Rangers to police our border."

"Can your Game-guards arrest people?" Alice asked.

"*You* could arrest somebody if you saw them breaking the law," he smiled. "And so can we. Game laws are strict."

"Are your Bantu Game-guards to be trusted?"

Rusty frowned. "They used to be. The natives are very good about accepting the principle of game preservation and its responsibilities, but just lately I've had my doubts about some of our people. We have even wondered if a Fifth Column is not being slowly but surely built up right here inside Velaba." He turned briskly to Nelmapius.

"By the way, Jan, I hear that Boryslawski has been burning off grass along his boundary."

"Yes," said the Ranger. "He has." He added to Alice: "This farmer, Boryslawski, has a big property that runs with the Sanctuary boundary. When he burns grass and the new shoots come up it lures the game. Naturally he has a licence to shoot a certain amount of game, but we suspect that he exceeds his rights by a long way. He's a bad man, Miss Lang. The natives call him Radinoxa, the King of the Snakes."

"His farm is here." Rusty's sinewy forefinger rested on the chart between Camp Two and a point marked Sweet Spruit. "Adjoining it is the old Chief's kraal. And here, at Sweet Spruit, is where Amos met his—accident. We will go there today and investigate the Tokoloshe tale a little further."

How grim he can look, thought Alice. Suddenly his face changes. All the boyishness goes out of it and it is hard as iron, coldly cruel.

Nelmapius said : " Job tells me that March—Amos's opposite number—has friends in the Chief's kraal, and that he must have been somewhere near when the attack was made. He'll be on his way back to the picket by now."

" He should get there some time this morning. And so will we. I have a good many questions to ask our friend, March. Then we'll outspan here on the hill above the river for lunch, and I'll inspect the road construction work afterwards. But we won't take the direct route to Camp Two. We'll make the big detour that includes Sweet Spruit—and the Tokoloshe and the Chief's kraal. Possibly Boryslawski's place, too, on some pretext or another."

" You'll be late getting in to Camp Two. If your brother comes though at eight-thirty tonight he may miss you."

" If he does, tell him to call again at nine-thirty. And now I want a word with Job. Alone."

While Rusty talked to the old Game-guard who was Nelmapius's companion on his inspections and treks, the young Ranger took Alice to the skin-room opening off his office. It was a dark little room which led out into the compound. It had a close, sickly smell of tanneries.

Unpolished horns and strips of hippo-hide lay upon shelves ; and, slung over a line down the centre of the room, were innumerable hides and skins. Nelmapius selected a few and spread them in the sun outside.

" Zebra, giraffe, wildebeest, impala," he said. " And this is a leopard skin with the rosettes—different from this cheetah with its spots. And here's the lion who was maimed—the one Esau shot the night before last and whose meat was drying by the fence. And here's a spotted hyena skin. I hate hyenas, they are cowardly scavengers, but this poor devil got his snout into a wire noose. Somehow he escaped, but the noose had tightened and acted like a muzzle. We found him trailing the rest of the wire, his cheeks had been cut through to the bone and he was slowly starving to death. All these skins are damaged by traps."

" So cruel," she said, shuddering. " So cruel, these traps."

" And there's nothing to them," said the young man. " See here's one." He took a long loop of wire from a shelf. " Just a noose and a slip-knot. It's placed in some game-trail leading to a drinking-place, and it will catch anything and strangle it. They use the gin-traps, too, but they are all very old-fashioned because it's illegal to sell them."

" Have you tusks among these . . . trophies ? "

" Elephant tusks ? No. The elephant country is in the north. You'll find tusks at Camp Three, I dare say."

She wanted to talk to him about Andrew. Some way she would try to lead the conversation to Andrew. She had moved a little way from the skin-room—away from the unpleasant odour and the sad associations of dumb suffering.

" Do you often go to Camp Three ? " she asked.

" Whenever I can find an excuse."

She saw the fair, sun-reddened skin deepen its tinge, and she smiled, wondering what—or who—he had to blush about.

" Is Camp Three so attractive then ? "

" It is to me."

Alice laughed. " Who is she and what is she like ? "

" She is Dorothea Hurley, the prettiest girl I have ever seen."

" The missionary's schoolgirl daughter ? Andrew has mentioned her in his letters——" She caught herself up sharply. She had spoken as if Jan knew about Andrew's letters and their meaning in her life. But he had noticed nothing.

" Thea's not a schoolgirl any more," he said. " She's eighteen. My mother was married at eighteen."

" So Thea is your girl ? "

His face fell. " I wish that were so, Miss Lang."

" Is there somebody else then ? " She did not wish to appear curious, but she had the feeling that he was eager to confide in her.

" At times I think so. But she doesn't say so."

" I'll tell you what. Try shaving your beard."

His hand flew defensively to the fluffy golden growth, and she realized that it was the symbol of his manhood—that he was insecure here in his youth.

" It's just that some girls don't go for beards," she said. " Others do—like Meg, Rusty's sister. Her husband has a proper pioneer's beard."

" I'll think about it. In the meantime, would you give her a message ? I've saved a puppy for her. One of Smokey's— one of the very best. As bushveld dogs go, you couldn't get a better. Next time I come north I'll bring it with me."

" Of course I'll tell her. Anything else ? "

" Just give her my love, please."

" I'll do that."

" You are very understanding," he said with a quick smile, and she wondered how the missionary's pretty daughter could resist the devotion of this young Adonis of the bushveld.

Was she really understanding ? The strong morning sun seemed to pour right into her veins as she stood next to Jan Nelmapius. If being understanding meant feeling yourself to be a part of the life about you then no doubt she was. Never before had she felt more intensely alive, more completely herself. Her new-found sense of freedom rang in her consciousness with a clear, secret note as sweet as the flick of a fingernail on a crystal goblet. It was a prism reflecting rainbow colours and flashing them through her system till she too had the illusion of being light and dazzling. The knowledge of freedom had expanded her sensibility to embrace this whole unfamiliar world to which she was giving herself with abandon. Yes, Jan was right. There were no limits to her understanding any more. She was as much one with this young man in love with Thea Hurley as she was with the dark tragedy of Amos mutilated by the mysterious forces of African evil ; she belonged to this bright, sun-drenched land ; she shared the frivolous rapture of the birds warbling in the thorn-trees, and she suffered with the poor beasts whose skins lay on the ground, creatures who had met their painful death through the greed and cunning of man.

" What are you thinking ? " asked Jan Nelmapius. " You are thinking something deep, not so ? "

She pointed to the seedy lion-skin lacking a paw, lying beside that of the spotted hyena who had died of slow hunger in the bountiful bush.

" I was thinking that every trap leaves its wounds and scars."

" Every trap ? Ja, naturally. And the worst wounds come in the effort to get free. One must always remember that a trapped creature—so long as there is life in it—is at its most dangerous."

She looked at him steadily. The smile had died out of her dark eyes. Her face was sombre.

" I know that, Jan. That is one of the things I understand."

8

Something to Fear

IT was not yet nine o'clock, but the sun was hot. Rusty and Alice had the front windows of ' Sweet Sue ' wide open, while Nimrod, at the back, peered through the glass pane and Smokey sat beside him wearing that expression of noble canine patronage peculiar to the dog whose master is his chauffeur.

The veld through which they drove had the open charm of parkland, though the red grass was tall enough to hide a lion. The delicate foliage of the terminalia trees stirred in the warm breeze and every now and again their silvery monotony was broken by the rich spreading green of a wild-fig or a shady tambouti and the feathery yellow blossom of the cassia. The country was veined by innumerable dry *spruits* and water courses where palms and bushveld-willows grew side by side with tall fever-trees festooned with the nests of yellow buffalo-weavers. Here too the creeper, burning-bush, put out its clusters of bright red flowers.

Rusty, who had driven so fast over the long road from Duikers' Drift to Velaba, now travelled at a leisurely twenty-five miles an hour or less.

" It's a peaceful pace," said Alice. " I like it."

" One doesn't exceed the speed-limit in a residential area."

" I would hardly call this a residential area."

" It is. And in depth at that. The population lives at various levels here as it does in a city. There are the basement people in their burrows, the ground-floor folk, like the buck and the lions, the upstairs monkeys and all the other tree-dwellers—to say nothing of birds and insects. And we have our water-gypsies too—hippos and crocs and the fish that are lucky enough to survive. And, although these various people travel from season to season as necessity demands, they love their homes and come back to them like anybody else. Look, Alice, on your left, a herd of wildebeests grazing with their friends, the zebras. They like open country—so does the hunter for that matter, he can get a better shot at them. My grandfather was a great hunter before he became a Ranger— robber turned policeman."

As ' Sweet Sue ' slowed down, the lugubrious, bearded gnu faces turned to watch her, while the striped, pink-tinged zebras raised their pretty pony heads inquisitively. Foals trotted near their mothers, and most animals carried dark, narrow tick-birds sitting upright on their backs and pecking occasionally at the parasites that formed their diet.

" Oh, Rusty, how enchanting ! I know these faces so well from the stamps on Andrew's letters. A miniature portrait gallery is coming alive for me ! "

" You know their faces, but you'll have to learn their habits just as you'll have to learn Andrew's. The wildebeest is a melancholy clown, and the zebra is quite a joker too. He loves to stampede our horses and pack-donkeys when we go on trek. Just for the fun of it—real schoolboy mentality. A bit farther on we may find a pair of sable antelopes. The sable is an aristocrat, if ever there was one."

Within less than two miles Rusty was able to show her the ridged scimitar horns of a magnificent sable bull who froze into the landscape at their approach. His mate, with horns less dashingly curved, grazed quietly at his side.

" How did you know they'd be here ? " Alice asked.

Rusty smiled. " These people don't behave aimlessly. They go to certain restaurants for meals at fairly regular hours, and they frequent their favourite pubs and meet up there with their pals. Of course, during the dry season a number of popular pubs close down and they have to go farther afield to new water-holes, but one learns to know where to expect them. And if a bad man—a dangerous person—comes into the bar, everybody else walks out. The carnivora are the gangsters round here, but man is still the arch criminal—Public Enemy Number One."

" You say that as if you didn't think much of man."

" I like animals better. You know where you are with a wild beast. He kills for food, or because he is wounded or afraid. There are a great many men who kill for gain or blood-lust—like my grandfather in his unregenerate days."

His blunt, humorous profile was averted as he studied the rough earth road and the veld with trained, experienced eyes. Suddenly, in answer to an exclamation from Nimrod, he stopped the car opposite an enormous jakkalsbessie tree. Enthroned upon the ant-heap at its base sat a full-grown leopard, solitary and regal.

" There's one of the gangsters," said Rusty. " More ferocious than the lion, quicker on the draw."

" He's beautiful," she said. " Fascinating."

" Dangerous people often are."

To her surprise they met women and children trudging along the road. The women in their bright sarongs, with babies strapped to their backs, carried bundles of gourds on their finely balanced heads, the piccaninnies frisked merrily and waved to ' Sweet Sue '. Many of them were stark naked, but a few wore little hide or monkey-skin sporrans. The women were always in pairs or parties.

" Where are they going ? " Alice asked.

Rusty laughed. " Father wants his home-comforts—his beer and his wife. The women brew the marula beer and bring it to their menfolk. We use a good deal of seasonal labour, construction gangs, road-menders and fire-squads during the dry months, and they build their temporary huts and form squatter settlements. Then they send for one of their wives to keep them company."

" *One* of their wives ? "

" Sure. And when she bores her husband he packs her off home and tells her to send another of his wives. Good idea. Keeps them up to the mark."

" How many wives does a man average ? "

" Depends entirely on his means. Four, if he is rich. Nimrod has two. Amos—the boy whose tongue was cut out—has only one, but she's a little beauty. He gave thirty head of cattle for her—a high bride-price in any company. He prefers quality to quantity."

" Don't they mind sharing their man ? "

" Not a bit. They know that a normal man is as polygamous as the animals."

" Oh, come now, you enjoy shocking me."

" Do I shock you ?   I doubt if you are easily shocked."

She said :   " Do these women have far to come ? "

" Some do, some don't.   Their kraals are outside the border of Velaba.   Perhaps a day, or two, or three."

" But this is lion country.   They must be afraid."

" They are brought up in it—used to it.   Every now and again someone is taken by a lion or a crocodile or a leopard, but it's all in the day's work.   You take your risks in the cities, they take theirs in the wilderness.   You get your accident cases in your hospitals.   We get ours too."

" But they must *feel* afraid," she persisted.   " How can they not be with so much real danger on every side ? "

" We don't all have the same fears," he said.   " They have theirs, you have yours, Andrew, no doubt, has his.   Maybe I have mine.   They are all different.   What frightens you doesn't disturb me.   There is only one fear common to every-body—fear of the unknown.   To the natives this country is the known—something to respect.   To you it is the unknown —something to fear."

" To me it will become the known."

He threw her a sideways glance.   Her features were hardened by her strength of purpose, as he had seen them harden last night when she had fought and conquered one of her fears— when she had made up her mind to talk to his brother over the radio-telephone.

" Possibly," he agreed.   " You are capable of anything. You master your fears."

" There are so many to master—the unimportant outside fears like being afraid of snakes or lightning, and the deep ones —the inside fears."

" Ah, the deep ones.   There you have something.   These people realize very well that no lion is a person to be trifled with.   But they are much less afraid of the natural lion lurking in the long grass than they are of one of Ndlovukasi's paper lions.   The paper lion is the unknown—the supernatural. He embodies the sense of doom that precipitates death.   What are *your* deep fears, Alice ? "

" I have never tried to analyse them.   What are yours ? "

" Mine are my own business."   He grinned.   " Look over there, in that acacia grove."

Two young giraffes were standing in the speckled shade of the thorn-trees, caressing one another's short, velvety horns.

" Like Eskimos rubbing noses," Alice laughed. " And look at the little birds hovering round their heads—in their ears ! "

Not far off, a fantastically tall bull giraffe was nibbling the spring shoots of a branch twenty feet above the ground, the lighter-coloured cow browsed near him with her honey-dappled baby between her forelegs—powerful, slashing legs and hooves that could inflict mortal injury—even on a lion—in defence of her calf.

" Astonishing creatures, aren't they ? "

" Unbelievable," she said. " The deeper one looks into the woods the more one sees. I am learning to penetrate the camouflage better already."

He braked as ' Sweet Sue ' wound down the hill into a dry watercourse scored with the spoor of innumerable animals and birds. It was there, between the willow-fringed banks where the red and gold finches and flashing honey-birds darted among the rushes, that they came upon the troop of impala. Their flickering tails were tucked close against muscular, white-banded hind-legs, and many of the sleek, auburn ewes had lambs with them. It was a sylvan scene : Alice half expected to see the slender form of Artemis, patron of all wild things.

" They are worried about something," said Rusty. " Not us. A leopard, perhaps, or a lion."

Even as he spoke some hint of danger communicated itself from one animal to another, and, as a flock of birds takes to the wing upon a single impulse, so the red-gold buck sprang away up the bank with soaring bounds.

" Perhaps they are nervous on account of their lambs," suggested Alice. " Everybody round here seems to have babies." She had fallen into Rusty's way of talking of the animals as people.

" October is the month of birth and life-giving," he said. " In October the rains come and the whole veld flowers."

The month of life-giving. To Alice the words held a more profound significance than he had intended. Was October—this spring month of light and warmth—destined for her own mystic rebirth into this primitive world to which she already spiritually belonged ? It was a strange sweet fancy. She felt the goose-pimples rise on her skin, and awe pervaded her being as if she stood on the threshold of some unexplored truth. For a moment it seemed to her that she saw her own face looking back at her from a dark pool, wavering and uncertain. Then the water settled and she saw that the mirrored eyes held an old fear—the deep fear that had haunted her for four years. She recognized it now, the fear that her dreams and her youth might wither together behind the invisible bars of a loving servitude she must not refuse. Yet, although she had been given her freedom at last, although it was not too late for her to live and love, and, in her turn, give life, she was aware that she had exchanged one fear for another. Was she strong enough to face an existence of solitude and danger ? Yes. If Andrew should be the right man—yes. But was Andrew the right man ? The nearer she drew to him, the less she seemed to know him. In the moment of their meeting her inmost fears and ultimate hopes would be released. She desired that moment and she dreaded it. She was not ready for it.

Rusty's voice ruffled the surface of the secret pool in which, for an instant, she had seen herself so faithfully reflected. The image shivered and broke and vanished.

" There'll be something over there—near that leadwood tree," Rusty was saying ; and, as her gaze followed the direction he indicated, she saw the tall tree covered with big birds. They were perched in the branches with brooding patience. " Vultures. They are waiting."

" Waiting ? For some animal to die, you mean ? "

" Waiting for the lion to leave his kill. Scavengers don't sit at table with the King. They eat afterwards. We'll go in and take a look. Close your window. We don't want Smokey jumping out."

" Or a lion jumping in," she laughed. But her mouth was dry with excitement.

" Nimrod'll scout about first. They may be anywhere."

Rusty turned ' Sweet Sue ', ready to put her into the long, red grass. The engine ticked over gently. Nimrod left the car, and the dog sat staring out of the window as if he too were on look-out duty.

Alice observed that Nimrod's first instinctive movement as he left the car was to feel for his hunting-knife in the impala-foot sheath. It was attached to his belt ready to his right hand. His loosely jointed limbs tensed as he advanced warily into the concealing grass. His concentration was absolute. Upon it might depend his life, for, once away from the car, he was undisguised, he was man, the scent and the shape of the Enemy. Lions were unlikely to be hungry with a kill close by, but on the other hand a lioness with cubs might well be menacing. He hesitated and looked round in all directions.

" Would you do that ? " Alice spoke in a whisper to Rusty.

" Look round and sum up the situation ? I should say so ! "

" I meant get out of the car with lions about."

He stiffened. She felt his resentment and knew that all his antagonism towards her had been renewed. When she had tended Amos he had yielded a part of his hostility, but her question had proved her insensibility to a fundamental principle —something she should have understood without being told.

" No ranger asks a Game-guard to do something he would hesitate to do himself." Rusty spoke with a contemptuous curl of the short upper lip, blue eyes narrowed to slits. She remembered his words: " Nimrod is my brother of the veld."

Suddenly Nimrod, who had moved farther forward, came back to the car with long, leaping strides. Rusty had the door open for him and the boy flung himself in with a broad grin that showed his splendid white teeth and rosy gums. In the tawny grass he had seen the dark twitch of ears and the shadow of a black mane, and then another pair of ears and a lashing tail. He exchanged a few words with Rusty, and they laughed together. Alice was excluded. These two understood each other perfectly. Here, in the bushveld, they spoke the same language in every sense of the term, they had their private jokes.

" Does he talk no English ? " Her tone was sharp.

" He can say ' Good morning ' and ' Good night ' in English and Afrikaans. Perhaps a few sentences. Very little else."

Rusty's good temper had returned as he headed the station-wagon into the long grass under the boy's directions. He was quick to anger, she thought, and quick to laughter—a fiery, hot-blooded man with somewhere in him a hard, bitter streak. ' Sweet Sue ' rocked over the rough veld like a boat riding a choppy sea. Alice's tongue was dry, it clung to the roof of her

mouth, making speech difficult.   Am I scared ? she wondered.
I am going to see a killer at close quarters and not in a cage.
Might the lions attack the car ?   Rusty had said nothing to
reassure her.

"There, a few yards away, on my side," he said.

In the feathery grass she saw the magnificent black-maned
head staring straight at them.   The dark-tufted tail lashed
slowly to and fro.   How different they were—the blazing,
amber eyes of the lion or the leopard, clear and cruel, and the
soft, dewy eyes of giraffe or buck—the eyes of the killer and the
victim ?

"So long as we are in the car he can't get our scent," said
Rusty.   "And Smokey won't get his.   In any case, Nimrod
says this one is not dangerous."

"How does he know ? "

"He has looked into its eyes.   That is a language he understands.   He looks into an animal's eyes and knows whether it
will attack him or not, and he looks into a woman's eyes and
knows when she is ready for him to make love to her."

Alice was conscious chiefly of the lion, but somewhere in her
mind a question formed unspoken.   How could Rusty know
so much about Nimrod—personal things ?   What did they
talk about when they were days and nights alone together in the
bushveld.

The lion rose and moved slowly away, and, as it did so,
Smokey saw it and gave tongue.

"Shut up, old boy, we're not worrying now."   Rusty
turned and patted the dog, who still growled his warnings.
"I'll say that fellow is a beauty.   Let's find his family."

'Sweet Sue' ploughed forward again towards a solitary
sycamore-fig round which the earth had been trampled bare
by the hooves of some big animal.   The vultures in the neighbouring branches remained undisturbed.   Two magnificent
lionesses lay in the shade of the tree watching 'Sweet Sue'
intently.   Three young cubs played near them, gambolling
like big, yellow puppies.   Smokey barked and flung himself
against the window, but to the lioness he was only some unruly
part of 'Sweet Sue', the large, new beast which invaded their
territory at intervals and had so far proved itself harmless.
They neither smelt the dog, nor saw his form.

" What a marvellous sight ! " Alice whispered.

" Rather a sad one. The old man's home abandoned, occupied only by his murderers."

" What old man ? "

" An old bull wildebeest, I should guess. His signs are all round this tree. It is his home and his stamping ground. When the sex goes the wildebeest often becomes unsociable and prefers to leave the herd and live more or less by himself. He must have been easy meat."

The two lionesses had risen languidly and strolled off into the woods with their cubs. They were the apotheosis of lazy latent power and hunger appeased. Rusty drove towards the vultures' tree, and there, beneath it in a *donga*, lay the remains of the wildebeest's half-devoured carcass.

" There he is—what's left of him—poor old chap."

He spoke of the kill as if it were some old man who had been his friend and who had died in violent circumstances. It grieved him to come to the empty house and find the invaders and the scavengers upon the doorstep. Yet he accepted it, for such was the law of the wilds.

" Last night you heard the lion's voice," he said. " Today you make his acquaintance. Do you like him ? "

" I am tremendously impressed."

Presently, when they were back on the track, she said :

" There's something I notice. Every creature we have seen looks so healthy—so sleek and perfect, as if they'd all been carefully groomed. How is it done ? "

" Everybody looks healthy because they are healthy. The law here is a harsh one and a good one. It is the law of Nature —survival of the fittest. The old and the lame provide food for the swift and the strong. Witness our old friend back there. He'd had his chips, his hour had come, and he was taken in the night without time to say his prayers. Fair enough."

" How cruel it sounds, how callous ! "

" Is it, though ? In your profession you help to keep the living dead lingering on. Isn't that the true cruelty ? Your profession is the very negation of Nature's law."

He saw her shiver in the sun.

" I'm sorry," he said. " It's my turn to apologize. I had forgotten."

He took his broad, strong hand from the wheel and put it over hers. Its unexpected gentleness weakened her. The left corner of her lower lip trembled and she blinked the sudden tears from her eyes—she who seldom wept.

" You've had a tough time, Alice. Forgive me. We can't find God and ask Him what is right and what is wrong. We have to do the best we can. I went straight from the school-room into the war, I was taught to kill my fellow man, not to cherish him ; since then I've lived too much by Nature's law. You are a healer, and that is right."

His hand left hers and returned to the wheel. The moment of sympathy passed and they were separate again, each with their own hidden fears and their own inescapable isolation.

9

Oasis

" THIS track is pretty rough," said Rusty, as ' Sweet Sue ' bumped over the dusty pot-holes, " but it's only a firebreak leading up to the Game-guard's picket shared by Amos and a man called March. Our Game-guards work in pairs. It's safer."

" Will March be there this morning."

" He should be back by now. I hope he will be because I have a few questions to ask him. My talk with Job before we left Camp One gave me a good deal to think about."

" Is Job the elderly Bantu who was holding Amos across his lap when we met the jeep yesterday ? "

Yesterday ? Surely it was not only yesterday that Rusty had met her at Duikers' Drift—that they had set off together for this new world of Velaba ! Already the gulf between the past and the future had widened beyond any conceivable limits. She felt that she had come infinitely farther in time and space than a few score hours and a few thousand miles.

" That's right. Job always goes on trek with Nelmapius. They were together when they found Amos in that ghastly condition yesterday morning. There's a point that interests

me. Amos was crawling *away* from the nearest village when
he was found—the old Chief's village. Now, wouldn't you
expect a man so hideously injured to make for the nearest
human habitation in search of help?"

"Yes," she said. "But he was half out of his mind with
shock and pain. And he couldn't see." She shuddered.
"How could he know where he was going."

"These people act by instinct most of the time, and Amos
knows the district backwards. I should have thought he
would have made for that village instinctively—unless, of
course, he had some strong reason *not* to do so."

"What reason could there be?"

"That's what I'd like to know. When they found Amos,
the first thing they did was to get him across one of the pack-
donkeys. Then, while Nelmapius went on to Camp Two with
Amos, Job followed the blood-spoor back to the scene of the
crime. It led him to Sweet Spruit—a stream-bed, dry at this
time of year, which the natives believe to be haunted by a Tokoloshe. When Job got there he saw March standing staring at
the signs of a terrible struggle. March told Job that Amos
had gone there in the night to meet a certain girl and that the
Tokoloshe must have attacked him in a fit of jealousy."

She shrugged her shoulders impatiently. Tokoloshe indeed!

"Where had March and Amos spent the night?" She
spoke in a voice that preferred facts to fairy-tales.

"If March is to be believed—which I doubt—they spent it
at the old Chief's village. March has relatives there and he
told Job that the girl in question was from the village. When
Amos didn't show up next morning March went to look for
him."

"Did Job go to the village and question the girl?"

"No. He told March to get back to the picket as soon as
possible, and then he rode after Nelmapius to report what he'd
found. I intend to go over that ground myself today. And,
when I've seen March and got his evidence sorted out to my
satisfaction, I shall pay the old Chief a visit and have a chat
to the girl in the case."

Rusty's face was stern. What a strange case to unravel,
thought Alice, all tangled up with sorcery and fictitious
creatures with outrageous habits. She said in her practical way:

" It is quite fantastic, Rusty, that March or Job or anybody else could believe in a mythical dwarf capable of performing such an obvious atrocity. Human hands tore out that man's eyes and a knife cut his tongue out."

" Do you believe in ghosts or evil spirits ? "

" I believe in plain factual human wickedness," she said firmly. " I have seen plenty of it in the course of my training—people brought into hospital knocked about by their husbands, slashed by razors, men with bullets in their bodies and little children near dead with malnutrition and ill-treatment, but I do *not* believe in spirits capable of committing crimes of physical violence."

" What about a poltergeist—the chap who throws things around ? Do you believe in him ? "

She hesitated. A week ago she would have mocked at the notion of a poltergeist, but now she was no longer so sure where the border-line of credibility began and ended. Only this morning she had looked deeply into groves and bush that at first sight had seemed to her to be utterly untenanted, only to discover that the more she looked the more she saw. Anything might exist anywhere—even in dimensions outside her experience.

" Many people do," she admitted.

" We all have our superstitions and beliefs," he said. " And these people have theirs. But theirs pervade every aspect of their lives. Witchcraft is in the marrow of their bones. The Tokoloshe is just as real to them as Smokey is to me."

She smiled. " Tokoloshe is a funny word. It sounds like an insect."

" And looks like an ape. I'll tell you something. The Pretoria Zoo has animals from all over the world and a while ago they acquired their first chimpanzee. Chimps are not to be found in South Africa, they come from the Congo and West Africa, so this fellow was a rarity. Soon after he arrived the natives began to pour into the Zoo from all over the country. They came in such numbers that it was more like a pilgrimage than anything else, and the object of their journey was the chimpanzee. The rumour had got around among them that the Pretoria Zoo had a Tokoloshe in a cage ! "

She laughed. " I give in. All things are possible in Africa."

" Here we are at the picket," he said. " And it's a quarter to eleven—just the right time for a cup of coffee."

The little native outpost consisted of three thatched huts inside a high stockade of strong termite-resistant branches. Like everything else in the bushveld it appeared to be part of the landscape. The silvery terminalia woods had given way to the thorn-veld beloved of the giraffe, who browsed on the young leaves of the tall acacias, and of the impala, who liked the cover of the thicker bush, and of course of the hungry lion.

As they got out of the station-wagon a kaffir-dog ran out yapping and snarling and Smokey retaliated with threatening growls until he discovered that the watch-dog was a lady. The gate in the stockade was open and Alice and Rusty and Nimrod entered a miniature world apart.

A spreading wild-fig tree cast its generous shade over the little compound ; date-palms and paw-paw trees backed the three mud huts, and tobacco flowers distilled their sweet fragrance side by side with a meagre patch of kaffir-corn. A few fowls pecked about in the dust under a small thatched hen-coop on stilts to keep it safe from rodents and snakes. A three-legged iron cooking-pot stood in the ashes of a burnt-out fire ; near it was a log which could serve as a seat, a wooden stool and a deep, leadwood mortar and pestle. The mortar contained some pounded monkey-nuts. The usual strips of *biltong* were drying under a thatched shelter against the fence. But this humble setting only served to frame the picture of the girl and her baby.

She sat on a rush mat in the shade, her thin, dark legs stretched straight out in front of her, her child in her lap. She wore a short, gaily coloured cotton sarong and turban and a shining array of brass necklaces, bangles and anklets. Her full breasts were bare and her firm skin had the quality of indigo satin. Her face was carved in the same proud classic mould as Nimrod's ; the features were neat and flat, the wide lips soft as purple grapes, and the lobes of the small ears had been pierced and loaded with heavy brass ornaments. Her large black eyes, turned upon them with no particular interest, reminded Alice of those of the gentle buck who had gazed from thorn and thicket. Her son, perhaps eighteen months old, was naked save for a string of beads and a bangle. He was, Alice thought, the loveliest child she had ever seen.

The young woman did not rise to greet them or alter her position, but she responded to Rusty's questions in her own language, and when Alice smiled at her she answered with a slow, furtive half-smile that never quite broke.

Nimrod was already squatting over the embers, adding twigs and lighting a fire to boil water for coffee. The brass gypsy ear-ring which he wore in his left ear and the three bracelets on his bony left wrist sparkled in the sun. The girl made no attempt to get up and help him. He was not her man.

Rusty's wide-brimmed felt hat shaded his eyes, but Alice could tell that he was disconcerted by the presence of the girl.

Here was a factor on which he had not reckoned.

" She is Oasis—the wife of Amos," he said. " I didn't know he'd sent for her, but she's been here for the past month and now she's waiting for him to come back from his patrol. She has been here quite alone for a week—but today she expects him back—before the rains break."

Alone—quite alone for a week, with the leopard and the lion outside her garden fence, and only a mongrel dog to protect her—waiting for her man to return. And that man cruelly mutilated in circumstances none of them could understand. Alice remembered the ashen, tormented face of the injured man, the quick, light pulse, the stained and swollen lips as he sprawled limp and near to death across the knees of his sombre comrade, Job.

" And March will come back without Amos," she said. " March will come alone."

Rusty had taken off his hat. He sat on the log, thoughtful and frowning.

" Yes," he said. " March will come alone."

" Who will tell her what has happened to her husband ? "

" Nimrod will tell her. I will take you into those huts and show you how a Bantu Game-guard lives away here in the wilds, and then Nimrod will tell her."

" He must explain that her husband will get better—that he is in good hands," she said earnestly. That was what one did in a hospital. One always reassured the relatives with those words—' in good hands '.

Rusty had taken his leopard-skin pouch from his pocket. He was plugging his pipe. His face was grave and sad.

" This is a savage land, Alice. Men and women like their mates strong—unspoiled. No doctor can make Amos whole again. And he can never be a Game-guard any more. We will find him work he can do, but the adventurous life is over for him."

How little I know of this country, she thought. I am no wiser here than that child on his mother's lap.

While Rusty spoke to Nimrod, Alice watched the girl, Oasis. She was still sitting on the mat playing with her baby, clapping her pink open palms against his chubby ones. He chuckled and grasped at her fingers—surprisingly delicate fingers. Alice had known a masseuse once with hands like this girl's—small, soft, and strong as steel. Suddenly the child made an upward bound to touch his mother's face. The movement seemed to stir her heart. A smile of sheer delight parted her lips to show her gleaming teeth and she caught her son close to her naked breasts and made tender kissing sounds as she seized his little hands and placed them against her mouth. Alice turned away, deeply moved. Madonna and child, she thought, young, black Madonna, the very essence of maternal love.

Rusty had risen. He made a gesture to Alice to follow him and they stooped to enter one of the three huts.

They saw at once, by her cotton skirt and a blouse hanging on a line beside a child's blanket, that they were in the hut of Oasis. After the hot brilliance of the sun outside it was wonderfully cool, and, when Alice's eyes were adapted to the gloom, she observed, with a sweeping glance, that it was also spotlessly clean. A rush sleeping-mat was rolled against one mud wall beside a wooden head-rest. Inside the doorway were cartons of dried beans, monkey-nuts, mealies and *biltong*, a small axe, a rush-broom and a spade. On a shelf was a calabash and a pot of some herbal unguent.

" Look," said Alice. " Pictures on the wall ! "

Primitive white clay drawings of birds and animals decorated the dark mud walls—a crocodile, an ostrich, a giraffe and various buck.

" She does them to amuse herself. You must remember that she is here alone for days and nights with nothing much to do except play with her baby and weave a rush-mat, or so."

The hot lonely days and long perilous nights with only her child and a dog for company seemed to haunt the girl's sleeping-place. Alice could see her crouched here, crooning to herself, her baby creeping about the mud floor, as memory and imagination inspired the crude clay portraits of wild beasts as familiar to her as a household dog and cat might be to Alice herself. Was this what Andrew's sister, Meg, had meant when she had said, " You'll live with fear knocking on your door . . . you'll learn the meaning of the word loneliness . . . ? " It could be the same for a white woman as for a black one. Meg's own grandmother had been found dead with her three-year-old son trying to warm the hands that would never clasp or caress him again. Meg's mother had died in the arms of a native servant while they sought her husband. " The mamba's poison kills in half an hour. . . ."

She put her hand to her throat. How strong are you, Alice Lang ? How brave ? How great is your love for the man you mean to marry ? She thought, with sudden panic, it's not even alive yet—how can my love be alive till he has held me in his arms—till our lips have touched—till my body has melted with wanting his ? Her heart was pounding. What did she really know of love and sex and child bearing ? The theory—no more. The physical sacrifice and suffering, the ecstasy and fulfilment lay ahead—if Andrew was the man for her—the only one.

" Come," said Rusty. " We'll go into Amos's hut. We'll reconstruct the family life of a Bantu Game-guard."

" Is Nimrod telling her now ? " she asked as they stepped into the sun.

" He'll take his time. They don't blurt things out. The knowledge will come to her gradually from his talk—but it will come. All of it."

They stood for a moment in the clear light between the girl's hut and the man's. There was a sheaf of rushes on the ground and another of the long tamboekie grass used for thatching ; an old bicycle tyre lay next to them. Strips had been cut from it to make veld-sandals. Across the compound Alice saw Nimrod squatting in front of the fire as he boiled the kettle for their coffee. He was talking softly to Oasis in the language that was like bird-song. She sat near him suckling her child. Alice could not see her face. Surely, she thought, that boy is too old to be at his mother's breast. As if in answer to the thought, Rusty said :

" They believe that as long as they are suckling one child they will not conceive another."

He guided her into the second hut.

" That is an old wives' tale everywhere," she said crisply. " It is quite a fallacy."

He smiled. " You are so professional sometimes. You turn from a woman into a nurse all in a moment."

"Do I ? " Her voice was startled. She stood in the cool twilight of the hut and looked at him with a quickening of her pulses, a sensation so unfamiliar that for an instant she wondered whether the heat and change of climate had affected her. And then she realized, with momentary bewilderment, that she was glad that he saw her as a woman first, and, only in flashes, as a nurse. For years she had forgotten how to be a woman. The nurse had been dominant. The starched uniform of Alice Lang, the hospital nurse, had armoured the heart and soul of Alice Lang, the woman, as a plaster cast armours and immobilizes a broken limb. " I don't seem to know myself any more," she added.

" Can we ever really know ourselves ? Or anybody else, for that matter ? "

" Deep down, you must be a very lonely person, Rusty," she said.

" Who isn't ? "

She smiled as the image of Betty Swanson, always so gay and uncomplex, came to her mind.

" My friend, Betty Swanson, is never lonely," she said. " She is either too busy or too much in love to be lonely. She is going to be married any day now to a man she adores. I don't think Betty has ever considered what the word loneliness might mean."

" Work may be an antidote to loneliness," he said. " It certainly isn't a cure. But you reckon love and marriage is ? "

" It could be."

She half expected to hear him deny it, to see the upper lip

curl in the ugly bitter way that distorted his features. But he looked round the little hut with pity in his face.

" Maybe you are right."

She knew that he was thinking of the girl out there—the young Game-guard's lovely wife whose soft doe eyes had told him when she was ready for love—eyes whose message he would never read again. Here, with laughter and love-play, passion and possessing, they had made an end of loneliness. Everything in this little shelter from sun and rain and the long nights told some part of a primitive life that was nevertheless touched with its own simple sophistication. Amos had not slept on the floor like his brothers in the kraal, he had been issued with an iron bedstead, a mattress and a pillow, and grey army blankets. On an upturned case stood his hurricane-lamp, a torch, a notebook and pencil, for he had received a limited mission education and could read and write in his own language. A small hide case held sewing materials and spare uniform buttons. Next to it was a bottle of scented hair-oil. Rusty took the stopper from the bottle.

" Smell it," he said to Alice. " He is something of a dandy, is Amos."

She took a sniff at the oil. Its fragrance was overpowering. She grimaced, but Rusty laughed. " Oasis would go for that in a big way. A matter of taste."

His spare tunic, shorts and police belt hung against the wall near two uniform hats with the brims pinned up dashingly on one side. His bicycle tools, wrapped in a wildebeest skin, lay next to his axe. His assegai and a *knopkierie*—a heavy truncheon—leaned against the wall just inside the door.

" A Game-guard's weapons," said Rusty. " He takes one set with him and leaves another behind. And here are bits of his magic."

He showed her an unidentifiable collection of dried herbs and strips of meat and skin wedged between the thatch and the framework of the hut. " This is a tsessebe's foot. The tsessebe is the fleetest of the buck. If a devil plagues a man he can wear a tsessebe's skin to help him escape, and here is a fly-switch made of a wildebeest's tail. Witch-doctors usually carry whips of wildebeests' tails—but for different reasons. If a man is mad and blunders about making a clown of himself like a wildebeest, a few flicks across the face from the whip will sober him down."

"Look," she said. "His guitar."

The guitar lay on his bed next to a vivid mustard-coloured cardigan.

"He was quite a troubadour," said Rusty.

Alice touched the guitar with diffident finger-tips. What songs of love and valour had echoed round the camp-fire under the stars ? And now the minstrel would sing no more . . . the story-teller would bind no more spells . . . the whispered words of love would lose their music . . .

She turned and looked up sharply as Rusty's hands caught her shoulders. The harsh, sudden grip sent a rivulet of fire through her veins.

"What . . . ? "

"Hush—listen——"

Outside they heard a high keening cry—a bird-note of anguish rising and falling, rising and falling in a rhythm of unbearable pain. Alice trembled. Sorrow in others was no stranger to her, but never before had she heard this high-pitched keening.

"She knows," said Rusty softly. "Poor little thing—now she knows."

The bird-note had fallen to a low, prolonged moaning, threaded by the loud wailing of the child infected by his mother's grief.

"It's dreadful," whispered Alice, her voice shaking. "Like nothing I've ever known . . ."

The injuries to the man—deliberate, barbaric—the lament of the girl, wordless and inhuman, lay beyond her experience of accident and suffering. Rusty released her shoulders gently.

"This is Africa," he said. "It's a cruel land, Alice. You're a long way from home."

Silence fell between them, broken only by the moaning of Oasis. At last Alice said in her most matter-of-fact tone :

"Where is her home ? Where do her relatives live ? "

"Amos comes from a kraal not far from Camp Two. She belongs to his people now that she is his wife."

"Can we take her there ? "

" Yes. It is almost on our way."

" I will go out there and look after her baby while she gets ready."

" You don't think she will be safe here alone any more ? "

" Safer alone than with March," said Alice grimly. " It can't have been much fun for March—the odd man out in this picket. Don't forget there is a third hut in this corner of the Garden of Eden."

He saw her bow her head and shoulders as she went through the doorway of the hut, and the way in which she straightened up outside and braced herself to walk briskly across the hot little compound to the moaning girl who sat rocking her child frantically to and fro in her arms.

There she went with the determined efficiency of her profession, taking charge of a woman and child in distress—Alice Lang, the nurse. His pipe had gone out and he relit it with careful deliberation. All the same, he thought, it wasn't the nurse who had guessed what this charming little set-up might have meant to a man like March, sex-starved and brimful of latent savagery. It was feminine perception that had led her to her conclusions, and feminine perception that had recognized the menace implicit in the return of March—alone.

10

March

THE girl had made no protest at leaving the picket. She had wrapped her few possessions and those of her husband into two neat bundles and Nimrod had stowed Amos's provisions and the bicycle tools in the wildebeest skin into ' Sweet Sue '. On top of them he had carefully placed the Game-guard's weapons —the axe, the assegai and the *knopkierie*.

They had been travelling for about half an hour when Rusty stood on the brakes.

" There he is—our friend, March."

A man in the uniform of a Game-guard was riding towards them on a bicycle. As he came up with ' Sweet Sue ' he stopped and dismounted.   He saluted Rusty and stood waiting.

Rusty got out of the car, and instantly Nimrod did the same, with the gesture of feeling for his sheath-knife that Alice had observed before.

Oasis withdrew still further into her corner at the back of the station-wagon.   She had put on the little blouse that Alice had seen hanging on the line in her hut, and her baby lay in her lap, asleep.   Tombazane, the mongrel bitch, was curled up next to them, and Smokey sat in his attitude of aloof dignity, gazing out of the window that Nimrod had rudely shut in his face.

Alice stared at March with frank interest.

He was more powerfully built than Nimrod or the injured Amos ; his features were coarsely negroid and totally inexpressive.   Alice thought that his night-black complexion added to the look of impenetrable stupidity that masked his face.   He stood at attention beside his bicycle which was loaded with his camping equipment—a small canvas sleeping-sail, an iron cooking-pot, water-bottles, the inevitable assegai, hatchet and truncheon, and a bag of dried beans, mealie-meal and *biltong*. His sheath-knife hung from his highly polished belt, and across his shoulders was slung the ·22 rifle that had been issued to his senior, Amos.   If he remarked the presence of the girl and her child in the station-wagon he gave no sign of surprise or recognition.

Rusty's attitude to March was very different from the friendly manner he always adopted towards Nimrod.   He was not as tall as the big Bantu, but the set of his coppery head and the out-thrust jaw gave the impression that he was looking down upon March.   He spoke the native language with fierce, threatening sibilance.   His questions were brief and persistent, and March's replies appeared to give him little satisfaction.   At last Rusty dismissed him with a curt order to carry on and report at Camp One in case Duikers' Drift police might wish to question him.   Even the word ' police ' did not ruffle March's impassivity.   He merely said, " Yeez, Nkosi," in his deep, resonant voice.

It was the girl who threw the pebble into the pool of March's complacency that till then had seemed inviolable.   Up to that moment she had ignored him completely, now suddenly she

leaned forward and called to him on the shrill note that seemed
to Alice scarcely human. It was the cry of a bird robbed of its
eggs, furious and veined by hysteria. For the first time the
big Bantu showed feeling. His face darkened ominously, his
hands that had been dangling limply at his sides clenched con-
vulsively and his eyes stared at her with hate and fear. The
whites, Alice noticed, were yellow and shot with blood like the
eyes of a man who has spent a debauched and sleepless night.
But, in spite of the girl's provocation, March made no answer.
He saluted his Chief, mounted his bicycle and pedalled away
down the dusty track.

Oasis sank back into her corner. Alice could see her re-
flection in the central driving-mirror. She seemed drained of
life. The vital sparkling beauty that had characterized her
only an hour ago was gone and her face was putty-coloured and
bloated with grief in sickly contrast to the moist, healthy skin
of the child who still slept peacefully in her arms.

" What did she say to him ? " asked Alice as Rusty started
up the engine.

" She said she was going to buy a lion. He knows she is
Ndlovukasi's niece and that this particular lion will be created
with extra strong magic."

" Is he really frightened ? "

" You saw his face. She has pronounced sentence. A lion
will get March before the year is out."

Alice shook her head, mystified, but no longer astonished.

" I wonder why she should hate him so much ? " she said.

" I wonder a good many things."

" What was March's story ? "

" Much the same as I got from Job. He doesn't seem to
vary it. He declares that he and Amos were patrolling the
border near the old Chief's kraal and that they decided to sleep
the night there. Amos then confided in March that he intended to meet a certain woman that night at a rendezvous near
Sweet Spruit. The woman's husband has been working in the
Mines on the Rand for some months and it seems she gets up
to mischief in his absence. March says he arranged with Amos
that they should leave at dawn next day, and he then went to
sleep in the hut of his cousin. When dawn broke and Amos
was missing, March made enquiries. The woman swore that

she had thought better of the plan to meet Amos and that she had never left her hut. So March went to look for Amos."

" How did he know where to go ? "

" He says Amos is like a brother to him and had told him where he meant to meet the woman. I asked him why Amos should have chosen a spot believed to be haunted, and he said Amos had hoped that nobody would risk following the woman there if she were seen leaving the kraal. March found that the Tokoloshe must have got Amos. The Tokoloshe is notoriously savage and vengeful if he catches a man with another man's woman."

" If March is to be believed, the Tokoloshe couldn't have caught Amos with somebody else's woman. By all accounts the woman stayed at home." Alice spoke with the irritation of someone whose intelligence is being insulted. Rusty smiled. She was very much the ward-sister refusing to accept a junior's far-fetched excuses for some gross neglect of duty.

" What's more," she added, " I simply don't believe that Amos was in the least interested in anybody other than his wife."

Rusty raised his eyebrows with amused cynicism. " A faithful man—even if he is a mission-trained Christian like Amos—is as rare as a bird with teeth."

" That may be," she said with the obstinacy he was beginning to know in her. " But this case is exceptional. I am sure of it."

" How so ? Because the girl is beautiful. You think that beauty can hold a man ? "

" Not necessarily. But respect might. You told me yourself that Amos preferred quality to quantity in the matter of wives. Well, he has got it. Anybody can see the quality of that girl. She's as proud and as pretty as a princess. And Amos gave thirty cattle for her. You said that was a high bride-price."

He was interested. " It certainly is—a generous lobola, the value of an aristocrat."

" Well, surely a man respects his property when he has given that much to possess it ? I should think those thirty cattle paid to her father would make for great mutual esteem and affection." She smiled widely. " If a man reckoned I was worth thirty cattle, my self-respect and self-confidence would soar. And I should love him very much for being willing to part with them on my account."

He laughed. " And he wouldn't part with them, in your opinion, unless he wanted you very much. And, having got you at so high a figure, he wouldn't treat you lightly. You work things out to a nicety, don't you ? You know something, I'd like to see you lose your head and your heart and your sense of proportion, Alice Lang. Human beings aren't adding machines. They are flesh and blood, moved by sudden storms and passions—by emotions you would never understand. There's something called temptation—quite a force in human life."

She uttered a little gasp. Temptation ! Did he think she knew nothing about temptation ? Did he imagine that she was incapable of passion—of understanding the hot blood of youth ? Could he really believe that she was satisfied with a paper love-affair—she, who for years had banked down a fiery temperament with the thin, dusty slack of duty ?

She said in a low, tense voice : " You don't have to tell me about . . . something called temptation . . . or even about human follies. Perhaps I know more about those things than you could possibly guess. But in this case—the particular case of Amos and Oasis—I am naïve enough to believe in love. They love each other, and I'd stake my life on it that there was no other woman he wanted to meet at Sweet Spruit that night. He was on his way home to his wife. All he wanted was to get back to her."

So back she came to her original point. That was her way. But, in spite of his own deep-seated disillusion, Rusty found himself half convinced by her vehemence. Her fine dark eyes glowed as she spoke, and he knew that in the Game-guard's hut up in the lonely picket she had sensed some lingering, elusive aura of a simple primitive love that had touched her heart. But he only said :

" You base your faith in Amos's fidelity on feminine intuition."

" Yes. And I base my mistrust of March on the same hunch."

And, remembering the way in which Oasis had screeched

her threat at March, he had to admit that possibly her hunch
was right.

" I don't discount your opinion."

" Thanks," she said dryly.

The noonday sun was blazing hot. It burned down from a
cloudless sky. The bush seemed deserted, most of the animals
had gone to their resting-places to lie up in the shade. And
then the baboons came through the thorn-trees on their way
across the road and down to the river. The troop loped
through the woods completely indifferent to the presence of
' Sweet Sue '. Even when Smokey and Tombazane barked
at them, their intelligent, deep-set eyes expressed no malice.
The baby baboons sat happily astride their relatives' rumps,
while the infants clung to the soft fur under their mothers'
bellies. If a little one lagged behind, any handy uncle or aunt
scooped it up and gave it a ride. The animals crossed right in
front of ' Sweet Sue ', and Alice shook with laughter when a
mother, suddenly impatient with her youngster, cuffed him
smartly and sent him scampering into the bush.

" How your nephew, Dicky, would love them ! " she
said. " His favourite toy is a dilapidated monkey called
Lily."

" When the boys are a bit older they can come and spend
their June holidays in the bushveld," he said. "That is if Meg
toughens up enough to risk their falling in love with a Ranger's
life."

" She won't," said Alice. " Not if I am any judge. There
they go, the last stragglers. What fun they are ! "

" They are very funny," agreed Rusty. " First-class carica-
tures of the human race, but even that doesn't endear them to
me. On the contrary, they are mean and destructive just for
the hell of it. And once I caught an old dog baboon dis-
embowelling one of our impala lambs. To be frank, I loathe
the baboons. I'm not like brother Andrew, who loves all
animals regardless, good and bad. Even elephant."

Andrew ? How strange. Since leaving the picket she had
forgotten about him. For months the thought of him had been
constantly with her ; he had been a shadow-man for ever at her
side. Yet here in Velaba, in his own territory, he had suddenly
retreated and left her free to live briefly in the moment without

R—D

him. She had been given over to the present completely, with her own past and future out of mind.

" Even elephant . . . ? " she echoed.

" I love trees," said Rusty. " So I hate elephants. The darn beasts are like great bulldozers. They push their way through everything, they rub their huge shoulders against the trunks of trees, tearing off the bark and literally skinning them, or they shove them right over to get at the roots or the sweet young leaves at the top. Every time I see what elephant can do to our woods I get mad. But Andrew has a heavenly love for all his creatures. He makes excuses for them, fits them into Nature's divine design and approves it. He will tell you that when an elephant pushes a tree over he is automatically bringing the young shoots and the roots into reach for other browsing or rooting animals who may need them. My brother holds the long view on almost every subject. But then you know that. He has been telling you his thoughts and theories for quite a while."

She was silent, oppressed by her new awareness of the great gaps in her knowledge of her lover.

" We don't see eye to eye on a good many subjects," Rusty added.

" I should know." Her wry smile weakened the left corner of her mouth.

" Sure, you are one of them. You are a very important part of Andrew's passion for a theory. Theoretically, you are the girl for him. You have proved yourself to be a person of character, sensible and self-sacrificing, and you have a mild obsession for Africa—also in theory. You are—mentally—in love with each other. It will be interesting to see what happens when you put your respective theories to the test. I happen to be a matter-of-fact individual. For instance, if I see a badly wounded animal, I shoot it. That's my idea of humanity. Not so Andrew. He reckons it's God's will for that animal to be handicapped—that there's a pattern behind it. A buck has been wounded in a fight and is running terribly lame—he's sure prey for a lion. Very well, the lion will take that lame buck, and, in doing so, it may well be that a healthy doe will be saved. The weak one is devoured and somebody else survives. That is the law."

" What about an animal caught in a trap—like the hyena who was starving to death because his jaws were muzzled by the noose ? "

" Andrew would put that hyena out of its agony just as Jan Nelmapius did. He would argue that it was not the intention of Nature that an animal should die in that fashion. The hyena would be the victim of one of man's crimes against Nature."

Suddenly Rusty half-turned to say something to Nimrod, who answered quickly and pointed into the woods.

" See what I mean, Alice ? Look at those trees ! "

She saw half a dozen slender bushbeld trees lying on their sides with the shallow, wide-spread roots torn out of the earth ; others had broken boughs, and tattered ribbons of bark trailed from their trunks. The grove looked as if a tornado had struck it, and recently, for the torn wood was still green and bleeding with the rising sap of spring.

" That's why I hate the ruddy elephant," said Rusty. " He's the Destroyer around here. The lion is the King, but the elephant is God, and nobody disputes his will—except man, puny, presumptuous little man who will catch even God in his wire snare or his fancifully prepared pit."

When he is angry, she thought, that upper lip of his gets shorter, curling up under his nose, and his jaw comes out in the most aggressive way. He's a fighting sort of man and I can understand how he hates dealing in theories. He deals in facts. Yet he doesn't discount the supernatural. He looks into the minds of people like Nimrod and Amos—and even Oasis—as I might look into a stew-pot. He can take a pretty good guess at all the ingredients simmering in there, he can smell out the spices, however unlikely they may be. Rusty knows things instinctively that Andrew would need to analyze.

A picture rose in her mind of Andrew, the prisoner of war, reading doggedly through tomes on anthropology, ethnology, zoology, ecology and the construction of the Bantu languages. She could see him striving to apply some sort of philosophy to the frustration of imprisonment. It was that experience—the years behind the wire—that had imbued him with his hatred of seeing a bird or an animal caged. His inherent love of wild creatures had inevitably translated his personal sufferings of war, wounds and captivity into terms of the hunter, the hunted and the cage. The mere thought of a leopard behind bars, padding to and fro, beautiful and tragic in its confined space, never again to bound through the bush under the hot, clear sky or stalk its prey as nature willed, distressed Andrew so profoundly that it could cause him to sweat and tremble in sympathy with the unhappy wild prisoner. These things Alice knew. These things he had told her, and they had drawn her to him. She too had endured the secret dread of the cage, the nightmare of invisible bars holding her in a grip stronger than steel, shutting out freedom.

' Sweet Sue ' wound down to the river and they crossed the stone causeway between the rushes and willows. The shallow water chuckled sleepily between outcrops of smooth flat rock where crocodiles sunned themselves. Ten minutes later they ascended a steep rise above the wide valley. At its summit Rusty turned off the road into the cool shadow of a glade of yellow flowering cassias.

" Here we are—our midday outspan. And the world at your feet, Miss Lang."

Nimrod sprang out and held the door open for her with the smile that showed his gleaming teeth and pink gums. She got out and walked a few yards to a spot which commanded a vista of bushveld spreading away to the Black Mamba Mountains. A delicate blue heat-haze shimmered over the scene ; the sky was hyacinth blue, the mountains jacaranda blue. I have come here ' into the blue ', she thought. This is it—the ethereal, indescribable African blue one reads about.

She stretched her arms above her head in a gesture of delight.

She held the gesture for a long, deep-breathing moment, standing straight and slim in her shorts and thin shirt, her small round breasts thrust up and out by the movement of her lifted arms. Her mouth was soft and relaxed, her olive skin glowed with an even apricot tan, her eyes shone beneath the strong brows that were winged at the outer corners.

She is changing as I watch her, thought Rusty. She is opening to the sun like a tightly closed bud saved from frost.

" Worshipping the sun ? " His throat felt dry. Time for a drink.

Her slender neck lengthened as her arms dropped to her sides. She tossed her head back and violet and gold lights danced in her smooth black hair. She laughed like a young girl intoxicated by some new entrancing discovery.

"Worshipping my freedom, Rusty. Freedom—what a wonderful, lovely word that is !   Freedom."

11

The Outspan and the Dream

THERE was a drowsy quality about the noonday heat—a sense of life suspended. Only the cicadas shrilled an accompaniment to the heat-haze dancing over the grass. Everything else was still. Even the birds had retired into the silent, windless seclusion of the branches.

Rusty had spread a rug and cushions for Alice under a big wild fig-tree and she lay back gazing up at the breathless mosaic of leaf and sky. Clusters of russet figs clung untidily to the grey bole and twisted boughs of the tree. Rusty sat on a smooth granite boulder and lit a cigarette. Alice, he had discovered, never smoked. "Too expensive in England," she had said, "and there's no point in beginning now." The light, filtered by the foliage, gilded the golden down on his bare arms and legs ; Smokey lay with his head on his master's ostrich-skin veld-shoes, and Tombazane sprawled sociably next to him. Oasis had strapped her baby to her back and was collecting firewood. She had evidently decided to make some gesture towards ' working her passage ' home. Nimrod had selected a strong forked stick and was sharpening the two prongs with his hunting-knife. Alice rolled over to watch him. She was fascinated by his dexterous hands and the delicacy with which he worked.

"He touches everything so lightly," she said, " so precisely. He uses his finger-tips extraordinarily sensitively. In repose his hands hang limp at his sides as if they didn't belong to him, and then suddenly they spring into life, deft and strong."

"That's typical of his people. Nimrod always takes his own time ; he'll fiddle about for ages getting something just right to his way of thinking. See how he lays that fire. Not haphazard, the way I should, but making an art of it."

The Game-guard was using his long fingers limply now, as if they were feather dusters, sweeping a clearing among the dry leaves and grass under a tall cassia—a space wide enough to ensure no risk of the fire spreading. Oasis heaped the wood into a pile near the tree and Nimrod then arranged it as though each twig were part of an elaborate jig-saw puzzle. When he had set a light to the fire he skewered chops and a skein of *boerwors* on to the two pointed horns of his forked stick and squatted near the fire, his body masked by the tree-trunk. Alice guessed that he had sited the fire with the intention of using the tree as a screen. The only visible part of Nimrod, the cook, was one long supple hand holding the home-made spit. The end of the stick was embedded in the ground, the horns, weighted by impaled meat, were bowed naturally over the fire and all Nimrod had to do was to turn it from time to time. The bangles on his wrist glinted where the sun caught them, and the quiet air was soon fragrant with wood-smoke and chops and spicy, farm-made sausage. The baby lolled contentedly in his sling against his mother's back as she gathered more fuel.

" I knew a young African surgeon once," said Alice. " He had hands like Nimrod's. I notice hands."

" You notice most things. A surgeon is a craftsman, so is Nimrod. Was your African friend a good operator ? "

" Yes, very. So long as nothing unexpected happened. What he had learnt he knew very well." She hesitated. " But sometimes it struck me that he lacked imagination. He didn't allow enough for the effect of pain, or for the *mental* suffering of a patient—anxiety, apprehension. . . . But that's one of the things we nurses have a bee in our bonnets about. We always find the surgeons inhuman. Patients are cases to them. To us they are people."

Rusty stamped out his cigarette carefully. Fire—even the smallest germ of fire—was a living threat in this dry, grass country.

" Pain is like fear," he said. " We all suffer it in different degrees, depending on our mental outlook. And it's difficult for us to gauge the extent of somebody else's pain—or even the cause of it. One person feels pain at the mere sight of the dentist's drill, another doesn't worry till the nerve is exposed.

Africans are incredibly brave about physical suffering—if the injury is visible. Their minds work in the opposite way to ours. We see a bloody-looking wound and it increases our sense of fear and agony. They see it and understand the cause of their pain. And somehow that makes it easier for them to endure it. But the invisible pain—the headache and the bellyache—gets them down. All the old superstitious fears rise up in them. They have been bewitched. It is hard for our doctors to understand their mentality towards pain, and I dare say an African doctor has to turn all his ideas upside-down when he is coping with a European temperament."

" I suppose so. But time and training will get that into focus. There are hundreds of African medical students in London these days. Nurses, too. Even ward-maids. Betty says they have a Jamaican maid in her ward who sings calypsos all the time she is sweeping and dusting. The patients find it soothing—like a lullaby—endless repetition in a minor key."

" Music is in the African—music and dancing."

They were silent, thinking of the guitar on Amos's bed. At the last minute Oasis had gone back to fetch it. Sightless and voiceless her man might be, but he would play for others to sing and dance.

" The music of Africa—so sad and haunting. Plantation songs, negro spirituals . . ."

" Those were the songs of slavery," said Rusty. " Most of the Bantu songs are brave and gay and warlike, full of pride and boasting. The native of South Africa was never enslaved by white man or black. Even invincible Chiefs, like Dingaan and Shaka, didn't enslave their enemies. They absorbed or exterminated weaker tribes."

" But there were slaves in the old Cape Colony. I've read about them."

" Sure there were. But they were imported—usually from the East, or from Madagascar. Very expensive too, considering there were plenty of natives on the spot. But it was the policy of the Dutch not to enslave the locals. Bantus—like Britons, my dear—never have been and never, never, *never* will—be—slaves."

His white, uneven teeth gleamed in the tan of his face, which wore its cynical look. She gazed at him sombrely. She has the eyes of a giraffe gifted with a mind and a soul, he thought, soft eyes with long lashes.

" I hope that's true," she said.

" Master and servant there will always be in any land. The Queen is the mistress and the servant of her subjects, the Archbishop is the servant of God. And, at this moment, I am the slave of my appetite."

When they had eaten, Rusty put the remainder of the meat into a paper napkin and gave it to Nimrod, who received it with pink palms cupped together in a gesture that was both polite and dignified. There was nothing subservient about his attitude, and, for an instant, as Rusty spoke to him, his expressive smile lit up the noble impassive darkness of his face. But Oasis would not eat. She shook her head and turned away.

" She's too upset," said Alice.

" Probably. In any case she is not accustomed to a midday meal. It is the habit of her people to have a late breakfast and supper after sunset. A mash of kaffir-corn or beans, and meat from time to time."

Presently they saw Nimrod pour a kettle of water over the dying fire to make quite sure that not a spark remained. He packed the picnic-basket with characteristic exactitude and put it away in ' Sweet Sue '.

Rusty rose, lazy and reluctant.

" It's a darn nuisance, but duty calls. I have to inspect our road construction gang about ten miles from here. I'll be away about an hour or thereabouts. Nimrod and Smokey will take care of the woman and child. You'll be all right, Alice, but, if in doubt, climb a tree."

She laughed. " It's quite a while since I climbed trees. But, if pressed, I could probably perform."

" You'd be surprised ! "

He called Nimrod and told him to take the lighter of the two guns from the station-wagon. Shortly afterwards Alice heard the whine of ' Sweet Sue's ' engine fade away down the hill.

She lay back on the cushions as the silence gathered round her once more. The little sounds that broke it only heightened the vast solitude of the bush. A cicada shrilled intermittently and the little grey bird with the crest and the long tail flitted in and out of the branches over her head. He was building a nice snake-proof nest for his mate. Lucky little hen, she thought, to have a mate and a home—somewhere to lay her eggs and hatch out her fledglings.

Alice closed her eyes and fell asleep.

She was on the road again, near journey's end, with the last bend in sight. When they rounded it she knew that they would find Andrew's house—her home in the wilderness. " When we get by those trees you'll see it," Rusty said. The trees were wild-figs, thick and spreading. She knew what to look for— the white bungalow with the red tin roof backed by the iron scaffolding of a windmill. Giraffes looked down at ' Sweet Sue ' disdainfully from their fantastic height, a lion peered from the long grass with glassy, amber eyes, and then they came upon a herd of impala. She cried out, " No ! We must go back and shoot the lion, Rusty. He will kill an impala if we don't." And Nimrod said, in English, " I have looked into the eyes of Ratau, the lion, and he is dangerous. He is one of Ndlovukasi's lions . . ." But Rusty was laughing. She was terribly aware of his muscular strength, of a thrilling, ferocious vitality glimmering round him in a golden aura, like the heat-haze dancing over the veld. He was Ratau, the lion—*he* ! He was cruel, he was her enemy. They were all her enemies, and they knew something that she did not. What did they know ? Oasis was twanging the guitar and singing softly to herself. " It is the hidden pain that kills—the wound that leaves no scar——" Crooning it over and over again in a sad, sinister calypso. They turned the bend of the road, and there was the windmill ahead, just as she had known it would be. But the house in front of it was not Andrew's house. It was the cottage at home. Rusty drew up in the dust outside the gate. " Go in," he said. " You must go upstairs—you know the room— he will be waiting there." She tried to cry out—to refuse, but no words came. They had torn out her tongue, yet there was no pain . . . one man's pain is another man's pleasure, one man's pain is another man's poison . . . They were pushing her up the stairs and into the room of death.

" There he is ! There is Andrew ! "

He was standing with his back to the door, framed in the window. What was he doing ? He was holding something up to the light. A syringe ? No, a little carton ; and he was counting aloud in that light voice that had surprised her on the radio-telephone. " One, two, three, four, five—but there *should* be six. One, two, three . . ." And it was becoming a beat, a rhythm. Oasis was there by the window too, strumming on the guitar with her beautiful, slender hands. She was singing with him, " One, two, three, four, five—but there *should* be six . . ." The refrain was endlessly repeated, like the beating of a heart, the throbbing of a pulse. It would go on for ever— unless he turned round, unless she saw his face. If he turned round and she saw his face the heart and the pulse would cease to beat. The face would be the face of an elephant—the face of Fate. The lion was the King around here, the elephant was God . . . the elephant was God . . . was God . . . God . . . He began to turn from the window—slowly into the room. But his face was still invisible, black against the light. She could not see the face of the elephant, the face of God. But he was coming towards her. When he touched her she would die. . . .

He was putting out his hand, his long, limp hand, dark and dangerous, the nails livid, the palms pink. Could *this* be the hand of God ?

Ah, he was touching her now ! Stroking her bare arm. Her flesh was cringing away from him—her flesh was shrieking because they had torn out her tongue and her mouth was dumb . . . Her flesh was shrinking and screaming, imploring him to go away, but her mouth was silent, choked with the entreaties she could not utter.

His cold finger-tips were on her dying skin, stroking, patting with the touch of death . . . " One, two, three, four, five, but there *should* be . . ."

" Nkosikasi, *Nkosikasi* ! "

She woke drenched with sweat, her heart pounding, her lips mouthing words that would not come. Her terrified eyes looked up into other eyes—the moist, dark gaze of the girl, Oasis. And the girl's small hand lay upon the pale skin of her outflung arm. The delicate hand withdrew itself, the beautiful, troubled face looking down at hers relaxed and receded. The girl said something Alice could not understand, and she answered faintly, " Thank you." She lay exhausted, staring up, up, up. The little bird with the crest and the long tail flitted among the branches, the glimpses of sky were pure blue.

But they had changed. They were different. Suddenly she knew why. A breeze stirred the leaves, the pattern was no longer motionless and dead. It was alive again, shifting and whispering. Movement and sound. These things were life. The breeze was warm, it fanned her hot cheeks. She raised herself slowly on to her elbow, she stood up and leaned against the trunk of the tree with her head back. The faint wind lifted her hair from her clammy forehead. She closed her eyes. She must know if the dreaded picture still lingered behind her lids. But she saw there the quiet gaze of the girl, Oasis.

" The devil has gone out of her," said Oasis to Nimrod in the singing language. " He was a strong one. He was a hawk with his talons in the heart of Likwezi. But now he has flown away."

How long had Rusty been gone ? Alice looked at her watch. An hour had passed. He had said he would be back in an hour's time. Far away she heard the hum of the motor. She looked back along the road and saw the cloud of golden dust. At the foot of the hill a hideous gear-change tore ' Sweet Sue's ' innards apart, and Alice smiled. She would tease Rusty about that change. It was not like his touch with ' Sweet Sue '. She waved as the station-wagon turned off the road into the glade. Never had she been so glad to welcome anything or anyone. Relief surged through her. Her heart was light.

But it was not Rusty at the wheel.

A little, wizened monkey-man crept out from under the steering-wheel. His ancient face was black as a moonless night, and seamed with wrinkles and tribal scars. His wide nose was so flat as to appear almost concave, and a fuzz of grey hair covered his head. His skinny body was naked save for a loincloth, a long necklace of leopard, crocodile and lion teeth, and a python-skin belt. There was a knife tucked into the belt and a monkey-fur pouch depended from it, evidently containing a few treasured possessions.

" Where is Nkosi ? " she asked him.

He answered in the language she could not understand.

" Nimrod ! " she called. " Nimrod ! *Somehow*—I don't care how—somehow you must tell me what has happened to Nkosi. *You must tell me !* "

12

Dumela

WHEN Rusty had driven away from the outspan he had put 'Sweet Sue' across country until he came to the new game circuit in course of construction.

Wherever he looked there were signs of elephant. He was puzzled. Elephant did not generally roam as far south as this, but in time of drought it was not unusual to find a pair of pilot bulls scouting out new territory, and, if they approved of it, they would return and collect the herd, leading it to better feeding-grounds and water.

Man had also been felling trees in this district, but with greater method and accuracy than the elephant. Soon the road would be cleared, ready for the bulldozers to growl back and forth, raising the dust and scaring the game. Then the graders would arrive, the camps would be built and the tourists would enter Velaba. Rusty regretted the necessity for roads. He would rather have seen Velaba intersected only by woodland paths and game-trails, but the tourists could not come without their cars and the Sanctuary could not exist without its tourists, so roads were of primary importance.

The car was the 'new animal' in the Sanctuary. It would presently appear in great numbers, and it would follow its regular trails from sleeping-place to grazing-ground, water-hole to sun-bath, mud-wallow to salt-lick like any other beast. It would establish its habits and its harmlessness, it would disguise the human scent and shape of its occupants, and gradually it would become accepted by the animals as one of themselves—a new breed, but one with the usual accessories, eyes and teeth, a roar of its own and a regular behaviour pattern which would adhere to the rules of time and place and seasons. His brother, Andrew, had developed a theory about the 'auto-animal' in the Sanctuary. It must be diurnal and properly disciplined if there was to be real safety for the tourist. "Remember, Rusty, it would take only one disaster to finish the whole principle of

Game Sanctuaries!" And, although Rusty was often impatient of his brother's theories, he had to admit that Andrew
was on the right track here. To Andrew the tourist was a
necessary evil, a tiresome animal peculiarly vulnerable except in
the shining armour of a car, an animal which must at all costs be
protected from its own folly.

It was the silence that struck Rusty first when he reached the
roadwork near the squatters' tents. Why were the picks not
striking the ground, the axes not thudding against wood, the
spades not digging round roots? Why was there no chanting
of men hauling on ropes to bring down the taller trees, no song,
no talk, no laughter? Then he saw the grim, grey-faced group
in the glade. He drew up and sprang out of the car to go
among them. They stared at him with eyes reflecting the un-
speakable horror of recent violent death.

"What is it? You tell me, Dlameni, my Old One."

The little wizened foreman stepped forward, the necklace of
carnivora teeth ivory-white against his dark, sunken chest
ridged by the aged ribs.

"Mbula is dead, Nkosi. Dumela raised him high in his
trunk and dashed him to the earth. Then he knelt upon
Mbula and trampled him. Nothing is left to show that so
short a time ago Mbula was a man."

The group parted and Rusty saw the red smear that had been
a young man in the prime of life.

"How did he come upon Dumela? How did he anger the
elephant?"

"Mbula came through the trees from the tents, not knowing
that the great elephant had wandered so near. Dumela was
standing there, Nkosi, under that big marula, quiet as a rock,
asleep perhaps. Mbula touched him before he saw him, and
then it was too late to cry for mercy. The Great One had
seized him."

"When did this elephant come to these parts? And
why?"

"For three days he has been seen—now here, now there.
He is cast out from the herd and he seeks a mate. He is a
mighty one, Nkosi. Never have I seen such splendid tusks,
and I have seen many in my long life. But his eye is red with
rage and his temper is that of a man maddened by dagga. He

is a rogue and a killer and filled with wickedness.   He must die."

When a man employed in a Sanctuary is killed by a wild beast while carrying out his normal duties and molesting no living creature, that beast's life is forfeit.   If Rusty failed to honour his obligation in this matter no man would feel safe.

" You are right, Old One, Dumela must die.   Mbula will be avenged this day.   One among you will come with me and we will follow the spoor while it is fresh."

Although he spoke confidently, Rusty was far from happy about his self-appointed task.   If only Nimrod were here with his second gun !   But to return to the outspan to fetch him would waste too much valuable time, and in any case it would be wrong to leave Alice, Oasis and the child unprotected.   That was the hell of having a woman tied round your neck in this sort of job.   The emergency arose and you were heavily handicapped.

He looked round the group.   Who would volunteer to be his companion ?   A lad with bold eyes and a glossy, muscular body spoke up.

" Let me come.   Mbula was my brother."

' Brother ' might mean friend or tribal contemporary, or it might imply full blood relationship.   It made no difference. Rusty recognized the young man as Mahuli, a useful tracker who had served as a Game-guard, but who was now more profitably employed as a lorry-driver.

" Good," he said.   " It is settled.   You will come with me, Mahuli.   And you, Dlameni, will drive my car back to my outspan on the hill of the cassia trees.   You will tell my Game-guard, Nimrod, that I will not return until the Rogue is dead. Am I right in believing that you can drive ? "

Dlameni replied with pride that he was in fact a driver of great skill and experience.   Moreover, he knew the hill of the cassia trees and Nimrod was the nephew of his sister's brother-in-law's third wife's fourth daughter.   A close relation.

Rusty knew that Nimrod would be deeply chagrined that anyone other than himself should accompany his master upon such a dangerous hunt.   He would be sorely tempted to set out on his own in an attempt to find Rusty and Mahuli.   That must not happen.

" Tell Nimrod that he is to remain at the outspan. He and the girl, Oasis, must make a *scherm* round the place, for we will have to sleep there tonight. And they must gather plenty of wood so that our fire will not fail. And he must look well after the white Nkosikasi who travels with me lest the Rogue moves in that direction."

He looked at the bloodstained earth, the tattered flesh and crushed bones of a brave boy, and he said:

" Was Mbula a Christian ? "

They shook their heads.

" Then bury what is left of him according to the custom of his tribe. After that continue with your work." He turned to Mahuli. " Which way was Dumela coming when Mbula stumbled into him ? "

" He was standing still, but he was only resting before crossing the road to go to the water. He came from the mopani groves."

It was as Rusty had guessed. The Rogue was returning from his feeding-ground to the river. And the outspan lay between the two.

He went over to ' Sweet Sue ' and took out his heavy ·375 Holland and Holland and passed it to Mahuli.

" You will carry this gun till we draw near Dumela. Then I shall take it."

Dlameni, the little monkey-man, clambered into the driving seat and started ' Sweet Sue '. He went his way with a series of gear changes that tore through Rusty's hardened nerves. Poor ' Sweet Sue ', his trusted friend ! He buckled on his cartridge belt with an inward groan.

" Let us be on our way," he said to Mahuli. " We may have many miles to go."

The monster plate-like spoor led them across the dirt road into the woods south of it. Uprooted trees, peeling bark, broken boughs and flattened grass told their tale of the great brute's progress. Green flies buzzed over a heap of steaming dung. Dumela had no great start on them.

The sun blazed down upon the veld. No leaf stirred, no blade of the long, red grass shivered. Mahuli walked ahead of Rusty. He was familiar with every inch of this district. Had they been south of the river Rusty would have taken the lead, for that was territory as intimately known to him as this was to Mahuli. No distinction of authority or manners dictated the order in which they walked. Here only experience and discretion counted.

They had been trekking across country for more than half an hour before the first touch of the breeze relieved the breathless heat.

"It is lucky that the wind blows this way," said Mahuli. "Dumela will not get our scent."

"It is a pity it does not blow for rain," said Rusty.

"It will change at sunset, Nkosi. That is often the way. When the heat is great the rain is near."

"I hope it may be so."

They spoke seldom and softly as they tracked the elephant through the wrecked woods. Although Dumela—He Who Charges—was their goal, the long grass might well conceal lions, a leopard or a deadly snake. There was no such thing as safety.

Rusty felt excitement mounting in his veins, the old primordial thrill of the chase, the rising blood-lust. His grandfather, the ivory hunter, must have felt this way when in pursuit of his quarry and taking a chance on death. Man was a hunter by nature, and, Rusty thought, with sudden contempt, that man, the game-conservator, was a mere artificial creation born of a decadent intellectual approach to wild life. *This* was the fundamental intention—to pursue, to hunt down and to kill. The other course—that of preservation—was for the idealist, for cultured, highly civilized men like Andrew.

We're an odd pair, Andrew and I, Rusty reflected. We love the same things, we always have done, but the emotion takes different forms. If Andrew were in my place now, he'd honestly regret the necessity for shooting the Rogue. He'd feel no enmity towards the killer of Mbula—only that divine compassion which embraces all his creatures. He'd set about this task with no sense of glee in having a valid excuse for doing a hunter's job, he'd go about it with the cold, judicial omnipotence of judge and executioner combined. As for me, I never see a herd of game without picking out the best pair of horns and speculating on the angle I'd shoot from if I were out for trophies. Andrew's too high-minded for me. Look how he goes courting—with pen and ink! Why, if I'd wanted Alice Lang, I'd never have sent my brother to get her. I'd have said, "To hell with the poachers and the Sanctuary Board!" I wouldn't have waited to see what she thought of me on the station either, I'd have taken her in my arms right away and kissed the mouth that trembles at the left corner when she's caught off guard, I'd have . . .

"Nkosi! It is clear from the spoor that Dumela goes towards the hill of cassias. There are mopani trees on the slope of that hill. He will pass by there on his way to the river."

"We must go faster. That place is near my outspan. The breeze which blows this way will carry the human scent to Dumela. If he is in an evil mood he may destroy the people who are there. We must hurry, Mahuli!"

Mahuli had assessed the Rogue's movements well. The elephant had followed a well-worn game-trail to the pan at the base of the long hill. For a time he had remained there, trampling the wet mud until it oozed sufficiently for him to slake his thirst. Then he began to make his way up the slope towards the mopani grove not a hundred yards from Alice Lang, who stood on the summit of the hill, shading her eyes against the setting sun as she stared out across the thickly wooded valley.

Nimrod stood beside her, the ·303 rifle in his hand. Watching, listening.

To Alice the afternoon had seemed endless, surely the longest in her life. Ever since Dlameni, the scarred old monkey-man, had climbed out of the station-wagon, she had been possessed by fear—fear for Rusty and fear for herself. Between them, Nimrod, Oasis and Dlameni had made her understand that Rusty was tracking down a killer elephant. The girl had told the tale in little drawings on the sand, and Nimrod, Alice had discovered, knew more English than she had supposed. Even so, she found it hard to believe that a man had been trampled to death only a few miles from here, and that Rusty was following up the murderer.

She had watched Nimrod and Dlameni chop branches from the thorn-trees and build a stockade round the outspan. She had realized that, whatever happened, they would have to

sleep here tonight, and she had helped Oasis to gather firewood.
Any activity was better than none. From time to time Nimrod
had left them to spy out the land, but when she had wanted
to go with him he had shaken his head. At last, however, her
nervous restlessness had overcome his resistance. "Now I
go with you," she had said. And, like an animal who takes
his meaning from the tone and not the words, he had accepted
her decision. What Likwezi meant to do she would do.

As they stood together on the hilltop with the welcome
breeze ruffling her hair and cooling her skin, and the heat of
the day abating with the approach of evening, Alice was
suddenly aware of Nimrod's body tensing and his hand tighten-
ing on the gun. He had frozen as she had seen the animals
freeze at the first hint of danger, he was listening with all his
being—with ears, eyes, nerves and all the subtle, invisible
antennae of the hunter. He was locating the exact direction
from which a curious new sound was coming. How far away
was it? Where was it?

Nimrod began to move cautiously along the flat summit
of the hill until he was able to see down the gradual incline.
Somewhere there he would find Dumela. The elephant's
belly-rumble had betrayed his presence. Nimrod peered into
a grove of mopani trees, and as he looked he saw the snake-like
trunk hook down a bough and break it off.

"Dumela!" he whispered. "Dumela!"

Farther down the slope he could just see the small figures
of his master and Mahuli drawing nearer to the elephant.

Alice had followed Nimrod, but although she looked where
he was looking her untrained eyes did not immediately distinguish Dumela. In the long shadows of the late afternoon
the huge form might have been a twelve-foot ant heap or a
granite boulder. But, as the human scent was borne towards
him, the Rogue raised his head and the fine ivory tusks shone
in the light. The long trunk began to wave gently this way
and that, testing the air for danger. That was when Alice
saw him and gasped. Even at this distance she found him
incredibly alarming—a prehistoric killer. Sooner or later the
issue would be between Rusty and this mastodon—Rusty's
life or the Rogue's.

The elephant spread his great ears and flapped them to and

fro. He was on guard, uncertain what to do. His temper was irritable and the human taint grew stronger as the breeze freshened. He had killed and he might kill again. The fever of *musth* ran through his blood and reddened his vicious little eyes, but the ancient habit of avoiding man was deeply ingrained and it was not Dumela's habit to charge uphill. Slowly the great tusker wheeled. As he did so Nimrod made Alice a sign to remain where she was while he moved with silent speed in a semicircle that brought him on to the Rogue's flank. Nimrod was a dark, running shadow drawing in on the huge beast who neither saw nor smelt him. And now Alice picked out the figure of Rusty raising his rifle to his shoulder.

There was little more than twenty-five or thirty yards between Rusty and the Rogue. But till then the elephant had been screened by thick thorn-bush and had had his back to the hunter. Now, as Dumela half-turned, Rusty slipped back the safety catch and took aim.

The massive head was lifted, angry and suspicious, the great ears flapped, the trunk waved. The animal was in profile to Rusty, partly masked by foliage, with the rays of the setting sun slanting on to the great grey bulk, shining on ivory. The tremendous thrill of the hunter in the moment of testing gripped him. There was nothing hot or tremulous about this excitement. It was crystallized into an ice-cold determination to put the shot into Dumela's brain. This was a match to the death between him and the Rogue. There was in it no element of surprise. The elephant was out to kill, so was the man. And there was, as far as Rusty knew, no second gun to back him up should he fail to strike his target. It must be the brain. His narrowed gaze sought the precise spot between eye and ear, it penetrated the thick grey skin right into the grey matter of the brain that must be shattered by the bullet. Rusty *saw* into the brain. He was not aiming *at* the great head, but *into* it. His hand was strong and steady, the long, hot hours of tracking that had led to this crucial point had not weakened him. He was master of himself and of the situation. Now. Now . . . let him have it !

But the bullet that whined into Dumela's cheek struck a fraction too low and only served to enrage the great animal further. And, as he slewed round towards his enemy, his inflamed, short-sighted eyes fell upon the man reloading his rifle farther down the slope.

Dumela did not hesitate. He took the few backward steps that presaged a charge, he spread his mighty ears like two great sails, lifted his head, curled up his trunk and opened his mouth wide to let out an atrocious, ear-splitting shriek of pain and fury. Then he came.

" Nkosi ! Nkosi ! "

Mahuli, a few paces behind Rusty, sprang out of the monster's path and climbed the nearest tree with simian agility. The earth shook and the woods trembled as the maddened elephant pounded down the slope, screaming his shocking primeval battle-cry. Everything in his way came with Dumela. He wore bush and bough like camouflage upon his mighty chest and head. Rusty levelled the rifle at the open, shrilling mouth. Through the mouth and into the brain. It was the only chance. There would be no third shot if he missed this time. It would be the end.

Alice watched with hypnotized horror as the brief drama played itself to a close. Through the hideous animal screaming she heard the second shot ring out ; and then, from another direction, came the third. The Rogue faltered and seemed to swerve, he sank to his knees and slowly subsided like a grey battleship pitching into a deep sea of foliage. She saw Nimrod dash down towards the dying beast, and then the little monkeyman, Dlameni, was rushing past her into the valley with Smokey at his flying, bare heels.

She wanted to go after them, but terror held her paralyzed. Had Rusty fallen beneath that monstrous weight ? She put her hand to her throat. She felt sick and faint. She leaned against a tree and closed her eyes. Her knees were shaking and her hands were clammy. What horrible sight awaited her there in the valley ? This was the nightmare—the dream of fear translated into living fact. Down there was something she dared not face.

A light touch on her arm made her open her eyes with a deep shudder that shook her whole frame. The girl, Oasis, stood beside her, ashen-faced. The child strapped to her back yelled lustily. She knows that Rusty is dead, crushed and mangled, thought Alice. She is sad for me as I was sad for her. This is the language of the eyes. Hers are telling me of her fear, of her sorrow and her sympathy that my man, like hers, has come to dreadful harm.

She said aloud: "But Rusty is not my man, Oasis . . . he is not my man . . ."

The sound of her own voice strengthened her. She braced her shoulders and drew a long, deep breath.

"Don't go down there, Nkosikasi!" Oasis implored in her own language. But she knew that her warning was useless. Likwezi's features had set in the strong mould, her eyes had darkened like the sky before storm, and the spirit commanded the body. She was going forward—into the valley to whatever might await her. Nothing would stop her.

Oasis watched her go. A devil had died this day. Earlier in the afternoon Likwezi had been possessed by this devil in her sleep, and no doubt it had left her to enter into Dumela. It had sought to destroy Nkosi and had itself been destroyed. Oasis squatted on the hilltop, watching and waiting. Already the vultures wheeled against the glowing sky and dropped. The breeze faded with the setting of the sun. The dog, Tombazane, crept near and licked her hand, and she made a movement of affection with her slim, dark fingers.

She began to croon. It was a sad song, a lullaby of lamentation, but as the child listened, his sobbing ceased and he fell asleep.

13

Thea

ANDREW looked up from his desk. The door of the fly-screen had opened and closed and a light step crossed the stoep.

The familiar figure of a girl was silhouetted in the doorway of his office—a figure he had known and welcomed for four years. But how she had changed! Thea Hurley, the plump little schoolgirl who had so frankly and childishly hero-worshipped the Senior Game-warden of somewhere as exciting as Velaba, had grown into a tall, willowy creature who surprised him every time she came home for the holidays.   The years between fourteen and eighteen were, he thought, very formative in every sense of the word.

" Am I disturbing you, Andrew ? "

" Yes.   Do you mind ? "

" No.   Do you ? "

" In principle, yes.   In fact, no.   I ought to get on with this darn project."

" What's it in aid of ? "

She came into his office and perched on the corner of his desk, swinging her long, bare legs.   A broad red belt girdled the waist of her printed cotton dress—a very small waist, he observed.   What had happened to the ' puppy-fat ' of his little friend ?   Had it melted away overnight, or had it happened so gradually that it had taken a scarlet belt to draw his attention to it ?

His short-sleeved blue shirt was open at the throat and he wore crisp white shorts and veld-shoes.   His sunburned arms and legs were bare and covered with soft dark hairs.   His expression was troubled and distrait.

He said, rather sadly :

" It's in aid of Velaba—or is it ?   We have to open it to tourism as soon as is reasonably possible.   That's any day now.   I'm working on a list of requirements and proposals— the camps we'll need to establish, the construction gangs we'll want, the type of stores that'll be essential, new Rangers—in fact the skeleton of a working organization that will turn a lovely liability into a financial asset."

She put her blunt, dimpled finger on the chart that lay on his desk and turned it so that she could study it without altering her position.   Her thick, brown lashes, tipped with gold, cast spiky shadows on her cheek.   In spite of the summer sun that had tanned her pale skin, she was so fair that it seemed to Andrew that you could see the blood moving underneath it. Her hair was silvery-gold.   She had a look of innocence, per- haps because she used so little make-up—only a faint dusting of powder—or it might be that he always associated her with her missionary background.   Surely a girl brought up by such devout parents in this remote place would be less sophisticated than her urbane contemporaries.   If Meg were to be believed,

the teen-agers of today could teach their elders a great deal
on an astonishing number of subjects.   But of course Thea had
been to boarding school in Pretoria.   And no doubt she had
learned more than the three Rs at school.   Her exclamation
came as a cry of pain.

" Not a camp *here* !   Oh, Andrew, you can't suggest that—
you mustn't ! "   Her forefinger pressed on a point that he
had marked about fifteen miles from Camp Three.   " This
is our special place . . ."

He brushed his hand over his forehead in a gesture she knew
well.

" But, Thea, it's an ideal spot for a small camp.   The
water-hole is only a mile away—and the tourists will be in the
heart of elephant country.   Yet the camp can be placed high
so that the elephants won't make a mash of it.   I can't very
well hide it up—pretend it doesn't exist."

The colour that had risen to her face ebbed again.   " It's
sacrilege."

" That's no word for a missionary's daughter to use lightly."

He took off the glasses he had been wearing for writing and
she saw that his fine, tired grey eyes were laughing at her,
indulgent, affectionate.   But she did not respond to his smile.
She jumped off the desk impatiently and walked away to stand
staring at a group of charts attached to the wall.   VELD MANAGE-
MENT, CARNIVORA CONTROL, INCIDENCE OF POACHING, VELD
BURNING.   The headings blurred before her tear-filled eyes ;
she was oppressed with a sense of change and loss—of relationships that could never be the same again . . . Andrew . . .
Velaba . . .

" What can one do ? " he said.   " Tourism was, after all,
the object of this rather prolonged operation—the preparation
of Velaba, its establishment as a Wild Life Sanctuary."

" Everything is going to be different—everything ! "   Her
fists were clenched.   " I can't bear it."

He missed the full significance of her distress.   He knew
that she loved the Sanctuary.   In her holidays it had always
been her greatest delight to accompany him when he inspected
one of the existing game-circuits or planned a new one, and
the water-hole that would be such an attraction near a tourist
camp was her favourite spot. They had spent many happy,

tranquil hours there together watching the animals come down to drink in the cool of the evening. It was her joy and her boast that he took her there—where no other woman had ever been. No wonder she hated the idea of sharing that privilege with scores of eager tourists armed with their cameras.

"We'll have to bear it, Thea. I shall hate it, too. But we mustn't be selfish. Think of the stately homes of England— all their privacy gone, and the owners tucked into a few rooms on week-days and acting as guides to the *hoi polloi* on high days and holidays."

" Don't preach, Andrew ! I get enough of that at home."

" All right, I won't. But, talking of your home, do they know you're here ? "

" I didn't tell them I was coming. I just made up my mind quite suddenly. I was passing the Sanctuary gate on my bike and I decided to come. Old Saul was on duty there, and he got on his bike and followed me here. He needn't have. We didn't meet a single lion or an elephant or anything except a few buck."

" Won't your mother worry ? "

" Why should she ? I'm grown up—old enough to take care of myself."

" Are you ? You've never seemed very grown-up to me."

" That's the trouble," she said in a choked voice. " I've taken too long growing up—left it too late."

He put his papers away in a drawer and crossed the room to her, his leg dragging.

" What's the matter, Thea ? "

" Never mind. You're limping more than usual."

" A good thing. It's a sign of a change in the weather."

She turned quickly to face him, her rather formless features soft with sympathy. " Your leg hurts. Poor Inyanga ! It's a mean old wound that makes the Wizard of Velaba suffer when the rains are coming. But we do need them badly."

" It's been a very dry season. You can see the accidental fires on that chart behind you—the huge devastated areas painted red. All the same, I'd like the weather to give us another twenty-four hours before it breaks—time for Rusty to get here with Alice Lang."

" Naturally. As a matter of fact, I really came over this

evening to ask you if you'd like me to arrange some flowers for
you here tomorrow. The feminine touch . . . to welcome
Alice Lang."

"That's sweet of you—but she'll be staying at your place—
at the Mission."

"I thought you might want her to get a good impression
of your home. After all, it's going to be hers——"

"Who told you that ? " he cut in quickly.

"Mummy. She seemed to think I'd better know. I wish
you'd told me yourself. I can't imagine why you didn't."

She went to the open window and stood looking out at the
garden, her face averted.

It was a garden of fruit and flowering trees. Camp Three
had once been part of a ranch, and the original owner had based
a small shooting-camp on the site now occupied by the Warden's
house. He had planted it out with flowering shrubs, citrus,
mango and paw-paw trees. So now the evening breeze wafted
exotic perfumes to Thea from frail bauhinias, fragrant frangi-
pani flowers, oranges and lemons and delicately scented mango
blossoms. The sky flamed through the moving tracery of the
leaves, and beyond the simple outline of the house she could
see the gaunt shape of the mountains. How she loved this
place—how she loved it ! Andrew was standing beside her.
She felt his nearness as if he were touching her—the warmth
and substance of him, its tallness and length of limb, the dark
hair sprinkled with grey, the sun-browned skin, the aroma of
cigarette smoke that hung about him. He smoked too much,
his fingers were stained with nicotine. She did not need to
look at him to know that his eyes—dark grey and gentle with
the crow's feet scored at the outer corners—would be at a loss,
wondering how he could have hurt her. He would never want
to hurt her—or any living thing.

"Just what did your mother tell you about Alice Lang—
and me ? "

"That you expected to marry her. That she couldn't come
to you sooner because she was nursing her mother through a
hopeless illness."

She heard the deep intake of his breath. "Ah . . . what
else ? "

"That you and she had never actually met—that you'd been

writing to each other for over two years—that your minds were attuned. Attuned. That's Mother's word."

" What do you make of that ? "

" I don't know. Can one fall in love with somebody's mind —with just their mind ? How should I know ? I'm an ordinary person. Love to me means someone I can see and talk to—and touch—a face I can picture and dream about at night."

" What do you know about love—at eighteen ? "

Her laugh had a break in it. " Your house-boy, Maxim, has a wife of fifteen. She is going to have a baby."

" Native girls are different."

" I don't think so."

" They mature young—these children of the sun."

" I am a child of the same sun. Maturity, surely, is the ability to bear a child."

She was intense. He had never known her like this before. She was flushed and little beads of moisture stood on her upper lip. Eighteen. Of course a girl could have some experience of love at eighteen. So Jan Nelmapius was the lucky one— Jan, whose heart was in his eyes whenever he looked at Thea, a heart as young and soft and golden as the youthful beard on his chin. He was a good lad. They would make a splendid pair one of these days if the calf-love lasted. But if ever the young devil harmed her he'd have to answer to Andrew for it ! A wave of fierce, protective jealousy engulfed him. Perhaps this was how a father reacted to the news that his only daughter wanted to become engaged. The emotion subsided, leaving tenderness in its wake.

" So you are in love too, Thea ? "

" Maybe I am."

" Why didn't you tell me ? "

" Why didn't you tell me about Alice Lang ? "

" That wasn't plain sailing."

She said, with the laugh that wasn't happy : " Perhaps it wasn't—isn't—plain sailing for me either. I don't want to talk about me. Alice is on her way. Tomorrow—tomorrow she'll be here."

Yes, tomorrow he would have to face the physical fact of Alice Lang, and he thought, with twisted humour, that it would be easier to meet a rogue elephant unarmed than this young nurse whom he so greatly admired and whose courage and character had won his heart. It was a very different matter for Thea. The course to true love might not be running perfectly smoothly, but at least it was all on a normal everyday basis. Jan Nelmapius was not yet of age, and he was posted quite a long way from Poinsettia, but he found excuses for trekking north fairly often and the years would pass soon enough, testing the two young people in the process.

" The thing between Alice and me is so nebulous . . ." he said, and found that it was a great relief to speak of her openly and easily. He had never been able to do that before—not even to Rusty. Rusty had been so hostile to the whole situation, so sceptical and unsympathetic, that he had put Andrew on the defence. He had taken all the warm, tranquil reality of a friendship between kindred spirits and transformed it into a snare laid by a scheming spinster for a lonely hermit. Rusty had been embittered by the failure of his own marriage, his respect for the integrity of women and his belief in love were dead. His outlook was distorted. Thea saw life and love with the eyes of innocence. It was suddenly very important that he should try to tell Thea how he felt about Alice. She wouldn't spoil it. She might even understand. The young had ideals—as he had himself.

" But now," she said, " it can hardly be nebulous now. It's coming true."

So she saw this strange romance as a dream materializing? That was the way in which he had seen it too—at first—before the fears and doubts had got their talons into him. Yet she spoke a little sadly as if the legend might, after all, have the wrong ending.

" Even now I don't know all the answers about Alice and me," he said. " When I first wrote and asked her to come to me here she refused. She said that as long as she was needed at home she would stay. That might have meant years. It was an indefinite postponement of our meeting. We settled into a groove of waiting."

Thea shivered. She put the palms of her hands on to the window-sill behind her and jumped up so that she was sitting on it, her back to the light.

" Waiting for someone to die, really ?   How ghastly ! "

Andrew had lit a cigarette and was smoking it feverishly.
He was so quiet in speech and movement and yet there were
many things he did nervously.   Smoking was one of them.
He said :

" Sometimes I was haunted by the thought of time slipping
by and taking the remains of our youth with it.   I wrote again,
begging her to consider her own life—and come to me—if only
so that we might meet each other.   I felt it was *intended* that
she should come to Velaba.   I wrote in that mood, sure of
myself, sure of her, sure that our coming together was inevitable
and right."

" And then ? "

" And then . . . suddenly—unexpectedly . . . she was free.
She could come."

" That must have been wonderful for you—both of you."

" It *was* wonderful, Thea.   A bit frightening too."

He pressed out the stub of his cigarette under his heel.

" I can understand that," she said candidly.   " Letters are
queer things.   People aren't always like their letters."

" Why do you say that ? "

" Well, if you are writing to somebody you know well, who
knows your friends and all about you, it's easy.   You can be
yourself, just chatter.   It was that way when I wrote to Mummy
or my sister from school.   I could tell them if I was pleased
about something, or browned off with somebody.   They knew
what it was all in aid of.   But sometimes Daddy's sister—my
aunt who lives in England—sends me a book or a present and
I have to write my thank you.   What does she know about me,
or my life at Poinsettia, or anything else to do with me ?   Just
nothing.   So I write her a letter that isn't really me at all—
something polite—the sort of thing I think she'd like.   I try
to make it interesting—about Velaba and the people and the
animals and so on, but it isn't *me*."

" If you wrote to each other often enough your letters would
reflect your personalities.   I am sure they would, whatever
you may think."

" They'd only reflect my best behaviour side—the Sunday
side.   Not the everyday grumbles and growls I wouldn't mind
writing to my sister in Durban."

The everyday grumbles and growls. There had been very few of those in Alice's letters. He had always assumed that she wasn't the grumbling sort. Was it possible, perhaps, that she had feared that grumbles would bore him, and so she had treated him to her ' Sunday side ' ?

" Letters aren't ever quite like talking," she said. " You talk to people and they make you laugh or they make you cross—or they may even make you cry—but you are close to them——"

" You mean that when you are close to people you get spontaneous responses—you can blaze up into a quarrel ? "

She looked straight into his eyes that were both amused and interested.

" Into a quarrel—or into making it up—into kissing—anything. You don't have time to think and consider and rewrite and tear up ! Words are thoughts out loud and when people are together words can lead anywhere."

He laughed. " Dear Thea, you are so alive, so sweet, so completely *of the moment*. It must be hard for you to understand this affinity between Alice and me."

" It *is* hard. You love a shadow. When you see her it'll be like seeing the print after looking at the negative."

" It'll be a lot more than that, my dear."

" Oh yes. I know." She spoke on a sigh, as if the knowledge hurt.

Andrew said : " Would you believe in the possibility of twin souls ? "

She turned her head towards the garden where the birds twittered in the sunset. Her profile was blurred and tender. How malleable she looked, as if the young waxen features had not yet set.

" I'm not good like Daddy and Mummy. Souls are part of their daily lives like God is. *I* think people only get glimpses of each others' souls occasionally—and then it's very exciting and beautiful. I don't believe souls are always on view—out in the open like the starlings and doves in the Sanctuary—you have to look out for them like looking for an oryx or a leopard or a specially lovely bird, and, when you do see them, it's just for a second—a sort of proof that they exist. I'm sure Alice Lang has a fine soul, but most of the time you'll be living with all the rest of her."

He laughed aloud.   He felt more light-hearted than he had done for a long time.

" All the rest of her is highly practical.   She's a well-trained, self-reliant hospital nurse.   She has wanted to nurse in Africa ever since she was old enough to have a point of view, and she certainly hasn't had an easy life.   She'll be just the right wife for a Game-warden.   There's one thing that does bother me, though. But she knows about it and it's not anything I can alter."

" What is it ? "

She put her hands lightly on his shoulders and slid down from the window-sill.   They were very close together in the darkening room.

" I am nearly ten years older than she is.   That's too much in this day and age when we all know that women are tougher than men—that they wear better and last longer."

He heard her gasp and felt her fingers tighten on his shoulders as if she meant to shake him.   You talk . . . and you quarrel . . . you are close enough to make up a quarrel—or kiss . . .

" Ten years !   Oh, you fool, you fool !   What's ten years between people who love each other ?   What's *twenty* years ? Nothing—nothing—nothing ! "

Her face was buried against his chest and she was sobbing stormily.   He stroked her pale, silky, ruffled hair.

" But Thea . . . please, Thea, don't . . ."

14

" . . . *Nor the Moon by Night* . . ."

RUSTY stood in the failing light and stared at the massive bulk of the dead elephant.   Eight tons of maddened, charging rage had thundered down upon him and only a miracle had saved him—the third shot.

In all his hazardous life, never had death come so close to him—the screaming voice, the hot breath, all the elemental fury of a violent end.   The head-shot, fired through the roof of the open mouth, might have killed the Rogue, but the heart-shot, fired from the flank, had brought him down just in time.

Nimrod came up with his master and leaned down to stroke the prodigious curved tusks. They were the longest, the heaviest and the finest he had ever seen. Mahuli and Dlameni touched them too. Presently Dlameni would take magic from the monster carcass, for he was an elder of the tribe, a sage, and he would have first pick. He would collect some of the secretion from the musk gland, a scraping from the teeth and tusks and other virile ingredients that would yield potent *muti*. Tonight there would be a feast for all. Warned by the road-gang, and assured by the vultures of the position of the kill, people would find their way here from far and wide. The women would bring beer and soon the drums would beat their invitation to the dance. Dlameni's scarred and wizened face was bright with Pagan worship as he said :

" This is a Mighty One, Nkosi. Dumela was a Great Chief when he walked with men."

Rusty knew that the old man meant it literally and that in his own heart Dlameni probably claimed some secret kinship with the Mighty One.

" Yes. He was a King."

And now men would dispute his carcass with the scavenging birds and beasts. Rusty pointed to the small hole in the great animal's side, the wound over the heart.

" You shot true, Nimrod."

The Game-guard's wide, white smile flashed proudly.

" Dumela died twice, Nkosi. First his head was killed and then his heart."

" You will cook the heart tonight, Nimrod—and the tender part of the trunk. Mahuli and Dlameni will chop out the tusks and bring them to the outspan. Then let the people feast, for there will be many in the valley this night."

His wide-brimmed hat, banded with snake-skin, lay a few yards away. Mahuli brought it to him and Rusty took it, but he did not put it on. He stood bare-headed by Dumela. The breeze that had carried the human scent from the outspan to the Rogue and caused him to turn and see his pursuers had dropped with the setting of the sun. Nature held her breath in the interval between day and night. Leaf and grass had ceased to nod and whisper, and even the dark figures round Dumela seemed caught in the motionless spell of silence broken only by the Bantu girl's chant on the lonely hill-side—a solitary requiem for the passing of the Mighty One.

Rusty looked up and saw Alice coming towards him. But what had happened to her? Where was the jaunty head-in-the-air hustle of the nurse who could not throw off the habit of hurry? She was coming down the wooded slope hesitantly, groping her way. He knew that she was afraid that she might find him crushed to death as he had found Mbula earlier in this long, arduous day, and the knowledge of her fear and of his safety gave him a feeling of triumph and a renewed joy of living. A great threat had passed and he was more acutely conscious of the glory and the value of life than ever before. Was this how a matador felt when he strutted round the bull-ring with the ear of his dead antagonist held aloft, when he bowed before the lovely lady to whom his bull was dedicated? Dumela should have been dedicated to Alice, Rusty ought to lop off one of those vast ears, and wave it at her now, but he would just as soon shake out a carpet. He gave Mahuli his gun and his hat and went to meet her.

" You're safe," she said. " Thank God you're safe."

All the dusk of evening seemed to have gathered in her eyes, cloaking her fear, but now, as she looked at him, relief shone soft as starlight in a deep pool.

" I'm safe," he said.

He linked his bare arm in hers and felt her skin tremble at his touch. He was tremendously conscious of her skin—firm and smooth, cold with her recent terror. A whole host of memories shook him. Italy. The respite after battle, the wonder of death cheated once again, the love of life a thousand-fold stronger by virtue of its very precariousness, the need for a woman . . . Flora. Burning desire transmuted into pure love—first love. Flora . . .

" Do you want to see Dumela before the rats get at him? "

Already the first Lilliputians were at work on mighty Gulliver, carving him up. The branches of the surrounding trees were heavy with vultures, and along the game-trails more and more dark figures converged upon the dead elephant.

" He's magnificent," she said. " He must be the biggest in all the world."

Death, she thought. An end of sound and fury, the peace

after the storm of living. But this was ignoble. The lion is the King, Rusty had said, the elephant is God, and here, under her eyes, this God of the Wilderness was being reduced to carrion. Rusty's arm still held hers tucked warmly against his body. He laughed.

"One of those feet would make the base of a splendid umbrella-stand. With toenails nicely polished. Quite a good wedding present. Heaven knows, we followed that huge spoor far enough for a hot afternoon's stroll."

The foot would be a souvenir and a dedication for Alice. He gave Mahuli orders to bring it to the outspan with the tusks. Then he walked slowly up the hill with Alice. The dog, Smokey, ran ahead of them.

The moon was high by the time they had eaten, and a fire burned in the entrance of the thorn-*scherm*. Dlameni and Mahuli had joined the revellers in the valley, but Nimrod and Oasis with her baby remained at the outspan.

"You're quite a girl," said Rusty. "You ate that elephant heart as if you enjoyed it."

Alice laughed. "Maybe I did. And I'm sure there was big magic in it."

"Crocodile's heart is the thing for that." He cupped his hands round his pipe and the glow as he drew on it threw up the mischief in his eyes.

"For what, precisely?"

"A love-potion. A little bit of croc's heart in your stew and you'll fall for the first man who crosses your path."

"*Midsummer Night's Dream* stuff. Won't elephant heart do?"

"Luckily not. Would you like to go to the hill-top and watch the fun and games down in the valley?"

She hesitated for an instant, and he grinned. "Yes, it's the lion's hunting time, but there's enough noise going on to keep any self-respecting beast at a safe distance."

She was sitting on a camp-stool, and he put out his hands and drew her to her feet. Once again he was intensely aware of her skin. Her hand was cool but it fired his blood. This, he knew, was part of the aftermath of danger. The faint night breeze that blew now from the rainy quarter stirred her hair so that her face, lit by firelight and moonlight, seemed small and defenceless with its dark frame blown lightly back and away from it.

"Your coat. You'd better take your coat. It'll be cool up there on the hill."

"No. Just my cardigan. It's in the car."

He fetched it for her and put it round her shoulders. He carried a rug over his arm. They sauntered through the glade to the summit where the wide valley spread beneath them. So radiant was the night that he did not need a torch. She wished he had taken a gun, and then she saw the shadow that went with them, neither near nor far from them—Nimrod, his assegai in his hand. And Smokey was ahead, weaving to and fro through the grass.

Oh, no, she thought, None of this is possible, none of this is true! This can't be me—Alice Lang. I don't know myself any more. What's happening to me here in this world that is as foreign to me as Venus or Mars? I've dreamed of Africa all my life, but I've never pictured anything like this—anything so savage, so sinister, and so beautiful, so strange and yet, somehow, familiar. Rusty, too. I know so little about him, but he is as deeply familiar to me as Andrew is remote—always more remote. But it is Andrew I love. His essential goodness, his loneliness and his need of me are the stars I have followed. I am on my way to him. He is my goal.

"What will happen when Andrew tries to make contact with Camp Two?" she asked.

"The Bantu caretaker will listen in at the usual times. He will tell Andrew that we have not arrived."

"Will he worry?"

"He may do. Tomorrow we'll send him a message through the Police Post at Poinsettia. We'll call in at Boryslawski's farm and telephone the Post direct from there."

Lightning forked and flashed continually along the horizon, and somewhere in the Black Mamba Mountains thunder rumbled. But the storm was far away. The moon blazed—not pale and chill like an English moon but white-hot in its high, starry firmament. A moon to fear. ". . . the sun shall not smite thee by day, nor the moon by night . . ." The psalmist of old had known the perils of the sun and the moon, the real and the intangible dangers of the forces of nature.

Rusty spread the rug on the rim of the hill and they sat and looked down into the valley. Somewhere near, Nimrod squatted. Smokey, nose to the dry earth and grass, explored.

A girdle of separate fires encircled the remains of Dumela, camp-fires and cooking-fires that also served to keep wild animals at bay. Tiny dark figures capered in diabolic silhouette against the flames, stamping, posturing, chanting in a dance that would go on till dawn. The African drummers beat their loud tattoo, ever faster and more furiously. Women had brought beer from the squatter camps and the high voices of children joined in the explosive monotonous song of Africa, the song with a heart-beat and the rhythm of pulsing blood and the mounting barbaric frenzy of an atavistic orgy.

"There you are," said Rusty. "The noble savage. Not much like your African surgeon in London, Alice Lang."

"Not much. But it was there in him—this side. It must have been. It's in all of us, I guess."

"I doubt it. It may be in me—the latent savagery—I'm a wild man. And it may be in you, deep down under all that self-control. But it isn't in my brother, Andrew. He isn't close enough to life for that. He is the referee, standing on the touch-line. Those dancing baboons down there are the players—and pretty rough too." He spoke with the curious mixture of pity and respect that she had come to associate with his attitude towards his brother.

"A wife and family should bring Andrew into the game," she said stiff and resentful.

"They should. But will they? To marry is to entangle yourself in an intimate—an inextricable—human relationship. Andrew mistrusts human relationships. That is the essence of his love affair with you. It has not yet come to birth as a full-blooded human relationship. He may still——"

She broke in. "Rusty! It is *you* who are afraid of human relationships! You—you!"

Her voice, breathless and sharp, penetrated the armour he had grown slowly and painfully during the years since Flora. After Flora he had sought neither love nor companionship from women, only physical solace and the brief satisfaction of the passing adventure. He had mated like the animals, without affection, much less love. But he had observed caution.

There must be no consequences of his acts, no ties of any sort. Never again would he lay his heart open to the pain and grief of love.   He heard Alice say :

" How did she hurt you so much—your Italian wife ?   How did she make you so bitter—so disillusioned ? "

The drums beat in the valley and the breeze blew stronger. The moon silvered a distant loop of the river.   Rusty saw another river under the moon on another spring night long ago —a world away—the night before the last advance up the ' boot ' of Italy.   There had been another girl beside him then, a fair girl with a thin, starved body and eyes haunted and saddened by experience of war.   Flora.   Hunger and sorrow had rendered her beauty naked—worn it down to the frail, finely-bred bone.   She had entered his life between one battle and another ; she had symbolized, for him, love in war-time, the butterfly on the cannon's lip.

Rusty said :   " You want me to tell you about Flora ? "

" Yes," said Alice.   And she thought : This is the key.   If he will tell me about Flora I will know him—and Andrew too. What happened to Rusty has left its mark on Andrew.   They are closer than they guess.

" It was spring in Florence," he said.   " We were resting there before the last Battle of Italy.   Flora was a translator in an Allied Unit.   They hardly paid her enough to buy a loaf of bread a day, but they gave her meals in an Allied Mess for locally employed Italians.   Hunger was the problem of most Italians and she was thankful for the job.   She came of a very old, very proud family, and she lived with her aunt in a medieval palace on the banks of the Arno.   For what it was worth, it was Flora's palace, because her father and mother were dead.   They had sheltered Allied escaped prisoners— and paid the price.   It seems very far away now . . . all that . . ."

" I know," Alice said.   " I feel like that too—as if everything before I came here belonged to another existence."

He looked at her as if he were seeing her with new eyes. " Yes.   Andrew is right.   You fit here.   You belong—just as Flora never could."

A thrill of sheer delight ran through her.   For the first time in all this queer adventure she felt confidence in herself, justification for her faith in the future.

" Flora was beautiful," said Rusty. He wondered why he talked of her as if she were dead. She was probably still beautiful. " She was very fair. You see them in the north—the fair Italians with faces like Renaissance angels. I had never met anyone like her before . . ."

Alice heard the echo of wonder in his voice, as if he had once again fallen under an old spell.

" She was part of an ancient culture. It was born and bred in her. She was only eighteen—three years younger than I was—but she was centuries old, she was as much a part of Florence as the palace in which she lived. She loved her city so much—too much. We used to go out together. Sometimes we ate at a little restaurant in the hills—black-market food with a delicious white wine called Tears of Christ. We fell in love, but we were too young to know how foolish that was. We believed in love."

He was silent, remembering the night he had stood with Flora on the balcony outside her room looking over the Arno—his last night in Florence. Soldiers and their *signorinas* strolled along the Lungarno past the iron Bailey Bridge where once the Ponte Trinità had spanned the river with historic grace. Flora had said in her perfect English that lent equal weight to every syllable :

" The Germans had to mine our roads and blow up our bridges when they retreated, but it was sad for us. The Ponte Trinità was so lovely, so graceful. I wish you could have seen it. We were warned when they were going to destroy it, and that last night of its life my aunt and I stood here and wept. It was as if we said good-bye to a dear friend condemned to death."

He had felt her sorrow and her mourning, and he had put his arm about her thin, sweet body.

" I can't bear what has been done to my country, Rusty. I would like to go away and forget all this misery and destruction."

" Let me take you away—if I come through. I love you. I never knew that love could be like this."

His memories came upon him like a flock of migrant birds returning home, some winged and strong, some sad and broken.

" We were married in Italy just after the war," he said. " I brought Flora to South Africa. I thought I was the luckiest man in the world, especially as I had been given a job as a Ranger in a glorious little Game Reserve not far from Durban. We had a nice house and a garden with flowering trees that were always alive with sun-birds. You could see the hills and vales of Zululand for miles."

He had taken Flora there with pride and joy.

" Can you be happy here ? " he had asked, sure of her answer.

" Sanctuary . . ." She had spoken the word slowly in her soft, Italian voice, so that it had seemed to him the most melodious word in all the English language. " This, I suppose, is sanctuary—escape from all that man has created and destroyed."

She had lifted her face in the clear sunlight and he had held it between his hands, searching the classic features for some assurance that she would indeed be happy. But humility and a flash of insight had warned him of what was to come. The shadow of a phantom palace had risen to obliterate their simple home. The stone courtyards with silent fountains, and the long, desolate galleries, peopled with the marble busts and statues of her ancestors, had claimed her in that sunlit moment as surely as they were to claim her later.

" What happened ? " asked Alice gently.

" There are trees you can't transplant, animals who die away from their own kind and climate. If we had been less young and less in love we would have realized that Flora was like that. She couldn't exist without her own sort of people, without art and music, and what she called the immortal creations of genius. God's creations weren't good enough for Flora."

Ah, the bitterness—the cry because the wound had never healed. Alice said :

" You couldn't give up your job ? "

" What use would I have been in Italy—except to fight there ? In peace-time I belong here just as Flora belonged there. After a while she went home. Italy had made a wonderful recovery from the war. So had Flora."

" And she never came back ? "

He stood up, and Alice rose too. The drums throbbed in her blood. Rusty was smiling down at her, but his face was hard as granite, the tenderness and absorption in the past gone from it.

" The story has a happy ending. Flora's palace had been rented by a wealthy international art collector. He collected my wife too."

" And you ? "

" Our marriage was annulled. Her guardian—her old aunt —had never sanctioned it, and Flora was under age at the time. One way and another, words were spoken that wiped the slate clean. She could begin life again. And I got my legal freedom after a time. For desertion. All quite neat and tidy. And I had learned a very important lesson. Love is not enough to make a marriage work out right."

" Is anything in life ever as neat and tidy as that ? I don't think so, Rusty. Lessons can leave ugly scars."

" What's done is done, and what's finished is finished. This tree we are under right now is called Ndivata—the Tree of Forgetfulness. We chose a good spot to talk of what is past."

" The Tree of Forgetfulness . . ." She looked up at the delicate leaves and clusters of flowers, pallid in the moonlight. " If only there were really such a tree ! "

" You too ? Are there things you want so much to forget ? "

" Yes," she said. " My mother's suffering. The way that girl, Oasis, cried when she knew what had happened to Amos ; even the way your face changes when you try to be tough about someone you loved as much as you loved Flora. And other things." She shivered. One, two, three, four, five—beat the drums—one, two, three, four, five, but there *should* be six . . .

As they went back to the outspan, Nimrod moved silently ahead of them, and every now and again Smokey barked violently as he put up a night-jar or some small nocturnal animal.

" This fence," said Alice. " Will it really keep out lions ? "

" No, it will only discourage them. If we had donkeys or horses with us we'd need a *scherm* three times as thick and deep. Will you sleep in ' Sweet Sue ' ? We can unpack the back and rig a sort of bed. Or there's a lilo Nimrod can blow up for you."

" What will you do ? "

" Sleep by the fire under the stars."

" So will I. I'd like the lilo, please."

Oasis had kept the fire going, and she lay beside it on her rush mat. She was covered with her blanket and her son nestled in her arms against her dark, naked breast. When he woke and cried she suckled him. The bitch, Tombazane, was at her feet.

" Women and children one side of the fire, men the other," said Rusty, and told Nimrod to put Alice's lilo near Oasis.

When Alice was ready to go to sleep, Rusty tucked the rug round her. " Don't worry if the dogs suddenly go off like bombs. They give the alarm for all sorts of unnecessary things, not just lions and leopards."

" I won't worry. I've never slept under the stars before. It's so clean and cool and fresh."

He stopped on an impulse and touched her shining hair.

" They have given you a name—a native name. I heard them talk of you just now. Likwezi."

" Likwezi ? " The touch of his hand was comforting. She knew that she would not be afraid if he were near.

" The blue, glossy starling. They call it Likwezi—the Morning Star—first in the sky, unique of its kind. You are the first white woman in Velaba—unique of your kind. And your hair is as glossy and bright as the starling's wing. Sleep well, Likwezi."

The moon shone full on her face and into her eyes as she looked up at him. The throb of the drums was more distant here. The night was fragrant, and the fire sent showers of little red sparks into the darkness. A night-bird called mournfully and was answered.

" Don't look at me like that," said Rusty. " My name is Ratau, the Lion, and I am dangerous."

She closed her eyes. When she opened them again he was on the other side of the fire with the dark form of Nimrod near him.

15

Haunt of the Tokoloshe

ALICE found sleeping under the stars more unrestful than romantic. Whoever happened to wake up fed the fire from the pile of wood collected in the afternoon. Every few minutes —or so it seemed to her—the dogs sprang up and barked furiously. The drums beat incessantly ; extraordinary huffings and gruntings sounded round the *scherm* ; once they heard the cough of a hunting-cheetah and the *yow-yow-yow* of the saddle-backed jackal, and dwarf-owls and night-jars called to one another eerily. The girl, Oasis, moaned constantly in her sleep.

" Men and women like their mates strong—unspoiled . . ." Rusty had said of the Bantus. Could it be that the tenderness Oasis bestowed upon her child, Shinhenani, would not include her husband, when he returned to her. Would she be unwilling to play protector to her man—to be his voice and his eyes ?

I am a nurse, thought Alice, with her sleepless gaze on the girl and her child by the fire. Tending the bodies of men and women is my job, yet Oasis there has learned more about Nature's intentions than I have. I know the body when it has been subjected to injury or accident, when it is sick and de-graded, or sterile for the surgeon's knife, and she knows it young and lusty for love, a healthy instrument for procreation and delight. Did love in a primitive heart boil down to a res-pect for physical power and perfection alone ? Did a man ask of his woman only that she bear him healthy children and brew good beer ? And did a woman demand nothing more than a potent lover, hot in passion, cool in danger ? The sharp eye, the iron nerve ?

She saw again the small, steady figure of a man with a rifle raised to his shoulder—a man facing death. But he was here, so she too was safe. Or was she ? " My name is Ratau, the Lion—and I am dangerous . . ." What was safety anyway ? Was that only physical by the standards of the Wilderness ?

No, not here, where things like the Tokoloshe hid in the reeds of the riverside! Safety, like civilized love, embraced the spirit as well as the body. She had said good-bye to safety. For her safety lay neither in England nor in Velaba. It lay in the past.

She turned and hid her face from the moon. From time to time she dozed.

At dawn Nimrod put a mug of strong, sweet tea and some biscuits beside her. Rusty and Smokey had disappeared. It seemed they had gone to the river. Oasis was moving about, her baby strapped to her back. The fire had burned down to a bed of silvery ash, but Nimrod had warmed a pot of water on it. He brought this to Alice with soap and a towel, and then he left the women alone in the outspan.

Alice changed her shirt and crumpled slacks for shorts and a clean blouse, she brushed her hair till it shone, and her bright lipstick flamed against the olive pallor of her skin. Likwezi, they called her—the glossy starling—and, as the last stars faded, she heard the sweet note of the bird whose name they had given her. The drums were silent at last.

When Rusty returned to the outspan his hair clung to his head in damp curls and he had the healthy glow of someone who has just taken a cold plunge. Alice said:

"But what about crocs and hippos—to say nothing of bilharzia?"

He laughed. "I know what risks I can take, and where. Nimrod keeps guard if the crocs are around."

Dlameni and Mahuli had appeared and were helping Nimrod to secure the Rogue's tusks on the roof of the station-wagon. Rusty and Alice strolled to the summit of the hill. He showed her traces of the visitors of the night. There was the spoor of a cheetah, a hyena and a warthog and his family, a scattering of porcupine quills and the droppings of the little buck who inhabit stony heights.

"No lion?" she said.

"Not last night."

"Only Ratau."

He was amused. "No other lion, Likwezi."

Her red mouth smiled. "I like the names the Bantus give people. What does Tombazane mean?"

" Young girl, and when that scrawny little bitch gets old they'll call her something else. The names they give are descriptive or hopeful. For instance, Shinhenani is a hopeful name. The baby is called Shinhenani—little warrior— because he is a strong, fearless child."

" Descriptive, too," she smiled. " He lives up to it, bless his little heart. And why Oasis—or Nimrod ? "

" Who knows ? They choose their European names from the Bible, or a legend, or somebody they admire, or just a thought—an aspiration. Oasis—it certainly suits her. And Nimrod the Hunter. A good Game-guard is born of a good hunter."

When they looked into the valley there was little to be seen. Deep, pale ground-mists covered the bones of mighty Dumela and the little slumbering mortals who had devoured him and danced round his grave. Here and there leafy tree-tops rose from the chill shroud, or a plume of blue smoke spiralled upwards.

" Did it ever happen ? " she asked. " Did you really shoot that monster ? "

" Nimrod and I. The tusks are on ' Sweet Sue '—close on two hundred pounds of the best ivory, I'd bet."

" Can you keep it ? "

" Property of the Sanctuary Trustees, my dear. I shall leave them at Boryslawski's farm later today and Nelmapius can pick them up in the lorry some time."

" Is that where we are going now ? "

" First to Sweet Spruit, the home of the Tokoloshe. Then we'll decide what next."

They followed the course of the Fulene River towards the western boundary of Velaba. Rusty drove carefully to allow for the extra weight of Dumela's tusks on ' Sweet Sue's ' roof. Herds of buck and wildebeests and zebra grazed in dewy glades ; giraffe nibbled the young leaves of tall acacias ; and down in the hollows of dale and *donga* the dawn-mists began to melt and drift away. Apollo raised his burning red disc above the shoulder of a mountain peak and at once the promise of heat thinned and dried the early morning air.

" It really is the Garden of Eden," said Alice. " All this is so much more beautiful than I could have dreamed."

Past and future no longer had any significance for her. There was only this strange, perilous present. It was all she wanted.

"The Garden of Eden is a term for the brave and the foolish," said Rusty.

Alice shook her head. "For the happy."

"Are you happy?"

"At this moment—entirely."

"So am I. But when we leave this road and go down the hill to Sweet Spruit the mood will change."

Was happiness so ephemeral, so vulnerable?

Alice turned and put out her arms for Oasis to give her Shinhenani. She had made friends with the child, who no longer regarded her pale skin with suspicion. Yesterday, at the outspan, she had played with him as his mother did, and after a while he had crowed with glee and bounded up and down in her arms. The firm sturdiness of his naked chocolate body had entranced her. He was a fine baby—a 'little warrior' indeed. But now Oasis held him against her heart and Alice saw terror in her large eyes.

Nimrod leaned forward to explain: "Oasis no like thees place, Nkosikasi. Frighten for Tokoloshe."

'Sweet Sue' wound down into the green gloom of a forested incline. At its base they came to a dry stream-bed strewn with boulders. Rusty stopped the car on the verge.

"I am going to explore with Nimrod and Smokey, Alice. You'd better stay here in the car with Oasis and Tombazane."

"I'd rather come with you."

"The girl will be very nervous without you."

Alice glanced at him quickly, but there was no irony in his expression and he meant it when he added: "This is different. This doesn't just concern wild animals. If anything alarms you, sound the horn. On no account get out. You may not see us, but we won't be far away."

This time he buckled on a cartridge-belt and took his rifle with him. Nimrod armed himself with his little axe and his assegai and together they went into the sunlit stony bed of the *spruit*. They moved forward with silent caution, Rusty a few yards ahead of the young Game-guard. For, to Nimrod also, the hazards of this excursion were not merely those of wild beasts. This was a haunted spot. Here a man had lost sight and speech at the hands of—*what*? And that man had been his comrade, the husband of the girl who waited with her child. Nimrod was glad that Likwezi had stayed with Oasis. Likwezi had strong magic. What it was he did not know, but her eyes said that she possessed it.

From where 'Sweet Sue' was parked, only a short part of the *spruit* was visible before it curved away among the trees. The section Alice could see was scored with the spoor of innumerable pads, hooves and claws, and human foot-prints. The sand was still dark in parts where blood had soaked it, and Alice saw the two men stoop to examine these marks.

Oasis had retreated into her corner of 'Sweet Sue' like a shadow. The Little Warrior slept. Tombazane sat with her muzzle pressed to the window. Amos's small axe was near the hand of Oasis. Alice found that her own fingers rested on the steering wheel and that her palms were damp and tingling.

She looked round her at the scene of recent violence, and it seemed to her that Sweet Spruit belied its name with obscure emanations of evil. Even the trees were held captive in a mesh of grey liana ropes. And on the opposite bank of the dry stream a tall, feathery stand of reeds formed a dense screen from which rose the slender, sulphur-yellow trunks of a grove of fever-trees, their twisted boughs laden with the nests of weaver-birds. Red and gold finches and brilliant kingfishers darted in and out of the rushes in all the spring glory of their courting plumage. The breathless air, stirred only by the wings of birds, shrilled with the song of cicadas, a sound so high and monotonous that it was the very voice of fever—the 'singing in the head'.

When Tombazane suddenly barked ferociously every nerve in Alice's system started and jangled. Even the sleeping Shin-henani woke and sat up and rubbed his liquid black eyes. Then he pointed a chubby finger at the commotion that had caused Tombazane's outburst and showed his tiny white milk-teeth in a joyous grin. He bounced and chortled and called incomprehensible endearments to the troop of grey monkeys who peered out of the green twilight at 'Sweet Sue'. As if his approval reassured them, they swung by hands, feet and tails from the liana ropes, chattering, chirruping, and throwing themselves gaily from branch to branch and tree to tree. Alice found herself laughing aloud with sheer relief at the antics of these furry acrobats—and then they were gone. All the fathers, mothers, aunts, uncles and mischievous little ones had vanished. The leaves settled once more, Shinhenani demanded nourishment, and Alice wondered if the hairy dwarf— the Tokoloshe—might not even now be peering at them from some hidden fastness of his own.

A few hundred yards farther downstream, Rusty and Nimrod stood in the shade of a large tamboutie tree. It was an old tree, and hollow.

Nimrod said, " It would make a good hiding-place for a bird or a snake."

" Or for guns," added Rusty grimly.

" I will look, Nkosi."

Seconds later Alice heard a shot crack through the silence. One single shot.

Ten minutes passed—perhaps fifteen—before she saw Rusty. But that little space of time was all eternity.

He came lightly and quickly through the *spruit* and up the bank to ' Sweet Sue '. Nimrod was with him, his face ashengrey.

Alice opened the door of the station-wagon, and Rusty stood there, his hand held out to her.

" Come with me. Nimrod will stay here with Oasis."

She got out of the car, but her knees were weak. She did not know that he had seen the trembling of her underlip and that he took her hand to find out if that too were shaking.

" Stay close to me," he said.

She followed him along the stream-bed, her mouth as dry as the sand under their feet. He still carried his gun.

" Where is Smokey ? " She tried to steady her voice.

" On guard."

He led her to the hollow tree. At its foot lay a writhing tenfoot snake about the thickness of a man's wrist. It was dark olive-green on top with a light belly, a tapering tail and a narrow head. The spine at the back of the neck had been broken by the shot and torn by the dog's teeth. Smokey stood by the reptile, suspicious still and growling in an undertone. Alice had all the normal horror of snakes, and this one, beautiful as it was, filled her with the utmost revulsion. There was something obscene about the sinuous, mindless life after death in the squirming muscular coils.

" What is it ? "

" A mamba."

" A mamba ! But——"

" Yes. A mamba killed my mother. This is one creature I never spare—the fiercest, deadliest snake in Africa."

" Where was it when you saw it ? "

He jerked his head upwards. " There in the tree. This is a hollow tree. The hollow is deep and the entrance above eye-level—a good hide-away. It could hold guns. Nimrod was climbing the tree to look. But carefully. No one explores a hollow, or a hole in the ground, or any cave or dark place rashly—and then suddenly, in the branch above his head, I caught sight of the snake. I shot it and it fell. Smokey did the rest. The mate may be near. This may be their breeding-ground, and they are full of poison now, after the winter."

" Rusty, let's go away ! This place is bad ! "

He took her cold hand in his. " Come and look up here—into the branches."

She peered through the leaves, fearing to see the mamba's mate, but presently she made out strips of meat hanging from a wire suspended from one branch to another.

" That's a trick the poachers have learnt from the leopard," he said. " The leopard uses a tree as a larder for his kill. The vultures don't see the meat among the leaves, and scavenging animals can't get at it. They can't even smell it because scent travels along definite levels. Sweet Spruit appears to have been a poachers' pantry with the Tokoloshe as unpaid watchman. I should guess that most of the game and all the guns have been taken from here already. They'll be getting their meat away to the Rand as soon as possible—before anyone in authority sniffs it out, and before the rains break and the roads become impassable."

" Why do they dry it first ? "

" It's lighter to carry and it keeps. But the white *bakkie*-bandits go about things differently from the native poachers.

They operate along the border between Camps Two and Three. They make their raids in light trucks we call *bakkies* and shoot up herds of game with machine-guns. They kill, cut up, and clear out. I'd gladly pepper them with lead if I got the chance ! "

" Let's get out of here, Rusty."

He tipped up her face and looked into it. The dappled, greenish light made her clear skin appear livid. Near them the dead mamba twisted and twitched.

" I haven't spared you much," he said. " You've had a hard introduction to Velaba. If you see it through . . . if you can take it . . ."

" Then what ? "

His eyes held hers, narrow and challenging under the level brows darker than his hair. " Then I shall apologize to my brother. I shall know that Andrew was right—that you are the one woman in the world for him. Come."

16

Wife of Radinoxa

RUSTY drove ' Sweet Sue ' through the dry bed of the *spruit* and up into the thorn-veld.

" About here Jan Nelmapius and Job found a scattering of empty cartridge-cases," he said. " Animals had evidently been shot and carried away—probably down to that Sweet Spruit hide-out."

" Do you suspect any of your own people ? " Alice asked.

He made no sign of having heard her and she did not repeat the question. Presently he said :

" We are going to Boryslawski's farm a few miles from here. Mrs. Boryslawski will give us breakfast and then you can have a bath and a rest while I go to the old Chief's kraal."

" Are you going to the kraal alone ? "

" With Nimrod. I don't want Oasis there, she may make trouble. And I don't want you, for that matter. My business will go quickest if there are no distractions."

He always knows his own mind, she thought with disappointment. She had wanted to see the Chief's kraal, but Rusty's profile did not encourage argument—not now, at any rate. He had withdrawn into himself to concentrate on the threats to the principle—even the very existence—of Velaba. The animal inhabitants of his beloved Sanctuary were being shot and trapped and, in certain places, massacred wholesale, while his natives were being corrupted or near murdered. And although he believed all these crimes to be connected he could find no definite evidence to help him fix the blame on any particular group or individual.

They crossed the stone causeway over the Lower Fulene, and, as they did so, a flock of emerald-green parrots rose squawking from the trees and flew towards a settlement of native huts not far away. Rusty increased speed and ' Sweet Sue ' shot forward and rumbled rapidly over the corrugated earth road. Here the country was open and undulating, and the golden grasslands were grazed to the quick.

" Look at that herd ! " exclaimed Alice. " What——" She broke off and laughed. " Why, Rusty, they are cows ! "

Nimrod's broad grin lit his face, and Rusty laughed too.

" The river is the boundary. This is the old Chief's tribal territory. Boryslawski's farm cuts a wedge through it to the border of Velaba. It's very isolated and unproductive. He got it cheaply when the last owner died. The only money he's likely to make out of it is when those trees mature." He made a gesture towards a swathe of gum and pine plantations flanking the western hills. The road ran parallel with the river between the hills and the towering Black Mamba Range to the east. Here were none of the rich citrus and mango orchards of the south, no farm-houses set in gay gardens and paw-paw and banana groves. The only suggestion of the influence of civilization was a tin-roofed Indian general store and a modest native schoolhouse which also served as a church. For the rest, the scattered kraals and cattle-folds huddled behind the strong thorn-fences designed to keep out marauding wild beasts who recognized no boundaries. Little herd-boys capered and cheered at ' Sweet Sue ', and women with various bundles on their heads turned their straight shoulders and waved. The shadows of fleecy white clouds driven before some wind of the upper air raced across the veld, and once again Alice wondered at the magnitude of the scene, the high sky and the sense of light and space.

"Boryslawski has been burning grass to attract our game!" Rusty scowled at a belt of scorched black stubble along the banks of the river. "As soon as the young shoots come up after the rains our buck will be tempted into his lands. Then he'll mow them down no doubt."

"You dislike this farmer?"

"See what you make of him. Draw your own conclusions and we'll compare notes."

"Jan Nelmapius—or was it you?—told me the natives called him King of the Snakes."

"Quite a guide for your judgment! Yes, they call him King of the Snakes—Radinoxa."

He turned 'Sweet Sue' up a long avenue of tall blue-gums. The bark was peeling from their pale trunks, and it seemed to Alice that they were sloughing their skins—like snakes. They drew up in front of a rambling house with a green corrugated-iron roof, and surrounded by a wide cement stoep. Radinoxa might be King of the Snakes, but he did not want his subjects on his stoep, and a snake on cement is at a disadvantage, for it can get no grip on the smooth surface. The house was shaded by exotic trees, and the whirring wings of sun-birds hovered over the gaudy trumpets of flowers Alice had never seen before.

A man came down the steps to greet them. He was slightly built, but his figure had the quick, whippy quality of the rhino-hide *sjambok* he carried in his hand. Like Rusty, he wore khaki shorts and a bush-jacket open at the throat. His fair hair receded at the temples—curious temples that looked as though two giant thumbs had clamped the narrow skull in infancy and left their hollow indentations on either side of the light, close-set eyes. To the left and the right of him walked a honey-coloured ridgeback and a young lioness.

Smokey and Tombazane hurled themselves at the window of the station-wagon and barked wildly, and instantly the ridge-back leapt forward and thundered insults at them, while the lioness lowered her head with a sideways movement and drew back her lip to show the teeth of a killer.

Boryslawski flicked his *sjambok* and shouted an order in a rasping, arrogant voice, and the two animals reluctantly retreated backwards.

" Wait ! " he called to Rusty. " I'll shut these two up. Then you can let your dogs out."

Alice was impressed. As the two beasts followed him round the side of the house, she said to Rusty: " He has all the tricks of the ringmaster. A sort of cruel, courageous authority."

When he returned a few minutes later a squat, blonde woman was with him, her pasty, sagging face wreathed in smiles.

" Rusty, how nice ! Have you come for breakfast ? We've had ours, but we'll soon get some more cooked. And who is your friend ? But of course, she's Miss Alice Lang ! We always listen in to your Camp-to-Camp conversations. And why not ? There's nothing else to do of an evening in this God-forsaken hole except put on the wireless and try to get a bit of news from somewhere—even Velaba ! Anton, tell that lazy kaffir, Klaas, to get busy and fry some eggs and bacon and make fresh coffee ! And what about your natives, Rusty ? Our servants can give them some food—and the dogs——"

" Christina, you talk too much."

The words, quietly spoken in the harsh voice with the R a trifle guttural, silenced her at once like a radio switched off at the turn of a knob. Alice was sure that, for a second, everything in Mrs. Boryslawski ceased to function, even her heart. Boryslawski was smiling at his wife, but his light eyes, set flat on the surface of his face so that the muscles round them worked visibly, were neither affectionate nor amused. He opened the door of the station-wagon on Alice's side, and she got out with the dogs tumbling after her.

" You were right, Mrs. Boryslawski," said Rusty. " This is Alice Lang from Middlesex, England, on her way to Poinsettia Mission Station."

"Then you're a missionary! Who'd have thought it? They have a certain look. You don't look a bit like a missionary ! "

" I'm not a missionary," smiled Alice. " I'm a hospital nurse."

Boryslawski said : " Come along in. You mustn't let my

wife tell you all her ailments, Miss Lang. It takes too long. I know Middlesex. I was stationed there in the war—in a fighter squadron."

His smile was thin and drawn down at the corners. Of course, Alice remembered now, Rusty had mentioned that he had been a fighter-pilot. His countrymen had become a legend in her district—men whose reckless valour was born of their hatred of the enemy who had ravaged their country, men who had nothing in the world to lose, except life itself.

Boryslawski turned to Rusty, with a flick of his *sjambok* at the Rogue's tusks on the roof of ' Sweet Sue '.   " You have some magnificent ivory there.   How come ? "

" A rogue elephant trampled one of our road-gang.   I had to shoot it."

How odd, thought Alice.   That's the first time I have heard Rusty talk of an animal as ' it '.   And the Rogue at that—such a formidable enemy !   He's talking Boryslawski's way.

" Life for a life, eh ? "

" Where a human being is concerned, yes.   I'd like to unload that ivory and leave it here.   Jan Nelmapius can collect it later in one of the lorries and take it to Poinsettia."

" Sure.   And we'll weigh it.   I'd estimate you've got two hundred pounds of the best there.   Pity you can't keep it for yourself.   I'll send a boy to help your native unload it, and then he can give your people some food."

They were still grouped in the sun by the station-wagon, and Alice saw the Pole's cold calculating eye run over Oasis as she stood quietly with her baby in a sling resting on her hip.   He seemed to be assessing her value as if she were a slave to be bought, or ivory to be weighed and sold.

Mrs. Boryslawski led Alice into the house.

" Breakfast will take some time to prepare.   These kaffirs are so slow and lazy, Miss Lang.   All they want to do is squat in the sun and gossip and laugh and boast.   You can't hurry them ; if the house was on fire they'd still be loitering and shouting to each other.   It drives me mad to see them polishing a floor—little slow movements as if they were stroking a pet cat ! You and Rusty were expected at Camp Two last night, but when we listened on the Sanctuary wavelength at the usual time Rusty didn't come in."

"We didn't get that far. Rusty had to track down the elephant, and that took most of the afternoon. We slept in the open."

"In the open—in Velaba! How horrible! All those lions and hyenas and wild dogs—to say nothing about snakes and scorpions!"

"It wasn't very restful. I wonder if I could have a bath while breakfast is cooking?"

"Of course, my dear. Come this way."

Alice followed her through a bleak living-room and down a passage into a bare little bedroom opposite a bathroom with an old-fashioned geyser. Mrs. Boryslawski called to a houseboy to light it—yelled would describe it better, for her hostess, Alice discovered, had a special voice for her servants.

"That wasn't the native language," said Alice.

"It was Afrikaans. They have a smattering of Afrikaans and English. They learn them at school."

"Three languages. That's quite an achievement."

"And in the end all they talk is the language of the baboons."

Alice looked round her. The house, like the garden, had a derelict air. Nothing had been done to make it attractive or homely. The linoleum on the bedroom floor was faded and cracked, the furniture was cheap and the window uncurtained. She opened the little dressing-case she had brought from the car and took out a few cosmetics and a change of underwear, and her linen skirt. Mrs. Boryslawski watched her with interest.

"I don't know that face-cream," she remarked. "Imported, I suppose—but then of course you've just come from London. How you must hate it here in the *bundu*."

"I think I'm going to love it." Alice started as the sound of an explosion came from the bathroom.

"Don't worry. That's just the geyser warming up. It's tricky, like my husband. Did it scare you to see that lioness with him? I hate the brute—Sheba, he calls her. I keep telling him she's dangerous, I've seen her stalking the farm-hands, and she ought to be sent to a zoo, but Anton says it's too late for that. He's had her since she was a cub. The mother was caught in a trap in Velaba, and the cub was found nearby, and some old kaffir brought it here. Anton can do anything with her, and she adores the dogs. He uses Sheba as a sort of special watchdog. She sleeps in the hangar he's prepared for our new aeroplane, and I promise you no kaffir would dare go near the place, though my husband swears she would never really harm anybody. But, as I keep saying, what can one do with a full-grown lioness about the house ? If she'll pine in a zoo, he'll simply have to shoot her. She could never live in her natural state now. She wouldn't have a clue how to hunt her food. But he won't bring himself to put her down. Sometimes I think she's the only living creature he really loves."

She spoke breathlessly, the words coming in rushes. Alice felt that if she moved Mrs. Boryslawski would hold on to her desperately and go on talking.

" Anton likes his own way in everything—and gets it," she went on with pathetic masochistic satisfaction. " Do you think I'd stay here if I wasn't forced to ? I was born and brought up in a city. I'm accustomed to life and lights and friends you can have in for a cup of tea or a game of bridge. I like the cinema and a bit of fun—all the things a woman of my age and position has a right to expect. In a few years time I'll be middle-aged, Miss Lang, and I don't like to think of the last years of my youth—I'm thirty-five—slipping by while I'm being buried alive in this hole. That's why I won't make it nice for Anton. I won't arrange so much as a flower. He might get to like the place."

" If he bought it and brought you here," said Alice reasonably, " he probably *does* like it."

" He was persuaded into it by Marcus Gottlieb. They put all their money and most of mine into this wretched farm. But does Gottlieb live here ? Not he ! He sits pretty with his diamond-studded wife on the Rand while Anton runs the farm. Oh, I admit he comes here occasionally. He's the only regular visitor we ever see. Do you wonder I talk too much when another white woman turns up and I get a chance to let off steam ! " Her plump fists clenched and a patchy, unhealthy flush flooded her throat and face. " I tell you, Miss Lang, this life is killing me ! "

" Maybe you should take a holiday, Mrs. Boryslawski. Go home to your own surroundings for a while."

" And leave my husband here ! You don't know Anton. Did you see him look at that pretty kaffir girl in Rusty's station-wagon ? No, I won't leave him."

She rose and went to the window, her face averted. " He's a foreigner, Miss Lang. He's not like you and me. He has different ideas, and he's had a terrible life. I have to make allowances. Anyway, it won't be long now. He says we're making good money and we'll sell out in a few months time. In the meanwhile he's ordered a little aeroplane. It'll arrive any day now, and then he'll take me to town every now and again for a jaunt. He was a pilot in the war—a fighter ace."

" Yes, I heard so. But to have your own private plane—how exciting ! "

" Anton thinks expensively, Miss Lang. It's in his blood. He changed his name when he escaped from Poland and made his way to England in the war. He comes of a very old and noble family." She seemed to grow a little taller as if for a moment she borrowed some of the dignity of her husband's proud lineage. " And what has he now ? Nothing but his memories—and his hates. The Germans confiscated his family's great estates and then the Russians went in and finished the job. If he's not an easy man it's to be understood and I must put up with it." She turned to Alice, her flabby features transfigured with a combination of love and pride. She had married ' above herself ' into the ruined nobility of a country despoiled by war, and she rejoiced in her achievement. The fact that her husband might have discarded his principles with his titles did not concern her, nor did she resent it that he preferred her own small fortune to herself. The fact remained that she had got him. But it was a grave trial to her that she could not flaunt him. Here, in the back of beyond, she could not display her treasure—her cosmopolitan, arrogant, worldly man. She was frustrated by her empty triumph.

Frustrated. The word slipped into Alice's brain. How many forms of frustration were there ? How many cages could fate construct to bruise the wings of the human spirit, however ugly or unworthy those wings might be ?

She went to the window and stood beside Mrs. Boryslawski,

looking out at the undulating grasslands.   There was the burnt
umber of the newly turned earth and the brilliant green of
young corn in the morning light, and on the hill a team of oxen
ploughed slowly along the skyline.

" Perhaps your husband enjoys all this," she said.   " Perhaps
in a way, it reminds him of what he left behind."

But Mrs. Boryslawski shook her head and stupidity settled on
her face once more.   " This ?   Oh, no, Miss Lang.   *This* isn't
the sort of thing he left behind."

The houseboy, in his dark blue cotton tunic and shorts, stood
in the open doorway.   " *Die bad is klaar,* Missus."

" Your bath is ready," said Mrs. Boryslawski to Alice.
" Here, across the passage.   I'll just get you fresh towels
and a new cake of soap.   I keep everything under lock and
key."

" Is that really necessary ? " asked Alice as she took talcum
powder, face-tissues and cleansing cream from her dressing-
case into the bathroom.   Her hostess opened a large cupboard
with one of the many keys she wore on a chain at her
belt.

" I take no chances.   I don't trust human nature one inch,
do you ? "

" That's quite a question.   I'll think it over."

" I'd put nothing past anybody, be they black or be they
white.   Sin is born in all of us and it only takes temptation to
bring it out.   I don't tempt my servants."

" You think then that to trust is to tempt ? "

" *Ja*.   Consider the matter when you relax in your bath, and
you will realize that you can't trust anybody all the time—not
even yourself."

It struck Alice as an odd conclusion, one that had its roots
deep in a suspicious nature.   Or in past experience, or even in
uncertainty of the future.

" Don't hurry," Mrs. Boryslawski added, putting the towels
and soap on the chair by the bath.   " There's nothing like a
good hot soak for steaming away tiredness—and you must be
very tired."   In the doorway she turned.   " By the way, do
you know Andrew Miller well ? "

The question took Alice by surprise.   For a moment she
hesitated, seeking the truth in her own mind.   Then she said :

" I hardly know him at all, Mrs. Boryslawski. What is he like ? "

" He is a true Christian, Miss Lang—one of the very few people I know that I *would* trust."

17

The Old Chief

" WE'LL take our coffee on to the stoep," said Mrs. Boryslawski. " Rusty's call to Poinsettia Police Post should come through any moment."

Klaas cleared away the breakfast dishes and put the coffee tray on the wicker table on the stoep. From where she sat Alice could see across the unkempt garden and the open veld to the tree-fringed river and the woods and thickets of Velaba. The heat was already intense. It shimmered among the leaves and made an illusory marsh of the thirsty grass-lands, it veiled the bush in hazy blue and sapped the substance from the mountains. They were painted in flat, pallid mauve against the blanched sky. The cicadas' tinny scraping, accompanied by the hum of innumerable insects, sounded to Alice like loose tappets marring the music of a smooth-running engine.

Boryslawski flipped the toe of one soft veld-shoe with his *sjambok*.

" I don't understand the delay," he said. " We put that call through almost an hour ago—immediately after you arrived."

In the dining-room behind them the telephone rang.

" That'll be it." Rusty rose and went into the house. Through the fly-proof swing doors they heard him answer in Afrikaans.

" An indefinite delay," Mrs. Boryslawski translated for Alice's benefit. " Now why ever should that be ? The line must be down somewhere."

As Rusty came back on to the stoep he said, " It seems they are keeping the line clear for Pretoria to talk to Poinsettia. Something must be going on."

" At Poinsettia ! " Mrs. Boryslawski laughed bitterly. " What would ever go on in Poinsettia ? "

Rusty turned to the Pole. " Look, Borys, I have to be on my way. When the call does come through, will you take it and ask Sergeant van Wyk to pass a message to my brother at Camp Three ? Tell him we expect to be at Camp Two this evening, and explain that elephant trouble delayed us."

" Certainly, I will. Is Miss Lang going with you now ? Or will she wait here while you complete your business at the old Chief's kraal ? "

Alice had risen. Her dark eyes threw Rusty an expressive look—one of frank pleading, which he found hard to resist. He said :

" Alice, why did you put on a skirt instead of shorts ? "

" I thought a skirt would be more suitable for a call on the Chief."

He grinned and shrugged his broad shoulders. " You win. Come along."

Mrs. Boryslawski's face crumpled. " Why drag her off to that smelly old kaffir's kraal ? Much better let her stay here and rest. You have to pass back this way in any——"

Her husband cut in. " You interfere too much, Christina." He added to Rusty. " Will you be taking your boy ? And what about the girl ? "

" We'll take Nimrod. Not the girl and her baby. She is the wife of Amos, the man who was mutilated. She may make trouble. We'll pick her up on the way back, if that's all right by you. And I'd like to leave Smokey, he'll only get into a fight among the kraal curs. The girl, Oasis, can look after him."

" You'll come back to midday dinner with us ? " asked Mrs. Boryslawski.

" I'm afraid we won't be able to spare the time. We'll just have to collect the girl and the child and the dogs and move on."

" Well, don't let the Chief keep you too long, Rusty. You know what these kaffirs are—talk in riddles for hours and in the end you never get a word of truth out of them."

" She's not far wrong there," Rusty said to Alice as they drove down the avenue of blue-gums. " If I get any sense out of the Chief it'll be a miracle."

" It was nice of you to let me come."

" I hadn't the heart to leave you with that old gasbag. She never draws breath."

" Poor thing ! She's up to the brim with chatter and no one to chatter to. But things are looking up for her. She says her husband is doing very well out of the farm, and that he's bought an aeroplane especially to take her for jaunts to Johannesburg. Better still, he's promised her they'll sell up and clear out in a few months time."

Rusty whistled. " Three interesting facts. If he's making quick money it's not out of the farm—not yet. If he's buying an aeroplane it's not solely for his wife's pleasure ; and if he's considering getting out of the farm it may well be because his racket—whatever it is—seems likely to blow up. He's right in one respect. Old Ma Boryslawski *does* talk too much. One of these days that lioness of his is going to eat her up. What did you make of our Polish farmer ? "

" I rather liked him. He's attractive in his own caustic way."

" He's as dangerous as a damn leopard—and yet you find him attractive ! He hasn't one scruple——"

" You asked me my opinion," she smiled.

" I'm sorry I didn't leave you behind to enjoy his company."

He turned ' Sweet Sue ' sharply off the earth road and they bumped along a rutted wagon-track in the direction of the native settlement near the causeway that marked the border of Velaba.

" That's the Chief's village, only a couple of miles from Sweet Spruit and right on our boundary," said Rusty. " There's a rumour that the old man's sight is gradually failing. If it's true it might well have a bearing on the case of Amos."

At the core of several scattered kraals was a larger kraal with the huts arranged in a semicircle round a spacious, well-protected cattlefold.

Rusty parked ' Sweet Sue ' outside the high reed screen which encircled the Chief's compound, and Nimrod sprang out to go in search of the Chief. Just inside the entrance of the compound he turned and said something to Rusty, who burst out laughing. One of their private jokes, thought Alice with a flash of resentment, but Rusty included her.

"Nimrod says the Great Elephant must be expecting me. He has observed the spoor and somebody here is wearing shoes."

But his smile faded and he frowned as he said, "I wish Andrew were here to interview the old boy instead of me. He understands their double talk and plays up to it, whereas I get impatient and rush my fences."

"Does the Chief talk English?"

"Much more than he lets on, I suspect. But never unless he's compelled to."

The Chief was sitting on a wooden bench under a thatched shelter between a large hut and the cattle-fold. A venerable crone in a cow-hide toga squatted on a rush mat at his feet, and near her was what appeared to be a small bell-tent fashioned out of a striped blanket, but when Alice looked more closely she saw that the tent was fastened with an enormous safety-pin at the scrawny neck of its owner, who turned a scaly, tortoise-like head towards them. Nimrod addressed himself to an elderly man clothed only in a baboon-skin sporran, who approached his master with much kow-towing and announced the self-evident presence of visitors.

The Chief was wearing a light-weight suit of Air Force blue and a wide-brimmed hat of the same shade. In spite of the heat, a canary yellow polo sweater added a touch of gaiety to his costume, his socks were to match, and his mustard-coloured shoes were new and highly polished. His broad features were adorned with straggly grey whiskers and a pair of tinted glasses. He rose awkwardly to his feet and stood waiting for his guests to approach him.

"Welcome, Lion of Lions," he said in the native language as Rusty took his outstretched hand, and he bowed gravely in Alice's direction when Rusty introduced him to the "Nkosikasi with a great knowledge of the white man's medicine who has come to Velaba from across the water". Then he clapped his hands and uttered an explosive shout. Instantly two children plunged into the large hut and reappeared with small wooden chairs for Nkosi and Nkosikasi, and a little wooden table.

Alice looked about her with interest. Round the large hut were grouped smaller dwellings, each as neat as a weaver-bird's nest. High reed screens afforded their owners protection from sun and wind and a certain measure of privacy, and in their shade squatted old folk and young children, while the more audacious piccaninnies crowded round to stare at the new-comers. Flies buzzed about them and settled in the corners of shiny black eyes, but they were evidently used to these pests and did not even trouble to brush them off. There were few young people to be seen. The women were working in the fields and the men were either employed by Boryslawski on his farm, or in Velaba, or they had gone to seek their fortunes in the cities of the Rand and in the mines. The boys were at school or herding cattle. A few fowls pecked about and a tethered goat bleated from time to time. Mangy kraal-curs lay in what shade they could find, their lean bodies studded with the bloated bladders of greyish ticks. The breathless air smelt suffocatingly of dust, cattle-dung, goat, hot human flesh and the cow-hide gar-ment of the ancient dame who had been presented to Alice as the Mother of the Chief and Keeper of the Rain-making Medicines.

Since Alice could not understand what was said between Rusty and the Chief, she contented herself with observing them closely.

Rusty had taken off his hat, and his sunburned face and powerful throat seemed extraordinarily exposed in contrast to the dark Bantu features shaded by the blue hat and the tinted glasses. The Chief, she thought, gave the impression of wear-ing a disguise. But then she had expected him to be dressed in beads and skins. She knew that Rusty would not find it easy to play the part of a wily African diplomat, but however great his inner impatience might be, he gave no sign of it.

" I have come, Great Elephant," Rusty was saying, " to fetch the bicycle of my Game-guard, Amos—he who was known for his far-seeing eyes and his witty tongue, he whose tales of valour could inspire the puniest creature with the courage of the warrior ancestors of his people."

Alice saw the Chief's face set as that of March had done when Rusty had talked to him near the picket-post. She had the feeling that she was looking into a dark room. They hide behind the colour of their skin, she thought.

" What makes you think this man's bicycle is here, Lion of Lions ? "

" I have been told so by Game-guard March, the companion of Amos, who returned to his post alone."

The Counsellor with the head of a tortoise clapped hidden hands beneath his tent-like blanket, and the man in the baboon-skin sporran leapt to do his bidding. The bicycle would be found. It would be placed upon the roof of Nkosi's motor-car. At once there was a flurry of activity among the children, who ran in all directions to help in the hunt for the missing bicycle.

The Chief removed his glasses and wiped them carefully with a red silk handkerchief with yellow spots. His next remark dismissed the matter of the bicycle.

" It has come to my ears that Dumela, He Who Charges, has been destroyed, and that there was great rejoicing in Velaba last night."

But Rusty did not let go so easily. " News, both good and bad, has the fleet foot of the tsessebe, Great Elephant. Dumela had trampled a man in the Sanctuary, and when a man going about his duties in Velaba is harmed he must be avenged. Mbula was killed by Dumela, and Dumela is dead. Another man has suffered grave injury. Amos will neither see nor speak again."

" It will not be easy to avenge Amos, for Amos is the victim of the Tokoloshe. Before March went his way he came here. He told us what Job had found near the Sweet Spruit—a man rendered blind and dumb, dying like an animal in the bush."

" He did not die. But you know that, Great Elephant. You have a wireless and hear us when we speak between ourselves from Camp to Camp. There is a woman in this story of the Tokoloshe. It would please me to talk to her."

" Yes, there is a woman," put in the dame in the cow-hide mantle. " She shall be summoned." She called to a child, who scampered off among the huts.

The Chief spat in the dust and reached into his pocket for a miniature meerschaum pipe. Rusty immediately drew out his tobacco pouch and his own pipe.

" You will take a fill of tobacco ? "

The dark hand groped towards the proffered pouch and the Chief plugged the little pipe. Rusty gave him a light and then slowly lit his own pipe.

" The Tokoloshe clothes himself in the blanket of invisibility," said the Chief. " It is hard to find the Tokoloshe."

Tokoloshe, Tokoloshe . . . they were still on that tack then ? Alice watched the sparring and the fencing. Sometimes the Counsellor intervened with a few words and a deferential look at the Chief, and every now and again the crone in cow-hide put in a shrill interjection. And as regularly as if it were a habit of long standing, the Chief took off his glasses and polished them with the red silk handkerchief. Once, as he did so, Alice uttered a sudden cry, and the old man, taken unawares, turned his naked, defenceless orbs towards the sound. The milky pupils stared into the bright light unfocusing, and with a spasm of pity Alice realized that to him she was a figure in a thick fog.

" Bitten by a horsefly ? " Rusty asked, leaning towards her.

She laughed and made a show of rubbing a spot on her leg. " Please don't interrupt your conversation," she said, and added in a quick, whispered aside, " He must be nearly blind, Rusty— a double cataract."

Rusty said : " Nkosikasi is not accustomed to the teeth of our horse-flies, Great Elephant."

The Chief smiled and put on his spectacles.

" This woman the child has gone to see—why do you wish to see her ? "

Rusty told him March's version of the night of the attack on Amos, and the old man listened attentively.

" You shall ask her what you wish," he said at length. " Now we will refresh ourselves with beer."

The man in the baboon-skin sporran placed a calabash of kaffir-beer on the wooden table in front of the Chief, and Rusty turned to Alice.

" This is a loving-cup. No shirking ! . . . And—thanks . . ."

The Chief took off his hat and placed it on the table. Then he dipped his wide face and sparse whiskers into the calabash and drank a copious draught. He wiped his full, purplish lips on his silk handkerchief and passed the calabash to Alice graciously. She held her breath, took it in both hands and forced herself to sip the sour, warmish beverage. Rusty took it from her, followed by the She Elephant, Mother of the Chief and Keeper of the Rain-making Medicines, who handed it on to the tortoise-headed Counsellor and last of all the man in the baboon-skin sporran helped himself to a deep, thirst-quenching gulp. The beer of the Great Elephant, brewed by his youngest wife, was famed for its potency and the richness of its flavour.

As the calabash was replaced on the table the piccaninny who had been sent to find the woman with knowledge of the Toko-loshe reappeared in the company of a fine, sullen-looking girl in a striped blanket with a wide bead collar and gauntlets. Her head was shaven but for a small topknot, and was partly covered by a bead headdress, large brass rings were passed through the lobes of her ears and her cheeks were marked by tribal scars. At first she maintained an obstinate silence when Rusty addressed her, and then, at the Chief's command, she answered him. Her replies were short and thrown at him with studied insolence. Strange, thought Alice, I know him to be a hot-tempered man, yet he doesn't seem to resent her attitude. He's quite poker-faced. Maybe he feels as if it's all acting. He doesn't hope for a word of real truth. He's just getting impressions by talking to these people.

" Why did you tell the man, Amos, that you would meet him at Sweet Spruit ? "

" I did not intend to meet him anywhere."

" Yet it is said that you offered to meet him at Sweet Spruit— a place you knew to be haunted by a Tokoloshe."

" I was angry because he took me for a strumpet."

" You hoped then that he would go there—and that the Tokoloshe would get him ? "

" I did not care."

" Why did he go to such a place ?　He must have known it was haunted ? "

" He thought nobody would go there to look for us."

" But he knows that the Tokoloshe is jealous of a man with a woman."

She shrugged her shoulders and the black iris of her eyes smouldered in the yellowish whites. The old crone in cow-hide cackled.

" When a man wants a woman he is madder than a wilde-beest ! "

Rusty turned to her.

" Tell me, Great She Elephant, has this Tokoloshe ever taken anybody before the man Amos ? "

When she did not answer he made a gesture of unconcern. " It does not matter. I can find out from the police records. I seem to remember reading of a young girl . . . it was before we came to Velaba—before Sweet Spruit was part of a Sanctuary."

The old Chief said portentously :

" In the year of the Big Drought the Tokoloshe ravished a young girl and took from her living head the eyes."

Alice saw the quick horror reflected in Rusty's face. He held up one broad hand and counted off five fingers.

" The Big Drought was five years ago. It is as I thought."

He looked from one to another of the night-black faces. The tortoise-head of the Counsellor seemed to shrink farther into the tent-like blanket, the old dame's expression was that of a chocolate blancmange, the girl's haughty mask remained impenetrable, and the man in the baboon-skin sporran crouched like a figure carved in ebony. The old Chief smoked his little pipe inscrutably. Rusty knew that he would learn nothing more from any person here. Whatever crime had been committed, and wherever blame might lie, there would be only one answer—that which he had already received. The Tokoloshe. He took a long chance. He stood up and spoke with impressive emphasis. He spoke as his brother Andrew would have done.

" In that year, the year of famine and sorrow for this nation, it is known to me that a Great Elephant walked for the first time into the mist—into the long twilight that darkens even as the sun shines in the heavens."

Alice felt the weight of the words she could not understand, the unspoken threat and deep compassion that lay behind them ; she guessed the significance of the immobility that held Rusty's audience. They had frozen like animals scenting danger. Only the bare prehensile toes of the old dame moved ; they seemed to clutch at the sand beneath her feet. The goat bleated and somewhere a child wailed thinly. A gust of warm wind put up a spinning gold dust-devil that went whirling across the compound. The Chief rose with sombre dignity and Rusty put his hand on the old man's shoulder. For some reason the gesture moved Alice. It was both filial and protective.

"We have far to go, Great Elephant.   We must be upon our way, for there are storms ahead.   The clouds are a herd of white cattle driven by the rain-magic of the Great She Elephant, your venerable Mother.   Soon the streams will run like rivers, the thirstlands will drink, the frogs will croak, and the wind will hold its breath to hear the growing of the young grass."

He smiled as he spoke the singing language and there was music in his deep voice, but Alice saw that his eyes were sad.

Here was tragedy—but she could not tell where it lay.

18

Poinsettia Police Post

SERGEANT VAN WYK stood in the doorway of his office that served also as a court-room once a month when the Magistrate came to Poinsettia to try offenders.

In the depths of the Sergeant's mind excitement stirred heavily like a monster waking from slumber.   The long telephone call he had just received from Pretoria had stimulated his personal and professional interest to an extent which surprised even himself.   Man, here was something that it would take real skill to handle—a true challenge to his gifts !   "You will have to proceed with the greatest tact," he had been told.   Well, that suited him fine.   His lessons in tact had been wasted out here in the *bundu* with nothing but a bunch of baboons who wouldn't recognize the difference between tact and the tail of a hyena.

His little deep-set eyes under the scowling black boss of eyebrow observed the handful of convicts with contempt as they worked in his garden.   They went about their occupations with the peaceful contentment of men who have no cares.   Jail, for them, was security, with food and lodging and even their red shorts and singlets all found.   And, for these privileged few, the work was as light as any man could wish to find.   Two were engaged in reconstructing a thick hibiscus hedge through which a warthog had pushed his way ; two more tidied the flower-beds, chanting as they dug up the weeds and flung them into a large basket made by women prisoners; and yet another dragged a sack on a wooden frame to and fro along the path to sweep it clear of the scattered mauve petals of the jacarandas that shaded the police compound. A pair of women in gaily printed sarongs carried water from the pump—only a few cans, for water was rationed now until after the rains—and the Sergeant had to admit that they looked more queenly than criminal with the cans balanced like crowns on their high heads, and that stately, unhurried saunter of theirs. But the men! He spat. What petty miscreants! A couple of stock-thieves, a man who had beaten his wife unconscious after a beer-drink, a poacher, and mad Absalom dragging the sack. Absalom was a ' regular '. Every month when the moon was near the full he gave himself into ' protective custody ', and his occasional shouts and bursts of maniacal laughter rang through the Police Post for a few nights.

The Sergeant's house was semi-detached from his office, and, as he contemplated the scene before him, he could hear his wife threatening to whack their youngest son. His face softened. That little *skelm* was a fine boy, but on him too the art of tact was wasted. At four years old he could talk English, Afrikaans, and the local Bantu dialect, but the only language he really understood was the palm of his Ma's hand warming the seat of his pants. It was accepted in the van Wyk family that Pa caught the criminals while Ma punished the kids. At home van Wyk was a man of peace, good-tempered and fond of a joke. He saved his ferocious demeanour for the evil-doers he locked up in the *tronk*. And ferocious it could certainly be, for in his day he had been a champion wrestler, and there wasn't a bad man within three hundred miles who did not respect the rumbling voice and massive frame of Sergeant van Wyk and those unexpected grips and throws that in the blink of an eye rendered a strong man as helpless as a tortoise on its back.

A jeep drew up outside the hibiscus hedge and the Sergeant strolled down the path to meet the Senior Game-warden. Now what would Mr. Miller be wanting this morning? Van Wyk's eyes brightened as if two small candles had been suddenly lit in a pair of dark caverns. Here, at least, was an opportunity of practising a bit of tact—getting his hand in, so to speak. He noticed that the Game-warden's limp was more than usually marked, and, like the Bantus, he recognized the sign. The rains were not far off.

"Morning, Mr. Miller. What can I do for you?" He rolled the normally silent Rs at the end of Mister and Miller, thereby endowing those innocuous words with a special virility all his own.

Andrew was about to reply when Absalom threw down his sack-sweep, flung up his arms and abandoned himself to a fit of demoniac laughter. Nobody took any notice and presently he sobered down and resumed his task.

Andrew smiled. "So *he's* back."

"Mad as a wildebeest. Same thing every full moon."

"That's really what I came about—the full moon."

"Come inside—but there's not much I can do about the full moon. That's the Almighty's province."

He led the way into the office. A witness-box and two hard benches faced the Sergeant's desk, behind which glowered the mounted head of a buffalo. Van Wyk had put it there to help intimidate the unruly, for his wife had often remarked upon its striking resemblance to himself. "It's the boss," she had said, "and the expression." The expression was most malevolent and it always gratified him to see the eyes of those under interrogation flicker nervously from the buffalo's face to his own. He greatly admired the buffalo, especially the great boss of the horns.

"A glass of beer?" he suggested, going to a filing cabinet, from which he produced two mugs and a quart of beer. "Not very cold, I'm afraid, but wet."

The khaki sleeves of his tunic with the three gold stripes were rolled up and he wore khaki trousers and a blue shirt with no collar. "About the moon," he said. "Now *what* about the moon?"

Andrew accepted the mug of beer and put it down on the desk while he went over to one of the maps of Velaba and Poinsettia that hung on the wall.

"It's my bet that the *biltong*-bandits are going to make a raid tonight. Once the rains have come they've had it, and with the full moon they won't need headlights. They can run their truck into Velaba here, a few miles south of Poinsettia, and go across country parallel with the border. Between the Seekoei and Hlaru rivers they'll get a slaughter. That area is full of game. Then they can break out in the direction of Boryslawski's farm and make for the main Johannesburg road by the veld track."

His long, narrow index finger, stained with nicotine, traced the direction of the raid as he visualized it. Van Wyk studied the map with him. "Yes," he said. "It is possible. It's now or never this season. What did you have in mind to do?"

"I think we should make a patrol along this border tonight. You take a couple of your men in your Land Rover and I'll go in my jeep with two of our Game-guards."

"We'd have to be armed. Those bastards would as soon train their machine-guns on us as on the game."

"I agree. We must take guns."

"Man, I'd like it! There's nothing I'd like better. But I don't think I can manage it. Have you any definite information?"

"Nothing. Just a hunch. They must have done well out of that last raid and I can't believe they won't try again. The wind's gone round to the rainy quarter, and, as I see it, it's tonight or not at all. You could put a call through to Duikers' Drift and get them to keep an eye on the Johannesburg road down there in the south."

The sergeant looked crestfallen. "I see your point. But the devil of it is I'm stuck here. I've got to wait for an important call from Pretoria, and it's very unlikely to come through before midnight——"

"But surely the possibility of getting these bandits takes precedence over any other business. Let's face it, there isn't much other business worth bothering about in this area."

"You'd be surprised," said the Sergeant. "*Very* surprised, Mr. Miller." He drained his beer and slapped down the mug on top of the filing cabinet. Andrew waited for further revelations, but, since none appeared to be forthcoming, he said, "Well, if you can't manage it, I'm sorry, but it won't prevent my going."

"If the call comes through in time, I'll be with you. By the way, your brother and the young lady didn't get through to Camp Two last night. I listened on your wave-length as usual, and it struck me that you must have felt a bit worried."

Andrew frowned. He had, in fact, been prey to gnawing anxiety all night, and his determination to take some sort of action on the chance of tracking down the *biltong*-bandits had been very largely born of a feverish restlessness and the need to take his mind off useless speculation about Rusty and Alice. Many causes might have accounted for their delay, not all of them unfortunate or disastrous. Rusty's journey was in the course of duty and Andrew knew that Alice's presence would make no difference whatever to his brother. If Rusty deemed it necessary to make a detour he would do so. The comfort of a young woman whom he firmly believed to have 'designs' on Andrew would certainly never be allowed to interfere with the interests of the Sanctuary. Andrew took a cigarette from his case and offered one to the Sergeant, but van Wyk shook his head. "A pipe of Boer tobacco for me," he said, "and that only after meals—ah, there goes the blasted telephone! That'll be Pretoria again, I expect."

He hesitated before putting out a brawny arm to take up the instrument, and Andrew said with a swift, sensitive movement, "If it's confidential, I'll clear out."

"*Nie, man, wag,*" said the Sergeant. "We'll soon know. Hullo . . . *Ja*, van Wyk here . . . Oh, it's you, meneer Boryslawski . . . a message for Mr. Andrew Miller? Well, it just happens that he's here. Hold on a minute."

He handed the receiver to Andrew.

Van Wyk watched the thin, ascetic face of the Game-warden gradually clear as he listened to Boryslawski. Even his voice, as he cut in with exclamations of pleasure or dismay or with a few quick-fire questions, had lost the irritable nervousness that had marked it a few moments ago. As he put down the receiver his eyes glowed with relief. He lit another cigarette from the stub of the one in the ashtray and said to van Wyk :

"Thank heavens they're safe ! But it must have been quite an ordeal. It appears Rusty fetched up at Boryslawski's place with a pair of superb tusks on the roof of his station-wagon. That rogue elephant the natives call Dumela had evidently roamed a long way south and trampled one of the road-gang working near the mahogany grove. Rusty spent all afternoon yesterday tracking him down and shot him towards evening. They had to camp out on the hill of the cassia trees."

Van Wyk chuckled. "Rather a tough experience for your friend, Miss Alice Lang. I don't expect she was tracking the elephant with Rusty, and waiting alone in the bush isn't much fun for a woman."

Andrew's head jerked up and his eyes darkened. What the devil did van Wyk mean by that ' your friend ' ?

"Come now, Mr. Miller, you can't pull wool over my eyes," continued the Sergeant with elephantine good humour. "I passed Miss Lang's cable to you *and* relayed your answer telling her to hurry up and come here. You can't have forgotten that."

"In fact I had. Or perhaps I should say I hadn't quite appreciated the significance you would attach to it." How absurd it had been to hope that knowledge of the situation between himself and Alice Lang could be confined to his own brother and sister and Mrs. Hurley. Mrs. Hurley had mentioned it to Thea, and no doubt van Wyk had elaborated on the subject to his *ouvrou*, who would add a few thrills when she confided her information to the storekeeper's wife. And, of course, there had probably been other listeners-in that evening when the Sergeant had broken in on the Camp intercom. Even Jan Nelmapius must have drawn his own conclusions. A man would hardly be likely to invite a young woman to an out-of-the-world place like Velaba unless he had some strong personal interest in her.

"I merely assumed that you were very well acquainted with the young lady," said van Wyk. "I thought at first that she might be a relation——"

"At first?"

"Afterwards I had reason to change my mind."

"Now why?"

The Sergeant resorted to tact. His deep voice was smooth and sweet as honey.

"I heard you two talk on the inter-com the night before last—and I thought to myself: Now, that's not the way relations talk! And it struck me that there was a fine English lady Mr. Miller had got for himself. Man, but she had that quiet way of speaking that makes a person think. Not like my *ouvrou* who blows off like a steam-engine when she gets excited, but *sommer* soft and sweet."

Andrew threw back his head and laughed. "Was that how Alice Lang sounded to you?"

"*Ja,* man. But then I haven't met her—I don't know her voice like you do."

Again the Sergeant noticed the other's recoil.

"You know," he went on conversationally, "I'm not one for the blasted missionaries. I like Dr. Hurley all right when he's curing a sick nigger's body, but once he gets busy on their souls it makes me vomit. You'll never purge these beggars of their magic and feed them Jesus Christ instead. They go to church for what they get out of it—*muti*, a bit of reading and writing, the chance to sing their heads off, and the pleasure of hearing the bloody missionary tell them that a black skin is as good as a white one in the eyes of the Lord. Believe me, the Lord knows better than that!" He paused and snorted belligerently like a buffalo about to charge. "Now your friend—this Miss Alice Lang—she's not a missionary, is she?"

"No. She's a fully qualified hospital nurse. Her job is with bodies, not souls."

"That's what I heard."

"Who from?"

"Young Thea, if you want to know. Man, how that *meisie* has ripened this last year!"

"It'll be nice for Thea to have another girl around—someone nearer her own age. She's cut off from her own sort of young person here."

"That's so, Mr. Miller. And, if you ask me, Thea will never follow in the footsteps of her Pa and Ma. A blind baboon could tell you that."

A blind baboon could probably have told him that Thea's hero-worship of her friend, the Game-warden, might well grow into love, he reflected ruefully—calf-love, of course, but none the less painful for that. He thought of her with his old protective affection mingled with a new sentiment, half pity, half gratitude. He had been profoundly moved by the revelation of her feeling for him—and by the young, pliant warmth of her body as he had held her to him and felt her sobbing in his arms. He had recognized—and been both flattered and dismayed—by the intensity of her emotion and his own automatic response to it. He had experienced a strong uprush of confidence. This could be Alice, he had told himself. I can make Alice want me as Thea does! Everything is changing, everything is different . . . Thea, Alice . . . The child, Thea, is gone and a girl in love has taken her place—and the writer of the letters is a woman on her way to me—a woman of flesh and blood, *my* woman . . .

" Some beer ? " The Sergeant's voice brought him back to the present.

Andrew shook his head. " I must go and tell them at the Mission that Alice Lang will *not* be there tonight. They expect her this evening."

" Where will she be, Mr. Miller ? "

" At Camp Two. Rusty couldn't get through on the phone himself; that's why he got Boryslawski to pass the message for me. He left Boryslawski's farm to go to the old Chief's kraal. Near Sweet Spruit."

" To see him about that Game-guard of yours, Amos, I suppose ? "

" Yes. It seems they had Amos's wife and baby boy with them. Rusty was going to take her to the kraal of Amos's family—Ndlovukasi's kraal."

" If Rusty learns anything from the old Chief it'll be a wonder. They don't talk, Mr. Miller. You know that. Not if there's anything *we* want to know ! "

Andrew nodded. If a Chief should chance to be involved in a crime the conspiracy of silence was absolute. It might include a whole village, or entire district; scores of people might be closely concerned, even the victim's closest relatives, but no man, woman or child would utter so much as a single word to give a pointer to the police.

Sergeant van Wyk sat behind his desk with his eyes on the empty witness-box. Dark, silent ghosts stood there to haunt him, the remembered faces hiding their own guilt and the guilt of others behind the black, impassive mask of assumed ignorance or some unbreakable alibi created by African superstition and a terror of what would befall them if they betrayed those whose hands were red with blood. He said heavily :

" Before you came here—about five years ago—a girl was raped and mutilated there by the Sweet Spruit. Her eyes were taken—for *muti*, of course. A blind baboon could see it was a medicine murder to strengthen the Chief, with the Witch Doctor and that wicked old She Elephant in it up to the ears, and that lizard of a Chief Counsellor, too, and a dozen others. But could we get one single scrap of evidence? No! It was the Tokoloshe who took the blame, Mr. Miller. The Tokoloshe did it."

Andrew was pacing up and down, smoking restlessly. Funny fellow, the Game-warden, thought van Wyk. Seemed so calm and casual, but underneath he was a bundle of raw nerves. No wonder, perhaps . . .

"It's shocking," said Andrew; "horrible, the things they do! And I agree with you that the missionaries with all their Christian teachings—and the law with its hangings, for that matter—will never eradicate their particular type of crime. You see, van Wyk, to them it's not wicked. It's a dreadful necessity, one which they deplore. A person has to look at it from their point of view."

The Sergeant gave his buffalo snort. But Andrew paid no attention.

"Don't you understand that the Chief and the tribe are identified as one? If a Chief is weak or ailing, if something bad happens to him, the whole tribe suffers. Crops will fail, cattle will die, and something has to be done about it. The strongest medicine in the world is human sacrifice, so that is what they regard as necessary. It's Old Testament stuff plain and simple—and the missionaries give them whacking great doses of it! God says to Abraham, 'Take they son, thine only son and offer him for a burnt offering . . .' and Abraham sharpens his knife and builds the altar! The fact that the victim is reprieved at the last moment has nothing to do with it. The point is that Abraham was perfectly prepared to murder his own and only son, Isaac, for the good of the tribe at the will of Jehovah. Medicine murder is the same thing. They can't see it as wrong. How can they? You can hang them in twos and threes and half dozens, but it won't make any real difference. The Witch Doctor—the High Priest, if you like —says human eyes taken from a living girl are needed to strengthen the vision of the Chief, and a victim is selected. They call it 'the buck'. No one will dispute the decision or the selection. They are not killing for gain or revenge, they are not tampering with a person's will. They are killing one human being under ghastly circumstances for the general good —to ensure that the Chief will be powerful, the crops good and the cattle healthy. There's nothing personal about it. From their misguided angle it's an Old Testament sacrifice ! "

Sergeant van Wyk was a staunch man of the Church and he strongly objected to the Game-warden dragging the name of the Almighty into the ritual crimes of the bloody kaffirs.

" Medicine murder has nothing to do with the Bible," he rumbled pugnaciously. " Never in the history of creation has the Almighty commanded men to rape first and kill after, or to cut flesh from the living body. Neither has He encouraged human beings to eat portions of their victims and drink their blood ! It is blasphemy to suggest such things ! "

" The Holy Sacrament," murmured Andrew, " the Body and Blood . . ." He broke off and sat on the desk with one long leg swinging. " You're right, of course, van Wyk. But you must realize that the Old Testament is very easy for these Bantus to understand—and misunderstand—with its accent on polygamy and burnt offerings, the annihilation of your enemies, blood and thunder. It's right up their street. I've argued that with Dr. Hurley. I've shocked him too by trying to tell him that these people will put their own interpretation on his teaching—and that it would surprise him a good deal if he could read their minds."

" Surprise him ? I should say it would ! " Van Wyk laughed. Then his black brows drew together in a thunderous frown. " But this matter of your Game-guard, Amos. I don't like it. I'd give a deal to read the old Chief's mind where that is concerned."

" What is your opinion on the case ? "

" Since you ask me, I'd say it was a plain case of making an example. Amos is a trustworthy native with the good of the Sanctuary at heart, whereas the old Chief is in some sort of a racket—a two-way street, running guns into Velaba and *biltong* out along the Nyamazane Road, the *biltong* trail. He may have made *muti* of that boy's eyes and tongue, but it's a side-line—a pity to waste good material, if you get my meaning. Let me tell you, if Amos hadn't been the strongest nigger in the territory we'd probably have had another bloody murder case on our hands!"

"And small chance of solving it."

The Sergeant was stung. He rose and loomed over the Game-warden, who remained half-seated on the desk, lighting another of his everlasting cigarettes.

"We overcome our difficulties, Mr. Miller. We solve our murders in time—and apprehend the criminals. And in this country we still hold to the law of the Old Testament. A life for a life."

"There are murders and murders." Andrew's light, gentle voice was mild, almost apologetic. "Surely you see that they can't all be lumped together?"

"Thou shalt not kill. That is the law of God and man."

"With the fighting-man and the executioner exempt?"

Oh, these blasted students, tying a man up with the strings of his own argument! To hell with tact and bumbling around the point?

"There's right and there's wrong," he said bluntly, "and we all damn well know which is which."

"There's black and white, but you can't deny there's plenty in between."

"There's bastards in between."

"Shades of colour, let's say. And in the same way there are degrees of murder—with punishments and dispensations of mercy to match."

"That may be. But the result is the same. A dead body. And it's a Policeman's job to find out how and when and where it got that way. The sentence is up to the Judge, and mercy is the business of the Almighty. The corpse won't care."

Andrew flicked the ash off his cigarette.

"Well, this time, Sergeant, you're not dealing with a murder."

"Thanks for telling me."

Something in the ponderous sarcasm of the remark made Andrew Miller raise an eyebrow. The Sergeant was standing under the head of the buffalo. The resemblance really was astonishing—the jutting, swarthy brows meeting over the pugilist's nose and the small, deep-set eyes that could look so threatening.

" I mustn't keep you from your investigations." Andrew rose and went to the door.

" On the contrary." The Sergeant was smiling now. He put out a huge hairy paw and thumped Andrew on the back. " It's been nice to see you—very stimulating, Mr. Miller. If that call comes through in time I'll be with you on patrol tonight."

He stood for a while in thought, staring after the tall figure walking down the path. Argumentative fellow, the Game-warden, always full of high-falutin ideas. His limp gave him an oddly hesitant look—not quite in character. If he had a point he stuck to it like a mule. A lonely chap—somehow lonely in himself as well as in his way of life. Ought to have a wife and kids. You couldn't be lonely with a woman and her brood about the place ; you might want to kick the whole bunch out from time to time, but you'd soon be bellowing around if you did, calling them back again. Yes, that was what the Game-warden needed—a woman of his own. And now this girl, this Alice Lang of Middlesex, England, with the cool, English voice, was on her way to him. A *very* cool customer, Miss Alice Lang.

" Hey, Sampie," he said to the Afrikaans operator in the bantering, flirtatious voice he adopted for her benefit. " Head-quarters, Pretoria—'n maak gou-gou, my girl ! "

19

The Maker of Lions

WHEN Rusty and Alice returned to the farm they found that Mrs. Boryslawski had prepared a picnic hamper for them, but she refused to allow them to go without taking a *sopie* first.

" A sherry for Miss Lang," she insisted, " and a beer for Rusty."

Rusty grinned. " We've already had a loving-cup with the Chief."

Her flabby face folded into a grimace of disgust. " Then

you'll need something to take the taste away. What did you think of the old Chief, Miss Lang ? "

" I felt very sorry for him," Alice said. " He must be almost blind."

Boryslawski glanced at her with his light mesmeric eyes suddenly alert. " What makes you so sure ? "

" He gropes. And he keeps wiping his glasses as if they were cloudy. Once, when he looked up at me without them, I noticed the milky pupils. Cataract, I guess."

" My, how you notice everything ! " Mrs. Boryslawski set a glass of sherry beside Alice. " I hope you like it sweet—I do. My husband prefers it dry, but I always say ladies prefer things on the sweet side. As a matter of fact, Miss Lang, you are quite right about the old Chief. He went to see his oculist in Johannesburg again about a fortnight ago, but his eyes aren't ready for the operation yet. They keep telling him to wait—for years they've told him that, and it makes him mad. But Marcus Gottlieb—my husband's partner—knows of a surgeon in Switzerland who can do the cataract operation *before* it's strictly speaking ripe—a most remarkable man. But naturally that would cost a lot of money. Not that the Chief is poor—these tribal Chiefs bleed their people when they want something—you'd be surprised. All the same, these people round here aren't as well off as some tribes—not like the Basuto, for instance, or the Swazis. The Basuto made a packet out of the wool boom and——"

" Christina ! Rusty has no beer."

The breathless torrent of words ceased with a gasp at the sound of the grating voice. He's switched her off, thought Alice. She's gone dead. But Mrs. Boryslawski recovered herself.

" Your beer, Rusty—and for you, Anton. Though why you didn't pour it yourself, I can't imagine. This husband of mine expects to be waited on hand and foot, Miss Lang. He was brought up with scores of servants——"

Boryslawski's chilling glance silenced his wife once more.

" By the way, Rusty," he said. " I got your call through to Poinsettia Police Post about half an hour ago. I spoke to your brother. He happened to be there at the time. He said to tell you he'd be calling you at Camp Two as usual tonight."

"Thanks." Rusty tossed back his beer and rose. "We must be off now." He turned to Mrs. Boryslawski with his quick engaging smile. "You've been so kind and hospitable. Even a picnic lunch!"

"I only wish you were staying. We always like seeing you, Rusty, and it isn't often I have the chance of a chat with another white woman. Come again soon." She sighed. "Oh, well, it won't be so bad when that little aeroplane is delivered here. Any day now we should get it and then Anton will take me back to civilization quite often."

"Is that the hangar—there in the field?" Rusty asked as Boryslawski and his wife went with them to 'Sweet Sue' where Nimrod waited with Oasis and Shinhenani and the dogs.

"It is," he said briefly.

"Quite impressive. Make a good storehouse too."

"I use it for that. And Sheba, my lioness, keeps guard at night. That's where I have stored your elephant tusks. They will be perfectly safe."

His manner was arrogant, and his eyes, light and unfeeling as a cat's, seemed to Alice to be warning them off. He reminded her of a certain notorious London gangster—a Sicilian by birth—who had been brought into the hospital while she was a student nurse. He had been severely knifed by a rival and his presence in the ward had created a stir. Betty Swanson and Alice had agreed that his personality was both repellant and attractive, and even at his most helpless he had given the impression that he was dangerous—as dangerous as a wounded leopard. This Pole had the same callous wary aura about him—a man who held life cheap.

Rusty and Alice bade the Boryslawskis good-bye, and soon they were following the river road outside the border of Velaba. Rusty travelled fast. In less than an hour they were at the kraal of Ndlovukasi, the Maker of Lions and aunt of Oasis. She came to meet them as if she had expected them, and with her came a swarm of children and old folks. The father of Amos was out with the cattle, but his wife, who was the mother of Amos, greeted the girl and her child with dignified sorrow. The grievous news of their son's misfortune had already reached them.

It was clear to Alice that Ndlovukasi was the Queen here. Unimpressive and shrivelled as she was, her whole bearing suggested authority. Her naked breasts dangled against her protruding ribs like two deflated bladders, and round her skinny loins was wrapped a short blue cotton skirt held in place by a python-skin girdle hung with various little sacks containing magic charms and medicines. Her hair was wild and fuzzy and her scrawny neck was adorned with a string of carnivora teeth. She carried a wildebeest-tail switch. When she spoke everybody fell silent.

When she had welcomed Oasis, she thanked Rusty for bringing her to them, and he answered in her own language. Alice liked hearing him speak the Bantu tongue when he did so formally. Something in the sonorous quality of his voice at such times made her feel that the words he used must be beautiful.

Oasis stood shyly beside 'Sweet Sue' with Shinhenani in the sling resting on her hip. Suddenly, upon an impulse, Alice got out of the station-wagon and held out her arms for the child. Oasis lifted him from the sling and gave him to her with a fleeting furtive smile. It was as if a butterfly of great beauty had flitted across her dark features and vanished. Shinhenani bounced and crowed as Alice caught him to her, he patted her smooth cheeks with his chubby chocolate fingers and laughed, moist black eyes shining. She turned her head with a swift bird-like movement so that her lips brushed his little hands.

" Good-bye, Little Warrior," she said softly. " God keep you."

She gave him back to his mother who clasped him as if he had grown more precious.

Ndlovukasi stepped forward and took something from one of the little pouches at her waist. She presented the small object to Alice and as she did so she intoned an incantation. Rusty stared as he gathered the gist of her words, but Alice, uncomprehending, only smiled her thanks and bowed her dark gleaming head.

" Come," said Rusty shortly. " We are getting late."

The group outside the kraal watched them till the golden dust-cloud settled on the veld and the station-wagon crossed the stone ford of the Fulene River into the woodlands of Velaba.

Alice still held Ndlovukasi's charm in her hand. She spread her palm and gazed at what lay there.

" Why, it's a claw, Rusty—a big curving claw ! "

" It's the claw of a lion."

" Now why should she give me that ? "

" For luck. She belongs to the Lion clan. She is the Maker of Lion Magic."

Alice looked at him with sparkling eyes. Her blood danced through her veins. She was at once sad and joyful and strangely excited. It had been sad to bid good-bye to Oasis and Shinhenani, the Little Warrior who had won her heart, but it was profoundly satisfying and thrilling to feel the new life winding itself about her like a cocoon. She was wrapped in its mystery, enmeshed and quiescent until the moment that would surely come when she would emerge from the chrysalis and enter fully into her paradise of many perils. When that happened she would be free of the past, she would yield herself body and soul to the present and the future.

" Ratau," she said, with laughter rippling in her voice. " Ratau, my friend. I think that you believe in lion magic. I think that you have eaten the flesh of the lion, and that you— like Ndlovukasi—belong to the Lion clan."

" Hush, Likwezi ! It doesn't do to think and talk like a Pagan. Not here—not in Velaba where spells can work."

" What did the old sorceress say when she gave me the tooth ? "

He shook his head.

" Tell me," she pleaded.

But he did not answer. He was driving slowly again, at the pace of Velaba, the pace that measures time by the setting of the sun and the rising of the moon, by the hunger in a man's belly and the distance between one water-hole and the next, by the coming and going of the seasons and the space between the blossoming of a tree and the falling of the fruit.

" Tell me ! " she repeated.

He took his eyes from the track and the glades where he sought the wild creatures of his kingdom, and he said : " Don't ask me, please."

How strange, she thought, how very strange ! His expression, his whole face has changed. I hardly know him in this mood. What has changed him so? And how is he different? And then she knew. The blunt features, the blue eyes under the narrow brows, the stubborn, slightly cleft chin, the upturned mouth that could be gay or bitter, had set into the secret impenetrable mould she had observed that morning at the old Chief's kraal. *They* had looked like this with masks drawn over their dark faces. Now he too was wearing a mask. There was something he knew, something he was determined to hide from her.

Rusty had become her friend during their trek, now it seemed to her that he was no longer her friend. He had withdrawn completely. From the beginning he had resented her intrusion—this woman who had come so far to 'catch' his brother, this huntress intent upon tracking down and capturing her man—but gradually she had discovered little chinks in his armour. From the moment she had tried to help his Game-guard, Amos, his suspicions had weakened. She had even dared to hope that he had grown to like her. And once or twice a message had flashed along her nerves to tell her that he found her attractive. Now, for no reason she could fathom, he had retreated once more.

She put the lion's claw into her handbag and she looked away from Rusty, out of the window. For some inexplicable reason tears stung her eyes.

Rusty saw the averted profile and the working of her throat. He knew that the left corner of her lip would be trembling. His grip tightened on the wheel and his jaw hardened.

" Nkosi, stop ! "

Nimrod's narrow black finger with the livid nail pointed into the grass, and Smokey growled.

Only a few yards away, on Rusty's side, the dark ears and tufted tail of a splendid lioness twitched as she crouched with her pitiless golden eyes fixed on a kudu bull grazing in the shrunken shade of noonday. If they stopped now they might well see the lioness make her kill. But Rusty did not stop.

" We are going on," he said to Nimrod.

Alice turned her head.

" What is it ? "

" A kudu bull."

She said : " I thought—I hoped—that you'd stopped hating me."

" You're too sensitive, Likwezi."

" You hate me again. I know it."

He moved his hand from the wheel and laid it for an instant on her knee. The touch of his fingers burned through her thin linen skirt and into her skin. She was aware of him with every leaping nerve in her body.

" We hate what we fear," he said.

20

The Law of Velaba

THE intense heat of the day had begun to abate when Rusty said, " Well, here we are—Camp Two."

Rusty had not prepared Alice for the beauty of this riverside Camp. The triple thorn-hedge surrounded it on three sides, but the fourth was bounded by a loop of the jade-green Python River—the Hlaru—which flowed in a winding canyon between steep banks fringed with bamboo, feathery rushes, a profusion of palms, and luxuriant flowering trees. Between the river and the range of the Black Mamba Mountains spread the bushveld with a froth of mauve and yellow blossom over the young burnished coppery leaves of spring.

The Camp was shaded by tall well-established trees and giant baobabs, the homes of innumerable birds, animals and reptiles and—so the Bantus said—ghosts. The Camp kitchens, small laundry, kennels, stables and boys' quarters were at some distance from the neat semicircle of guest *rondavels* and separated from them by exotic shrubs and the starry pink of impala lilies. A little apart, on the highest point of the Camp in full view of the river, was the Game-warden's simple house consisting of two thatched *rondavels*, each with its own shower, and connected by a spacious stone verandah which backed on to a light pleasant living-room.

Nimrod took Alice's bags to one of these *rondavels* and Rusty's to the other, and waited for further orders.

"We will go to the hippo-pool later," said Rusty, "before the setting of the sun." He turned to his smiling house-boy, Philemon, and said in English: "What have you got for our dinner tonight?"

"Tin-soap, Nkosi, chicken in castor-oil, and pineapple."

Rusty's eyes narrowed with laughter as he glanced at Alice.

"Don't be alarmed. Tin-soap—tinned soup—is quite innocuous, and the cook-boy makes an excellent chicken in casserole." To Philemon he added, "Get tea now."

Alice laughed. "I didn't much fancy castor-oil with the chicken! Better elephant trunk any day."

She stood looking down at the fast-flowing river and the far mountains. "This is the loveliest place I have ever seen—the loveliest yet."

"It's my nearest approach to a home. Come and see."

She followed him into the thatched living-room.

For the first time since entering Velaba she was aware of a hint of permanence—of possessions other than guns, charts and a radio-set. The room in which they stood had a lived-in air. At one end was an open stone fireplace, rough-hewn, and flanked with inset redwood cupboards under shelves filled with books that looked like old much-read friends. A set of ivory elephants marched across the mantelpiece. A well-stocked ebony pipe-rack hung to one side of the hearth, and on top of the cupboards were heavy pottery ash-trays, a cigarette box of stamped Florentine leather, and an enlarged framed snapshot of Meg Broeksma with her husband and sons. Alice took it up and saw that the sunny cheerful little picture had been taken in the Pretoria garden where Meg had warned her of the hardships of life in the wilds.

"It's extraordinary," said Alice. "This time three days ago your sister met me at the airport . . . only three days ago . . ."

"Has it seemed such an eternity—being in my company?"

"You may laugh, but in fact it *is* uncanny. I seem to have shed the past—at last."

"Does one ever?"

His glance picked out a large impressionist painting on the long back wall broken by two gaily curtained windows. Alice looked at it with interest. A narrow street, curved like a sickle, lost itself in a dark archway where an old woman sat behind a barrow of bright spring flowers. A little Romeo and Juliet balcony jutted out above a Gothic door, and beneath it, in the foreground, stood a ragged debonair urchin with a shepherd's pipe to his lips. The scent of flowers and the thin music of the reed-pipe seemed to come from the picture. It was alive, it breathed. You felt that you could walk down that narrow street through the shadowy archway into the past . . . into Rusty's past.

" What did you expect ? Skins on the floor and mounted horns on the walls ? "

" Not this," she said slowly. " Not this—unusual—picture. It's Italian, of course. Florence, I suppose ? "

" Yes, Florence. It doesn't fit here, does it ? "

" I don't know. I only know that it's arresting—unforgettable."

She turned away and perched on the arm of one of the comfortable easy chairs in front of the fireplace.

" A woman helped you with all this," she said. " I love the plain neutral rugs and these rough-woven mustard-coloured covers—and that long blue wall. It's full of personality."

" Meg's. She helped me choose all this stuff in Pretoria. She wouldn't allow any of the sort of furnishings she thought a Ranger might go for. No zebra skins or lion hearthrugs, not even a jackal kaross. But she couldn't confiscate the ivory elephants. They were carved by an Indian craftsman out of the tusks my grandfather brought home. He was a great old hunter. If he could see Andrew and me at our job he'd disown us for a pair of decadent cissies ! "

His wicked grin lit his face ; and she said, " You're like him, aren't you ? "

" Yes. Andrew's not, though. He's genuine. He isn't full of evil back-sliding and blood-lust like I am. When he has to kill something he says, ' This hurts me more than it does you '—and it's true. Whereas I thank the fates for a chance to justify a shot."

She wandered over to his bookshelves and ran her finger along a line of volumes.

" *South African Eden, Memories of a Game Ranger, Shangani,*

Shaka Zulu—and oh, these delicious books of Durrell's. Didn't you love *The Overloaded Ark*? Somehow I hadn't imagined you being much of a reader——"

" I'm no student like my brother, but the nights can be long and lonely, and books help. On the other side you'll find my real escapist literature—crime and adventure."

Philemon came in with the tea-tray, and a sleek black cat sailed in at his heels and came over to Rusty with arched back and hoisted tail. As it flirted round his legs it gave little trilling mews of pleasure and welcome.

" Hullo, Lucky, old girl. You see, Alice, we are really quite domesticated here."

" Shall I pour the tea ? I know how you like it by now."

" Yes, do."

It pleased him to watch her moving about this room with her light quick step and that bird-like turn of the head. She managed to look cool in spite of the heat. When they had finished their tea, he said :

" I suggest you change that nice blue skirt for a pair of slacks. We have to climb on to a tree-platform at the hippo-pool. It's a bit rough."

" Sounds exciting."

" I think you'll be interested. A number of drinking-places dry up at this time of year and so more and more customers have to patronize the few bars that remain open. After the rains they disperse again and everybody goes to their favourite pub."

" I'll go and change. My room is to the left, isn't it ? "

" That's right. There's a shower attached. If there's anything you need, just shout. Philemon hovers around."

Alice unpacked the few things she required for the night. She cleaned her face and showered, and dusted her body with talcum powder that had the same astringent scent as the perfume she dabbed behind her ears.

When she was ready she found Rusty waiting for her on the stoep. His hair was damp and curly from his shower and he was freshly shaved.

" The hippo-pool is about four miles away, down a fork of the Hlaru that we've dammed. Nimrod will come with us, but we'll leave old Smokey behind."

The sun was low over the horizon, a sultry raspberry ball behind the dark filigree of the thorn-trees, and the mountains were washed in topaz light. They left the main Hlaru River and followed the smaller offshoot which had been contained by a rough wall at the point where it would otherwise have cascaded down a boulder-strewn ravine. Here Rusty parked ' Sweet Sue ' in a small clearing.

" One day this will be a show spot for tourists," he said. " Like the idea ? "

She had a fleeting vision of orange peels and paper-bags littering the sylvan scene. " No," she said. " I don't."

" Look," he said. " We have to walk the length of that wall to the far side. There could be anything about at this time of evening. Afraid ? "

" Not with you."

" Good. Nimrod will go first, then you, then me. Whatever I tell you to do—don't argue or stop to think, just obey."

She nodded. She was relieved to see that he carried his rifle under his arm. During the few hours she had spent outside Velaba she had forgotten that the Sanctuary belonged to the wild beasts and that man was only here on sufferance. She saw the dense verdure on the banks of the hippo-pool trampled into well-worn tracks by innumerable hooves and she wondered what eyes were watching them from the tall concealing rushes.

Nimrod went ahead of her. His right hand had felt for his sheath-knife in the gesture she had come to know, and in his left he carried his assegai. He walked lightly and surely as a cat along the narrow wall and she knew that no sign or sound in his surroundings escaped his eyes and ears. Rusty was close behind her and she had an impulse to pause so that he would touch her. She wanted the physical reassurance of his hand on her arm. I *am* afraid ! she thought. I am afraid of the spring of a lion, the teeth of a crocodile, the crushing coils of a python. I am afraid to look down at the jagged pink rocks in the ravine, afraid of losing my balance and falling. On her right the deep wide pool reflected the delicate pinks and golds of the evening sky and water-lilies swayed gently on the polished pads of leaves. She heard the tree-cicadas, the croaking of frogs and the twittering of a myriad little birds, and then out of the reeds flew a magnificent rainbow-coloured bird tossing itself into the sky and performing aerobatics that showed off its jewelled plumage. Rusty saw her head lifted to watch it and he said softly, " It's the purple roller-bird. The Bantus call it the Blue Lily, or sometimes the Wedding-Ring."

The wedding-ring . . . Andrew. Her heart contracted with a new fear that had nothing to do with the perils of the hippo-pool.

Suddenly Nimrod hesitated and put out his hand in a gesture of warning. She saw the rosy palm and the tense narrow fingers. Her breath came fast as a deep bellow reverberated across the water, answered by another and accompanied by lusty snorts and blowings. She turned her head and saw Rusty smiling.

" Hippos—over there."

Small stiff ears, gaping nostrils and bulging eye-sockets floated on the surface of the water, and every now and again a grunt and a swirl of bubbles showed where some submerged monster was breaking surface. Over on the bank they had left was an old Auntie Hippo clambering up into the clearing, chivvying three fat babies in front of her. Their thick hides were folded collarwise across the tops of their necks.

" Will they harm ' Sweet Sue ' ? " Alice whispered, laughter dancing in her eyes.

" No. It's live and let live here—unless you are hungry, frightened, or duelling for possession of a mate."

A few steps farther took them to the end of the wall. On one side loomed a hilly rampart of rose-red granite rocks, and on the other an open grassy sward. Between the rocks and the grass was a glade of tall trees growing to the water's edge. Alice could almost feel the intense concentration of Rusty and Nimrod. A careless step or lack of observation might result in tragedy, for this was the hour of danger. Every animal knew that. Here the killer would lie in wait for the prey who must come to the drinking-place at the risk of his life.

At the base of a tall tamboutie tree Rusty paused and looked up to be sure that no snake or leopard was there before them.

Alice followed his gaze and saw a platform suspended in the fork between two strong boughs. A little rope-ladder depended from it. The lower branches had been chopped and the plat-form commanded a perfect view of the various game trails to the pool, the open sward behind them and the expanse of gleaming water. In one place the rushes had been trampled flat and this muddy area was clearly the wide track of a herd of regular visitors.

Rusty climbed the ladder first while Nimrod held it taut, and Alice came next. He took her hand and drew her on to the platform beside him among the cool unstirring leaves, and she sat with her legs over the edge as a child sits in a swing On one side she held on to a guy-rope, and on the other she was guarded by Rusty's body. His rifle lay along the back of the platform where Nimrod took up his position, pulling the rope-ladder up after him.

In this confined shadowy place Rusty and Alice were so close together that they might have been carved of the same substance. Her thigh rested against his, her shoulders were in the crook of his protective arm, the warmth and nearness of her body lit fires in his, and the faint scent that clung about her stung his nostrils. He could feel the glossy silk of her hair against his chin, and he thought, This is the hour of danger—don't forget it!

A water-buck stepped delicately down a hippo-path, and, after sniffing the air cautiously, boldly entered the water to drink. It seemed no hungry crocodile was lurking there that evening. A snake, head in air, swam swiftly across the pool, the wake of its weaving length closing swiftly after it. And then, from the open grasslands, came the wildebeest sentries, tails switching nervously. Alice saw them almost as soon as Rusty, and her total stillness pleased him. He had often noticed that she combined her habitual brisk manner with a genuine gift for relaxation or deliberate quiet. He could imagine her, with this alert stillness of hers, at the bedside of a patient gravely ill, watching for the dawn of renewed life or the shadow of death. She was not—like so many women—terrified of silence. On their journey she had chattered or asked questions as the spirit moved her, but he had never known her attempt to make conversation, she had preferred to lose herself in her own thoughts, and he had been grateful that this was so.

The wildebeests, reassured by their patrols, came in strength, and soon a score or more of the melancholy bearded gnu faces drooped over the water. With them came the zebras, shy and halting, raising their pretty Arab heads and neighing before adding their striped reflections to the many already mirrored in the pool. A family of wart-hogs joined them, and presently a pair of ostriches strutted ludicrously through the reeds with a fine parade of feather bustles. Suddenly a sentinel zebra tossed his head and uttered a shrill *qua-ha!* and in a flash the whole troop of smart striped ponies stampeded back into the grass-lands whence they had come.

Alice's amusement and interest enhanced Rusty's own never-failing enjoyment in the drinking-time of the game. Never did they come to this ' bar ', or any other, without the knowledge that a gangster might be there as well, biding his time.

A little later Nimrod touched Rusty on the shoulder and pointed to a wild fig-tree not far from the water's edge.

Alice felt Rusty's arm tighten about her shoulder. She swayed towards him. She was part of him, as a dancer is part of her partner, without volition of her own. Her skin accepted every signal his touch or the pressure of his hand might give her, her nerves were an extension of his, her gaze followed his, and, as she saw the movement among the leaves, she too tensed and held her breath.

The leopard flickered, flame-like, through the foliage and crouched along a branch, the black rosettes of its markings scarcely distinguishable in the light and shade of the leaves. He was intent upon a thicket stirring in the gilded sunset though no breeze sighed.

The little troop of impala ewes came through the bushes with their lambs. They displayed the same hesitant caution of every wild animal approaching water, but they could neither see nor scent the enemy in the tree. The leopard, with a soundless fluid movement, dropped to a lower branch, a better springboard.

I can't bear it—Alice thought—I can't bear what's going to happen. Rusty, for God's sake, shoot that leopard ! But he only held her as if they were both spellbound. This was the strange meaning of Sanctuary. You didn't take sides, you didn't interfere with the course of Nature, however cruel. She wanted to call out, but his will forbade her to utter any warning.

The graceful antelopes with their young grouped themselves

near the hippo-paths, they began to move towards the pool. The leopard crouched low, waiting for the last ewe to pass beneath the fig tree. The lamb followed his mother, long-legged and charming, baby-fair, with his short tucked-in tail flicking gaily, and the twitch of leaf-like ears. The next moment the leaping death was upon him and the fangs of the slayer were in his throat. There was a brief hopeless struggle and then the leopard was climbing the tree once more, dragging his kill after him, staining the grey bark with the fresh blood of his victim.

At once the bush was alive with the springing auburn forms of the fleeing impalas, and Alice's face was buried against Rusty's broad chest.

" No . . . oh, no . . ."

His arms folded about her and he felt the fast bird-flutter of her heart and her trembling warmth.

" That's the law of Velaba, Likwezi—that's the way it has to be."

21

The Lure of Tombazane

RUSTY took Alice back to the Camp by way of a new game-circuit which retrieved and followed the course of the main Hlaru River.

With the setting of the sun and the proximity of water the temperature had dropped and the motionless air was cooler. The moon had not yet risen and the short African dusk cast its soft purple veil over the bushveld so that the prevailing drifts of mauve and yellow flowers were blanched, their faint fragrance mingling with the thirsty tang of dry grass.

Alice leaned away from Rusty, her arm resting on the open window beside her. The slight breeze created by the leisurely progress of ' Sweet Sue ' lifted her hair gently from her hot forehead. She felt empty and at a loss. This isn't *me*, she thought. That's the whole trouble. And then, terrifyingly, it occurred to her that perhaps it was the other way about.

Perhaps this new unknown young woman *was* herself—Alice Lang!

But she refused to accept the notion. I'm not a fickle woman, she told herself severely. And I'm certainly not . . . *light*. I've sublimated and subdued every natural emotion and desire in my body for four years, thinkingly and deliberately. First I gave myself to work and what I believed to be my duty, and then I allowed myself to drift into that strange happy relationship with Andrew—a relationship that made so few demands upon my time and less upon my heart. It was there, with all the thrilling human potentialities and the promise of this country that has obsessed me ever since I can remember, but, for all that, it left me free to care for Mother—poor Mother who never knew of the temptation that so often tormented me, the temptation to find somebody else to look after her (though heaven knows where the money would have come from!) and to lead my own life regardless of her need for me. Only Betty knew that.

Oh, I wanted Andrew all right—in the plain sex sense of wanting. I used to go to the cinema and see Stewart Granger whenever I could and identify him with Andrew. I was always the woman in the story—Granger's woman, whoever she might happen to be—and when I got home I suffered in a sharp exciting physical way. That suffering was the dream of being loved, the spinster's makeshift for passion. I had no illusions. I always try to be honest with myself. I'm trying to be honest now, to sort myself out. I knew what it meant—that lonely aching longing in the night, the desperate craving to be possessed by Andrew—Andrew as I pictured him, with the face and the greying hair of Granger. I'd have given anything to break the chains of inhibition and necessity and abandon myself utterly to this man of my own whose letters begged me to come to him.

I suppose the happiest day of my life was when I got that letter—" I am in love with you, Alice. We can't go on like this much longer . . . I want you to join me here . . ." I read it in the summer-house, my hands shaking, my limbs dissolving. Here at last was the beginning of the reality of love! And later—when I was actually in the plane on my way to Africa— there was such a sick excitement inside me, such pins and

needles in my nerves that I thought I should die ! I daresay
that was when the chains really began to loosen and the long
habit of emotional and physical control to break. A new land
on the horizon, a new life . . . a man and a life of my own !
Then there was Andrew's sister, Meg, with her warnings. All
the warnings in the world couldn't have shaken me. I was so
sure of the rightness of this undertaking. And that night
something else happened. It happened when Dickie gave me
that shabby toy lion—" He can sleep on your pillow . . . his
name is Ratau . . ." I can still see the smile on Dickie's face—
elusive, so sweet that it hurt—a smile you'd angle to get, hold
in your memory and cherish. I thought about it, hugged it to
me, trying to recall if it was mostly in those blue eyes of his,
or on the soft childish mouth. That night I knew how deeply
I wanted children of my own and another chain broke. I felt
my body cry out to bear a child. It cried as one cries in a
nightmare—dumbly, with anguish and effort, struggling to
make itself heard. One way and another, my body seems to
have got the upper hand of me. Here, in Velaba, it is late
spring—' the month of life-giving ' Rusty calls it—it is hot
and elemental. Nature is the boss. I've broken out of a sort
of bondage and my freedom has gone to my head. I *must* keep
my sense of proportion. What really matters is the fact that I
love Andrew. I love his ideas and his way of expressing them.
I admire and respect his character and we have everything in
common—except experience of each other. When we meet—
when we are together—everything will be all right. It won't
need crocodile's heart, or any other love-potion, to make us fall
in love completely in every way.

Alice seemed oblivious of her companion and her surroundings. Rusty thought that she appeared sad and exhausted
with her small dark head leaning against the window-frame,
her eyes closed and her profile pale and drawn in the fast
fading twilight. Seeing the leopard take the lamb had upset
her.

He looked away from her and back to the road. The soft
dust on either side of the earth track was patterned with the
spoor of many animals, and it did not surprise him when he
heard Nimrod say, " Lion has passed this way, Nkosi." He
nodded. He too had seen the big pugmarks among the lesser

prints of jackals and hyenas and the neat indentations of hooves.
They saw the lioness when they rounded the next bend in the
road.   She was only a few yards ahead of them.

Alice opened her eyes.   Rusty had changed gear and slowed
down to walking pace.   The superb beast did not even trouble
to turn her head at the mechanical sound of the ' new animal '.
She was intent upon her own affairs.   To her the earth road
was just another game-trail pushed through the bush by the
comings and goings of the harmless ' motor-animal ' with the
noisy purr, and very convenient for a lioness on her way to her
hunting-ground.

"Look at that walk!" said Rusty.   "Lazy and tireless.
Minnie-the-Moocher.   She'll have hard work to get her kill
tonight with the moon at the full.   Like most killers she prefers
the dark.   There must be others of her kind about.   Listen to
the baboons!"

In the darkening bush they heard the baboons scolding and
swearing from the trees, but Minnie-the-Moocher paid no
heed, just went her way with long graceful strides, powerful
muscles relaxed, tufted tail dangling almost to the ground.

"She looks as if she knows exactly where she's going,"
murmured Alice.

"Sure.   She's a girl with a purpose.   She's hungry."

He switched on the headlights and dimmed them.   Still
Minnie-the-Moocher took no notice.   To her all eyes blazed
in the dark, some more than others.   ' Sweet Sue ' kept close
on her heels at her own unhurried pace.   At a fork in the road
the lioness hesitated and Rusty stood on the brake while she
played with the idea of turning right towards the high open
thorn-veld and then changed her mind in favour of the river-
road.

Rusty said, "That's a reprieve for some wildebeest or
zebra, and probably it's sentence of death on a bush-buck or
a wart-hog."

He heard Alice's half sigh—" The law of Velaba."

He increased speed till the bonnet was level with, and then
ahead of, the lioness.   From the car window Alice could
have put out her hand and stroked the tawny coat.   They
were walking practically hand-in-hand with Minnie-the-
Moocher and she suspected that Rusty was testing her nerve.

The lioness, without altering the measure of her stride, looked up and straight into Alice's eyes. The noble face with its impersonal pride humbled her. Here was neither the aggressiveness nor the subservience of the dog, not even the aloof egoism of the cat, only the sublime pitiless indifference of the Queen with the power of life and death in tooth and claw.

Rusty pressed his foot down on the accelerator.

" Well, did you look into her eyes ? "

" Yes."

" Did you find her dangerous ? "

" To someone else. Not to us. She was very regal and beautiful." Alice looked behind her. The lioness was no longer to be seen. " She's gone, Rusty."

" She must have reached her hunting-ground. And, come to that, I'm hungry, too."

Philemon had set dinner for them on the stoep. " Maybe rain come, Nkosi," he explained. " Better under roof."

And, indeed, while they were eating, there was the constant flash of lightning along the horizon, and in the mountains thunder rolled and muttered. A chill breeze rose and blew the corners of the yellow-checked table-cloth, and Rusty said, " There's the feel of rain in the air."

At eight o'clock they went over to his office across the compound to tune into Camps One and Three. But although Rusty was able to make contact with Jan Nelmapius and Andrew it was difficult to give or receive a message through the atmospherics that crackled furiously in the room. It seemed, however, that reception to Camp One was better than to Camp Three, and Rusty was glad of that, for there was something he was determined to put over to Nelmapius.

" Listen, Jan, you must collect a pair of elephant tusks and Amos's bicycle from Boryslawski's place. Can you hear me ? Over."

" I hear you loud and clear. Where did you find the bicycle ? "

" At the old Chief's kraal, exactly as we knew it would be. Do you get that ? Over."

" I get that. What about Sweet Spruit ? Any sign of the Tokoloshe ? "

" Only a hollow tree—might be his hiding-place. Over."

But, when Camp Three came in, Andrew said, " I can scarcely hear you. Reception here is shocking. Over."

" It's bad here, too. All's well with us. Call me tomorrow at six forty-five. We hope to leave here at seven a.m. Over."

" Six forty-five . . . I'll call you then. Over."

Rusty glanced quickly at Alice. " Want to try and talk to Andrew ? "

She shook her head. " I couldn't—with all that inter-ference. I can hardly hear anything except the crackles. Give him my love."

He passed her message rather grimly through the angry ether.

". . . and that's all now. Out."

" There's a dry electric storm in the mountains," he said, as they walked back to the Game-warden's house. " It always makes a hash of communications between Camps Two and Three. It's never as bad in the south. And thank goodness for that. Jan will understand what I was trying to tell him without listeners-in guessing too much."

" What exactly did you want him to know ? "

" That other things beside the bicycle were probably to be found at the old Chief's kraal. We arranged beforehand that if I told him the bicycle had been found at the kraal he must tell the Duikers' Drift police that they'd be well advised to search for smuggled guns round there. I also said that if I gave him some reason to call at Boryslawski's farm he could take it that Boryslawski was in the racket."

" Are you so sure he is ? "

" Yes. If Gottlieb is urging the old Chief to go to Europe for an expensive operation it's because he wants to establish a hold over him—make him vulnerable to bribery. The old Chief is their contact-man—I believe that's the word. And I'd be interested to know what Boryslawski keeps in that new lion-guarded aeroplane hangar. Guns—drying game-meat ready for transport ? Might be——"

He broke off as a flash of lightning forked down the sky, followed by a clap of thunder.

They had reached the height above the river and with one accord they stopped and stood looking across the dark canyon and the thick secret bush to the Black Mamba Mountains.

The heavy scudding clouds above the jagged peaks were edged with the silver of the rising moon, and every now and again the whole primitive scene was lit by a blaze of lightning.

Rusty said, " If the rains break tonight we'll be stuck here for twenty-four hours or more. There are no bridges over the rivers and the causeways will be flooded and impassable."

The sounds of the night seemed to Alice to have grown loud and ominous in the silence that followed Rusty's words. Frogs and crickets filled the air with croaking and chirping, and somewhere a bird called with an eerie screech. Grunts and weird animal laughter echoed in the bush.

" You mean," said Alice evenly, " that if the rain comes we'll need to stay here till the rivers go down—another day and night, perhaps longer ? "

" That's exactly what I mean.   Any comment ? "

She shook her head and there was something like despair in the droop of her shoulders.

" You don't trust me, do you, Alice ? "

" Does it matter ? "

" I think so."

She tried to smile.   " Mrs. Boryslawski says one can't trust anybody all the time—not even oneself."

" Mrs. Boryslawski occasionally talks sense."

" People are unreliable.   Only dogs are to be trusted. Smokey, for instance.   Smokey would never let you down."

She stooped to pat the snuff-coloured dog lying at Rusty's feet. Smokey was never far from his master if he could help it.

" Not even Smokey *all* the time.   If a native makes up his mind to rob my house he takes precautions.   He finds somebody like Tombazane when she's in season and ties her to my fence.   Then he may be sure that Smokey's instinct will make him forget his duty.   My faithful watch-dog will leave his post to chase the old, old call of nature."

" Even your loyal Smokey ? "

He gave a short laugh.   " Smokey's a flesh and blood dog. The lure of Tombazane makes mincemeat out of loyalty.   Can you understand that ?   I can, Alice Lang.   There are women with the lure of Tombazane who'd make a man let down his own brother ! "

R—G

His words degraded a situation that had risen between them without their knowing or inviting it. She felt him hating her, wanting her, and fighting the instinct to betray his brother's trust. Anger flamed in her, it flashed and burned like the lightning spasmodically reflected in the deep chasm of the Hlaru River.

The lure of Tombazane! So that was how he thought of her—of them both! Her nails bit into her palms and she trembled from head to foot. Shame and fury rocked her as if with the force of the distant storm. Heat and violence boiled in her blood. Tombazane—Tombazane! How dare you, Rusty . . . thinking of me like an animal! Her heart pounded, her mouth was too dry to speak. She raised her hand and struck him a stinging blow across the cheek with her open palm, and then another.

In the sudden white fire of sheet-lightning she saw his eyes narrow and his chin come forward as he seized her hands in a grip that made her gasp with pain.

" No one does that to me! " He spoke through clenched teeth. "*No one*—not even you, Likwezi! "

She was in his arms, her own pinioned to her sides, his hands clasped across the small of her back pressing him to her so that it seemed he must break her. His mouth on hers was hard and cruel, and she knew that unless he voluntarily released her, she could never resist his strength. Her taut body slackened, her lips parted, and when he let go she would have fallen but for his arm which was still about her waist. She gathered herself together with a supreme effort of will and drew away from him. She threw back her head and faced him. The chill rain-wind blew back her hair and cooled her hot cheeks.

" I hate you, Rusty! " Her voice was low and intense. " I know now that in all my life I've never even guessed the meaning of the word hate—not till tonight."

He watched her walk slowly and steadily towards the house, he saw Philemon rise from the gloom outside and open the fly-proof stoep door for her. She paused to speak to him and he bowed and disappeared. Her silhouette as she stood waiting for him to return was small and slender and very still, but it cast fantastic shadows as the hurricane-lamps swung to and fro in the rising wind.

Philemon returned, carrying a lantern, and she took it from him and went into her *rondavel*. She drew the curtains, and Rusty turned away.

You're not the only one who hates me, Likwezi, he said soundlessly to the night. I hate myself, God knows.

Clouds, fleeced with silver, raced across the star-studded sky, and a loom of luminous light spread over the Black Mamba Mountains as the full moon rose above the bush and forests of Velaba—the old atavistic world of Dumela and Ratau, of Ndlovukasi and the old Chief, of Smokey and Tombazane, of Cain and Abel.

22

" *The Police Know Something!* "

THE two Bantu Game-guards, old Saul and his nephew, young James, waited beside Andrew Miller's jeep. They were armed with rifles and they had ammunition in their pockets. James was excited and Saul watched him from under hooded lids. James, in his opinion, would be better without a firearm, for he was as quick with a weapon as an angry bee with its sting, and as wild in his aim. Nkosi had warned them that they might find themselves engaged with violent men tonight. " If we have to shoot," he had said, " we shoot for the tyres of their *bakkie*. We have no wish to kill men."

" So remember what Inyanga has said," Saul warned his hasty nephew. " It is the hoof we must hit if we fire, not the horns or the heart."

They saw the Game-warden come on to the stoep of his house and stand talking to his houseboy, Maxim.

" The rain is near," said James. " The lame leg of Inyanga tells me so."

" The thunder also talks. In the mountains it has rained already and the rivers will be running fast. We should put up the hood, but Nkosi wants it down."

Andrew limped down the steps and was walking towards the jeep when a familiar sound made him pause. The Missionary's ancient car had its own unmistakable growl and splutter. What could Dr. Hurley want at this time of night—nearly nine o'clock.

But it was not Dr. Hurley at the wheel. Thea drew up and sprang out. In her light cotton dress she looked fey and wraith-like as she ran to Andrew's side.

"I must talk to you, Andrew! It's terribly important." She was breathless and agitated. "Mummie and Daddy don't know that I'm here. They walked over to the house of John and Venetia—some business about the school. I gave them a quarter of an hour's start and then I grabbed the car and came over."

John and Venetia were the young Bantu couple who taught in the Mission School. They were an earnest young pair and they would certainly keep the Missionary and his wife talking for some time. They would probably offer tea and refreshments. Nevertheless, there was a danger of Thea's parents returning home to find both her and the car vanished. Andrew was worried.

"Don't look like that!" she said. "Whatever you were going to do will have to wait. I *must* talk to you."

"Come inside." He took her arm and found that she was trembling. "What is all this about? What has happened, Thea?"

He led her into the house, into the shabby lounge with the skin rugs and leather arm-chairs, with the walls lined with bookshelves filled with dusty textbooks on Bantu customs and natural science side by side with works on psychology and philosophy, many of the classics, plays by William Shakespeare and George Bernard Shaw and the Bible Designed to be Read as Literature—which last always offended the susceptibilities of Dr. Hurley and entranced his daughter. On Andrew's big mahogany writing-desk was a photograph of Alice in a leather frame.

Thea went straight to the photograph and took it up. She studied the clean-cut austere features and soft dark eyes with a puzzled frown. Her own fair skin was flushed and her full lips pouted like those of a child in distress.

"Andrew, what do you know about her? What do you *really* know? I'm frightened of her. She's going to make trouble for you."

The harsh overhead light accentuated his frown and the iron-grey streaks in his dark hair. His mouth tightened.

" Thea, what nonsense is this ? "

She faced him with an expression that was both defiant and desperate.

" Those dark eyes of hers—what goes on behind them ? You can't see the thoughts behind brown eyes. They are hidden. They keep their secrets——"

He took the photograph from her impatiently and put it down.

" Neither of us has time for this play-acting," he said sharply. " I have to go out on patrol and you must get home."

She flinched at his tone, but she stood her ground.

" There's something wrong about Alice Lang ! I don't know what it is, but the police know something about her."

He knew the brittle pitch of her voice—it was her frightened voice. It belonged to her childhood, to the days when she was a little school-girl clinging to his hand, saying, " Andrew, will they charge us ? Will those elephants come at us ? " When she spoke and looked like that he had always soothed her and made light of her fears. He was gentle with her now.

" Please, Thea, pull yourself together. Why are you making these wild statements ? Try to tell me sensibly what it is that's upset you like this."

She sank on to the arm of his leather chair with the spun gold of her hair very bright and young under the light. The pink had left her cheeks, even her lips were pale.

" This evening—about seven o'clock when we were just going to have supper—Sergeant van Wyk came in to see Daddy and Mummy. They sent me on to the stoep, but I could still hear every word that was said. Maybe I shouldn't have listened, but when I heard Alice Lang's name, I did. The Sergeant was asking a lot of questions about her."

" About Alice ? But why ? I saw van Wyk this morning, and we talked about her. He knows all about her."

She shook her head obstinately. " Not as much as he wants to know. He asked Daddy endless questions, but of course Daddy hadn't got the answers."

" What sort of questions ? " Andrew's heart turned over and there was a sick feeling in the pit of his stomach.

" Had my parents ever met her ?   Was she—or any member of her family—really known to them ?   When did you first suggest that she stay at the Mission ?   When did my parents first realize that you were interested in her ?   What could they tell him about her friendship with you ?   All sorts of things. But of course Daddy and Mummy didn't know anything except what you'd told them—and that wasn't much—not when you boil it down."

Andrew felt the blood mount to his head.   Like most men who are slow to anger, the emotion, when it did grip him, was the more intense.

" How dared van Wyk go to the Mission behind my back and put your parents through an inquisition !   He knows very well that Alice Lang has come to Velaba at my invitation.   He probably knows that she has come here to marry me.   If he wants to talk to anyone about her, he should talk to me."

He bit off the words furiously, his voice shaking with rage, but under the indignation was alarm.   What was going on ?

Almost as if in answer to his unspoken question, the police Land Rover drew up outside his house, and the massive form of Sergeant van Wyk appeared on the stoep.   Andrew strode to the open door.

" Come in, Sergeant.   I'm glad to see you."

But van Wyk did not think the Game-warden looked glad about anything.   He looked as grim as Satan himself.   And there was young Thea with her face going from pink to white and back again and guilt written all over her.   The Sergeant prided himself upon knowing the look of guilt at a glance. So she'd borrowed her father's motor-car—without his permission, no doubt—to come rushing round to tell her dear friend, the Game-warden, that the police—represented by himself—had been making a few inquiries about Miss Alice Lang.   The situation clearly called for tact and the natural cunning which he had inherited in full measure from his *slim* Boer ancestors.   Van Wyk's little black eyes beamed disarmingly from under the jutting brow.

" I'm glad to be here myself, man," he said heartily.   " That call came through from Pretoria and left me free to come on patrol with you.   I've got two of my men out there in the

Land Rover—both armed, in case we have a bit of luck and catch the beggars."

" That's fine." The Game-warden lit a cigarette with nervous nicotine-stained fingers. " But before we go any further I'd like to know what the devil you've been doing up at the Mission—bothering Dr. and Mrs. Hurley and nosing into other people's business ? "

Van Wyk put up an enormous restraining hand as if to stop any further verbal traffic.

" I have my duty to perform."

" What duty ? Why should you be making inquiries about Miss Alice Lang ? "

" That I am not in a position to divulge. I suggest that it is time for us to proceed on our patrol."

Andrew hesitated, but he could tell by the Sergeant's heavily official attitude and method of expression that he was unlikely to learn much more from him.

" Very well," he said, " we will—as you put it—proceed." He turned to Thea, who had risen. " I'll see you to your car. Maxim will go back with you as far as the Sanctuary gates."

He called the houseboy and gave him his orders. At the car he said : " Thank you for coming, Thea. You were right . . . it was kind and thoughtful of you. But you mustn't worry. I am sure this is only some stupid misunderstanding. She's probably got herself tied up in some sort of red-tape regulation. There are so many these days. Perhaps she's come into the country as a tourist when she really intends to work here or take up residence—perhaps she should have called herself a Settler if she's going to marry here—I don't know. I've no idea what the immigration rules are. But, whatever silly thing she's done, I'll swear it's nothing serious— nothing she knew was wrong."

Thea was in the driver's seat and she had turned the ignition key, but before she put her foot on the self-starter she looked at him with wide anxious eyes.

" I hope not, Andrew. But the trouble is you don't know her. You don't *really* know Alice Lang at all."

The rattle of the self-starter drowned his answer, and as Maxim, her dark, unobtrusive escort, climbed into the back seat, she put the car in gear and drove away.

She's right, thought Andrew. In a way she's right. I don't *really* know Alice Lang—not like I know Thea. I know what Thea will do and say and the foolish and the good things of which she's capable. But Alice? Is there some dark side to her that I've never guessed at? Are there secrets behind those lovely eyes? Suddenly the face he had loved and studied and found so brave and self-sacrificing took on a suggestion of mystery. He had an overwhelming impulse to go back into the house and look at that photograph again and see if he could discover there some weakness—or even strength —that he had somehow missed.

But van Wyk had other ideas. He was standing at Andrew's elbow.

" I got through to Inspector Banks at Duikers' Drift. They'll keep an eye on the Jo'burg Road in the south tonight. It appears the Sergeant—Neethling—is at Camp One. He went there yesterday to interrogate that Game-guard, March, who was with Amos on the night of the crime."

" Good. I had a feeling that my brother was giving Nelmapius a lead over the inter-com this evening. But reception was shocking here——"

" Very bad. I was listening."

" Of course. You wanted to be sure of Miss Lang's movements."

" Correct, Mr. Miller." He moved towards his Land Rover. " Now will you go ahead? Or shall I? "

" I will." Andrew spoke curtly. " I know every inch of this territory. If I stop anywhere, you do the same. I've told my Game-guards that if there's any shooting from our side it's to be tyres only."

" Unless the beggars open up on us."

" In that case I shall naturally give other orders."

He's in a fine old temper, thought van Wyk. I wonder if he guesses what it's all about—*if he knows*? He's a deep one, like all these bloody scholars. It wouldn't surprise me if he tries to break away some time tonight and make for Camp Two to warn her what's in the wind. But I won't allow that. He won't give me the slip. I mean to catch that young woman off guard. That's the best way of telling if they're guilty or not. Get them when they least expect it, fling it at them suddenly, and they give themselves away. They blurt out things and sweat. You scare them and they sweat. They can control their faces, but they can't control their sweat.

" You intend to follow the route we discussed this morning ? " he asked.

" Yes."

" There's a chance that we may find the Seekoei River in flood. The storm broke in the mountains about an hour ago, though it hasn't reached us yet."

" We'll take the risk."

" Very well, Mr. Miller. Let us waste no more time."

Later, thought Andrew. Some time later tonight I must shake him off. I've got to get through to Camp Two. I *must* see Alice before he does. It's vital that I see her first. What have they got against her ? What could anyone possibly have against Alice Lang ?

23

The Chase

DRIVING without lights was not easy. Andrew forced anxiety about Alice into the depths of his consciousness where it rested, leaden and uneasy. He realized that his full attention was required for the immediate task.

The milky light of the full moon was continually obscured by gathering clouds, thunder rumbled in the Black Mamba Mountains, and a fitful wind with rain on its breath was rising stormily.

When Andrew left the earth road and took to the savannah country inside the eastern border of Velaba it was necessary for van Wyk to keep close behind him.

He could dodge me here, thought the Sergeant, and it wouldn't be easy to make my way to Camp Two without so much as a path or a guide-post to show the way. But the Game-warden had no intention of dodging the Sergeant—not yet—for he had already observed a number of signs that increased his conviction that the *biltong*-bandits had recently been active. Herds of game, grazing peacefully, stampeded in wild panic at sight and sound of the jeep, herds that normally accepted the 'motor-animal' as harmless. He was on the right track—he must be! Excitement began to purge his anger against van Wyk and he was genuinely glad of the support of the stalwart policeman and his two native constables. In fact his habitual preoccupation with the Sanctuary and its population had reasserted itself and his mind was no longer divided. There was evil abroad, a threat to his wild creatures, and all his energies, mental and physical, were concentrated upon their defence.

Andrew put the jeep down a winding natural declivity into a sandy drift that had once been the bed of a river which had long since altered its course. In the dark he braked suddenly and van Wyk's Land Rover almost rammed him. A herd of elephant stood facing them, grey, ghostly and prehistoric. The moon swam above a bank of cloud and by its light Andrew estimated that at least a hundred animals of all ages and sizes barred their path. Trunks waved snake-like in the silvery light, immense ears flapped and here and there one of the monsters blew sand over his head and back or browsed on the young leaves of trees growing in the wide drift. The herd was evidently passing through the drift on the way to higher ground and the jeep and the Land Rover were directly in the way of the easy ascent.

Andrew had a swift terrifying vision of the mangled mess that would remain when the herd had walked over them—not in malice, but with the deadly bovine calm of cattle crossing a country road regardless of oncoming traffic. Nothing would head them off. There was only one thing to do, and it must be done slowly and quietly in order not to alarm the great beasts.

Andrew made a sign to van Wyk to follow him. He heard young James in the back of the jeep load his rifle and Saul turn with a restraining mutter. The old man would keep the boy in check.

Very slowly he turned the jeep along the water-course at right angles to the herd, but, as he went forward, he heard the Land Rover rev up behind him with the wheels skidding helplessly in the loose sand. Van Wyk was making more noise than headway, and Andrew cut out his engine with a sign to the

Sergeant to do the same. Van Wyk had some experience of elephants and a profound respect for them. As he saw the herd begin to move he and his two Bantus abandoned their stranded vehicle and made for a patch of trees growing in the drift and a few moments later they were in the branches. Andrew fully expected to see the Land Rover crushed under foot like a beetle, but the elephants ignored it. They kept on their course, plodding up the gradual ascent from the drift to the uplands, the babies keeping close to the sides of their female relatives. The night seemed filled with the muffled sound of their ponderous march and the hollow rumbling of their bellies as they passed within a few yards of the Land Rover.

When the last huge shape had disappeared over the rise the Sergeant and his men somewhat sheepishly descended from their place of safety while Andrew and Saul studied the spoor.

" That was a near thing," said Andrew. " They passed close enough to lift you out of this open Land Rover without even extending their trunks ! "

" *Ja*, man, I don't mind telling you that lot gave me a *skrik* ! "

" I wasn't too happy myself. Now, look here, that herd— luckily for us—wasn't worried or excited about anything, and you can see the way they've come—from inside the Sanctuary. We'll take the other direction, keeping along the border. But first we must get you out of this sand."

When they reached the Seekoei River an hour later the cause- way was already under fast-flowing water, but they made the crossing without mishap. It was in this area, between the Seekoei and the Hlaru Rivers, that the density of game was always greatest in the dry season, and Andrew felt that it was here, if anywhere, that they were likely to come up with the bandits.

Suddenly old Saul touched him on the shoulder. " There, Nkosi ! "

They had left the thickly wooded riverside and emerged into open thornveld. Andrew parked the jeep in the shadow of a tree, and the Land Rover came up alongside him. The men remained in the cars surveying the scene before them.

Van Wyk shook his head. " God, man, it looks like a bloody battlefield ! "

The moon shone on the freshly dismembered carcasses of

wildebeests. The grass was darkly stained with blood, and the air stank of carnage. Hyenas and jackals, the scavengers of the night, tore ghoulishly at what remained of the decimated herd.

Andrew took his revolver and got out. " Stay where you are," he said to the others. " There may be wounded animals about."

But Saul followed him, his loaded rifle in his hand. Andrew stooped and picked up a scattering of cartridge cases. He gave a few to van Wyk. " They're using Sten guns."

The Sergeant held the small brass cylinders in his huge palm.

" *Ja*, that was their method before. Must be the same bloody beggars."

The sixth sense of the man of the wilds made Andrew swing round. He was just in time to see Saul raise his rifle to halt the charge of a wounded wildebeest, but young James was before him, firing from the jeep. The shot went wide, grazing the infuriated animal, but Saul's aim was true and the bullet in the brain brought the wildebeest to his knees almost at Andrew's feet.

Andrew examined the dead animal grimly. The wild spray of the bandits' fire had inflicted senseless and cruel injuries before Saul's shot had put the wildebeest out of its agony.

" They won't have heard our shots," said van Wyk. " They must be well ahead of us and the wind is this way."

The grass was not high and the tracks of heavy tyres were plainly visible.

" Let's go. But first get the hood up. It's going to pour any minute."

As Andrew spoke the stutter of a Sten gun was carried to them on the wind. " That's not far off," he said. " A few miles at most. It's from the direction of the thicker bush. They're probably shooting up a troop of impala. With any luck we'll get the damned murderers red-handed while they're carving up their meat ! "

" We must keep on these tyres tracks," said van Wyk, " but if we use lights they'll spot us long before they hear us."

Andrew nodded. " We'll manage without."

He took the lead once more, but the going had grown more difficult. The moon sailed fitfully between the massing storm-

clouds and the rain-wind blew more steadily. The sound of
gun-fire had ceased and it occurred to Andrew that the noise of
their engines could not fail to warn the bandits of their approach.
He welcomed the constant rumble of thunder, and the ever
more frequent flashes of lightning. But, even without the
moon and the lightning to show him the crushed grass, he could
guess where those tyre tracks would lead them. He could
picture the gentle antelopes mown down by the callous fire
sprayed into their midst, slender leaping legs broken, lambs and
ewes torn to ribbons and rendered fit only for *biltong* strips.
No lion or leopard could create such hideous havoc and destruction. The lion took his kill because he needed food, these
gangsters destroyed wholesale, leaving the wounded to perish
painfully in the bush.

His rage crystallized into an icy desire for revenge. He
hated these killers with a cold bitter hatred that had in it no
element of the human understanding that marked his attitude
towards the native poacher. The native, left to himself, snared
for food or for magic, and if he was cruel it was because cruelty
had little meaning for him. But the white gangsters used the
Bantu's meat-hunger and the greed or necessity of certain
Chiefs to exploit and corrupt the people of the Sanctuary and
to teach them new and evil ways. This sort of killing was
massacre. Damn the purr of the engines ! At any moment
they might overtake the bandits' *bakkie*. If only there were
some way of creeping upon them silently !

It was James who saw it first—the pick-up in the tree
shadows at the side of an open glade about a hundred yards
ahead of them.

" Nkosi—they are there—a man in the *bakkie* with a gun, and
three others taking the game meat ! "

But the flash of lightning that revealed the light truck to
Andrew and his companions also served to illumine the jeep
and the Land Rover. Instantly the native in the pick-up gave
the alarm, and in a second the men had abandoned their
operations and leapt into the truck. The driver switched on
the headlights and set off at high speed.

It had been impossible at that distance and in the darkness to
tell how many of the four men were white, and Andrew realized
that in their anonymity lay his danger. They would not

hesitate to shoot if, by doing so, they could get away unidenti-
fied. He put on his headlights and saw van Wyk do the same.
The massing clouds had now covered the moon, and, as they
bounced over the rough terrain, a streak of forked lightning
tore a gash in the overcast sky, and, with a mighty crash of
thunder, the heavens opened and the rain pelted down in solid
blinding sheets.

There were many obstacles in the veld to hinder both pursuers and pursued—tree-stumps, anthills, fallen logs, boughs
torn down by elephants, and once the form of a giraffe loomed
fantastically out of the inky night. But the need for caution
was gone. All that mattered now was speed. Saul had
Andrew's revolver in his hand, and if they could close the range,
he would aim for the pick-up's tyres. The two men in the
back of the truck, dazzled by their headlights, would not find
it easy to take accurate aim.

If the Hlaru causeway is flooded we've got them! thought
Andrew. It could be. The Seekoei had been in spate from
the mountain storms an hour ago, and the Hlaru had its source
in the same watershed, but it was a faster, stronger river, and
already the rains would be swelling the flood-waters. There
was only one possible crossing if the bandits were to get out of
Velaba and make for the road to the Rand, and, if they were
held up there, they would be cornered. In such a case he
fancied that they might well be desperate enough to shoot it out.
He hoped they would, for he, too, was killing mad.

Van Wyk was close behind the jeep, following the blurred
shape and headlights through the torrential rain. He had to
admit that the Game-warden could step on it and seemed to
know his way through this pitch-dark thornveld by instinct.
It was a good job Duikers' Drift were going to keep an eye on
the Jo'burg road in the south, just in case these bastards got
away. Hell, the Game-warden was charging down to the river
like a bloody buffalo! And there, ahead of him, was the
bakkie already on the causeway, swaying and skidding in the
flood-water, but more than half way across. Van Wyk brought
the Land Rover to a stop. He was a family man as well as a
policeman and he saw no reason to commit suicide.

But the devil must be in Mr. Miller tonight! There was the
jeep, still in hot pursuit of the pick-up, plunging axle-deep into

the torrent. He hasn't a hope of making it, thought van Wyk, not a snowball's hope in hell.

It did not enter Andrew's head to hesitate or try to reverse when he felt the drag of the raging flood-water on the jeep. He could hold her, he'd get across somehow, he wasn't going to give in at this stage. The pick-up was gaining the opposite bank, she was out of the river, struggling and slithering in the mud. She'd never get up there without chains.

" Shoot for the *bakkie's* tyres," he told Saul, who sat beside him.

In the glare of the intermittent lightning the Game-guard aimed for the truck's wheels. At the same moment the two men in the back of the pick-up shone a sudden dazzling spot-light on the jeep that was being forced, broadside on, towards the edge of the causeway.

" Shoot to kill ! " shouted the driver of the truck.

Andrew heard Saul's six shots and saw the truck ahead lurch and skid.

" Well done ! " he said. But he thought, It's no good, I can't hold the jeep against this racing current, it's too strong for us. Let me hang on—just a few yards more—and we'll be across . . .

The stutter of the pick-up's Sten guns hammered against the sound of rushing water and Andrew felt a searing agony tear through his chest and shoulder. As the Game-warden slumped over the wheel a shimmering blaze of sheet-lightning showed van Wyk a new wave of the rising flood surge towards the jeep and carry it, helplessly out of control, over the submerged stone causeway into the dark deep waters beyond. The swollen carcass of a little buck was borne with it on the turbulent tide.

The Sergeant swore mightily as he emptied his revolver in the direction of the pick-up.

" Bloody murderers, I'll get you ! And I hope you swing for this ! "

24

The Kill

WHILE the three Sanctuary Camps were in communication earlier that night Sergeant Neethling of Duikers' Drift Police Post happened to be at Camp One with Ranger Nelmapius. He had been sent there to continue the investigations into the assault on Game-guard Amos, and he had received further instructions to be at a certain cross-roads before midnight. If *bakkie* bandits were operating in the Sanctuary they would almost certainly break away towards the main Johannesburg road at that point.

Neethling had just had a curious interview with March, who had confessed that, on the orders of the old Chief, he was in league with the native poachers who frequently invaded the Sanctuary from the Chief's village.

" And now," March had added hopefully, " you will take me to Duikers' Drift, Baas, and shut me up in the *tronk*."

" I shall take you to the old Chief's kraal," Neethling had said icily, and he had smiled at March's discomfiture. Neethling was a fleshless grey-haired fellow known to the Bantus as ' the Axe '. His face was as sharp and narrow as a chopper and his eyes as steely. It was his strength and his weakness that he could never find in his heart one shred of human pity for any evil-doer.

" Well ? " he had said as Nelmapius turned from the radio telephone. " Anything behind Rusty's remarks ? "

" *Ja*, I think there's something doing at the old Chief's kraal. Gun-running, I guess. And he gave me a lead that Boryslawski's place would be worth a visit."

" Then let's be off. The rain's on the way and time is pretty short for what we have to do."

" What do we have to do ? "

" We'll go and give them something to think about at the Chief's village, and then I want to talk to Amos's woman—what's her name ? "

" His wife, you mean ? Oasis. She'll be at Ndlovukasi's kraal, March says."

" March has said a mouthful one way and another. We'll take him with us. He can come in the van with me and one of the constables, and you can take the other constable and a couple more Game-guards. What about that chap, Job, who found Amos ? "

" Yes, I'll take Job and Esau."

" See they're armed. We could run into trouble tonight. And I suggest you bring chains for your jeep just in case the rains break."

Sergeant Neethling in the closed police van had set a smart pace, ignoring the Sanctuary speed limit, and in little over an hour they had crossed the Lower Fulene into the old Chief's territory. The embers of the last cooking fires were still glowing as they neared the native village and the smell of burning cow-dung and dry grass mingled pleasantly with the cool scent of approaching rain. They parked their vehicles at a little distance from the village in charge of Esau and continued on foot. March carried spades and a pick and walked in front of a constable whose assegai occasionally prodded the small of his back.

There was evidently some sort of celebration going on in the village, for, as they approached the Chief's kraal, they could hear the stamp-stamp of dancing feet and the throb of the drums.

" They're beating up for rain," said Nelmapius. " The She-Elephant will be praying over her rain-medicines."

Outside the fence Neethling spoke to March.

" Now, you bastard, you'll show us exactly where those smuggled guns are hidden. If you don't, there'll be no nice safe gaol for you. We'll leave you here for your friends to deal with you as they dealt with Amos ? "

The constable's assegai prodded him in a tender spot. " Show the way, son of a hyena ! "

March chose swiftly between the safety of the gaol and the threats of Velaba and of those outside it who would know them-selves betrayed.

" The guns are hidden in the hut of the strumpet," he muttered.

" Lead us there," said Neethling. " And no palaver. We are in a hurry."

The drums fell silent and the dancers froze as the little party, with Neethling and March at its head, strode through the astonished merry-makers to the hut of the sullen handsome girl to whom Rusty had talked only twelve hours earlier. The hut was empty when they entered it and the two constables remained on guard outside while Job dug up the mud floor and revealed a coffin-shaped box containing a number of ·22 rifles.

It was then that the storm broke with thunder and lightning and a torrential downpour. All but a few of the revellers, who had grown ominously silent as they crowded round the girl's hut, fled for shelter.

Neethling neither asked questions nor invited explanations. He commanded his constables to take the box of guns and make his arrests. Before they fully appreciated the situation the old Chief, the Counsellor, the Witch Doctor and the girl found themselves being led out of the village and locked in the van. Neethling had hesitated for a moment about including the She-Elephant in his ' bag ', but the rain had come and her prestige was high. He had thought better of it.

" Now we'll go to Ndlovukasi's kraal, and have a word with Oasis," said Neethling. " We must cut it short though if we're to make the cross-roads before midnight."

Ndlovukasi's kraal was hidden by the driving rain when they arrived there half an hour later. While Neethling and Nel-mapius talked to the Maker of Lions and her niece, Oasis, the constables and Game-guards were busy putting chains on the wheels of the vehicles, for already the dirt veld tracks were quagmires. Only March was ordered to remain at Neethling's side.

The fury of the storm had wakened everybody in the kraal, for it seemed at times as if the grass huts might be swept away in the deluge or struck by the lightning that preceded every clap of thunder.

Ndlovukasi received her unexpected guests in her ceremonial hut. She looked wilder than ever with her fuzzy hair and turkey neck and dangling withered breasts. The necklace of carnivora teeth gleamed against her inky skin, and her python-skin belt held her short monkey-fur skirt roughly in place. She

used the wildebeest switch in her hand as if it were a magic
wand.   Oasis stood demurely beside her aunt.   She was more
conventionally clothed in a cotton *sari* and blouse, while Shinhenani rested sleepily in his sling on her hip.   A half naked
entourage and a few entirely naked children squatted round the
Maker of Lions.

Sergeant Neethling pointed to March.   " Do you know this
man ? " he asked Oasis in the Bantu language.

" Yes, Nkosi.   He shared my husband's picket."

" Was he your husband's friend ? "

" My husband thought so."

" Did you ? "

" I knew he was my husband's enemy."

" How did you know this ? "

She did not answer.   It was Ndlovukasi who spoke up shrilly.

" He looked upon my niece with hot eyes.   She was afraid
that if she told her husband so he would kill this man."

" I see."   Neethling turned to Nelmapius.   " Anything you
want to ask her ? "

Nelmapius addressed Oasis kindly.   " If there is anything
you need, you must tell me, Oasis."   He spoke her language
haltingly.

Her liquid oval eyes sought March as she answered Nelmapius.   There was hate in them.

" I need two pounds, Nkosi.   I owe five pounds to my aunt,
the Maker of Lions.   Three I have already given her, but she
is owed two more."

The rain drummed loudly on the thatched roof as the girl
put out her slender dark hands to receive the two pound notes
Nelmapius laid in her cupped rosy palms.   Although the air
was cold, beads of sweat stood on March's forehead, and his
face was grey.   Oasis went on her knees to Ndlovukasi in a
respectful kow-tow and placed the notes within reach of her
aunt's bare prehensile toes.   Ndlovukasi instantly trod on them.
Then she made strange passes in the air before picking them up
with a swift ape-like movement and tucking them away in one
of the many pouches attached to her python-skin girdle.   As
she did so her eyes rolled back in her head and she uttered a
weird inhuman shriek.

" I see it !   I see it ! "

As the words left her lips a roar of thunder shook the hut and a flash of lightning lit up her lion-tooth necklace and the sweating deathly face of March who shivered as if with ague.

" Let's go," said Neethling. He swung on his heel and left the hut without a backward glance at the old woman and her niece.

" There's a law against the practice of witchcraft," he said to Nelmapius as they hurried to their vehicles. " But I have a feeling that the old witch was breaking it right and left under our very noses."

" I didn't like it either," said Nelmapius. " Oasis was paying that money for some sort of a curse."

" You'll never breed witchcraft out of these people," said Neethling. " It's in the marrow of their bones. Now, listen, man, you just follow me to the crossing. If there are any *bakkie* bandits about tonight, they'll be bound to turn off there to get on the Jo'burg road."

" The Hlaru'll be in flood by now," said the Ranger. " They may be stuck to the north of it."

" In that case they'll be between the devil and the deep green river," grinned the Sergeant, " the devil being van Wyk, who's on patrol tonight with your boss."

Nelmapius got into his jeep and followed the police van through the pelting rain to the crossing a few miles farther south. They ran the jeep and the van into the shelter of a group of willows whose heavy drooping branches concealed them from the track. Then they settled down to a wait that might well prove fruitless.

But within an hour they heard the harsh purr of a pick-up's engine, and Neethling made a sign to the Ranger to take his place at the wheel and stand by to follow him.

As the *bakkie* loomed out of the gloom Nelmapius expected to see it break west towards the Johannesburg road, but, to his surprise, it continued straight on south in the direction of Boryslawski's farm. In the dark and the rain it was impossible to distinguish the men in the cab, but Nelmapius fancied that he could discern two dim figures huddled under the tarpaulin which covered the back.

Neethling did not come out of the shelter of the willows till

the *bakkie* was almost out of sight.   Then he followed slowly
and cautiously, without lights.   It was only when his quarry
turned off the main track into Boryslawski's avenue of blue-
gums that he switched on his headlights, increased speed and
sounded his police siren.   If they were innocent they wouldn't
worry, if they were guilty, they'd probably run.

But they couldn't run fast, for the glare of the lights revealed
that the *bakkie* was limping along on three wheels and one flat
tyre.   The constable next to Neethling emptied his revolver
into the other tyre and the pick-up skidded to a stop in the yard
between some farm buildings and a large shed.   A lantern
burned in a disused stable and a man's lean form appeared in
the open doorway.   At that moment one of the drenched
figures in the back of the pick-up trained the Sten gun on to the
police van and blew out the headlights, but before he could do
further damage, the man in the stable doorway had leapt into
the back of the *bakkie* and was laying about him with a *sjambok*.
The Sten gun stuttered into silence.

In a few moments the Sergeant and his constables, followed
by Nelmapius and the Game-guards, had hustled the occupants
of the *bakkie* into the stable and relieved them of their weapons.

" What the devil goes on ? " rasped Boryslawski, tapping his
rhino-hide *sjambok* against his shoe.   In the blaze of the
stationary jeep's headlights his features had lost none of their
natural arrogance as he faced Neethling furiously.

" That's for me to ask you," said the Sergeant grimly.   " Am
I right in thinking that this man is your partner, Marcus
Gottlieb ? "

" You are.   And what the hell he's doing here at this time of
night I neither know nor care."

" We'll see about that."   Neethling turned to Nelmapius.
" You and one of your Game-guards search the *bakkie*.   Its
contents could be of interest to the Sanctuary."

As the young Ranger went to the *bakkie* with Job, who carried
a torch, Boryslawski turned his contemptuous gaze on his
partner.   Gottlieb's pallid cherubic face was scared and his
plump hands were writhing in the pockets of his denims.
Boryslawski wondered how the hell Gottlieb had pulled this lot
on to his tail.   What did the police know ?   Who had talked ?
Was Neethling only wise to this one raid ?   Or had he got wind

of the fact that the old Chief was being steadily supplied with smuggled weapons? Supplying illicit arms to natives could carry a prison sentence. Pity they hadn't got out of this racket sooner. It had been very profitable while it lasted—running guns into the native territory and meat out of Velaba on to the Rand, with an occasional good killing in a *bakkie* raid—but things had got out of hand just lately. Since that Game-guard had been so brutally assaulted in the Sweet Spruit Boryslawski had felt sickened with the whole poaching racket. He was a hunter and an adventurer, both by inclination and force of circumstances, he was callous and cynical, an exile from all that had ever meant anything to him—a man full of hates and desires for vengeance, who had rejoiced at shooting down his country's enemies in time of war, and who now felt no qualms about destroying protected game in order to make a quick fortune. But to condone the silencing of a human being by torture was not in his line. Nor was black magic. The old Chief was getting good money to organize native poaching in Velaba—money which would have enabled him to go to Europe to regain his sight, yet he had permitted this ghastly crime to take place so that an example might be made of a too-loyal Sanctuary employee, and the most powerful of all *muti* added to his own medicine horn.

Boryslawski's calculating eye fell on March. He recognized the Game-guard who had worked with Amos and who had been the Chief's most useful contact in establishing a poachers' 'fifth column' in Velaba. Why was March here now? And why was Neethling keeping him under obvious surveillance?

As Nelmapius returned from the *bakkie* to report to Neethling, Boryslawski saw lights go up in the house across the un-kempt garden, and presently a torch bobbed like a glow-worm through the dark. He groaned. Here came another compli-cation.

Mrs. Boryslawski was gasping for breath as she hurried into the pool of light shed by the headlights of the jeep and the *bakkie*. One hand held an umbrella over her head and the other grasped a torch. She wore a mackintosh over her night-gown and her bare feet were thrust into goloshes. Her hair was done up in curlers. Raindrops glistened on her pasty face heavily anointed with cold cream.   She looked round her in bewilderment and panic.

"I heard shooting and sirens, Anton.   I looked for you but you weren't in your room.   Then I saw lights over here——" She broke off.   "And there's Marcus!   Whatever are you doing here at this time of night—or rather, morning?   And Jannie Nelmapius?   But where is your beard, Jannie?   What, in heaven's name is the matter, Anton?   I thought you were in bed—you told me——"

Her husband's cold eyes were on his wife's costume, and, suddenly aware of the ludicrous figure she must cut, she dropped the torch and umbrella and began to fumble with the curlers in her hair.

Boryslawski's sardonic smile spread.   "Don't worry, Christina.   This isn't a social occasion.   Marcus seems to have attracted a good deal of uninvited attention by coming here at such an unearthly hour—nearly two in the morning!"

"You were expecting him, Mr. Boryslawski," said Neethling. "He was going to deliver freshly killed meat and collect dried *biltong*.   Not so?   Mr. Nelmapius has found a very interesting load in Mr. Gottlieb's pick-up.   Wildebeest and impala carcasses shot up with Sten guns, the guns that did the job, and a spot-light."

Gottlieb shrugged his shoulders and Mrs. Boryslawski uttered an outraged cry of fury.

"You, Marcus—*you* a smuggler!   Anton, I've always told you he was a good-for-nothing, just using you as a cat's paw—inducing you to go shares in this hateful farm but never living here himself—oh, no, not he!   Nor his fancy wife!   And now he's getting into real trouble, dragging you into——"

"Christina, you talk too much!"

She seemed to choke on an indrawn breath.   To Neethling it was immediately evident that she had had no suspicion whatever that her husband might be more than a 'cat's paw' in his partner's illegal activities.

Neethling said brusquely: "I'm going to search that big shed across the yard, Mr. Boryslawski."

The woman gave a little cry and tried to say something, but Boryslawski interrupted roughly.   "Leave this to me, Christina!"   A sinister and sadly satisfying notion slid snake-like into his mind. " Have you a search warrant ? " he asked the Sergeant.

Neethling said : " I have something better than a search warrant. I have information that I will find unlicensed guns there and enough game *biltong* to feed an army. Would you like to prove me wrong ? "

" I would like to know your informant."

Boryslawski's cold unwinking eyes went deliberately over the men who surrounded him—the hatchet-faced police sergeant, the Ranger, the two native constables and the Game-guards, Job, Esau and March. He did not even glance at his wife or his partner, who were staring at him with undisguised anxiety. Nelmapius felt the chill of Boryslawski's searching look and shuddered. In his own way, he thought, this man is ' smelling out ' a witch, or something mighty like it ! No wonder the natives call him Radinoxa, King of the Snakes. There was something cruel and deadly about him.

" I am surprised that any man sees fit to tell tales in Velaba," he said finally, with his eyes on March. " Especially one who does not hesitate to deceive and torture his friends. I know this man, March, Sergeant Neethling, and he knows me. If *he* has told you what you will find in that hangar which I have built for my new aeroplane, let *him* show you its contents. I will give him the key. Let him unlock the padlock on the door and we will forget the matter of the search warrant."

The rain was no longer torrential. It fell with a steady hushed whisper, and from time to time the clouds parted to show the dazzling moon serene in the stormy sky. The big shed rose gaunt and dark against the stars.

Boryslawski took a key from his pocket and offered it to March, who cringed away from him.

" What are you waiting for ? " he said. " You, who stink of fear ! "

" Get on with it ! " Neethling pushed his loaded revolver into March's back.

" Go on," repeated Boryslawski.

A hush had fallen on the little group in the ill-lit stable. Gottlieb's face was ghastly and even Mrs. Boryslawski seemed to be deprived of the power of speech. Nelmapius touched his recently shorn chin with a nervous hand. He felt as he had done

in the hut of Ndlovukasi when her eyes had rolled backwards
in her head.   Macabre emanations of evil hovered in the cold
clammy air.   Only Neethling remained apparently unconcerned.

"Walk," he said, and jabbed March with the muzzle of the
revolver.

With Neethling behind him, March walked in a trance across
the yard.   Boryslawski's eyes never left him, and it seemed to
Nelmapius that the Game-guard no longer acted under his own
volition—that he was under a spell.

March reached the shed, and Neethling stood away a little
as if he suspected some trap.   The Bantu put the key into the
padlock and turned it.   The door swung inwards and March
stepped back with his arm across his face.

The moon swam out of the clouds and the watchers saw the
long crouching form and the swift relentless spring as the young
lioness, Sheba, brought March to the ground without a sound,
her teeth in his throat.

Neethling's revolver cracked and the lioness lay dead upon
her victim.

A cry burst from Mrs. Boryslawski.   "I told you, Anton!
I told you you'd have to shoot Sheba——"

Boryslawski's face was tormented.   "I couldn't have shot
Sheba.   I made Neethling do it for me."

25

Rain Magic

THE thunder-storm that had begun in the Black Mamba
Mountains earlier in the evening and raged across the bushveld
only struck Camp Two with its full force after midnight.

Lightning blazed with the brilliant persistence of Neon signs
in Piccadilly Circus and thunder shook the walls of the living-
room where Rusty was trying to concentrate a sorely disturbed
mind on writing a factual Sanctuary report.   He had got no
further than the heading : 'The State of Velaba Communications'.   After this, he thought, the state of Velaba communications would be damn all for quite a while.   If only he had

Andrew's gift for the written word. A pen in his hand had a paralysing effect on Rusty's brain. And the ' noises off ' didn't help, nor did the mental picture of Alice cowering in her *rondavel*, petrified with fear and too proud to come and tell him so after that idiotic scene by the river. She'd been frightened then, too—frightened of him and of herself—or she would never have turned on him and attacked him like a scared animal. Hell, that last clap of thunder had landed like a cannon-ball on the roof !

Rusty sprang to his feet as the shuddering wall dislodged the beautiful Florentine picture and sent it crashing to the floor, face down.   He bent and turned it over with a quick incautious movement that gashed his left hand with shattered glass.   When he lifted the torn canvas there was blood on the face of the boy with the reed-pipe to his lips.

" You've hurt yourself."

Rusty swung round and saw Alice, still in the slacks and shirt she had worn that afternoon at the hippo-pool. She was leaning against the lintel of the door and her face was drawn.

" It's nothing." He bound his handkerchief hastily about his hand.

" Show me." It was her nurse's voice. Bossy, he said to himself, damn bossy. She came into the room and took his hand, removing the impromptu bandage.

" That glass was splintered fine, and these two fingers are bleeding freely. You'd better come with me. I have iodine and Elastoplast in my dressing-case." He followed her along the stoep to her *rondavel*. These nurses were used to being obeyed when they were on the job. It amused him to see her take charge.

" Go in there," she said, pointing to the bathroom, " and wash that hand well, while I get out what's needed."

When she had dressed his two injured fingers and rinsed out his stained handkerchief, she said in her brisk professional manner, " You were lucky it wasn't worse. I've never seen anything so silly as the way you grabbed that picture. If it had been a hurt human being you couldn't have been in a greater hurry to pick it up."

Perhaps that was how he felt about it, she thought. Perhaps that picture still meant Flora to Rusty.

He grinned. "Thanks for the medical attention."

She seemed to droop. Where was the starch of a few moments ago?

"I was glad to have something to do—*anything*. Oh, God, that lightning!" She winced and covered her face.

He looked round quickly and saw that her pillow was crushed. So she *had* been lying here with her head buried like an ostrich —poor little thing. She wasn't used to this sort of storm. In England the rains didn't break with cataclysmic fury, they just kept solidly on for most of the year.

She sank on to the bed and sat with her elbows on her knees and her face hidden in her hands. Her voice was muffled. "I can't stand it. It's gone on for ages—like an air raid that never ends."

Almost as she spoke a zigzag of forked lightning streaked down on to the huge baobab tree behind the house and split the monstrous bole with a rending report. Birds, reptiles and little tree-animals were thrown, dead or stunned, from their nests and lairs, but their blighted host stood stolidly against the storm, unaware that a fiery elemental claw had destroyed its life.

The door of the bathroom led on to the garden, and Rusty opened it, letting in a cold draught that blew through into the bedroom and set the lantern swinging on its chain.

When he came back to Alice he sat down beside her and put his arm about her shoulders.

"You're right," he said gently. "It is like an air raid. A big tenement-house has just received a direct hit—the old baobab—and I should say most of the inhabitants have been blitzed into a better world."

He was amazed at the extent of her fear. He could feel it beating about inside her like a trapped wild bird. He had been conscious of this bird-flutter of her heart up in the tree-platform when she had seen the leopard take his kill, but now, with every flash of lightning and roll of thunder, the bird went mad and dashed itself against the slender bars of her ribs.

"Don't be frightened. The storm is over the worst—it's moving on. The thunder is farther away already. You should have come to me sooner. I didn't realize——"

"Why should you? This—this *terror* doesn't just belong

to now—it's more than that, much more.   It goes back into my childhood—the war.   That time, when the picture fell, when the whole place shook as if it was going to fall to pieces, I had to come to you then.   And when you hurt yourself—in some strange way it helped me for a few minutes, made me pull myself together——"

He chuckled.   "Dear Alice—is there anything more I can do for you?"

She smiled, with the corner of her lip trembling, but it was a smile on the verge of tears.   He was touched and distressed.

"There now, you aren't used to our storms.   How could you be?   Everything is violent—and sometimes dangerous—in Velaba.   Even me—but you know that by now.   And the danger goes over—it passes . . ."

Does it though?   Will it pass—this stormy longing, this terrible tenderness I feel for Andrew's girl?   He told himself that he must fight and master it.   Andrew was his only brother, closer to him than anyone else in the world.   They had had their disagreements, more than that—imperial rows—but nothing and nobody had ever really broken their friendship for long.   Not even Flora.   You didn't steal from your brother—from a shy lonely man like Andrew who had discovered companionship and love in his own strange sensitive fashion and who at last seemed likely to find permanent contentment with the one person in the world best suited to his reserved sincere temperament and solitary way of life.   He heard Alice whisper:

"The storm brought it all back to me . . . the horrible things I thought I had forgotten.   The blitz.   It sounded just like the blitz, Rusty.   Bombs, fires, guns—things that mean death. It was like the time my mother and I stood in our garden with the flares and the searchlights and the gun-flashes all round us— and, only a few miles away, the factory burning.   We knew my father was there—in his laboratory—we knew what must have happened to him . . ."

The remembered horror was in her eyes and voice.   She, too, had her wounds of war, the indelible agonizing memories, as he had his.   He stroked her hair with his bandaged hand, and she turned her face into the hollow of his shoulder and wept. Her body was racked as if her tears were a tide that must burst the dykes of flesh and bone.

" Cry——" he said. " Cry all you want Likwezi."

When did you last cry so bitterly ? he wondered. When your father was killed, perhaps : When your mother died ? Or was it four years ago when you went into your voluntary prison and locked the door on youth and freedom and all your big dreams of Africa ?

After a while she was quiet and he thought that she had fallen asleep like one of Meg's little boys worn out by some emotional outburst of childhood. Lightning no longer flickered over the Camp and the echoes of thunder were more distant, but the drenching rain continued to patter steadily on to the parched earth, the Hlaru River sang with a new full voice, and the chorus of frogs swelled to a raucous symphony.

Alice drew away from Rusty. She rose blindly and hunted for a handkerchief.

" All right now ? " he asked presently. His smile and his tone were those he used for Meg's children.

She came out of the bathroom, where she had been bathing her eyes, and saw him in the doorway, his sturdy figure outlined against the stoep light.

" Where are you going, Rusty ? "

" Into the rain. I'm going to take off my shirt and I'm going out into the rain. Want to come with me ? "

She heard the smile still in his voice. " Yes," she said.

" Then put on something that doesn't matter. No water-proofs and umbrellas tonight. If we go out into the rain it's because we want to feel it—this much-needed rain that will make the veld live again."

" Does it mean as much as all that ? "

" The end of the dry season—it means new life ! Drinking places for the animals, young grass for their grazing, crops for the natives, a good season for the farmers—with any luck. Why, rain-making is the most important magic in Africa. The old Chief's tribe send envoys all the way to the sea at certain times of the year to get sea-water by the light of the full moon. It's part of the She-Elephant's rain-making medicine."

" So you want to go and revel in this life-giving rain ? "

" Sure, I do."

He saw that he had diverted her from her fright and her sadness, that she was thinking about the rain and all that it meant to the thirsty earth, to the trees, the veld, the animals and the people.

" I'll be ready in a few minutes, Rusty."

When she met him ten minutes later she had changed her slacks for the linen shorts she had worn the day before, and he saw with surprise that her lips were innocent of her usual vivid lipstick. " No shoes ? No scarf for your hair ? All right, then, we're not going far, just across the grass to the river."

He wore only his brief khaki shorts. Alice guessed that, if he had had his choice, he would have gone naked into the deluge. He was a Pagan at heart, like Nimrod.

The wind had died and the rain fell in straight heavy rods. Without another word he took her hand and together they ran across the compound towards the river.

The wet grass under the soles of Alice's feet was cool and soft, the rain on her face and hair was wonderfully refreshing. All the stress and turmoil of the past few hours was washed away by this clean wonderful downpour. She put her tongue to her lips to taste the purity of the rain ; she felt her thin shirt begin to cling to her body and the drip of water down her cheeks and back.

On the height above the Hlaru they stopped. Away to the west the moon had broken through a rent in the clouds and by its light they saw the race of the rising flood foaming between the banks of the canyon.

" It's so much higher and faster ! How quickly the level has risen ! "

" That's what happens. In a few hours—less—every spruit in Velaba can become a raging torrent, every causeway impassable, every road a quagmire. But, when the sun shines again, the spruits and rivers go down amazingly fast, and, with chains on our wheels, we can be on our way."

She laughed softly.

" I seem to think that's where we came in."

" Yes, Likwezi, it is. The worst has happened. For at least twenty-four hours we'll be unable to cross the Hlaru. You are Camp-bound."

She put up her hand and touched his cold wet cheek. She felt him smiling.

" It still tingles," he said.

" I won't do it again—unless you give me cause."

" What cause did I give you before ? "

" You compared me with—with——"

" With Tombazane. That was bad of me. But I didn't
want to face the truth."

" What is the truth ? "

She looked up at him, her face small and wan in the diffused
light of the moon veiled by drifts of scurrying cloud. Her
soaking hair was swept back, and the rain—light now—fell
softly on her skin.

His hands clenched and his smile faded. " You know the
truth. Don't make me say it."

She laid her palms against his broad bare chest and felt the
heavy pounding of his heart. She heard the rain and the river,
the dripping leaves all round them, and the beat of her own
pulses singing in her ears. Her arms went up and round his
neck.

" We can't pretend any more, Rusty—not any more."

He held her to him. The chill of her firm body through the
rain-drenched shirt was pain against his skin, the indefinable
scent that clung about her, heightened by damp, hurt his
senses with its stinging fragrance.

" This is love . . . this is the only truth, my darling."

Despair was in his voice as well as wonder, and a deep knowledge of betrayal ached beneath his bitter joy in this woman
who was going to be his brother's wife.

26

Saul

IN the mad moment when Andrew Miller had driven his jeep
on to the flooded Hlaru causeway it seemed to Sergeant van
Wyk that everything happened at once. It was all—and then
nothing. The bandits' Sten gun spluttered into silence, their
spot-light, evidently struck by one of his bullets, blew out,
and then he realized that the pick-up had somehow got on to

firmer ground and was limping over the rise. It was then that a flash of lightning revealed the jeep being whirled downstream, and another showed her sinking beneath the rushing water. There was a roll of thunder and then a hiatus in the storm during which he heard the fading sound of the truck's engine, the steady beat of the rain and the surge of the swollen river.

What to do? He was trapped between the Seekoei and the Hlaru Rivers, both in spate, and although Camp Two was only about twenty miles south-east of the causeway there was no means of getting there until the floods subsided. Fortunately he had a small supply of tea, biscuits, tinned milk and *biltong* in the Land Rover in case of emergencies, and there was certainly no shortage of water. Brandy he did not carry because it was against his principles to drink hard liquor under the noses of his men to whom it was forbidden. He resigned himself to the prospect of waiting for Nature to take its course. His *ouvrou* would worry, he thought with satisfaction. His *ouvrou* was always the better for a bit of anxiety on his account. Her temper was sweeter and her cooking spicier every time he returned 'from the dead'. Keep them guessing—that was the secret of success with women—and there was no doubt about it, his *ouvrou* was kept on the hop. Even here in the *bundu*, where crime was raw and unsophisticated, you could never be sure what next.

" We'll go back a little way and find a place for the night," he told his constables. " At dawn we'll think again." He spoke in Afrikaans. He did not believe in pandering to their ignorance by talking their baboons' language as Mr. Miller did. A good native constable must know how to speak and write Afrikaans, and, if he had a little English up his sleeve as well, so much the better.

" Baas Miller and his Game-guards will feed the crocodiles," said the older of the two constables. He spoke with the reverence accorded to the recently deceased, but the Sergeant only frowned and snorted. Jason was inclined to be cheeky, and it annoyed the Sergeant that the bandits had given them the slip. True, he had other fish to fry, but it would have been a fine feather in his cap if he could have popped the bandits into the pan as well.

" I saw the heads bobbing on the water when the jeep sank," went on the constable called Jason. " And then they were sucked under. Gone."

Van Wyk knew that Jason was a man of the Crocodile Clan and that he probably hoped to gain some vicarious benefit from this involuntary sacrifice to the spirit of his ancestors, which owed nothing to his own initiative.

" Baas Miller is Inyanga, the Wizard," he said. " He will cheat the crocodiles, who will be much displeased when they have to put up with black meat instead of white."

He only hoped he was right. But he had every reason to fear that the crocodiles would indeed feast upon the Game-warden. He had seen Andrew Miller fall forward over the steering wheel like a man mortally wounded, and only one of the Almighty's swiftest and strongest angels could have whipped him out of those rapids in time to save his life.

The Angel of the Lord, in this case, wore the face of Saul.

The current that drowned the young native, James, who could not swim, swept Andrew and Saul towards a floating branch being carried in the direction of the bank. Saul, a powerful swimmer, caught hold of his wounded master and managed to grasp and cling to the branch and help Andrew to do the same. The branch was borne round the bend in the river where it became wedged against an overhanging partly submerged willow bough. They hung on to it, gasping for breath, as small animals and reptiles floated past them on the breast of the torrent.

The cold water that had taken the life of young James had served to revive Andrew and sluice the wound in his shoulder. The arc of the Sten gun's fire had been high, missing his heart but shattering his shoulder-blade as the jeep was swung round on the causeway.

Presently, supported by Saul, he managed to drag himself along the willow bough and on to the bank. There they found themselves in a muddy hippo-path through the reeds. They crawled up the well-trampled track into the shelter of a big sycamore-fig where Andrew collapsed in a trance of pain and exhaustion.

" It's my shoulder," he said faintly, as he regained consciousness. " Try to stop the bleeding, Saul."

" Yes, Nkosi. Rest now."

Saul's sheath-knife was still in his belt, and he cut away the legs of Andrew's trousers above the knee. One of these he tore into long strips to serve as a bandage and a sling, and the other he cut and folded into thick pads. He gently removed the wet blood-stained bush-jacket from the left shoulder, but even then it was impossible to see the extent of the damage. Saul could only feel the broken skin and bone and the warm gush of blood. Thus guided, he placed the pads firmly over the wound and tied them in place with the dexterity of the born craftsman. With Andrew's canvas belt and the strip of khaki he contrived a sling to take the weight of the useless arm.

Andrew stifled his groans as best he could while the old Bantu tried to make him comfortable. If only he had a cigarette ! He'd give his birthright for a smoke ! He was soaking wet and his teeth chattered uncontrollably with cold, shock and pain. Oh, God, he was going to faint again. He heard Saul speak to him in the resonant Bantu language, but his voice came from far away, and, as the world of pain and storm receded, Andrew felt the big native gather him into his arms and warm him with the dark warmth of his own body.

For four years these two had been inseparable companions of the veld. Saul had been Andrew's protector and mentor, for he had been wise in the ways of Nature before the Game-warden had been born. Andrew had never hesitated to ask his advice and had often deferred to his judgment. He understood Saul's superstitious fears in certain matters and he was always eager to learn from him about the medicinal properties of trees and plants. There was between them that intimate, almost mystical, relationship which exists between master and man who respect one another and share daily perils as a matter of course.

Gradually Andrew's shivering ceased and Saul realized that he had fallen into a feverish fitful doze. At dawn the big Bantu released himself from his cramped position. The wind had dropped but the rain fell steadily.

Andrew stirred and groaned. As he woke he saw Saul standing near him.

" I am going to seek healing leaves, Nkosi. And I will go
back along the river to the causeway to see if the police Land
Rover is still on the other side."

" No ! " The exclamation was smothered in a cry of pain
as Andrew made a quick move to stop Saul.

" But the Sergeant will fear that you are dead, Nkosi."

" Never mind. Dead men tell no tales."

Andrew felt light-headed. The pain was an animal gnawing through his shoulder. Who was it that carried a fox
hidden under his tunic and the fox gnawed through to his
vitals ? Where were your vitals anyway ? In the region of
your heart or of your stomach ? His back, chest and arm
burned and throbbed with the ravages of this animal who was
silently devouring his shoulder. He must get away from here
—get to Camp Two—to Rusty and Alice. He must warn
Alice of some unknown danger, and he must get help for himself. He must get there before Sergeant van Wyk, before the
causeway became passable.

" We have a trek to make," he said. " Help me up. We
are going to walk to Camp Two."

With Saul's aid he rose unsteadily to his feet. Images
danced before his eyes in the grey light. Thea holding the
leather frame with Alice's photograph. "You can't see the
thoughts behind brown eyes . . . they keep their secrets . . ."
Scenes of carnage left by the *biltong*-bandits—" Man, it looks
like a bloody battlefield . . ." The chase, the shots, the
searing pain, the pull of the current wrenching at his wounded
shoulder . . . still wrenching. There was nothing more he
could do about the bandits now. The rest was up to Duikers'
Drift. If they were guarding the Johannesburg road in the
south they might pick them up. The bandits didn't matter
to him any more, they'd done their dirty work, he hadn't been
able to stop that. But the police would get them—surely the
police would get them—" We overcome our difficulties, Mr.
Miller . . . we apprehend our criminals . . ." The echo of the
Sergeant's voice rumbled in his ears. What did the Sergeant
want with Alice Lang ? What could he possibly want ? Alice
. . . Alice . . .

Andrew swayed on his feet, gaunt and deathly in the dawn
light. His blue unshaven cheeks were sunken, his lips were

grey, the blood-stained bush-jacket hung loosely over his left shoulder. Saul drew it carefully aside and saw with relief that there was no fresh blood oozing through the improvised bandage.

"You are weak, Nkosi. You have lost much blood. It will take all day to reach Camp Two."

"We must start at once. Remember, Saul, a man with a purpose is never weak. His purpose—if it is strong—lends him its strength. I have a purpose. I intend to be at Camp Two before dusk."

The old Bantu shook his head. Inyanga was boasting to make himself brave. When a man was afraid he threatened and bragged, and his proud words, winged with false courage, bore him up. Perhaps, therefore, it was well that Inyanga should boast of the strength of his purpose, for there was little strength left in his body. Too much blood had flowed away on the waters of the Hlaru River.

But, as Andrew spoke of his purpose, it became a living power in him, and Saul saw his face change from death to life. Andrew said :

"We can take the shorter path along the river bank, or we can follow the car track. Which is it to be ? "

"Let us follow the car track. Nkosi. Someone may pass that way. Also on the car track we can walk side by side. On the river path we must go singly, and in the country of the lion, two pairs of eyes are better than one."

"Good. It shall be so. And these are my orders. The left side of the track belongs to you. The right belongs to me. If we meet a lion and there is a tree on your side and not on mine, so much the better for you ; if the tree should be on my side and not on yours, the luck is mine. But first we must drink at the river."

While Andrew knelt painfully at the water's edge to drink, Saul remained close by him, watching the river and the reeds, and when the Game-guard took his turn, Andrew stood sentinel. Although the level of the water was high it already seemed to Saul to flow a little less wildly. But the rain would continue to feed it. Until the rain had ceased for a day or more it would be impossible to cross.

Will-power, Andrew told himself as they began their trek.

With enough will-power a man can accomplish anything. A cigarette—what wouldn't he give for a smoke! Saul had found and collected certain herbs and these he gave to his master.

" Chew them, Nkosi. The juice is bitter but it will ease the pain."

But, as the pain gradually withdrew, Andrew was overwhelmed with drowsiness.

" No," he said thickly. " This *muti* is like the bite of a cobra—it makes a man sleep. It becomes hard to walk, hard to keep awake."

By noon they had only travelled a few miles, with constant rests, and Saul realized that his master could go no farther. They stopped under the dripping leaves of a big ntoma tree with a grass-grown antheap at its base. The rain had ceased. Andrew looked up at the little starry white flowers and said, " This tree bears the female flowers. We have come to the mother tree, Saul." He found curious comfort in the thought.

Andrew knew the place well. Under this tall tree he and Saul had often rested and exchanged confidences during their long treks through the Sanctuary. From here to Camp Two was at least fifteen miles, and he was forced to admit that even the strength of his purpose could not drive him on. Under the loose bush-jacket fresh red blood was staining the khaki pads, dizziness seized him and let him go, and when he looked about him the misty thornveld seemed to expand and contract as if the winding watery coils of the Hlaru River crawled over it, constricting and releasing a scene so familiar, yet suddenly strange to him. Hlaru, the Python, was dangerous today.

" A python is crushing my shoulder, Saul. He has broken my bones."

" A man cannot walk and also struggle with a python, Nkosi. I will leave you here and go on alone. By myself, I can run. I will reach Camp Two and return with help before darkness falls. Here is your revolver. The bullets are still in your pocket. See, I will load it."

Andrew made a supreme effort to assert his authority.

" You must take the revolver. There are many lions in this district."

Too many lions. Again and again the Sanctuary Trustees

had urged him to thin out lion in the Hlaru strip, but he had fought the decision, insisting that the balance of nature be left undisturbed in Velaba as far as was reasonably possible. But now he could see the charts on the walls of his office. They haunted his feverish imagination. " Density of Game and Carnivora in the Hlaru Strip." Too many lions . . .

" You must take the revolver," he repeated.

" I am of the Lion Clan," said Saul. " I eat the flesh of the lion and gain his power. I have lion *biltong* in my pocket now. I will be safe with my knife, Nkosi."

He put the loaded revolver on Andrew's lap and folded the limp fingers of the right hand gently round the butt.

" Nkosi, you must keep awake. You must grow as many eyes as a spider in your head, so that you may see on all sides of you. A man in the grip of a python dare not sleep."

Vaguely Andrew saw the dark face bent over him, the wise, troubled, slightly protruding eyes with the yellowish whites, and then the face receded and the figure of the Game-guard was loping down the muddy track with the long loose-limbed jog-trot that he would keep up most of the way to his goal.

Andrew's fingers tightened on the butt of the revolver. So Saul had refused to obey his orders. He had left his only sure protection against lion. Obstinate old devil—as obstinate as Rusty—but then they were both men of the Lion Clan—Saul and Ratau. Too many lions in the Hlaru Strip . . .

Early in the afternoon the sun broke weakly through the clouds. Saul slowed down to a walk as he chewed some of the sweetish dried lion-meat that he always kept in his pocket. Now that the sun was out there would be animals on the move —possibly lion—hungry lion. He must do as he had told his master to do and grow the many eyes of the spider so that nothing could creep up on him unseen. He must listen for every sound with the sharp ears of a zebra sentry.

Suddenly Saul stopped and stood still in the pale watery sunshine. His head was raised and pressed slightly forward as he strove to catch the purr of an engine on the road ahead of him. There was a fork in the road some three miles on. Which way would the car go? Saul implored the spirits of his ancestors to direct it well. With relief, almost sickening in its intensity, he heard the harsh motor of the Camp lorry come towards him, and saw it round the bend of the track. There were chains on the heavy double tyres, and at the wheel was the brother of Inyanga with Nimrod and the dog, Smokey, beside him.

Rusty brought the lorry to a stop beside the bedraggled weary old Bantu.

" Saul, what are *you* doing here—alone ? Where is my brother ? "

" Nkosi, your brother awaits you under the big ntoma tree. He has been shot, but he lives."

" Shot. Oh, my God ! Get in quickly, and tell me everything as we go. Nimrod, get in the back."

As they drove along the muddy track Saul explained all that had happened. ". . . he is very sick, Nkosi. He has lost too much blood."

When they reached the tree they saw Andrew sprawled across the grass slope of the antheap. There was something very frightening to Rusty about his brother's attitude. It seemed to him to be twisted, helpless and vulnerable. Was he asleep ? Had he lost consciousness ? The third possibility he refused to consider. Guilt, love and terrible anxiety possessed him as he sprang to Andrew's side and leaned down and put his broad hand over his brother's heart. He looked up at Saul. " His heart is beating."

Saul nodded. " We can save him, Nkosi."

Andrew's pain-filled eyes opened slowly, and gradually Rusty's features came into focus. They were part of a dream. They would dissolve and fade. But this time there was the deep, well-known voice as well.

" Take it easy, Andrew, old boy. We'll soon have you at Camp Two—safe and comfortable."

" You . . . Rusty ? Really . . . you ? "

" Really me. Let us help you now."

" First I have to know something . . ."

" What do you have to know ? "

" Is she there . . . at Camp Two ? "

Rusty looked down at his brother with love and compassion, as he said quietly :

" Yes, Andrew. Alice Lang is at Camp Two. She is waiting for you."

" Thank God.   Give me a cigarette, Rusty."

Rusty smiled.   " That's a good sign.   Sure, I'll light you a cigarette right now.   Then you'll have to grit your teeth. Getting you to the lorry is going to hurt."

27

" *This is How We Meet . . .*"

WHEN the sun came out Philemon took a deck-chair to the height above the canyon.

" This place, Nkosikasi ? "

Alice nodded.   She wanted to think.   She had been relieved when Rusty had said that he must make a tour in the lorry.

" My report on the state of Sanctuary communications requires some personal investigation after the rains.   Will you come with me ? "

" No, Rusty.   I want to be by myself for a little while."

" I'll be gone a couple of hours."

She had smiled in a mature, almost maternal, way that he had resented.   " I can wait."

" I believe you can ! "

He had wanted to take her in his arms, but she had held him from her with an expression in her brown eyes that he did not understand.

" I don't know you any more, Likwezi.   You've turned into a stranger.   You do that.   One moment I think that I know you better than I have ever known anyone in my life, and the next you are far away.   When I touch you I know every sensation that goes through you, your thoughts and fears, the things that make you want to laugh or cry, the things that please or excite you, and then suddenly you slip away and go back into your corner.   You lean your glossy black head against the window of ' Sweet Sue ', and you are a thousand miles distant—six thousand—in England again, for all I can tell."

He had left her then with the hurt angry look that made his face so boyish.   *When I touch you I know you . . .* ah, Rusty, but when you touch me I no longer know myself. Everything becomes different—vibrant, Pagan, frightening. *The sun shall not strike thee by day, nor the moon by night.* I've had too much sun and moon these last few days, too much storm, too much Nature.

She lay back in the deck-chair and listened to the tumult of the river. The cicadas shrilled once more in the trees, and frogs croaked. The earth and grass smelt delicious, and the whole bushveld steamed softly in this pale sunshine that was the tender aftermath of the rain. Just for a few hours the sun had ceased to be ferocious, it was kind. Every leaf and blade of grass sparkled and the sky with its banners and tatters of cloud was a pure washed blue. Weaver-birds twittered in the willows, and here and there some little hen complained shrilly because the nest she was offered by her mate was not to her taste.

Here, last night before the storm, Alice had believed that she hated Rusty. She closed her eyes and her cheeks burned as she recalled the hot uprush of shame and rage that had caused her to lose her temper and strike him like an undisciplined schoolgirl in a panic at the force of passions unguessed at in herself. We hate what we fear, Rusty had said yesterday —only yesterday?—after Ndlovukasi had given her the lion's claw. Could it be that she had feared his effect upon emotions grown suddenly unstable? They were like caged birds set free without any preparation, singing and swooping in an element foreign to them and fraught with danger, taking fright and enjoying their freedom by turns. She reflected sadly that emotions so uncontrolled were doomed to destruction, and she wondered at herself, this new passionate wayward self whose existence she had never even suspected

She took the claw from her handbag and held it in her palm —the curved sickle of yellowish unpolished horn that was her amulet against evil. What had the Maker of Lions said when she had presented it with such impressive dignity? Rusty had refused to translate the incantation, or the blessing— or, perhaps, the warning. Why? Suddenly Alice shivered. This was the land of magic. It was a land where you might lose your way. How strange last night had been! That angry scene, then the storm with its unbridled fury, the lightning that had struck the old baobab and those who dwelt among the branches, and Rusty's kindness—the kindness that had melted her terror into tears. They had run, light-hearted as children, into the cool life-giving rain and they had come here as if to an ancient trysting-place, and then, with the spell of his kindness still upon her, she had invited the admission of his love.

Kindness. Had she needed kindness so much ? Was kindness the true key to love ? If that were so, then Andrew had given her love and kindness in full measure—with his letters, his patient understanding, and his warm response when at last she was free. He had given her trust, too. Rusty had never trusted her. He had sought motives in her actions, for the poison of an old wound still tainted his simplicity. Andrew loved her for the qualities with which his lonely heart had endowed her—strength of character, courage to remain at her post, devotion to duty, whereas Rusty had recognized the strength in her only to suspect it. He had thought her capable of anything—even of coming all the way to Africa to spring the trap she had set slowly and carefully for his brother. With his earthy Pagan outlook and his sheer physical magnetism, he had discovered her weakness—the remembered thrill of his presence passed over her skin like a night-breeze—he had wakened pent up, dormant desires that had found a dangerous outlet in perils and experiences shared with him alone, in quiet moments of inevitable intimacy, in accidental contacts of skin that had later been sought. I've been intoxicated, she thought, drunk on freedom, drunk on sunshine and moonlight. I still am, but now I know what is wrong with me.

She felt herself to be unarmed in a borderland of great physical and spiritual danger, poised on the razor's edge between two worlds, between the past and the future. She recalled the first night in the aeroplane when darkness had shown her a trail of sparks flowing from the engine under the wing. She had thought with panic that the aircraft was on fire and a crash imminent, but the blonde air hostess had laughed and reassured her. She needed someone to reassure her now. If only Betty were here. It would be so easy to unload her heart to Betty, and her friend would examine her problem and explain her to herself. Betty would advise her with the ruthless candour that was the backbone of their friendship. There were no secrets between her and Betty. . . .

No secrets? Alice clasped her hands suddenly over her eyes. No, she could never say that again. That moment of perfect frankness was past. There *was* a secret between her and Betty—a terrible frightening secret, one so dark that it could never be shared.

She looked down with a gasp of alarm as a trilling mew sounded at her feet, and the next instant the sleek black cat had jumped on to her lap. She laughed shakily, grateful to see a cat and not a leopard.

" Hullo, Lucky ! It's good to find an ordinary animal in Velaba." She stroked the smooth coat and the cat began to purr. " But are you an ordinary animal ? Does such a thing exist here ? Or are you the familiar of some sorceress as black as yourself ? "

Lucky settled herself into the broad brooding attitude of a hen on a nest or a sphinx on the desert and made no answer.

" Cat," said Alice. " There are two men in my life. One is flesh and blood, and the other, so far, exists only on paper. If you are truly the familiar of a sorceress—of someone like Ndlovukasi, the Maker of Lions—you will substantiate my paper lover and bring him to me. I need him very much, Cat. I don't know truth from illusion any more."

Lucky purred on a louder note.

Andrew. Early this morning Alice had expected to hear his voice on the radio telephone, but Maxim, his house-boy, had spoken instead to say that his master had gone on night patrol with Sergeant van Wyk and that they had not yet returned. Rusty had also failed to make contact with Jan Nelmapius at Camp One, but Inspector Banks from Duikers' Drift Police Station had come through telling him to contact Duikers' Drift again at 8 p.m. on the usual Sanctuary wavelength when there might be further news.

Rusty had turned to Alice. " If Andrew and van Wyk have been caught by the storm between the Seekoei and the Hlaru they'll be stuck till the floods subside."

" Could they be in any trouble ? "

" On night patrol you can always be in trouble. They may

have gone after the *biltong* bandits—and those men are thugs. But Andrew and van Wyk are a tough pair."

Andrew tough? Andrew, who never killed any living creature except to release it from suffering. Somehow she found it hard to think of him as tough. The word fitted his brother.

Alice sighed and rose to her feet, spilling the cat out of her lap.

The sun was low and in the distance she could hear the lorry returning. Rusty had been gone two hours. It was the only time they had been separated—with the exception of the afternoon on which he had tracked the Rogue. How petrified she had been then—how anxious for his sake! Or had she been afraid chiefly for herself, scared of being stranded in the wilds with only a Bantu man and girl whose language she could not speak?

She looked down at the cat weaving round her legs. Do I face the motives for my actions? she wondered. Or do I dress them up to please my self-esteem? I have never indulged in self-analysis, I've been too busy all my life. Nurses don't have much time for contemplation, not even on night duty when the ward is dark and quiet except for the restless moaning of someone in pain or dreaming unhappily. The pool of light on the nurses' table doesn't often fall on the open pages of a novel; it falls on records and charts to be written up. We work and we play—oh, certainly, most of us play in our off-duty hours—and we go to bed dead tired with feet and legs that ache like an over-exercised athlete's.

The cat trilled. Too bad—it seemed to say.

Alice looked across the foaming river to the mountains. She could see the thin milky threads of waterfalls in the clefts of the range, and the trees along the spine were clearly etched against the glowing sky.

She heard the lorry draw up outside the Game-warden's house, but she did not go to meet Rusty. He would come to her here. She wanted to preserve this moment of peace for as long as possible. It had assumed for her the threatened beauty of the impala at the water-hole, ignorant of the snake or the leopard crouching watchful on an overhanging bough.

She heard his step, but it was so quick and urgent that she hardly recognized it. She turned towards him and her heart contracted.

His face was ghastly, his usual healthy tan had lost its glow and his eyes were sick with misery.

" Rusty ! What is it ? "

He took both her outstretched hands in his. " Alice, I have a shock for you—a dreadful shock. We found Andrew—shot up and horribly knocked about—some fifteen miles from here. We've brought him back—he's alive——" His voice shook and he turned his head away, his face working. That frightful journey home, with his brother lying in the back of the lorry—perhaps dying in the arms of Saul—had been a nightmare of dread and horror. " He's under morphia. I had my first-aid kit in the lorry—I always carry it in case of emergencies—and when we picked him up he was in cruel pain—had been for hours. I gave him an injection . . ."

Andrew—Andrew here ? Wounded, perhaps desperately ! She swayed on her feet, pale and trembling. Her momentary faintness seemed to brace Rusty and she felt his grip shift and tighten on her wrists.

" Listen, this is up to you ! We can't get him a doctor for forty-eight hours at best, and I don't know what to do for him. You *must* take charge. You're not a woman now, you're Sister Lang. And don't forget it ! No matter what you think or feel when you see him—you are Sister Lang—the boss ! "

Power flowed through his hard forceful hands and his will conquered her weakness. Her head lifted and her face changed under his eyes, gathering its strength.

" Come," she said.

They walked across the compound together, her step brisk and purposeful beside his long stride. She was Sister Lang going on duty in an emergency. He led her into his *rondavel* and she saw the form lying on the bed—quite still, as still as death. She looked down at the man who lay there—at the long, quiet limbs, the fine head with the dark hair streaked with grey, the closed waxen lids under dark level brows and the gaunt sunken features. It was a face of shadows and hollows, sensitive and strong, fine-drawn by strain and suffering—a hitherto unseen yet deeply familiar face. She saw the blood-soaked bandages under the open bush-jacket, the grimy sling holding the wounded arm and the long sinewy fingers of the limp left hand.

She knelt by the bed and laid her cheek against his breast, hearing the quick light beat of his heart. The tears gathered in her eyes and throat and the nurse was lost utterly in the grief of the woman and her memory of the long lonely years of their need for one another.

" It's you——" she whispered, " you—and this is how we meet . . ."

Rusty's voice was sharp. " We must do what we can for him before the morphia wears off."

As Alice stood up the nurse took charge, outwardly calm and reliable, responding faithfully to the demands of the situation. Rusty marvelled at her competence, at the quiet exactness of her orders, at the neat manner in which she removed the rough makeshift bandages and exposed the ugly wound. She's hard again, he thought, hard as nails ! And he thanked God for it. He could not guess at the horror and distress she was fighting down like nausea. Don't let him die, don't let it end like that ! Let me help him now as he has helped me through so many hard times at home, let me do the right things for him . . . please . . .

" What happened, Rusty ? Do you know ? "

He told her Saul's story while together they disinfected and dressed the wound and did all that was possible to make Andrew warm and clean and comfortable.

Sometimes he moaned, but the pain that had gnawed at his shoulder during the bitter hours of darkness and the feverish endless day had released its hold at last. He was aware of voices and figures, of gentle hands on his body, of brandy on his tongue, of warmth and comfort and an overpowering desire to sleep and never wake again. But deep down he knew that there was something important that must be done before he could allow himself to sink into this sea of oblivion in which he longed to drown. There was something he had come here to do, something which dared not wait. He did not want to open his eyes and float to the surface of consciousness and wake the sleeping pain, he only wanted to go on drowning. But there was a reason why he should not drown, one that had already saved him from such a fate. He groaned aloud and lifted his right hand to his head; he drew it down his face and felt the rasp of his unshaven cheek and chin. What was it he had come here to do? He tried to say something. Rusty—where was Rusty?

But it was the clear soft English voice that rang like a bell through his clouded brain.

" Try to lie still, Andrew. Try to sleep. You are safe here with Rusty and me. Go to sleep . . . sleep . . ."

The low voice, in spite of its lullaby quality, brought him back to his surroundings with a movement that was the re-birth of pain. He opened his eyes and saw her sitting at his bedside. Her cool hand had taken his very gently and her soft dark eyes looked down at him. How sad they were—her eyes—how beautiful. Echoes sounded through the confusion of his mind . . . " brown eyes keep their secrets . . ." But wait, it was coming back—it was all coming back . . .

Alice glanced across at Rusty, who sat on the opposite side of the bed with his back to the window. Her lips formed the words, ' He's waking '. She saw the little lines deepen between Andrew's brows and the grey eyes begin to clear. She had seen it hundreds of times—this process of coming to, this gradual return to reality. She knew every sign, every step of the way. Some came back reluctantly, they clung to the mists and refused to wake, while others forced themselves towards consciousness, bringing their pain and their problems with them. Why was Andrew driving himself so hard—past fear of pain, past exhaustion, past the drowsy effect of morphia?

His gaze began to focus, there was the dawn of recognition in his eyes and a faint, slow smile

" Alice . . . at last . . ."

" Yes, Andrew."

" To meet like this . . ." The smile twisted a little. " Not the way we planned."

" Nothing is quite as we planned."

How sad her eyes were. " Never mind . . . Alice . . . darling." His voice was stronger, the words less slurred.

" He looks better," Rusty said.

But Andrew hardly heard his brother. He did not try to

turn his head. He saw only the girl whose hand was on his, the girl of the letters and the photograph who was more beautiful than he had dreamed. His doubts and misgivings dissolved and faded at sight of her, and he was sure that all his life had led up to this painful, poignant moment, to this woman.

Her smile trembled at the left corner of her mouth. He had not known about that lip—it's slight weakness. He loved it.

She murmured, " Hush now, close your eyes, we can talk later."

" There is something I must remember . . ."

" Don't worry. It's not important. Nothing is important except that you should rest."

Rusty said, " Look old boy, you've been shot through the shoulder by the damned *biltong*-bandits. You and van Wyk were in a skirmish——"

" Van Wyk ! Is he here ? "

" No. He's stuck on the other side of the Hlaru."

Andrew's eyes had come alive. Rusty's words had brought him back to the present with all its significance.

" Van Wyk—that's it. Alice, I came to warn you——"

" Warn me, Andrew ? But why ? "

" Van Wyk—the police—are interested in you—asking questions. Why, in heaven's name, should the police want to know your movements, Alice ? "

The colour had drained from her face and lips and he felt her hand withdraw itself from his. The room was very still. The golden light of evening fell in a long level shaft through the open window on to her bowed head. She looked terribly alone, as if she had deliberately set herself apart. Her silence and her air of guilt and defeat caught at his heart. She had carried her own burdens and the burdens of others for too long. He was with her now to share this new trouble. And then, with one of those strange flashes of insight that sometimes come in moments of pain, danger, hunger or great sorrow, the answer to his question was engraved on Andrew's mind before she could utter it.

He saw his brother rise and cry out as if he had been wounded.

" Alice ! "

It was impossible to see Rusty's face against the light, but Andrew knew that there was dread in it, and the pity that had welled up in him for Alice reached out to embrace his brother. Rusty said :

" What could the police want you for, Alice ? "

She rose to face him across Andrew's body. Her eyes met his with sad fatalism as she answered him in her clear, quiet voice :

" They could want me for murder, Rusty."

28

" We Have News for You "

IT was 8 p.m., the usual hour for inter-Camp communication, and when Rusty failed to get any reply from Nelmapius at Camp One or Sergeant van Wyk at Poinsettia he made contact with Duikers' Drift.

" Yes, Camp Two, I hear you loud and clear. Ranger Nelmapius is with me in my office at this moment," said Inspector Banks, who was in charge.   " And we have news for you."

" I have news here, too, Inspector.   My brother, Andrew, is in the Camp.   Shot through the shoulder.   He can't talk to you himself, because he's in a pretty poor state.   He's been in a show-down with the bakkie-bandits.   But I can give you most of the facts—partly from his version of the affair and partly from Game-guard Saul.   Over."

" I'm sorry about your brother.   Is there anything we can do ?   Get a doctor to advise you on the inter-com ?   Over."

" No, thanks.   Andrew will make out till we get him to Dr. Hurley at Poinsettia.   Over."

" Not as simple as that, Rusty.   I'm going to need Mr. Miller here as a witness as soon as he is fit to travel.   I'll get in touch with you about that again tomorrow.   In the meantime, tell us what happened as best you can.   We may be able to fill in a few gaps later.   Over."

Banks and Nelmapius listened as Rusty described the chase,

the loss of Game-guard James and the jeep in the river, the escape of the bandits, and the rescue of Andrew. He concluded : " We reckon Sergeant van Wyk is stranded between the flooded Hlaru and Seekoei Rivers. Over."

Banks said, " That accounts for our failing to contact him at Poinsettia. We knew yesterday evening that he was going on patrol with your brother. He asked us to keep an eye on the southern intersections leading to the Johannesburg road. So I can give you certain sequels to your story—just bare facts that'll probably be on the nine o'clock news tonight. Over."

" Carry on, please. Over."

" Over to Ranger Nelmapius," said Banks. " It's his story."

Nelmapius told Rusty most of what had happened from the time he and Sergeant Neethling had left Camp One up to the moment of catching up with the bandits at Boryslawski's farm. Then Banks took over.

" Neethling found guns and enough *biltong* for an army in that big hangar," he said. " He brought Anton Boryslawski and Marcus Gottlieb directly back here with the other prisoners and witnesses. Over."

Rusty asked : " Did you get any further evidence about the case of Amos ? Over."

" I prefer to say nothing about that for the present. Can you tell me the state of the river crossings ? Over."

" Unless there is more rain the causeways should be passable by noon tomorrow. Over."

" In that case van Wyk will probably show up at Camp Two soon afterwards. If he does, tell him to call me on the intercom at three p.m. for further instructions. Over."

" I'll tell him—if he turns up. In any case, I'll contact you at that time. Is that all ? Over."

" That's all for now. My compliments to your brother We hope he'll feel better in the morning. Out."

As Banks switched off Nelmapius rose and lit a cigarette. The events of the past twenty-four hours had shaken him.

" You didn't tell him about March," he said to Banks. " Why not ? "

The Inspector, who was as lean and dry as a strip of *biltong* himself, and almost as brown, cleaned his nails thoughtfully with his pen-knife.

" I thought that was better left. A good many people are involved in this business, and if any of them happen to be listening-in it's just as well to let them think the informer is still in a position to inform."

He opened a drawer and drew out a paper and pushed it across his desk to Nelmapius. " You've seen a copy of this, I suppose ? Neethling had one."

" Amos's statement ? "

" Mmn. We had the devil of a job getting it out of the poor bastard. One of our native constables dragged it out of him bit by bit with hours of patient questioning and signs for answers. But what we've got here fits in with our theories."

Nelmapius turned the typewritten paper over in his hands. It was signed with the careful childish signature which he knew well—the laborious script of his best Game-guard—but written with more than ordinary difficulty, unevenly, in the dark.

The brief statement, so painfully elicited, told a tale of treachery.

Amos had set out on patrol with March as usual, never guessing that his comrade was in league with the poachers. He had confided in March that he believed the Sweet Spruit to be a hiding-place for drying poached game-meat and smuggled guns. March had appeared to agree. They had camped between the old Chief's kraal and the Sweet Spruit, intending to examine the area thoroughly at daybreak. They had taken turns on watch during the night as was their custom when there was no effective *scherm* round the camp. While Amos slept March must have gone to warn the poachers. Amos woke in the moonlight and firelight to find himself surrounded by perhaps half a dozen men. Before he could reach for his rifle or his assegai they had overwhelmed him. They dragged him to the Sweet Spruit. He was sure that March was among them, and also the old Chief's Witch Doctor, and he thought he had recognized the Counsellor, but could not be sure. His recollections of the ghastly climax of his sufferings was mercifully confused. Job's story of finding him in a near-dead condition supplemented the tragic story.

Nelmapius handed the statement back with a sigh. " Amos didn't know March was making passes at Oasis."

" Black or white," said Banks, " it's always the same old plot with a few variations. The eternal triangle. That's life."

Yes, thought Nelmapius. That's life. Thea wanting Andrew Miller—me wanting Thea . . .

He said : " What beats me is why March turned Queen's Evidence. I don't get it."

Banks snapped the pen-knife shut and examined his nails without much interest. He rose and put a horny hand on the young Ranger's shoulder.

"Listen, man, here's a thing worth remembering. Sometimes a person has to choose between their fears. March was afraid of the police, but he was a lot more frightened of other things. If you could get into the black soul of a Nigger you'd be surprised at the snake-pit you'd find there—fears crawling over each other like a nest of bloody mambas, swallowing each other, poisoning each other. We'll probably never exactly know what made March fancy a term in gaol, but I can assure you he never meant to go back to Velaba. Whatever happened, he was through with Velaba. Now, go along and tell Game-guard Amos some news to cheer him up. God knows the poor beggar needs a bit of cheer."

The hospital was just across the road from the police station, but Nelmapius walked the short distance with lagging steps. He wished that he possessed Andrew Miller's experience of the Bantu mentality. Andrew would know just how to talk to this poor wretched boy.

A young nun with a pink face and extraordinarily clear blue eyes answered the door.

" We expected you, Mr. Nelmapius. Inspector Banks phoned us that you were coming and asked particularly that you be allowed to see Amos."

" How is Amos ? " he asked, following her into the hall. " I mean how is he taking this—*really* ? "

She paused under the large painted wooden crucifix with its perpetual reminder that our Lord's agony transcended anything the patients might be called upon to endure. She said :

" Physically he is doing well. He is a healthy lad, and he

should be quite out of danger by now. But when you ask me
how he is taking this tragedy, I find it hard to answer you.
These people are strange . . ."

She broke off. She had a soft Irish brogue, and he thought
that she had the same look of innocence that was so sweet in
Thea.

" What do you mean, Sister. That he doesn't want to
live ? "

She hesitated. The clear blue eyes were no longer young.
They were too experienced in the tortuous ways of human
suffering.

" Mr. Nelmapius, I have a curious feeling about Amos.
Perhaps I shouldn't say this to you——"

" Please go on."

" I have an idea that he is waiting for something . . .
before . . ." She brushed her hand across her eyes. " No,"
she said. " I'm foolish. Come with me. This way. Then
you can tell *me* how you find him."

" I have a good deal to say to him," said Nelmapius.

She glanced at a plain heavy wrist-watch, and he pictured
her taking pulses and temperatures with her innocent, yet
experienced, eyes on the busy little second hand.

" Half-past eight. Don't stay too long. It's been a great
strain for him—all those questions the police had to ask him—
on and on."

" I won't ask him questions."

Her white-clad figure glided ahead of him down the passage.
She seemed to Nelmapius to sail along like a swan. She
stopped at a door with St. Francis written over it.

" He's in a room on his own. It was easier for the police
that way." She opened the door and switched on the light.
" Go in, Mr. Nelmapius. I'll come back when time's
up."

Amos was propped up against stacked pillows. The room
was very narrow and the bed was against the wall opposite
the window. A mosquito-net was folded back behind his
head, there was a mug of lemon and barley water and a packet
of cheap cigarettes on the bedside table. A small cupboard
and a wooden stool completed the furniture.

As the light went on Nelmapius saw the blind, expression-

less face turn silently towards the sound of the closing door.
The young Bantu's eyes were bandaged and his skin no longer
resembled dark satiny wood carved with noble simplicity.
It had the texture and colour of clay. His long supple hands
lay limply on the coarse brown blanket and his striped hospital
pyjamas showed the bruised throat with the prominent Adam's
apple.

Nelmapius, who had known him as the lynx-eyed Game-
guard or the gay young jester with the guitar, felt a hot prickling
sensation behind his eyes. He caught his lip between his teeth
as he approached the bed on his soft veld-shoes. He knew by
the flicker of the Game-guard's swollen mouth that he had
recognized the familiar footfall. He drew up the wooden
stool and sat down, and gently placed a finger on Amos's arm.
As he felt the sudden flinching of the skin, he realized that to
the blind every unexpected physical contact must be a small
shock. He was upset and he found it difficult to steady his
voice as he said :

" Amos, they tell me you are doing well, but I mustn't stay
too long. Listen, then, because I have many things to tell
you."

He spoke in Afrikaans for Amos had a better knowledge of
that language than the Ranger had of the Bantu tongue. But
he spoke simply and slowly, for he knew that neither expression
nor gesture could help to make his meaning clear.

" First I must tell you that your wife and child are well.
Baas Rusty took them to the kraal of Ndlovukasi, the Maker
of Lions, and they are there with your parents. I was there
this morning and Oasis sent you many messages. She asked
me for two pounds as she had some debt she wished to pay
Ndlovukasi, and I advanced it to her——"

He broke off as Amos made a strange little sound in his
throat, and for an instant the dead-looking features quickened
into some semblance of life, even satisfaction.

" Then you must know that as soon as you are recovered
there will be work for you in the Sanctuary. I cannot say
exactly what, but there will be something to enable you to
earn your living."

Amos turned his head away, and Nelmapius felt that he
had failed to relieve the boy's mind. Instead he had struck

an invisible and unintentional blow straight at the empty sockets under the bandage.

This was difficult and harrowing. If only Andrew Miller were here. Or even Rusty. His hand flew to his shaven chin, and he thought with shamed relief that to Amos he would still be bearded and mature. He took a grip on himself. There were things he could tell Amos that it had not been possible to say over the radio telephone to Rusty.

" March admitted many things," he said. " He told us that the men who captured and wounded you wanted strong *muti* for the medicine-horn of the Chief. The Chief, he said, was not guilty of that evil thing. He wanted to go across the sea to consult a white doctor who would strip the film from his eyes and make him see again. But those near the Chief are ignorant men. They did not believe in the power of this white doctor, they still put their faith in the old bad magic."

A curious expression came into the Game-guard's sick face, almost one of contempt. For a moment it put Nelmapius out of his stride. Was it contempt for the ' old bad magic ' or for the Ranger's disbelief in it ? He was acutely aware of his inability to probe the Bantu mind. He went on :

" March spoke much. He confessed that he was helping the poachers. And then he asked Sergeant Neethling to take him away from Velaba and put him in gaol for a while."

Again there was the little sound in Amos's throat and the putty-coloured face changed almost imperceptibly. It was expectant, faintly smiling. Nelmapius recalled the nun's words, " I have an idea that he is waiting for something . . ." Suddenly, with his flesh crawling, Nelmapius knew what it was for which Amos waited. And, with the knowledge, the scene of March's death rose so vividly before the Ranger's eyes that it was almost manifest in the little room. As he described the brief drama Nelmapius had the curious impression that the young Game-guard was no longer blind, that he *saw* the lioness leap upon her victim and sink her teeth in the jugular vein. This is what he had been waiting for, thought Nelmapius. This is it ! And the goose-pimples rose on his arms.

As the Ranger finished speaking Amos gave a long surfeited sigh, and turned his face to the wall.

The young nun entered and made a sign that it was time for Nelmapius to go.

"Amos will sleep now," she said, and drew the blanket a little higher.

Jan Nelmapius said nothing. He knew that Amos had decided his own fate.

29

"We Are Not Your Judges!"

IT was after midnight when Andrew woke from the long sleep induced by morphia and exhaustion. The pain and the fever had abated, but it was a moment or two before he was fully conscious of his surroundings. By the moonlight streaming through the window he saw Rusty, dressed in grey flannels and a sports shirt, lying on a camp stretcher. Rusty was awake, and now he turned his head and smiled.

" Well—how d'you feel ? "

" Hungry," said Andrew.

Rusty called to Saul, who was curled up dog-like on a mat outside his master's door. The big Bantu entered, his protruding eyes blinking and swollen with sleep.

" Tell Philemon to get Nkosi a ham omelette and some tea —plenty of strong tea for both of us."

" Yeez, Nkosi."

As Saul went to the kitchen quarters Andrew said :

" I've had a bloody awful nightmare. I had to warn Alice that the police were after her——"

" You did that."

" Yes—but the rest. She said they could want her for . . . murder."

" She said that. I was here."

Andrew passed his right hand across his eyes. " She can't mean it."

" It's hardly something she'd say for effect."

Rusty got up and lit the lantern on the table in the middle of the room. He reached up and hung it on the chain suspended from the ceiling. Then he put the cigarettes and a lighter next to Andrew.

"Where is Alice?" Andrew asked.

"Asleep, I hope. She said I was to call her if you needed anything."

Andrew felt his rough cheek and chin. "I need a shave. But I can manage that for myself. Help me up, Rusty, and find me a toothbrush."

"Aren't you being a bit ambitious?"

"I can make out." But Andrew had to grit his teeth as his brother helped him to the bathroom.

"Shout if you want a hand," said Rusty. "You look damn groggy to me."

"I'm all right."

Andrew was stiff and shaky and sore all over. His shoulder hurt with every movement, but the throbbing agony had left him and his head was clear. His attempts to shave drew blood, but improved his confidence, and by the time he had washed and eaten he felt stronger. Nevertheless he was grateful to go back to the bed which Philemon had remade.

"Bring brandy and water," said Rusty, as Philemon cleared the table, "and sandwiches too. Has Nkosikasi had anything to eat tonight?"

"Yeez, Nkosi. Nkosikasi has wake up now and eat toast and tea."

"Good. Then that'll be all."

As the boy left the room Andrew said, "Have you talked to Alice about this—thing?"

Rusty lit his pipe. "No."

"What happened exactly? I'm still hazy about it."

"You were doped, old boy. But you got your message home all right. And then she said, quite calmly—numbly perhaps—'They could want me for murder'. But saying it did something to her—upset her badly—and she stumbled out of here before I could stop her and ran to her room. I went after her, but she wouldn't talk to me, just kept saying, 'Go back to Andrew, and call me if he needs anything'. It was quite useless to ask her questions then, and I didn't even try. When I came back here you were pretty muzzy and soon afterwards you were out for the count."

Philemon set the tray of drinks on the table and bade them good night, and Saul returned to his sleeping-mat. The night was very still, almost soundless, except for the voice of the river and the frogs. Even so, they did not hear Alice cross the stoep in her soft slippers. It was only when she knocked lightly and pushed open the fly-screen that they saw her looking oddly tall in her linen slacks and a striped blouse. As she came forward into the room her hair gleamed under the hanging lantern and her lips were red, but her face was deathly pale and her eyes were like scorched holes in a paper mask.

" Philemon told me you had had a meal," she said to Andrew. " He thought you were much better."

She came and took his wrist and he felt the coldness of her fingers. But they were steady and it was evident that whatever emotional storm she had been through she was now calm.

" Never mind about pulses and temperatures," he said. " I'm all right. Just tell me what you meant when you said——" He broke off. " Rusty, give her a drink."

She shook her head. " I don't want a drink." She moved over to the table and stood behind it facing them defensively. Rusty sat on the camp stretcher with his head in his hands, not looking at her.

" My mother didn't die of natural causes," she said slowly. " She died peacefully in her sleep of an overdose of a sedative." She faltered then. " I don't know—I can't imagine how anyone found out—or why . . ."

She swayed a little, and Rusty sprang to his feet.

" Sit down, Alice—don't stand there like that ! We are not your judges ! "

She sank into the cane chair he held for her and rested her elbows on the table.

" I suppose one makes enemies without knowing it," she went on quietly. " Real enemies. I never thought such a thing possible, never guessed it, but it must be so. I've turned it over and over in my mind—wondering *who* would want to start something." She pressed her fingers to her temples. She seemed to be thinking aloud. " Harriet—my half-sister— hated me, and when she knew about the special legacy—the two thousand pounds my mother had left me—she was beside herself. She attacked me then . . . but even so . . . even if she had some means of finding out what had happened that night, she must have *known* it was the most merciful thing—something to be grateful for. She *knew* my mother's terrible hopeless suffering, and she knew that I loved her." Her voice broke.

Andrew said gently. " Try to tell us exactly what happened, Alice. Perhaps we can find some way of helping you."

" This isn't fair to you. This horrible thing is no concern of yours."

" Perhaps I'd better decide that for myself."

Rusty had helped himself to a brandy. He had gone to the window as if he found it hard to breathe. He stood with his back to the room looking out at the moonlit compound. He seemed to accept the fact that this issue was between his brother and Alice Lang. On its outcome might depend the future of all three of them.

She said in a low voice. " I never wrote you very much about my life at home during those last few months. There seemed no point in harping on all the daily tragedies—because that's what they were."

" How strange, Alice. You didn't feel you wanted to confide in me or let me share your troubles—not even at the end when we were so much more than friends ? "

" I didn't want to bore you. Our letters were on another plane. They lifted me out of myself—out of my ordinary life into this magic place. I told you a little, of course—but only enough to make you see why I couldn't come to you—why I was needed at home."

He thought, that's what Thea said. You write to your intimate friends and relations as you talk—the ' every day grumbles and growls ', as she put it—but to a stranger you are on your Sunday best behaviour. His grey eyes were deeply hurt, as if her words had damaged the sincerity of their relationship.

" Don't misunderstand me," she pleaded. " I didn't want to spoil the thing between you and me with morbid miseries. You'll never know how much you helped me, Andrew. You made everything bearable. Towards the end my poor mother began to have fears and hallucinations. She thought everybody was against her—even me. It seemed best for me to go

away for a while. That was when I took my holiday in London
—just before she died. While I was away she had a day and a
night nurse, but she turned against them, too. She wanted
me back, she was so pleased when they left and I was home
again to take full charge of her. But it didn't last. The fears
and suspicions got hold of her again—as Dr. Manfield had
warned me they probably would. Sometimes I was desperate
for her sake—desperate for both of us."

" You poor girl. I read between the lines, but I didn't
guess how bad things were."

" Betty Swanson was the one person who really understood
everything. She even knew about you, Andrew. We were
intimate friends, and, whenever she could, she came to spend
a day or a night. It was always a tonic to me to have her at
the cottage. She came soon after I was back from my holiday.
She was there . . . that . . . particular night."

Down by the Hlaru River the frogs croaked, and somewhere
a lion roared, but Alice was no longer in Velaba. She was
back in the cottage swathed in the English mists of early
autumn, with a fire burning in the living-room, a kettle on the
hob, and Betty tuning in to the radio programme they both
wanted to hear. She was about to settle her patient for the
night before enjoying a late cup of tea and the play they had
selected.

" When I went upstairs I found Mother in one of her
frightened moods. When she was in that state she hated to
be given her injection." Alice pressed her knuckles against
her eyes as if to shut out the scene. " I can't tell you what it
was like to have to give it against her will—knowing what she
thought—what she dreaded. I had to make myself into a
machine to do it. She was so helpless and pathetic, so pitiable."
Her voice and her hands shook.

Rusty went to the table without a word and poured her a
drink and gave it to her. She took it from him and he held
his hand over hers for an instant to steady it and to raise the
glass to her lips.

" Go on. Drink some of this."

She did as he told her. Then she went on.

" It wasn't the first time I'd forced myself to do it—with
her looking at me as if I were a stranger and an enemy—but

that night it broke me. I knew that I could never bring myself to put that needle into her arm again—that we had come
to the end. I can hardly remember what happened after that.
I know I put everything away as I always did. It was automatic to tidy away the syringe and the kidney dish and throw
the empty vial and the cotton wool swab into the waste-paper
basket, but when I went downstairs I couldn't speak for sobbing. Betty jumped up and put her arms round me, she tried
to comfort me and get sense out of me. I must have been
completely incoherent."

Rusty bit his lip. He, too, had held this girl in his arms
and felt the pent-up force of her sobbing. His brother's
girl.

Andrew said, " This is terribly hard for you, Alice. But
try to go on, my dear."

" I remember Betty said, ' Don't worry, Alice. Pull yourself together while I run up and see to her. I know where
everything is, and she's always good with me.' When she
came down again I'd got a grip on myself. I'd made the tea
and turned up the radio play Betty had been listening to. She
just squeezed my hand and whispered that Mother was all
right—that she was asleep."

Alice drew a long sighing breath. " When I went to her in
the morning I couldn't wake her . . . she had gone in her
sleep . . ."

Andrew exclaimed, " But it could have happened any time—
you said so ! "

Rusty had turned his back to the window and was facing her.
" Why do you blame yourself? Why should anyone else
blame you ? "

She said slowly, " I know now that Betty never realized that
I'd given Mother that injection. She must have thought that
I hadn't been able to do it. I only made that discovery after
she'd gone back to London. I was tidying the medicine cupboard and I counted the little vials remaining in the carton.
There were only five left. There should have been six. Then
I knew what had happened. Betty had given a second injection. I went to look in the waste-paper basket to make
sure, but Mrs. Withinshaw had already emptied it. I didn't
know what to do—who to go to ! "

She sprang up and paced the room with quick distracted steps.

" I couldn't tell Betty ! How could I ? It would have been like telling her that she—oh, God——" She leaned against the table, her face buried in her hands. In a second Rusty was at her side, his arm about her shoulders.

" Steady, Likwezi ! Take it easy."

His touch and his voice restored her self-control.

" Between us I suppose we were guilty of criminal negligence —at best. It seemed to me that if the truth were to come out it could ruin Betty's career as a nurse. My own hardly mattered any more. But . . . there were worse implications . . . You must see that ! If Dr. Manfield had been there I think I could have gone to him and told him everything—asked his advice—but he was still away."

" There seemed no reason why anything should ever come out," said Andrew. " Strange that it did."

Alice went on, " That scene with Betty—when I broke down—it went round and round in my mind till I thought I was going crazy. Everything was my fault—my responsibility. I wanted to get away . . . quickly . . . quickly. That was when I sent you the cable, Andrew."

" I see. Yes, I think I understand. You wanted to get away from your memories and your fears—from yourself."

It wasn't that you wanted to come to me, he thought. It was just that you wanted to escape. I was your means of escape. That's all I've ever been. He felt cold and deadly tired, but he spoke with the calm authority Rusty knew well.

" You must go and get some rest now, and then you must write down exactly what you have told us. They'll want a statement from you, and you'd do well to have it ready. Rusty, go with Alice now, and see that she has writing materials— whatever she needs."

She went to Andrew's bed and took his hand and held it against her cheek. It was dry and burning.

" You're feverish again."

" I'm all right. Look after yourself now. Good night, my dear."

She looked down at him with a feeling of helplessness. She

bent and kissed his forehead, and then she followed Rusty from the room.

" Come in here," he said.

They went into the big living-room. The lantern on the stoep shone through the door on to the long wall where the Florentine picture had hung before the storm. Under the blank space it had left was Rusty's desk. He opened a drawer and took out some of the sheets of foolscap he used for his reports.

" Do you need pen and ink ? " he asked.

" I have a fountain pen."

" You'd better take a bottle of ink—in case you want it."

He put the ink bottle beside the sheaf of paper and leaned against the desk, facing the door. She saw his face grim and strained in the light of the lantern. He stretched out his arms to her and she went into them without a word. Here was strength and safety—only here.

" I believe in you," he said. " I want you to know that."

" Yes," she said. " I know."

30

The Moth

SERGEANT VAN WYK forded the Hlaru River when the noonday sun was at its height.

The floods had subsided, but the jade green water still raced over the stone causeway and there was a moment when he wondered whether, after all, he would not have been wiser to wait another hour. The fate of the jeep, and—as far as he knew—of the men in it, was still fresh in his mind. The Land Rover, however, made the crossing safely, and, with chains on the wheels, the Sergeant had no difficulty in negotiating the slushy road to Camp Two.

He travelled as fast as he could, and to hell with scaring the blasted animals. If it came to scaring, they could do their share all right ! He had dirty work to do and he wanted to get it over and go home and sleep in a warm bed with his *ouvrou* snoring peacefully beside him.

The Sergeant had had a day and a night in which to realize just how nasty a task lay ahead of him, and the more he reflected upon it the less the situation appealed to him. Thanks to the storm, the bandits had got away, and the Senior Game-warden had almost certainly lost his life, with a couple of Game-guards thrown in for good measure. But the Game-warden had asked for death by charging that flooded causeway like a maniac. He'd meant to get across at any price. And why? To catch the bandits? Or to hurry to Camp Two and warn Alice Lang that the police were on her track? A nice packet of trouble she was in for now—a charge of matricide hanging over her head and the news that her lover was drowned. Rusty would take that hard, too. He and his brother were very close—good friends as well as brothers.

Van Wyk did not notice the blossoming thornveld and the young green grass spring up all round him in the warm sunlight, he didn't even slow down to admire a pride of lions lying lazily in the shade of a yellow flowering cassia. He was absorbed with his professional problems. To take a statement on behalf of Scotland Yard from a young Englishwoman was outside his experience, and, in the circumstances, he had ceased to fancy that delicate job.

He drove through the gates of Camp Two and straight to Rusty's office. Nimrod, who was squatting in the shade of the blighted baobab, rose and saluted at sight of the police Land Rover. He was well acquainted with the two native constables—one of whom was rather a wag—and he looked forward to hearing their version of the exciting tale he had already heard several times from Saul.

Van Wyk sprang out of the Land Rover and up the steps on to the stoep. The swing-door of the fly-screen thudded to behind him, and he hurried into the Game-warden's office. Rusty came forward to meet him.

" So you're safe, van Wyk! The lions didn't get you."

" No, man, they didn't, but——"

" And you didn't get the bandits."

The remark annoyed van Wyk, which made him feel better.

" How the devil did you know about the bandits? "

" From Banks on the intercom. He wants you to stand by to talk to him at three o'clock this afternoon. Neethling stole your glory. He arrested them at Boryslawski's farm—and Boryslawski and Marcus Gottlieb, too. There's been quite a clean-up. Pity you weren't in at the kill."

Chagrin was written across the Sergeant's scowling face and Rusty relented. He opened a cupboard and took out tankards and a quart bottle of beer.

" I'll bet you're hungry, too," he said, as he filled the tankards.

" I could eat a bloody hyena. But, look here, Rusty man, I have to tell you some upsetting news. Your brother was with me on that patrol and when the rains broke he drove his jeep into the flood-waters of the Hlaru after the bandits and the jeep was swept away. Last thing I saw in a flash of lightning it was sinking like a stone. Your brother hadn't a hope in hell."

" My brother is all right, van Wyk. Game-guard James was lost, but old Saul saved Andrew's life. We picked them up yesterday evening a few miles this side of the Hlaru causeway. Andrew'd been shot through the shoulder-blade and he was in a poor way when we brought him here. But he's mending. He has a very good nurse in Alice Lang——"

" It's a bloody miracle ! " gasped van Wyk. He tossed back his beer and poured himself some more. " But now, as to this nurse, I have some business with her—not very nice business at that."

" Can it wait till you've had some food ? "

The Sergeant gave Rusty a sly searching look. " It's waited too long already. I'll get on with it right now."

" She's over at my house with Andrew. You'd better come with me."

They found Alice in the living-room with Andrew, who was dressed and lying on a divan. The black cat, Lucky, purred at his feet. Van Wyk was so genuinely relieved to see him alive that he hastened across the room and wrung his hand with a grip that made Andrew wince.

" Og, man, it's fine to see you ! I thought the crocs had made a meal of you."

Andrew grinned. " Saul helped me cheat them."

R—I

There was a pause as the Sergeant turned to see the slim dark girl who stood with her hands resting lightly on the back of a big armchair. She had a smooth olive skin, untouched by rouge, but her red lips were like a danger signal in her quiet face. Her eyes were as large and liquid as an antelope's and as wary.

"Alice," said Rusty. "This is Sergeant van Wyk from Poinsettia Police Post."

"Miss Lang——" The Sergeant looked unhappy. He hesitated with one enormous hand fidgeting with the briefcase he held under his arm.

She took the initiative.

"If you have anything to say to me, please say it in the presence of Mr. Miller and his brother."

So she *had* been warned? And she was a fighter. Van Wyk reckoned that he knew a fighter when he saw one. He preferred it that way. He would like to be a little angry with this girl, he would like to think the worst of her. He said with his rumbling Afrikaans accent :

"I am acting on behalf of Scotland Yard, Miss Lang. An enquiry is being made into the circumstances surrounding the death of Mrs. Mary Jane Harriet Lang, who died during the night of October the tenth of an overdose of morphine believed to have been administered by yourself, her daughter, Alice Mary Lang. Would you care to make a statement ? "

He added the usual warning that any statement she might make could be used in evidence.

"I have already written a statement, Sergeant van Wyk. It is on that desk."

His swarthy brows knitted and his face hardened. So she'd known what to expect. She'd cooked up her yarn—probably with the help of the man she hoped to marry. He began to feel much better.

Rusty handed him the sheets of foolscap covered with the neat unpretentious writing, and van Wyk sat down at the desk to read what Alice Lang had written.

She moved round and sank into the armchair with her head thrown back and her eyes closed. A pulse beat in her throat and the palms of her hands were damp. "We are not your judges," Rusty had said last night. But, in her own mind, they were. Andrew and Rusty were the only people in the world whose judgment really mattered to her. " I believe in you," Rusty had said. But would he go on believing, or would this big policeman find some way of shaking his faith ? In all her life she had never been in a situation as terrible as this. How could anyone think this dreadful thing of her ? *How could they ?* In London now they would be making their enquiries, no doubt —talking to Harriet and Cyril Carver, to Mrs. Withinshaw, to Dr. Manfield—or would he still be away ?—to Betty—Betty, who had no idea, who would wonder what in heaven's name had happened. Would Betty guess ? Would she realize that she was in danger of being accused of criminal negligence . . . unless . . . She shuddered with a spasm of cold that shook her whole frame. Suddenly she felt a hand on her shoulder, strong and firm. Rusty, ah Rusty. Warmth and strength returned to her.

Outside the cicadas shrilled and insects hummed drowsily in the midday heat. Across the compound the camp-boys were laundering sheets and towels and singing their repetitive African refrains in a monotonous minor key. Smokey came in and looked round for his master and flopped down at Rusty's feet.

From where he lay Andrew saw the others in profile. He wondered if Alice was fully aware of the extent of her danger, of the shocking charge towards which these enquiries were leading—the worst surely that any nurse and daughter could be asked to face. As for his own position—that, too, was difficult. Andrew could guess clearly enough where they would seek the ' motive ' for the . . . crime. He would owe it to Alice to go with her, to stand by her and help her with every means in his power. And afterwards they could make a life for themselves somewhere else—if there was an afterwards—they could go to Central Africa where he had already been offered a post in a great new scheme for the Preservation of Wild Life. He would not mind leaving Velaba now that it was to be opened to tourism. In fact, he had kept the Central African offer in his mind, hoping to interest Alice in its possibilities.

He saw van Wyk raise his massive head. The man looked as menacing as a buffalo with those mistrustful little eyes deep-set under the overhanging brow.

"I should like to clear up a number of points that are not dealt with in this statement, Miss Lang."

"I will help you if I can." Her heart had begun to race. His tone was uncompromising.

"I shall try to keep them more or less in the order of events," he said. "So let us go back a little."

He took a folder from his briefcase and spread it open on the desk in front of him. He looked across at Alice whose chair faced the light. His blunt finger marked a place in the folder.

"It would appear from certain information I have here that at the end of September you were in London, and that you made preparations for a journey to South Africa."

Andrew cut in quickly, "You don't have to answer questions, Alice."

"It's all right," she said. "I understood the Sergeant's warning in the first place."

She gave her attention to van Wyk. Exactly what was he driving at?

"I was on my annual holiday," she said. "And I went to one or two travel agencies to enquire about the price of air passages to South Africa. You see, I had received an invitation to come here . . . I'd been interested in Africa for a long while . . ." She faltered and broke off.

"Your interest went a long way, Miss Lang. At that time— over a fortnight *before* the deceased passed away—you went so far as to have a yellow fever inoculation. You made ready to leave at a moment's notice."

Andrew started. Here was something on which he had not reckoned. He saw Alice's fingers grip the arm of the chair.

"Yes. I did have the inoculation."

"Why?"

"My mother was very ill—incurably ill. She might have— gone—at any time . . . any hour. She might have lingered on for a long time. There was no knowing." She paused while the Sergeant's pencil laboriously recorded her words. Her lip shook a little, for she realized now that every word she uttered might indeed prove damning. Truth—that was all that mattered—to stick absolutely to the truth. She continued :

"I had strong personal reasons for wanting to come here without delay if and when I should be free to do so. The immigration laws of the Union require air travellers to have a yellow fever certificate issued at least ten days before departure. It is valid for some years. There seemed no reason not to have it . . . just in case I should suddenly find that I was no longer needed at home."

" What were those strong personal reasons ? "

" I prefer not to answer that question." There were enough people involved in this already. She was not going to drag Andrew's name into it.

" Very well," said van Wyk. " And now we come to the night the deceased passed away. Your statement reads as follows : ' My mother was in a nervous overwrought condition when I went upstairs to give her her nightly injection of a quarter grain of morphine. She had lately become afraid of everybody who had anything to do with her—even me at times. When she was in that state it was very distressing for me to have to give her the injection which was ordered for her. But I forced myself to do so. Afterwards I tidied everything away as usual. When I went down my patient was quieter, but I broke down. I can only think that Miss Swanson jumped to the conclusion that I had been unable to give the injection . . .' " Van Wyk's buffalo head came up sharply.

" So we must assume, according to the rest of this statement, that your friend gave a second quarter grain of morphine— which proved fatal ? "

" I have nothing to add to my statement."

" *Ja*, but isn't it strange that next morning—when you counted the remaining vials in the carton and found one short— you did not mention such a serious discovery to your friend ? "

" I don't think so. For one thing she had already left to go back to London . . . and for another I could not bear to suggest that she . . . she . . . Surely, *surely* you must understand . . ." Her eyes brimmed and her chin began to quiver. " If I hadn't broken down it could never have happened . . . don't you see, if I'd told Betty, she'd know that she . . . she actually——" The words choked her and she turned her head away, overwhelmed once more by the horror she had felt when she had stood at the bathroom window with the little round carton in her hand— five vials, but there should be six !—and the sickening realization of what had happened penetrating her brain.

When she had herself in hand once more she said : " It may even be that I was trying to spare myself as well as Betty. I kept telling myself that there might be some other explanation for the missing vial—that it had been spilt out of the carton. I went to look in the waste-paper basket, but it had already been emptied. I didn't ask Mrs. Withinshaw—the help—if she'd found two empty vials . . . I realize now that I didn't want to *know* the truth for sure. I couldn't bear it."

She looked tormented as if her memories were more than she could endure. Sergeant van Wyk was not imaginative, but he had an unpleasant sensation between his heart and his stomach. He felt much as he had done the day he had found his small son staring with guilty fascination at the big blue pin-cushion on his ma's dressing-table. A very beautiful moth seemed to have alighted on the pin-cushion. Every few seconds it wings fluttered and whirred but it did not fly away. Then van Wyk had observed the hat-pin that impaled it. He had bellowed for his *ouvrou* who had come running from the kitchen with her hands covered in flour from the pastry she was making. She had sized up the situation at a glance and it was plain to van Wyk that it was not new to her. She had hammered her son on his bare behind till it was as rosy as a young baboon's rump, but powdered with flour. " That'll teach you to torture dumb creatures ! " she had shouted above the little *skelm's* lusty yelling. She had seized the hat-pin, removed the moth and crushed it under her large foot, leaving van Wyk with that nasty squeamish sensation that was with him now.

For some reason Alice Lang reminded him of that moth. He wanted to get this damn business over and clear out.

" One last point, Miss Lang. You inherited a legacy of two thousand pounds. Were you expecting that legacy ? "

" I was not." Her voice was low.

" You mean you had never seen the deceased's will ? "

" My mother never discussed her financial affairs with anyone. She made her last will when I was away on holiday about two years ago."

" Who witnessed it ? "

" Dr. Manfield and Betty Swanson."

" Miss Swanson was your great friend, yet she did not tell you the contents of the will ? "

" She didn't know the contents of the will. She only witnessed the signature."

The Sergeant nodded. He folded her statement carefully and tucked it into the pocket of his tunic. He rose with an audible sigh of relief.

" And now I'd be glad if you'd come with me to the office, Miss Lang. I want to get this statement straightened out and signed."

Alice felt the pressure of Rusty's fingers on her shoulder as he said, " Surely, Sergeant, Miss Lang has had about enough ! "

" No, Rusty," she said, standing up with her head held high. " The Sergeant is quite right. We must get these formalities over. I would rather go with him now."

When they had gone Rusty sat down on the divan beside Andrew with his head in his hands.

" It's Betty," he said. " Betty was guilty of criminal negligence I suppose. I don't see how blame can attach to Alice."

His brother shook his head.

" Alice had motives. She wanted her freedom, she wanted her legacy, she wanted—me. Above all, possibly, she wanted to be merciful."

He lit a cigarette and said : " There's one point van Wyk didn't make—a point somebody is going to make sooner or later."

Rusty looked up. " What point ? "

" Did Alice *intend* Betty to think that no injection had been given ? Did she—knowing her impulsive warm-hearted friend —produce that impression on purpose ? "

As Andrew spoke in a quiet objective tone devoid of all personal feeling, he was watching his brother intently.

Rusty felt his heart grow cold. His hands grasped at his thick hair and his eyes narrowed. He would willingly have struck Andrew across the mouth at that moment. He said through clenched teeth :

" For God's sake, Andrew ! Are you telling me that you didn't believe every word she said ? "

" I have to think about it," said Andrew, his eyes on his brother's face. " Don't you ? "

" No, damn you ! I believe in her completely."

He sprang up and towered over Andrew with clenched fists.

And then, suddenly, the sadness and sick weariness of his brother's expression melted his rage.

" I understand," said Andrew. " I understand how you feel, Rusty. But then you know her—you know her very well. I don't. I never have."

31

The Missionary

WHEN Duikers' Drift made contact with Camp Two at three o'clock that afternoon there were six people in Rusty's office.

Andrew leaned against the desk with his bush-jacket hanging loosely over his left arm in its sling, and his face haggard ; Rusty sat on a redwood stool by the radio-telephone with Sergeant van Wyk astride a wooden chair beside him. On the other side of the room Alice shared a small *rimpie* bench with Dr. Hurley while Thea was perched on the window-sill. Smokey sprawled across the boarded floor where anyone was likely to fall over him ; the black cat stalked in, brushed a feline kiss on the dog's hairy cheek, cast an appraising glance at the rest of the company and stalked out again with her tail in the air.

The Missionary had arrived with his daughter earlier in the afternoon. The Hurley family had listened in on the Sanctuary wave-length the night before, and, hearing that Andrew was at Camp Two and wounded, they had instantly decided that a doctor's professional assistance might be urgently needed. Thea had insisted upon going with her father and had arranged for one of the Sanctuary Game-guards to accompany them. They had taken what medical supplies and surgical instruments Dr. Hurley considered might be necessary, had picked up Andrew's mail and set off as soon as there was any likelihood of crossing the flooded rivers.

With Alice's help the doctor had examined Andrew's wound and dressed it again.

" He's in very good shape, thanks to a sound constitution and your care, Miss Lang," he had said. And Alice had thought, Poor Andrew, all I've brought him is trouble—and more to come. But she had given Dr. Hurley a grateful smile. In the little wiry man with the fierce fanatical blue eyes and the shock of bushy white hair she had recognized the selfless purity of purpose of the healer whose skill is employed for the benefit of others without any thought of personal gain.

Thea she had only met a few minutes ago. She had been interested to see the tall fair girl Jan Nelmapius found so attractive, but Thea had been reserved—almost antagonistic—and Alice had been hurt and puzzled by her attitude.

The dry clipped voice of Inspector Banks from Duikers' Drift, over two hundred miles away, came clearly through the grille.

" Yes, Camp Two, I hear you loud and clear. Is Sergeant van Wyk there ? Over."

The Sergeant answered. " Van Wyk speaking, Inspector. I arrived here shortly before one o'clock. Over."

" I shall require you at Duikers' Drift tomorrow afternoon. In the meantime wait for Sergeant Neethling who is on the way to Camp Two with Ranger Nelmapius. He has important dispatches for you. How is Mr. Andrew Miller ? Over."

Andrew limped over to the intercom.

" This is Andrew Miller, Inspector. Dr. Hurley has arrived here from Poinsettia. He reckons I can travel tomorrow, but he wants you to fix me up with a room at the hospital. Over."

" Sure, Mr. Miller. Glad you're doing all right. Ranger Nelmapius has some reports to make to you. We thought it best he should see you as soon as possible. Over."

Alice looked at Thea, but the young girl gave no sign of caring whether Ranger Nelmapius was on his way to Camp Two or not. Her eyes were on Andrew—and suddenly the truth dawned on Alice. She loved Andrew—this child was in love with a man old enough to be her father !

Andrew was speaking on the intercom. " What is the news of Game-guard Amos ? Over."

" He died early this morning. There seemed no reason for it. He'd been making good progress physically. I also have to tell you that Game-guard March met with an accident. He was mauled by that tame young lioness of Boryslawski's. Boryslawski swears she's never harmed anyone before. But she killed March. Nelmapius can give you further details of both cases. Over."

Rusty turned to Alice with a half incredulous expression that seemed to say, " There you are ! The curse of Ndlovukasi ! "

Alice's scalp tingled and a cold shiver passed over her bare arms and legs. The magic of Africa had for a moment chilled and darkened the room. She felt the Missionary shift his position next to her and she wondered whether the Inspector's laconic information had any deeper meaning for Dr. Hurley. She hardly heard the rest of the conversation on the intercom. She had been swept back to her first day in Velaba, the real beginning of her trek with Rusty.

In imagination she was back in the hot lonely picket in the thornveld watching Oasis play with her baby, Shinhenani, the Little Warrior. The girl's crooning voice and the child's gurgling infectious laughter echoed in her ears with the click of Nimrod's brass bangles as he set the fire and boiled their coffee. She stood with Rusty in the Game-guard's hut and looked down at the guitar of Amos, the minstrel and teller of tales. There, in the cool shadowy hut, with its ghosts of primitive love, long dormant instincts in her own body had quickened ; there she had trembled at Rusty's touch and heard the high keening note of the Bantu girl's grief. That day she had seen Oasis hurl a death-curse at March, and that night she had slept by the camp-fire with the drums of Africa beating into her blood-stream. The moon had shone into her eyes over Rusty's shoulder as he leaned above her with the firelight glinting in his copper hair, and he had said, " Don't look at me like that, Likwezi . . . my name is Ratau, the Lion, and I am dangerous ! "

Ah, Rusty, how dangerous ! I learned too late how dangerous.

Andrew's quiet voice recalled her.

" That's all then, Inspector. We'll see you tomorrow afternoon at Duikers' Drift. You want Rusty too, I gather. Over."

" That's right. And certain of your native witnesses. Neethling has the list of names. *Tot siens*. Out."

So Rusty would be going to Duikers' Drift with the others. Alice was stricken with panic at the prospect of being without him—alone again with her anxieties and her impending ordeal. The Missionary seemed to sense her feeling of abandonment and he said, " Shall we go outside. I think Andrew and Rusty and van Wyk will want to discuss their plans."

As they went on to the stoep with Thea, he added. " My wife and I thought you might like to come back to Poinsettia with Thea and me. We'll be leaving at daybreak tomorrow when the others will have to start for Duikers' Drift."

" I'd be very grateful," she said. But she wondered if she would be allowed to go to Poinsettia. Would she require Sergeant van Wyk's permission? Was she a free woman or was she already under police supervision?

Thea shaded her eyes with a dimpled sunburned hand as a jeep drew up under the baobab that had been struck by lightning. The leaves had wilted and begun to drop but birds still twittered in the branches. Alice saw them flitting to and fro— the glossy starlings with their metallic jewel-bright plumage, the black and white hornbills and a flock of yellow buffalo-weavers. Since the rain the air had been more than ever alive with wings.

" Why, it's Jan Nelmapius! " Thea ran into the sunny compound with skipping childish steps. She was laughing. " Jannie! What have you done with your beard? "

" You! " he said. " You here—but Thea! "

He had taken off his wide-brimmed hat and his hair was fine gold in the sun. He stood gazing at her, disbelieving his entranced eyes.

" He's like a young Apollo," said Alice to the Missionary. And, for the first time, he really noticed the charm of her smile and the beauty of her dark eyes. He laughed.

" There are enough Pagans as it is in Velaba, Miss Lang. We can do without Apollo."

Sergeant Neethling hurried to the office with a brief greeting to Thea and her father, but the Ranger looked glad to see Alice and paused to talk to her and Dr. Hurley.

" I took your advice, Miss Lang," he said with his hand to his chin.

" So I see."

" Did you tell him to shave his beard? " asked Thea on a slightly indignant note.

" I suggested you might like him better without it. Do you? "

" I'll think about it," said Thea, mollified.

" Do."

Alice thought that, curiously enough, the young man appeared more mature clean shaven. His chin was unexpectedly forceful and his lips firmly moulded.

She said : " We were very sorry to hear about Amos, Jan."

Nelmapius frowned. " He didn't intend to live. He waited till he knew that March was dead, and then he . . . went to join his ancestors."

Alice's experience had taught her the importance of the will to live. She had seen it drag the failing body from the borderland between life and death. She had known it perform miracles. Without it the arts of surgery and medicine could be rendered powerless.

She said sadly, " Perhaps he felt that—as things were—he had nothing much to live for. Perhaps he didn't care any more."

Dr. Hurley sighed. " It's more than the negativeness of not caring. With these people it's usually a positive death-wish or expectation. In this instance the death-wish was in Amos himself. But often enough it is in the heart of an enemy. A healthy man believes himself bewitched and he turns his face to the wall and dies."

She thought of March and Sheba, the lioness. March had known his fate and invited it with his fear and his fatalism.

" Jan, can you tear yourself away to join us ? "

Rusty was standing outside his office on the stoep. His grin embraced Nelmapius and Thea with sympathetic amusement.

The young Ranger coloured under his tan. " *Ja*, man, I'm coming."

As he joined Rusty Thea looked after him with puzzled blue eyes.

" It's like getting to know a new person," she said. " That beard was so silly. It was like a child showing off. Now, if Andrew grew a beard, it would be the real thing."

" I think you should go and have a rest, Thea," said her father. " We started very early this morning and we didn't have an easy journey."

" Oh, Daddy," she pouted. " Resting's a waste of time. I'm going to sit over there by the river."

She's hoping Andrew will go and talk to her there, thought Alice. Or Jan, perhaps. She rose with a smile.

" I didn't sleep well myself last night and I think a rest would be a good idea. I'm going to my room."

The Missionary watched the two girls stroll across the compound and part outside the Game-warden's house, Alice to go to her room and Thea to wander off in the direction of the canyon. There were worried lines between his brows as he made his way to the semicircle of guest *rondavels* where he and his daughter had adjacent rooms. He was disturbed on Thea's account. His wife had warned him that, in her opinion the girl was infatuated with Andrew Miller. As far as Thea was concerned, the elder-brother-little-sister relationship had entirely changed its character. That was why Mrs. Hurley had, to a certain extent, betrayed a confidence in telling her daughter of the understanding between Andrew and Alice Lang. She had hoped thereby to put an end to foolish dreams that could only end disastrously, for, even if Andrew had been in love with Thea, the difference in their ages would have made a marriage between them quite unsuitable.

Dr. Hurley was very fond of the Senior Game-warden. Andrew's broad humanity appealed to him, and, although there were many points on which the man of God clashed with the man of science, their differences only formed the basis for stimulating discussions. Both had learned tolerance through adversity. Dr. Hurley was genuinely anxious to see Andrew happily married, for a loving helpmeet and the blessings of children were not only in accordance with the Divine Will but they were also the best possible insurance against the subtle perils of a solitary life. Thus he had welcomed the news of Andrew's friendship with the young English nurse who had sounded just the right woman for him. And the moment Dr. Hurley had set eyes on Alice he had been confirmed in his opinion. The fact that their intimacy had developed on a mental rather than a physical basis seemed to him no disadvantage. If minds were strongly attracted and bodies were young and healthy Mother Nature could surely be relied upon to do the rest.

But when he had examined Andrew's shoulder with the assistance of this quiet competent young woman, who could even lay claim to a certain degree of beauty, he had been aware of an atmosphere of tension between them that troubled and baffled him. Questions had begun to jostle one another in his brain. Why had van Wyk come to the Mission to make enquiries about Alice Lang? What was wrong? That something was seriously amiss was no longer in doubt in his mind. Was it possible that this girl was guilty of some grave offence against the law? He found it hard to think so. Dr. Hurley had looked into those sad dark eyes and he had seen secret distress there, but no evil. The Missionary, like his Bantu flock, was not unaccustomed to the ' language of the eyes '.

It seemed to him that these two people—Andrew and Alice— had reached a crisis in their lives, that they were in danger, and in need of spiritual help. There was only one way in which he could help them.

Dr. Hurley went into his *rondavel* and closed the door after him. He sank on to his knees by the bed and closed his eyes. His palms were pressed together like a child's. If Alice could have seen him then she might have thought of Meg's little sons, so touching was his attitude, so complete his faith.

32

" *They are Waiting for You* "

ALICE flung herself on to her bed. Till now she had hardly had time to realize the extent of her own weariness and despair. But, as she let herself go, it seemed to her that her thin limbs and body were weighted with lead. I'm heavy, she thought, every bit of me is heavy—most of all, my heart. It was huge and aching in her breast, a dead weight of sheer misery.

For four years her own personal life had been suppressed and then, in as many days, she had lived with an intensity of which she had never dreamed herself capable. And what a mess she had made of this new life on which she had entered with such high hopes! Everything had run against her, every circumstance had been just wrong, from the initial tragedy that had set her free to Andrew's inability to meet her at Duikers' Drift.

If only she could have come to know Rusty under other conditions—after her relationship with Andrew had become established and secure—this emotional situation between them would never have arisen. But, as it was, the flame of his personality had set her alight, it had burned up the dry impotent love born of a bundle of letters and reduced it to ashes. She had learned too late that her love for Andrew had been as little alive as a paper flower. It had been exotic and alluring, an artificial bloom with a few shallow thread-like roots reaching flimsily into the mind and the imagination. The strong living roots of lasting love between a man and a woman must spring straight from the heart, they must be warmed by the spirit and nourished by the flesh. Yet she realized that such a love might well have developed between Andrew and herself—if she had not met Rusty first.

She tossed and turned and at last fell into a light doze filled with disquieting dreams.

It was late afternoon when she was wakened by a knock on her door.

" Come in," she called.

She saw Rusty's sturdy figure without surprise. He came and sat on the bed beside her.

" Van Wyk wants to see you. He's in the living-room with Andrew."

Alarm darkened her eyes. She sat up, dreading a new interrogation. Her shirt and shorts were crumpled, her features had sharpened in her shrunken face and now the colour left her skin and lips. She looked to Rusty like some small bird or animal in the hour of its death. His pity for her was more painful than desire. He took her in his arms and held her with his cheek against her hair.

" Don't look like that, Likwezi—don't be afraid. Be strong."

She rested silently against him, her face pressed into the hollow of his shoulder. She felt the steady beat of his heart, the warmth and strength of his body and his mouth on her hair. Tomorrow he would be gone, she'd never see him again. The inhuman machinery of the law would take her away and smear her into the dirt as the Rogue had crushed and broken Mbula. Hold me, hold me, Rusty—don't let them take me from you ! But, if they must, if there is no escape, at least I have had your love. You are part of me for always—as long as they let me live—you and that night of the storm, with your hair wet and curly in the rain and your skin cold and fresh against mine, and both of us knowing the truth . . .

She felt the beat of his heart quicken, and very gently he put her from him.

" They are waiting for you," he said.

He saw her will take visible command of her fears in the way he had come to expect. "*You know her very well*," Andrew had said with a sorrowful significance that understood, acknowledged and forgave everything. With those words this morning he had renounced her to his brother and made explanations and recriminations needless between them. And it was true. Alice was more deeply known to Rusty than Flora had ever been. He knew her as he knew himself.

" I won't be long," she said. " Tell the Sergeant I'll be with him in a few minutes."

She was already at the mirror brushing her hair. He came and stood behind her with his powerful square hands on her shoulders. She looked up into his mirrored eyes.

" Whatever happens," he said, " you can count on me."

His hands slid down and crossed over her breast, and she leaned against him with her throat working. If things had been different—if only things had been different—this moment might have been one of supreme happiness. She lifted his hands from her body and laid her cheek on them.

" Thank you, Rusty. Go now."

When she had changed into a neat cotton dress and applied her bright lipstick she felt better. " Be strong," he had said. She must prove her strength.

She found Sergeant van Wyk sitting at the desk with a number of documents spread before him. Andrew stood beside him, and his smile when he saw Alice was reassuring. He is my friend, she thought. If things had been otherwise we might really have learned to love each other. It could have happened. But it would have been a different love to the one that has set me on fire.

Van Wyk rose cumbrously to his feet. His heavy features were grave, but no longer hostile to her.

" Sit down, Miss Lang. I have here some new statements in

connection with the case of Mrs. Mary Lang. These are copies of depositions taken in London and transmitted to Pretoria. They were then sent to Duikers' Drift and brought to me here by hand of Sergeant Neethling."

The Sergeant was proud of the efficiency of the South African Police. Even here in the *bundu* they didn't allow grass to grow under their feet.

" I would like to read you the relevant sections of certain of these documents," he continued. " Am I right in assuming that you desire these two gentlemen to be present ? "

A half smile touched the corner of her mouth at the ponderous formality of his manner. " Yes, please," she said.

She refused the easy-chair Rusty offered her and perched lightly on its arm. She was very neat and compact even in that casual attitude, with her back straight and her head high and challenging.

Rusty went over to the fireplace. He stood in front of the empty grate with his legs apart and his hands clasped behind his back. Andrew sat on the divan and lit a cigarette, while the Sergeant seated himself once more at the desk and sorted his papers with the deliberation that characterized all his actions. When he was ready he looked up at Alice.

" Here is a deposition made by Sister Elizabeth Caroline Short, born Swanson. It was made yesterday on her return from Paris where it appears she was on her honeymoon." He cleared his throat self-consciously. " In it she gives her version of the night the deceased passed away."

The Sergeant began to read in a carefully expressionless tone.

" ' Alice was terribly upset that night when she came down from her mother's room. She was crying bitterly and she said, " Mother is in one of her frightened moods. I can't bear it when she's afraid of the needle—of me—when she looks at me like that ! It's more than I can stand ! " I tried to comfort her and promised to go upstairs and see what I could do to soothe the patient. Mrs. Lang was always very good with me. When I went into the bedroom her mood had changed. (She was often very variable—hysterically terrified one minute and rational the next.) She said, " What have you come for ? " and I answered, " To make sure you have all you need. If there's anything Alice didn't do for you, I can see to it." She put out her arm to me and said, " Then give me my injection. I wouldn't let Alice, but now the pain is beginning again." She appeared lucid and sensible. I had often helped to look after her and I knew where everything was kept. I knew her treatment, too, of course. When I had given the injection she thanked me and asked me to stay with her while she fell asleep. I did so. When I went down about twenty minutes later Alice had got herself in hand. She had made tea and she seemed to be listening to the radio play we wanted to hear. I whispered that all was well, and she nodded. The following morning, when she took her mother's tea in to her, Mrs. Lang was dead.' "

The Sergeant paused but he did not look up or he would have noticed the pallor of Alice's face and the dawning pain in her eyes. Oh, God, she thought, Mother meant it—poor, poor darling, she meant it—she saw her chance and took it. . . .

Van Wyk went on. " I have here also Sister Short's—or shall I say Swanson's ?—answers to certain questions. When asked if, at any time, she had reason to believe that an injection had already been administered, she said, ' When I threw the cotton wool and the used vial into the waste-paper basket I noticed that there was another used vial in it already. I thought that the basket had not been emptied since the morning injection. We always used spirit before inserting the needle, so there was no stain or smell.' Question two. ' Did you have no doubts next morning when the patient was found dead ? ' Reply. ' None. Mrs. Lang might have died at any time. There seemed no reason to think the injection had anything to do with it.' "

The Sergeant drew a second sheet of paper towards him.

" This is a statement from Dr. Quentin Manfield. He gives the sad details of your mother's last illness, Miss Lang, and then he goes on to say : ' During the past year it was necessary for my patient to have increasing doses of morphine to control the pain. Her system had developed a considerable degree of tolerance to the drug and a dose that would undoubtedly prove fatal to the average person would not have had a particularly adverse effect upon Mrs. Lang. The half grain administered on the night of October the tenth would not, in itself, have been sufficient to cause death.' Dr. Barnett, who was Dr. Manfield's locum and who issued the death certificate, is in agreement with his colleague's opinion."

Van Wyk shuffled his papers once more, and selected one with obvious satisfaction.

"Here is Dr. Manfield's testimony as to the character of Miss Alice Lang. 'I have known Alice Lang since her childhood and I am proud to testify to her absolute integrity. During the past four years Alice Lang's conduct, both as a nurse and a daughter, has been exemplary. She had nursed her mother with selfless devotion and unfailing care.'" Van Wyk took up another note. "The Matron of the hospital in which Miss Lang trained has borne out this testimony. Therefore, in all the circumstances, it is clearly evident that the Crown has no charge to bring against Miss Alice Lang."

The Sergeant, who had been entirely concerned with his documents and their import, looked up to offer Alice his congratulations and his sincere regret that she had been put to so much mental strain and distress. To his dismay he saw that the young woman opposite him was weeping silently and uncontrollably. Her shaking hands covered her face and tears ran between her fingers and splashed on to her cotton dress. Andrew Miller had moved over to the window ; his back was to the room and his head was bowed. It was Rusty who astonished the Sergeant by striding over to his brother's girl, and it was to Rusty that she turned, burying her tear-stained face against his khaki bush-jacket.

Outside there was the evening twittering of birds, but in the room was only silence save for the rustle of the Sergeant's papers as he gathered them up and put them away in his briefcase. He went out into the sun-set without another word. He drew a deep contented breath. Thank heaven that job was over ! And tomorrow he'd give his *ouvrou* a ring from Duikers' Drift. She'd be cross as a snake when she heard that the *biltong* bandits had slipped through his fingers into the grasp of that bloody fellow, Neethling, and she'd wonder about the English case to which he had foolishly referred once or twice. Fortunately he had not confided any names or facts to her, for his *ouvrou* had about as much discretion as a rogue baboon. But she'd goad him just the same. Well, he didn't give a damn ! It was a policeman's business to catch criminals, not to torture the innocent. He had not enjoyed his sessions with Alice Lang. Ever since he had associated her with that blasted moth impaled on the blue pin-cushion he had hated the whole affair. Now it was closed, and he had a sense of wings fluttering towards freedom and wounds that would heal. He took some Boer tobacco from his pouch and plugged his pipe. He'd go and have a word with the Missionary—and maybe a beer. Old Hurley would want some explanation for those enquiries that had been made at the Mission. They'd take a bit of laughing off, but a little tact should do the trick. He'd better go and get on with it.

33

Ndlovukasi's Prophecy

ALICE recovered herself and began hunting for powder and lipstick in her handbag.

" It's relief," she said shakily.   " I'm sorry to be so stupid."

It was more than relief that had moved her to tears, it was great joy. Not only was her own reputation cleared, but her mother had not, in fact, succeeded in making Betty the instrument of her sad intention. Of course Dr. Manfield was right. A patient habituated to increasing doses of morphine could have sustained that half grain perfectly well. If she had been less obsessed with the fear that she had failed in her duty and that Betty had been too hasty she might have realized that for herself.

Andrew limped over to the desk and half sat on it. He was smoking—not in the quick nervous way he sometimes did, but thoughtfully, blowing azure rings into the quiet evening air.

· Philemon came into the room and gave his master a slip of paper with a scribbled message from Sergeant van Wyk. Then he lit the lamp and drew the curtains. Rusty read the message and looked up quickly.

" Have the police cars gone already ? " he asked Philemon.

" Yeez, Nkosi. Just now."

" That's all then, Philemon."

As the boy padded out of the room Rusty said, " Van Wyk

and Neethling have left for Camp One with the Native Constables. They'll sleep there, pick up a couple of native witnesses and make Duikers' Drift well ahead of the rest of us tomorrow."

" What about Alice ? " said Andrew. " Do we take the poor girl all the way back with us ? "

She smiled. " The poor girl has been offered a lift to Poinsettia with Dr. Hurley and Thea—and she has accepted."

" Good work," said Andrew. " And now there's something I'd like to get settled with Rusty. No, Alice, don't go. In a way, this concerns you too."

He crushed out his cigarette and ground the stub into the ash-tray with needless force. He extinguished the small smouldering flame as if he were making an end of something in himself. When I saw her, he thought, I knew that we could find love and happiness together. She was all and more than I had dared to hope and my doubts evaporated like mist in the sun. And then, word by word, gesture by gesture, look by look, I saw what had happened to Rusty and her. They tried to hide it—they didn't want me to know, but, as the Sergeant would put it, a blind baboon could have guessed the truth. I pretended to Rusty that I had no faith in her and he believed it. He could have struck me ! Then suddenly he was sorry for me. He realized that I knew.

" Rusty," said Andrew. " I haven't had any opportunity of talking to you about the Chairman's visit. He's very keen on getting the Sanctuary opened to tourism. He even wants us to take a limited number of tourists next winter. There's a big programme to be carried out. You'll have to take charge of it."

" *I'm* not the Senior Game-warden. You'll be the boss."

" Not then. I'm drawing out in about three weeks' time. That'll give you a chance to have a holiday before you get cracking."

Rusty had taken up his position in front of the empty grate. His jaw was thrust forward pugnaciously.

" What are you driving at, Andrew ? I don't understand what you're suggesting."

" I'm through with Velaba. I belong to the pre-tourism period in any Sanctuary. You know that perfectly well. Meg knows it too. She wrote to me not long ago and said that as soon as a little human life came into the Sanctuary she supposed I'd be off. She's right. I'm seriously considering that Central African offer. You remember I went so far as to discuss it with you. I stalled in my answer—I was waiting to see what Alice thought about the idea——"

" Why don't you ask her, then ? "

" Because what Alice thinks or doesn't think is going to make no difference—now."

Shadows of pain and fatigue deepened round his eyes and he went on with an effort.

" When the Chairman was in my office, he picked up Alice's photograph from my desk. He asked if she was my girl-friend, and said it was a good thing for a man living out in the blue to get himself a wife." He paused and his face twisted as if what he had to say sickened him, but his quiet voice did not falter. " I told him then that I wasn't the marrying sort. The words slipped out. There must have been a grain of truth behind them." There, he thought, that's done it. That's freed her. And he remembered how he had felt when he had spoken those words to the Chairman, the prickling under the collar, shame at denying her, fear that what he had said was true. But that was before he had seen her—the woman who, in other circumstances, could have been every-thing in the world to him. That was when he had still been a prey to his doubts.

" So you're not the marrying sort ! " Anger flared in Rusty's blue eyes. " Well, then, let me tell you, Andrew— I *am* ! Even if I did make a damn mess of it the first time ! "

" Then take Alice away and tell *her* so."

Andrew sounded deathly tired. Alice made a quick move-ment towards him, but he shook his head and put out his hand as if to ward her off. For an instant their eyes met, and he saw that hers were no longer sad and haunted but glowing with a soft, radiant gratitude that told him more than any words could have done.

Rusty went to Alice and took her arm. " Come," he said.

Andrew watched them go out into the dusk. For a long time he did not move. Then he drew a letter from his pocket. Dr. Hurley had brought it with the mail from Poinsettia. It was from the Chairman of the new Central African Wild Life Sanctuary and it was marked urgent. Andrew re-read it with a wry smile. "We very greatly regret that the post of Chief Game-warden has already been filled. We would like to have kept it open for you but you will understand that we were compelled to . . ."

He crumpled it into a ball and threw it into the empty grate. As he looked up he saw the slight figure of the missionary in the doorway.

"Come in, Dr. Hurley," he said.

"I thought I'd take a look at my patient." The little man's shrewd eyes seemed to see through the injured body into the sick heart.

"Sit down," said Andrew. "A smoke? A drink? It's all here."

"I'll help myself to a beer. What about you? I should recommend a brandy."

Dr. Hurley went over to the tray of drinks Philemon had set on the table. He poured a strong brandy and water and gave it to him.

"Well," he said. "How goes it?"

Andrew sank into one of the arm-chairs and indicated the other, but Dr. Hurley shook his head and remained standing. He leaned an elbow on the mantelpiece and looked down at the younger man's drawn face. Andrew lit a cigarette and glanced up.

"That marriage licence——" he said. "You'll need to change it. It'll be for Rufus Maxwell Miller and Alice Mary Lang."

The missionary plugged his pipe thoughtfully.

"I see," he said after a while. "And what about Andrew Miller?"

"I'm clearing out."

"Where to, if I may ask?"

"You may ask—but I don't know the answer yet."

"What about that offer from the new Central African Reserve?"

"That post is filled. You brought the letter."

Dr. Hurley puffed silently at his pipe. When next he spoke he seemed to change the course of the conversation.

" Has it struck you," he said, " that while we out here in darkest Africa set aside vast tracks of fertile land for the pre-servation of wild beasts, in Europe there is less and less safety for human beings ? Your animals live with their food and water assured as far as possible, their territories are policed against the human invader and the killer. They live according to the laws of nature, but in Europe an iron hand has destroyed the whole meaning of the word Sanctuary. There is no security for millions of our fellow men."

The room was very quiet and the missionary's words filtered into Andrew's mind through the deep weariness that engulfed him. There was pain and strange healing in their significance.

" It's curious," he said at last. " For years I've been lost in the study of nature. I've turned away from human problems."

" You were a prisoner of war and you'd had your share of man's inhumanity to man. You didn't try to escape, Andrew. You accepted your fate—your imprisonment. But you've been escaping ever since—escaping people, escaping love and marriage, and all the normal demands of life."

" I saw my brother's marriage break his heart."

" Hearts mend."

" Do they ? "

" Most certainly—as you have seen. Of course, if the break is severe enough, it may leave its mark. You limp from time to time and no doubt your shoulder will ache now and again long after it has healed, but you're no less of a man for your scars. More so."

Andrew thought, I had my chance and I lost it. I let her go. She was the one for me. He said :

" I'm ignorant about human beings—except my Bantus. I understand them."

The missionary smiled.

" Forgive me, Andrew. But you only understand your Bantus because you regard them as part of the wild life of Velaba. You know them as you know the animals. *You are not one of them.* If you want to live, you must plunge into life itself. Time enough to be a recluse in your old age."

Dr. Hurley rose.

" I must go and find young Thea. You'd better turn in—

you've had quite a day. I'll come and see you later—unless you want a hand now."

"Saul will give me a hand. I'll think about what you've said. Maybe I'll take a look at Europe—plunge into life, learn something about those people who have less sanctuary than my wild beasts—try to help them——"

"Why not? There are organizations. Well, I must be off."

Andrew stood on the stoep to watch the wiry little missionary walk purposefully towards his *rondavel*. He called to Saul. *You are not one of them*, Dr. Hurley had said. But that wasn't true. Saul was closer to him than a father. When you have faced death with a man and he has saved your life he is part of you. But maybe it was more important to face life— as Rusty and Alice would face it together, for better or for worse. He passed his hand across his eyes. He was very tired.

When Rusty and Alice had gone into the dusk they had crossed the grass to the height above the river. Fireflies darted here and there among the leaves, and Smokey chased the black cat, Lucky, up the nearest tree. Only two nights ago they had run barefoot and hand in hand over this same veld grass. It had been tawny then and soaked with the rain that had brought new life to the whole bushveld world. Now it was young and green, transformed by the annual miracle of the spring, of October, the month of life-giving, of hot, strong sun and blinding moon, of flood and birth and blossoming.

Rusty stopped in the glade Alice knew so well. She could smell the sweet, insidious perfume of the acacias and the cool, indefinable scent of the river. In the half light the bush stretched mysteriously away to the Black Mamba Mountains, and the first stars glimmered in the luminous jade of the evening sky. Birds called sleepily before the long silence of the night should overtake them, and it seemed to Alice as if they were leaving a party—the last guests bidding one another good night and good-bye and promising to meet again with the rising of the sun.

Rusty said, "This is *our* place, Likwezi. This is where you accepted the truth about us—where you stopped fighting it. This place will always mean more to me than anywhere else in the world."

"To me too," she said softly. And she thought, Here I knew the substance from the shadow, here I knew that I belonged to you for all my life, no matter what the future might do to us. "And you? When did you know, Rusty?"

Her hand was in his as they stood looking across the canyon to the eastern range. He smiled down at her in the twilight.

"When you held Shinhenani, the Little Warrior, in your arms, and Ndlovukasi presented you with the lion's claw."

"Oh, yes, will I ever forget that extraordinary experience! And I know the claw has been lucky for me. I'm superstitious about it—as superstitious as any of your Bantus. But what did she say that day? You wouldn't tell me."

"No, I wouldn't tell you what she said. I couldn't then. You were my brother's girl."

"And now?"

"And now, my love, you are mine—with my brother's blessing. So I can tell you what Ndlovukasi said."

She was looking up into his eyes, and fire began to burn in his veins. "Tell me."

"Ndlovukasi prophesied that you would have sons of your own one day—as beautiful and brave as the Little Warrior. They would belong to the Lion Clan and be powerful and red-maned like Ratau the Lion who would be their father. You see, Likwezi, it was a bit tricky for me to tell you that at the time."

He put his arms round her and felt laughter shake her body. Her laughter was as soft as the sound of the river flowing through the canyon, and suddenly he thought that it was a long time since he had heard her laugh.

"You've just made that up," she said, "this very minute."

He brushed her lips lightly with his. "Hush! There is the voice of the lion. Can you hear it? Never despise the magic of Velaba."

Far away the call of the royal hunter reverberated through the darkening bush. They waited, bound together, while veld and forest held their breath before the sudden burst of distant mimicry echoed the thunder of the King.

He released her then to take her small, thin face in his hands. His grave eyes looked into hers.

"I love you. Everything that's happened between us—

the good and the bad—has only made me love you more. I didn't know it could be like this—such closeness, such understanding, such faith. I want to marry you. It's asking a great deal. Will you take us—Velaba and me—for better, for worse?"

Hardship, loneliness and danger; separation from those promised children; drought and storm and violence; the Camp-dogs baying at the invisible foe beyond the boundary of the thorn-*scherm*—these would be part of her life from now on. So would the gentle antelope browsing in the thickets and forests at the water's edge; birds spreading unbelievably bright wings in the clear golden light; and the high sky and the burning moon. There would be the camp-fire under the stars sending its shower of sparks into the fragrant night, and the arms of her lover whose embrace moved her to rapture akin to pain. Life without danger—without this man of hers— would be death.

" I love you," she said. The words were strange and unfamiliar on her lips. Never before had she spoken them to any man, and, as she said them now, it seemed to her that the whole new life about her quickened and possessed her. She was part of her lover, part of Velaba, and in the gathering darkness the bushveld seemed to stir and draw close and take her to its heart.